I0615841

SPECTRUM DUOLOGY
VOLUME two

UNCURSED

PART ONE
INDIGO STONE

Also by D.N. LEO
http://www.narrativeland.com

CHAPTER 1

Heat. That was all he could feel. A wave of fire that carried incinerating heat was flying toward him. Lorcan stared at it as if it was a movie clip shown in slow motion. Once that fire brushed over him, Lorcan knew all that would be left of him was a pile of ashes. He was stuck beneath a collapsed brick dome, half of his body was buried, and his legs were crushed. He didn't think there were any bones left intact, so even if the bricks and stones didn't crumble down upon him, he wouldn't be able to move out of the way of the fire anyway.

As death loomed close, he thought of Orla. He hadn't had a chance to marry her properly. He thought of his family in Ireland, too, and regretted taking their love for granted. If there were a God—and somehow that God was compassionate enough to grant him another chance—he would take Orla to Ireland to meet his family and marry her. On top of that, he would go to church every week.

Brandon's laughter still echoed in the air—the sound of evil. *How could a gatekeeper in a virtuous place such as the Daimon Gate turn dark so quickly?* Lorcan wondered. As he closed his eyes, awaiting the coming fire, he heard the sound of a spaceship moving closer. Turning toward the noise, he saw it had parked close to where he lay. From inside the spaceship, Ciaran jumped out and rushed over to Lorcan.

"Go away! There won't be enough time, Ciaran!" Lorcan yelled. *That man must have nerves of steel,* Lorcan thought. Without a word, Ciaran blasted his weapon at the loose bricks around Lorcan and then used his daggers as levers to lift the large stone from on top of Lorcan. Ignoring Lorcan's verbal abuse, Ciaran hauled Lorcan up and half-carried, half-dragged Lorcan into his spaceship.

The door closed and sealed immediately after their embarkation.

"Heat defense mechanism on!" Ciaran shouted. The spaceship shuddered, and they heard a click.

"Affirmative and ready," a robotic voice said.

Then the storm of fire hit them.

The spaceship tilted slightly when hit, but regained its balance soon after. As the counterbalance mechanism kicked in to compensate for the heat outside, the air inside the spaceship dropped to freezing. The storm continued to attack the spaceship from the outside. They heard the sound of hard objects hitting metal, and the force of the air blew through gaps in the outer body of the ship, creating a hellish howling noise.

Then it quieted down, the fire went past, and the spaceship seemed to settle.

Lying on the floor, Lorcan's vision became blurry. He knew he needed to pass out so that his body could begin the healing process, but he had to tell Ciaran about his healing ability first or he would think that his system was collapsing. *"Damn it,"* Lorcan thought. He couldn't force a word past his lips. And as he'd predicted, Ciaran was trying to prevent him from passing out because in the same situation, a normal person would pass out and go into cardiac arrest due to the shock of the injuries and the extreme changes of environmental conditions they had just experienced.

"Lorcan, come on. Open your eyes for me. You're not going to die on me. Come on." Ciaran shook Lorcan's shoulders so hard that there was no way he would be able to pass out and start any healing process. Lorcan wanted to scream, but again, he couldn't get any words out. Ciaran ran to a small compartment and pulled out an emergency medical kit. Lorcan opened his eyes and saw Ciaran preparing a syringe. It had to be adrenaline, Lorcan thought, which normally he wouldn't mind, but if that kick-ass chemical was injected into his system now, he'd be forced to remain conscious and deal with this excruciating pain.

Lorcan summoned all the strength he had left and said, "No."

Ciaran cocked an eyebrow. "No? It's only adrenaline. I know what I'm doing."

"No," Lorcan repeated, but Ciaran approached him, still ignoring his weak protest. Ciaran crouched next to Lorcan, but before he could inject the adrenaline, something hit the spaceship so hard that it almost tipped the craft over. Ciaran fell, dropping the syringe on the floor, and it rolled away to a far corner. He hurried toward a control window to look outside, mumbling some profanity as he went.

On the floor, Lorcan took his opportunity and slipped into his needed unconsciousness.

After a while, Lorcan opened his eyes to find himself alone, lying on the floor of the spaceship. His body had healed. Getting up, he went to the window to see what was going on outside. A short distance away, Ciaran and a group of soldiers had barricaded themselves behind the ruins of a gothic dome and were firing at a small army of space creatures. To protect Lorcan, Ciaran shot and killed any creatures veering toward the space vessel.

Lorcan immediately recognized the ambush attempt that had caught him off guard before. He searched the spaceship for the weapon compartment. He grabbed two long laser beam guns. He'd never used them before, but in looking them over, it didn't take him long to figure out where the triggers were. Unfortunately, as soon as he touched the handles of the guns, a line of text flashed on a small screen located above the trigger: *Unauthorized User.* Lorcan swore and ran to the control panel. He slammed his palm on the verification screen and, ignoring the machine's protest, hacked into the system. It didn't take him long to prompt the system to give him a pass for weapon usage. Lorcan scanned the receiver of the gun over the verification screen dashboard and the recognition mechanism on the gun flashed a green light.

Outside, Ciaran had nearly wiped out the small army, still keeping an eye on the spaceship to be sure no stray creatures wandered near it. He felt a sudden blast of heat and dust pressure coming from behind, an area that, oddly, backed up to a dead end wall of rock and stone. Ciaran was sure that nothing could penetrate the wall to come out at him from that corner. But it then dawned on him that he was fighting at a transitional zone in between universes. The dead end could be merely an illusion, and a dimensional hole could open before he had a chance to react. He whirled around to face the general direction from which the blast had come, but it seemed to be too late. He shouted to his soldiers to take cover and dove behind a rock.

The pressure came like an explosion. He and all of his soldiers were thrown feet away, tossed around like rag dolls. Dazed, Ciaran tried to sit up and see through the dust storm. He saw nothing but the shape of a man walking toward him. He groped for his weapons on the ground nearby but found nothing but dust. He could feel the warmth of his blood streaming out from a gash on his left shoulder. Ciaran tried to spring to his feet, but his body wouldn't obey. Looking up, he saw Brandon standing right in front of him, a cold smirk on his face.

"Never thought you would face death like this, did you, Ciaran?"

"Why? I saved your life."

"Well, you should have asked me if I wanted that. You think you know it all, Ciaran? You, the Host, and those stupid humans are trying to obtain what doesn't belong to you."

"The key of Psuche? What does it have to do with you?"

"I could take the time explain to you why you must die today, but I'm not feeling compassionate at the moment. So goodbye, Ciaran LeBlanc, king of Eudaiz. You will die on the battlefield like a common soldier."

Brandon raised his crossbow, aiming at Ciaran's head, but Ciaran swung his leg and kicked the weapon away. His second kick landed on Brandon's abdomen, sending him staggering back and falling to the ground. Still groggy, Ciaran struggled to his feet and was then assaulted by Brandon's two-leg kick. He skidded backwards and fell back to the ground. As Brandon stood up and ran to recover his weapon, two streams of laser beams blasted at his chest. His clothes became engulfed in flame, but he pulled a lever and the fire died out instantly.

Brandon released a black smokeball and fled the scene.

Lorcan hurried into the dome of dust and black smoke to drag Ciaran out.

"I've got this! Let go!" Ciaran shrugged off Lorcan's support and walked out of the dust on his own. He inhaled some clean air and coughed out the dust that coated this throat and lungs, recovering swiftly. Then Ciaran turned around, looking at Lorcan. "Are you okay?"

"Yes." Lorcan grinned.

"Did you know the best way to kill a creature in space is to aim at the head? You're using two laser beamers, and all you did was set Brandon's clothes on fire!" Ciaran exclaimed.

"I've never used these before, so that's good enough, isn't it? I didn't miss totally!"

"Brandon ran away—again," Ciaran mumbled, clutching his bleeding shoulder. He glanced around, taking stock of the situation. "And he killed seven of my best soldiers."

"Shouldn't you be relieved he didn't kill you, too?"

Ciaran said nothing and headed back to his spaceship. Lorcan followed, and Ciaran asked, "How can you walk like that now? A short while ago, you were dying."

"I knew that would be the first thing you'd ask when you saw me! I wasn't dying. I have the ability to heal myself, heal my injuries very quickly, but I have to shut my system down first."

They were inside the spaceship now. "You can heal yourself?"

Lorcan nodded. "Yes, as long as I haven't died, I can heal myself from injuries. To what extent, I don't know. It's all new to me, too."

"Right." Ciaran rolled his eyes.

"Ciaran, I know it's hard for you to accept anything you can't explain scientifically. It was hard for me, too. But when your life partner, the person you've spent your entire life with, tells you she's a sorceress, you kinda learn to accept things that seem a little beyond reality."

Ciaran nodded. "Are there any more special abilities you and your group have that I should know about?"

"Apart from what you already know—Roy and Mori are werefoxes, and Orla is a sorceress— nothing else. Anyway, why are you here? I thought you were taking Roy to Eudaiz."

Ciaran shook his head. "I got a message on way to Eudaiz with Roy. I came back for you, and the girls said you'd gone. What happened?"

"I was on my way to the Daimon Gate to get the guest pass for Mori. Brandon ambushed me exactly the way he did you just now. He thought I had the key with me, and when he couldn't find it, he left me buried in the ruins and went after Orla. We have to get to her."

Ciaran shook his head. "I've sent for her. They'll be here soon." He glanced at his wrist unit. "My officers just confirmed. They're safe and sound."

The sound of an incoming holocast interrupted, and a beam of light flashed inside the spaceship, inside of which stood the life-sized hologram image of the Host of the Daimon Gate.

"You're injured, Ciaran?" the Host asked.

Lorcan nodded, acknowledging the Host. The Host responded in turn.

Ciaran winced and walked toward the medical compartment. He pulled out a square medical patch and cleaned his wound. "I don't have the ability to heal myself quickly, but this will help clean things up. It should look better by the time my wife sees it." Ciaran flashed Lorcan a brief smile and then addressed the Host. "I called for you because one of the missions you sent people to complete on Earth might have caused collateral effects that I don't think you'll be happy about. I placed our intelligence system on Earth to keep an eye on things, and the system has just reported that a sea creature is gathering a massive amount of energy under the seabeds of all continents on Earth. That amount of energy could create a series of tsunamis."

Ciaran looked straight into the Host's eyes. "It's going to drown the entire human population. This creature has something to do with the Daimon Gate. What can you tell us about the key and the mission you ordered?"

The Host arched an eyebrow and stared at Ciaran. Ciaran shrugged. "I can certainly find out myself, but it will take precious time that we might need in order to save the humans on Earth. I still have interests on Earth, so I'd like to protect the people there," Ciaran explained.

The Host nodded. "There was a myth before my time that the key of Psuche can give the holder the ability to control the water level of any universe, given the correct lineup of all astronomical elements. For me, it's simply a key to secure one of our Eastern gates."

Ciaran nodded. "For creatures that live in an aquatic environment, water dictates their territories and is a prime motivation for invasion."

"I killed the woman who was supposed to give the key to the creature. It looked quite pissed. I'm not sure if it was because of the woman's death or because it couldn't get the key. But whatever the reason, if we go back to Earth to kill that reptile, do you think it would solve the tsunami threat?" Lorcan asked.

Ciaran nodded. "It's speculation, but it's better than doing nothing."

Lorcan pulled out a little pouch and put it on the floor. "Here is the key. I'll leave it with you, and we'll return to Earth for the creature." He looked at the Host.

Ciaran arched an eyebrow. "I thought you said you didn't have it with you?"

"I'd hidden it before Brandon attacked me. Just got it back now."

"Brandon?" the Host asked.

Ciaran nodded. "He was trying to kill me, too. He's taken residence in Xiilok, outside your jurisdiction. And now he—or the person who took him in—wants the key, too. Maybe the myth has some truth to it—perhaps the key of Psuche does have magical powers," Ciaran mumbled sarcastically. The Host stepped forward, moving the light beam up to encircle the pouch on the ground. He then bent down to pick it up.

"Oh, no." The Host shook his head.

Lorcan and Ciaran watched the Host as he pulled out the key and pointed to its top. "The stone is missing. There's an Indigo Stone that's supposed to be mounted right here."

"So the key won't work without the stone?" Lorcan asked.

The Host shook his head. "The stone carries the power, and the key unlocks the power. They won't work separately. This is now simply a metal key, and the stone an expensive decoration."

"But we took the key out of the patch lock at the temple. My guess is that it had to have the stone attached to it at the time— the Fire Fox clan wouldn't have spent generations and sacrificed many lives to guard a useless key with no power. And the woman grabbed the key from me and ran to the beach. It wasn't long before we caught up with her, and we killed her before she could give the key to the dragon. So what happened to the stone in between?" Lorcan exclaimed.

"Time is relative," Ciaran contemplated.

"How does that explain any of this?" Lorcan raked his hands through his hair and paced in agitation.

"Did anything strange happen between the time the woman took the key and when you killed her?" Ciaran asked.

"Not really. She locked us in the temple and triggered a mechanism so the temple collapsed, and we were buried. We escaped via the drainage system beneath the temple. The only thing that was strange to me was the drainage. It was like a tunnel—long, dark, and confusing . . ." Lorcan trailed of as a thought came across his mind. "Dimensional hole . . . do you think that's what it was, Ciaran?"

Ciaran smiled and nodded. "The woman was obviously going to give the dragon the key without the stone. There must be more to that woman than meets the eye."

Lorcan rolled his eyes. "Yeah, she stripped naked on the beach."

"I beg your pardon?" the Host asked.

Ciaran laughed. "Never mind," Lorcan rumbled and continued, "So I guess we leave the key with you here and go back to Earth for the stone and the dragon?"

Ciaran nodded. "You might be able to kill two birds with one mission. Take these." Ciaran removed handguns from the weapon compartment and programmed them. "These are specially designed for the transitional zone, so I think they'll work on Earth. They'll definitely be superior compared to the current technology there and won't be detected by any detecting device." Ciaran gave

Lorcan the guns. While Lorcan assessed the weight and the feel of them, the Host shook his head.

Ciaran merely smiled at the Host and muttered, "I'm sorry your peace-keeping mission isn't working out. But my friends are still on Earth. I'm not going to let them die because of this stupid reptile."

CHAPTER 2

Hot sand rubbed at her face. Orla rolled to her side, moaning. Her entire body ached, but it was not the pain of battle, it was the pain of overtaxed body muscles after a body combat session at the gym. She opened her eyes, squinted at the bright sunlight, and immediately recalled what had just happened. She jumped to her feet, searching for Lorcan.

Behind a small sand hill, Lorcan drew himself up, squinted his eyes groggily, and registered the situation. He swung around, catching sight of Orla, and grinned. "Are you okay?" he asked, glancing up and down her body.

Orla nodded. "You?" She turned him around, checking him over.

"I'm fine."

From behind a small shrub on their left, Roy and Mori stood up, taking inventory.

"How are you guys?" Orla asked.

"We're fine," Mori responded.

Lorcan ran back to the sand hill where he had landed and dug around in the sand. When Orla, Roy, and Mori approached, Lorcan explained, "I'm looking for my wrist unit."

"The one Ciaran gave you?" Orla asked.

Lorcan grunted a response and breathed a sigh of relief as he saw a black band sticking up from the sand a few feet away from him. Picking it up, he brushed the sand from it with the sleeve of his shirt. After blowing off the last bit of sand, he started coding. Everyone's eyes were on the device, the only tool they had at the moment to reopen the portal that would take them back to the transitional zone of the multiverse. The device flashed green, signaling that it was operational. Lorcan sighed a breath of relief and put the device away.

Orla rubbed at her shoulders. "It was a rough landing, wasn't it? I thought Ciaran was more skillful than that when he opened the portal for us."

Lorcan smiled. He came over to massage Orla's aching shoulders. "He is skillful. You should see him in battle. The transition was bumpy because we ran into some dust storms along the way. Anyway, I hope there won't be too many rough days ahead of us."

Orla rolled her eyes. "We can only hope."

Roy stood stiffly, looking at Mori. "We'll be all right. We'll find the stone, and then return to the transitional zone. I'll take you to Eudaiz."

"Is that what Ciaran promised?" Mori asked, arching an eyebrow.

"If we complete this task, Ciaran will take you in. You can trust him—he's that kind of guy," Lorcan said.

"And you know that because . . . ?" Mori asked.

"We've had a lot of dealings with Ciaran. He has more important things to worry than dishonoring his promise," Orla said.

Mori shrugged.

"He saved me and asked nothing in return, remember, Mori?" Roy asked. Mori looked at Roy. There was so much more she wanted to say to him, but she couldn't say it in front of Lorcan and Orla.

She tugged at the new weapon Ciaran had just given them to make sure it was secured, then walked away. "Where are we?" Roy asked.

"Ciaran showed me the map of the energy moments underneath the seabeds, but we didn't have a chance to convert the information to a surface map. But I think we're somewhere between Japan and some small islands in Southeast Asia. I could locate us by triangulating the wrist unit and the base station, but I'm reluctant to activate the signals unless it's absolutely necessary. We can ask the locals." Lorcan squinted, his hands on his hips, and glanced around the endless expanse of white sand.

"Well, this looks very promising," Orla said, rolling her eyes. From the corner of her eyes, she saw a small head with black hair popping in and out from behind a black rock. Without a single word, her hand was on her weapon, and she was charging toward the possible stalker. She moved too fast for the person behind the rock to react or run away. The group followed her.

Orla pulled her gun, pointing it at the rock. "Come out and raise your hands where I can see them." For Lorcan, she added, "Yes, I learned that from cop shows on TV."

From behind the rock, a small child stepped out. He was a boy about ten years old with short black hair and huge brown eyes, which were filled with tears. The boy had his hands in the air, suggesting he'd understood what Orla said.

"Hey, don't worry. I'm not going to shoot you," Orla soothed. She almost sounded like she was singing a lullaby. She put the gun away. The boy put his hands down, but his eyes still gleamed with tears. "I'm sorry I scared you. It's okay now. We won't hurt you. We're just a little bit lost. Do you know where we are?"

The boy stopped shaking, and a faint smile came across his face. Lorcan approached and pulled out the liquid map Ciaran had given him previously. He programmed it to reveal the surface map of the Earth and zoomed in on Asia. "Do you think you can point out on the map where we are now?" He laid the map on the ground where it flattened out and expanded like a paper map. Lorcan made a mental note to praise this technology to Ciaran. The boy crouched next to the map and reached his hand out, pointing to a particular location on the map, but before his finger could make contact, he turned his hand and pulled the gun holstered on Orla's belt. The boy jumped back to his feet, stepped back, and held the gun shakily in his little hands, pointing it at the group of people.

"Easy, easy, kid, that's not a toy," Lorcan said.

"If you put it down, and go away, we won't chase you. We don't mean any harm," Orla said.

The boy's eyes fixed on Roy and Mori. He stepped back as the group advanced. Then he lifted the gun, pointed it at Roy, and pulled the trigger. Mori yelped and dove at Roy, squashing him down.

The gun didn't discharge. It wouldn't work for him because he wasn't authorized to use it. It had been programmed only for the people in the group. The boy threw the gun on the sand and ran away.

Orla started to rush after him, but Lorcan held her back. "Let him go."

"He shot at us. The kid shot at us!"

"He didn't shoot at *us*, he shot at *Roy*," Mori said.

Roy pushed Mori off him and grabbed her shoulders. "Never, ever do that again, Mori. Do not jump in front of me to block an attack." Roy's eyes sparked with fury.

Mori waved her arms in the air in frustration. "You never know what's coming at you," she growled and walked away.

"Why did the kid shoot at me? Do I look like the kind of thug who would harm a kid?" Roy asked Lorcan and Orla.

"On the contrary, you're as beautiful as a character straight from Japanese comic books. The thing is, even the bad guys in those comic books are sinfully gorgeous. Maybe you look like a character from the dark side, Roy." Orla grinned.

"Not helpful, Orla. And since when do you read Japanese comic books?" Lorcan asked.

"I don't read them. There aren't many words. Mainly pictures."

Lorcan waved his arms in frustration. "Orla!"

"All right, all right. But my point remains. Roy might look similar to some dark character that scared the kid."

"He wasn't scared. He shot at me with hatred. With conviction," Roy said.

Lorcan nodded. "Roy's right. The boy wasn't scared. What could raise such vicious emotion in a boy who's, what, barely ten years old?" Lorcan shook his head.

"It has to do with his family." Orla looked down at the sand where the boy had stood before. She said that more to herself than in response to Lorcan's question. As a part of her training in sorcery, her family had tried to bring up evil spirits in her since she was as young as six years old. Orla felt a tug at her arm and saw Lorcan had grabbed hold of her hands. He pulled her into his arms. He said nothing, but she knew he could read what she was thinking.

"Mori found something," Roy said and ran toward Mori. Mori was crouching, examining something on the ground. Orla and Lorcan followed Roy. As they approached, she was staring at a small piece of black rock peeking through the white sand. Roy crouched next to Mori and then looked at Lorcan and Orla. "There are werefoxes nearby."

"Was the boy . . . ?" Orla asked.

Roy shook his head. "I can't tell."

Mori stood up and headed west. They followed her.

After walking for a bit, they approached a small village, a generous description of a handful of temporary shelters carved into the sandy hills. Sandstone cliffs stood tall, arcing into natural dome, bizarre patterns imprinted on the rocks by the wind and water. The breeze blew in between the cliffs and the patterned rocks, creating an eerie flutelike sound, soulful and haunting. The sun was drifting away quickly, leaving a last drop of sunlight on the shiny limestone of the cliffs.

Standing at the entrance to the village, they could see sparkling eyes from the shelters looking at them. They inched a bit closer, and the rumbling noise of growls became audible.

"Don't go inside. They'll become hostile, whatever they are," Lorcan warned. Mori continued on. Roy grabbed her arm, pulling her back. She hissed at him.

"They're werefoxes. They'll recognize us. You know that, Roy," Mori protested.

"No, I don't know that, Mori. They're definitely some kind of were-creatures, but if the boy came from this group, they obviously hate me for some reason. I don't think it's a good idea to go in."

A snarl came from the shelters, followed by hisses, howls, and barking. The shadow of a little fox darted out from a shelter. Then there were many others that ran out in a herd. They stormed to a corner between two large rocks arched like a doorway and disappeared into the darkness. Mori tried to give chase, but Roy held her back.

"We chased them off. They're firefoxes, and we chased them from their home!" Mori cried out. Roy's arms were like a pair of iron pliers, gripping Mori and lifting her off the ground.

"You're not going after them, Mori. It could be a trap. They're firefoxes, but they're not your clan. We can't be here. You can't go with them. Do you hear me?" Roy wiped away Mori's tears and held her in his arms.

Lorcan and Orla checked the shelters, finding none of the foxes left. Lorcan shook his head. "They obviously need a leader. Living in this condition and running away whenever anything that remotely resembles a threat comes knocking on their door—this clan won't survive for long."

Orla hushed Lorcan. "Don't give Mori any ideas. It'll break Roy's heart if she goes with the foxes and he has to go to Eudaiz."

Lorcan shook his head and sighed. Orla pulled him into her arms, tucked away a long strand of hair flopping on his forehead, and looked into his striking blue eyes. "We're the lucky ones, aren't we?" he said and kissed her.

CHAPTER 3

As soon as the sun climbed over the top of the limestone cliffs the next morning, the group left the shelter of the werefoxes behind and headed in the direction of possible civilization. Orla was utilizing the best of her psychic ability to sense the direction. The liquid map Lorcan relied on didn't seem to work consistently. They followed the coast for a while, with the endless open water on one side and the limestone cliffs on the other.

Roy pointed in the distance. "I think that's a town." He squinted his eyes, spotting the silhouettes of buildings.

"Finally," Orla sighed. Lorcan grinned and kissed her on the cheek.

They walked a bit further and finally arrived at a town. There were a couple of blocks of small houses, a few convenience stores, a gas station, and a grocery store on the main street. Lorcan glanced around, making a mental map of the place.

"There's one thing that's missing," Lorcan mumbled.

"People," Orla whispered.

"There are were-creatures nearby," Mori said. Roy's hand hovered over his gun.

They were standing in the middle of the road, and there was no traffic. It was the middle of the day, but there were no pedestrians, no shoppers, and not even shopkeepers inside the open shops. It was like a ghost town. Lorcan pulled Orla behind him. Then he realized that they could be ambushed from behind as well.

"Stay together and . . ." Lorcan trailed off as he saw the door of the convenience store in front of them swing open. The group gathered together, their backs to one another, their hands on their guns. They moved across the road toward a corner so as not to be too exposed. They waited. Nothing happened. The air seemed to grow heavy as the waiting continued. It was so quiet that they could hear their own breathing and the sound of dry leaves scraping on the ground in the light wind.

Lorcan broke the silence. "I'll take a look in the shop."

"Don't be crazy. You walk in there, chance is you'll take a bullet," Roy objected.

"Agreed," Orla said. "I prefer you alive, Lorcan."

Orla glanced around. The wind had seemed to stop blowing. The lack of sound made the silence seem artificial, the type of vacuumed quietness often experienced in recording studios. "We're getting out of here. Back to the water—then we'll find another direction," Orla said, wincing at the unpleasant squeaking noise in her head. She wondered if it was only her who felt the eerie silence. "You hear anything strange?" Orla asked.

"Not hearing things is stranger. It's too quiet—not normal in the middle of the day," Roy responded.

Orla could feel the presence of people very close by, and she heard the squeaking noise again. This time, there was something added to it. A sobbing sound.

"Watch out!" Lorcan yelled and dove at Orla, knocking her down as an arrow flew through the air and hit a cement pole.

Lorcan cursed and pulled his gun. Everyone else followed suit. They braced themselves against an attack, facing in the general direction of the arrow's origination.

From around the corner, groups of people emerged, marching toward them with crossbows in hands.

"We've just arrived here. If we're not welcome in your town, we'll leave immediately. There's no need for violence," Lorcan told them.

The group of people continued to advance, crossbows raised high in combat position, eyes fierce and jaws clenched. When they came closer, Lorcan continued, "We don't want to fight you.

"There's no reason for this. But if you shoot at us again, our guns will do more damage than your crossbows."

Five arrows flew in their direction. The group hit the ground fast enough to avoid the arrows. They pointed their guns, ready to fire, but before they did, the fire arrow shooters dropped dead, each of them with a knife in the head. The group turned to see a large group of menacing men approaching from the fence across the street. They were heavily armed with guns.

"Damnit, we're in the middle of crossfire. Let's take cover in one of the stores," Lorcan said, heading toward an open door.

Orla, Roy, and Mori followed. Inside the convenience store, they hid behind the counter and kept watch out the window. On the street, groups of people poured from the buildings to join the fight— a fight between those with firearms on the one side and those with crossbows, knives, and anything that could be fashioned into a weapon on the other. From inside the store, the group could clearly see who had the advantage, but at the moment, they weren't sure which side was friend and which foe. They couldn't risk helping either side.

"Where are the cops? Where's the authority?" Lorcan asked. "People weren't allowed to fight like that on the streets even in the Wild West."

"Are you sure this is the right dimension? Are we on Earth? And currently in modern time?" Orla asked.

"Judging by the guns, yes. We're in modern time, Orla," Roy answered.

At a corner of the battlefield, they saw the boy they had encountered yesterday. Orla pulled her gun and charged to the back door of the building, Lorcan trailing behind her. They ran around the block so that they could approach the boy from behind. As they came closer, they could see that he was watching the fighting on the main street. Turning around and seeing Orla and the group, he darted through a gap between the two houses and ran into a small alley, disappearing among the crooked walls and ruins.

They stood on an ancient-looking street lined with gothic-style houses. This was a world much different than the center of the town just a few blocks away. They no longer heard the fighting noises of the groups slaughtering one another.

"Do you hear anything?" Orla asked.

"Only the wind," Roy answered.

"Nothing," Mori added.

Lorcan approached Orla. He knew she'd heard something. He cupped her face in his hands. "Tell me what you heard."

A tear rolled her face. "I hear crying . . . sobbing . . . moaning. Someone is saying something about the stone," she said as more tears ran down her face.

"Can you block that from your mind?" Lorcan asked. A stream of blood ran from Orla's nose, and she grabbed at her ears, breathing heavily. "Oh no, don't do this to me! Block the noise . . . we can find the stone ourselves. I don't need you to do this. Please!" Lorcan begged.

Orla concentrated and closed her eyes. Then she suddenly opened them, and they were blank.

Lorcan said nothing. He'd been through this before, and despite the pain he felt seeing her like this, he didn't stop her. He merely followed Orla as she walked, his hand resting on his gun.

Soon they stood before an imposing medieval house decorated by many bird sculptures. "The Raven House," Roy whispered.

"They're here," Orla said.

"Who?" Lorcan asked.

"The talking people . . . the stone."

Lorcan shook Orla's shoulders. "Wake up, Orla. Honey, we can't do anything if you're not with us. Come back to me."

Orla gasped as she came back to reality, blinking her eyes and falling into Lorcan's arms. He held her for a while, kissing her forehead, waiting for her to settle. Once she seemed to be back to normal, he asked, "The stone is in this house?"

Orla shook her head. "The voice said something about 'stone' and 'seeking'..."

"What if it's a trap?" Mori asked.

"There's only one way to find out." Lorcan aimed his gun high and approached the house. Orla and

Roy followed. Mori hesitated, but then followed. Lorcan pushed open a heavy oak door. As it squeaked open, a swarm of ravens and hawks flew out from the inside. Some of the birds were similar to those that had attacked them at Roy's place, the Yakuz's hawks. But these birds didn't seem to be aggressive—they simply fled the house.

"What did we just open?" Lorcan mumbled to himself.

In response to his questions, bullets rained down on them. Roy grabbed Mori and dove behind a column. Lorcan covered Orla, running toward the other side. "Are you hit?" Orla asked. Lorcan shook his head. He scanned her up and down and was pleased she wasn't injured.

Five men emerged from a dark corner of the room with guns in their hands. Under the dim light from a torch on the wall, their scaled skin glowed, and their lizard eyes sparkled with excitement in anticipation of a fight. Lorcan made eye contact with Roy, who was taking cover behind the column across the corridor. They nodded at each other in agreement. Lorcan slid across the floor from left to right, and Roy did the same from right to left. The five lizard men were sluggish in reaction and were gunned down by two rounds of laser beams from Lorcan and Roy.

Their bodies dropped on the floor and began to disintegrate, ultimately evaporating into thin air. Roy and Lorcan approached their remains as the last of their body parts vanished, and all that remained on the floor were black puddles full of swimming worms.

"Xiilok creatures. I haven't seen them before, but I've heard of them."

"Say again?" Roy asked.

"They came from a universe called Xiilok. Ciaran told me it's full of multiversal outlaws. When the Xiilok creatures die, their bodies evaporate into puddles of maggots and worms.

They searched for other reptiles, but found none alive. Orla followed the sound in her mind, entering a small door which led down to a basement. As the door opened, the crying sound stopped. On the wall, they saw sixteen people, shackled. Orla searched for the locks to pick, but she found none. The steel chains were cemented into the wall. All sixteen people were still alive. A man in his late thirties looked at Roy, snarling and saying something in a language that made no sense. Roy didn't understand, but he could guess as to the meaning. He spoke to the man in English. "I am not who you think I am. We have just arrived, and we have nothing to do with why you are chained up here."

The man didn't seem to understand what Roy was saying and continued his verbal assault. A woman from the right corner uttered something to the man that calmed him down. They thought she had translated what Roy had said to the man because she turned toward Roy and spoke in English, saying, "One of the men who captured us and brought us here looks like you."

"I don't see any resemblance between me and the reptile men we just killed upstairs."

"They're not the ones who captured us. They're just guarding us. They have been locked in here with us for quite some time."

"How long have you been here?" Orla asked.

"A few days . . . or maybe a week . . . we lost track of time." The woman yanked at her chains.

"They're buried into the wall, just like the gatekeeper at Gate 313." Lorcan clenched his jaw and searched for something he could use to free the people. Veering off to a different wing, he noticed the handle of a small compartment. He touched it. There was no movement. The rusty handle looked as if it hadn't been opened for a long time. He jiggled it and pulled.

All Lorcan remembered was a sudden and unstoppable suction into the darkness.

The soothing voice of his mother echoed in his ears, making him smile. "Lorcan, you went to the river bank again. You know your father won't be happy about this."

"Then please don't tell him, Mother," answered six-year-old Lorcan as he blinked his innocent blue eyes at his mother. She smiled and pulled him in for an embrace.

"All right, I won't tell him this time, but only because it'll upset him. Not because you're fluttering those blue eyes at me again."

"What's wrong with the river, Mother?" Lorcan asked, nuzzling in his mother arms.

"There's nothing wrong with the river. It's just the people who use it. They're bad for you."

"She can't be . . ."

His mother looked into his eyes. "Who did you see, Lorcan?" Her voice shook.

"Just a little girl playing in the sand, Mother. She's very little . . . very pretty. I didn't talk to her . . . I just looked. Please don't be mad at me." Lorcan started to pout, and tears gleamed in his eyes. His mother smiled. "Oh, my little boy! She's your first crush! How could I be mad at you? Whoever that little girl is, her parents shouldn't let her wander to that river."

"Her mother was with her. They built sand castles on the riverbank."

His mother kissed his forehead. "I can take you to any river you want, but not that one. We can build a castle on the sand, and one day, you'll be able to give your princess a real castle."

Lorcan smiled. "Would you really help me do that? Would you help me build a castle for my princess? Can I find a princess? I mean, one who would like me? Will I be able to find a princess like the girl at the river?"

"You ask too many questions, my son. I don't have the answers for most of them. But I'm sure you'll find your princess, and I'll help you build your castle." She embraced him again and kissed his forehead. A tear found its way down his face.

Lorcan opened his eyes to find himself in Orla's arms. He sprang to his feet and asked, "Orla, honey, why are you crying?" He glanced around. He was still in that dark wing of the basement where he had been searching for a way to free those shackled people. Orla stared at him and burst out in tears. He pulled her into his arms. "It's okay, darling. I just passed out for a bit . . ."

Roy and Mori approached. Mori pulled Orla from Lorcan's arms. "Come on, we should go. People are waiting," Mori said.

"What's going on?" Lorcan asked Roy. "I just checked that door . . ." He pointed to the compartment door and found a solid wall instead. Lorcan exhaled and collected himself. "Okay, I might have passed out for a bit."

"You didn't just pass out. You didn't have any pulse when we found you, Lorcan. No heartbeat, no breathing, no response whatsoever."

CHAPTER 4

Lorcan stepped outside the door of the house with Roy. The sixteen people who had been shackled in the basement were waiting.

"How did you guys free them?" Lorcan asked.

Roy shrugged. "Not rocket science. I found a few shovels."

Lorcan nodded. "All right then, you proved me useless."

"No big deal. You scared Orla to death when you passed out. More earth-shattering to her than my digging out a few loose bricks."

Lorcan nodded. He went to Orla, but she looked away and walked toward the woman who had spoken English.

"What's your name?"

"Rose."

"I'm Orla. And they're Lorcan, Roy, and Mori. Anyone else in your group speak English?"

Rose shook her head.

"What language do you speak here?" Lorcan asked.

"A forgotten one."

Orla glanced at Lorcan, and then turned again toward Rose. "We should go back into town. Do you think you can find your people there?"

Rose nodded, glancing back at Lorcan, and walked away with Orla. Mori hurried along with them, leaving Lorcan standing alone. Roy approached.

"Give Orla some time. It was a shock." He patted Lorcan's shoulder, and they both trailed behind the group of people heading back into town.

The main streets where the fighting had occurred before seemed quiet. The group of sixteen strode through the main streets, followed by Orla, Lorcan, Roy, and Mori. In front of them, bodies and body parts were strewn across the street. Blood pooled on the ground in places. It was dead silent.

The people ran to the bodies, too shocked to even cry.

"That's my brother," Rose said as she ran toward the body of a young man in his twenties, lying half-on, half-off a sidewalk. He'd been shot in the chest. Rose sobbed and gathered his body into her arms. Orla crouched next to her.

"There was a big fight here this morning. Do you know who killed your brother? Are they likely to come back?"

Rose shook her head. "I know who they are. But I don't know if they'll come back."

They heard a door slamming and then footsteps around the corner. Lorcan, Roy, Mori, and Orla gathered quickly, their backs to one another, weapons drawn.

From a side street, a group of people charged at them.

"Don't shoot!" Rose shouted at the attacking people. The man leading the attacking group lowered his crossbow and looked at Rose.

"Rose? Rose! Thank God, you're all okay!" He said, surveying everyone and pulling Rose into his arms for an embrace. She hugged him back tightly. Then the whole group of people hugged one another and cried with joy. The man turned to explain to the group about the fight—and the bodies. They talked, shouted, and cried. Some started to gather the dead bodies, and others just stood dazed, unsure of what to do.

"How long will this reunion be?" Orla mumbled to herself. "We need to find the stone so we can go home."

"So the Daimon Gate is home now?" Lorcan looked at Orla. She looked at him, and then to the ground, saying nothing.

Before Lorcan could say anything further, the man and the group of people approached them. The man extended his hand to Lorcan. Lorcan shook hands. "I am Jay," the man said. "I help organize things around here." Jay lowered his heavy American accented voice when he glanced back at the dead bodies.

"By organizing, I take it that you're the leader of this group, and you might be responsible for the bloodbath this morning?" Lorcan accused.

Jay nodded. "Yes, I'm responsible. But it was necessary. I'll do whatever it takes to protect my people."

"Does that include the sixteen we found shackled in the house a few blocks from here?" Lorcan nodded at the group people.

Jay snarled, "You're in no position to judge us. You're strangers here."

Rose approached. "They saved us, Jay."

Jay nodded. "And I very much appreciate it."

Lorcan looked up and saw that the sun was starting to set for the day. He looked at Jay. "We need a place to stay tonight. Could you point us in the direction of a hotel?"

"We're on lock down. No business can be conducted in town."

"Lock down? If I'm not mistaken, your authority is enforced by a group of men with crossbows and butcher knives. Your adversaries are armed with machine guns. If it's your town, and you're locking down to prevent them from attacking, I think you've got a very slim chance," Lorcan said.

Jay smirked. "We chased them off." He gestured widely.

"At the cost of how many casualties?" Lorcan nodded toward the dead bodies.

"What do you want?" Jay growled.

"Let us know where we are, and where to find the next town, and we'll be on our way."

"Why don't you stay here for the night? I'm sure your people need a rest," Rose interjected.

Lorcan looked at Orla. "We sure need a rest, but we don't want to be in the crossfire again."

"Especially when you think we have no chance?"

"Rose!" Jay called out.

Rose swung around and snarled at Jay. "Come on Jay, there's no room for your ego. We need their help."

"We didn't say we were going to stay to help. We don't even know you. We've got things we need to do that require us staying alive," Roy said.

"Then you should leave. We can take care of our own," Jay said. "Follow the coastal line until you reach Japan."

"Japan? I don't think we're anywhere near Japan," Roy said.

Lorcan pulled out his liquid map and showed it to Rose. "Can you help us?" Rose glanced at the map, and looked up at Lorcan. "I'm sorry. I really want to help, but we're not on that."

"What do you mean?"

"We're not on the map."

Jay pointed to the middle of the ocean. "We'd be somewhere around there."

"Are you saying the map is missing an island?" Lorcan snorted.

Jay shook his head. "I don't know. It used to be a popular island. But it's been eleven years now that no one can get off the island. If you get on a boat and row out, you'll just go around in a circle." Jay shrugged. "We accept it now. No one tries anymore. So . . . what are you?"

"You mean, *who* are we?" Orla asked.

Jay laughed. "I used to be an English teacher. I know the difference between what and who. Only creatures can transport on and off of this island."

"Oh, I'm . . ."

"The ones you fought with this morning, are they human?" Lorcan cut in before Orla could finish her sentence.

"They're shapeshifters. Many are werewolves. But they stay in human form most of the time so that they can use weapons."

Lorcan glanced at his map, then nodded. "If you don't mind, we'll stay here tonight and figure out our next move tomorrow." Here would be better than being out there among the well-armed men he'd seen this morning, Lorcan thought.

"You can stay at my place. It's nothing fancy, but it's comfortable," Rose said. She glared at Jay then walked ahead.

Jay glanced at Roy. "No, I think the guests should stay with me. My house has plenty of room." Jay didn't wait for a response but gestured them to follow.

"He just wants to keep an eye on me," Roy grumbled.

Jay led the group to a two-story modern house. The decoration was tasty, Orla thought. She arched an eyebrow at the contemporary furniture and expensive antiques in a glass-encased cabinet. She hadn't dealt with antiques for a while, but she was sure these items were authentic. She approached the cabinet but was stopped by Jay on the way.

"Nice vase." She pointed.

"It's not for flowers," Jay said.

"Can I take a look?"

Jay smiled. "Tomorrow. Your room is this way." He pointed to a corridor at the far end of the living room and proceeded forward. Orla shrugged and followed, making a mental note to revisit the cabinet. If it was true that humans could not travel to and from the island, and Jay was one of the last human travelers here, where, then, did he get these valuable items? Orla wondered.

Jay had left the room, and Orla was pacing, agitated, still thinking about the antiques.

"Orla!"

"Huh?" She ignored Lorcan and channeled her mind back to the antiques.

"Orla!" Lorcan repeated. "I'm going to activate the wrist unit to see if I can triangulate our position using the system in the Daimon Gate. We need to know exactly where we are before we can find the stone."

Orla looked up, saw Lorcan's face, and bounced back to reality. The incident at the Raven House this morning came flooding back to her mind.

Lorcan cupped her face. "Talk to me, Orla!"

She shoved him away. "I need to be alone for a bit. I'm going out for a walk." She turned to exit the room. Lorcan grabbed her elbow.

"No. You're not going anywhere until we talk this out. What's the matter?"

"Let go of my arm." She shrugged him off and tried to head toward the door, but Lorcan grabbed her again. Orla whirled around, and before Lorcan realized what was happening, she'd slapped him across the face. He could taste the blood from his split bottom lip.

"Is that what you want? Okay, hit me then if that's what makes you feel better. But then tell me what the fuck is going on with you." Lorcan grabbed her, pressing her hands against his chest. But she shoved him away again and turned toward the door. He pulled her back against him. She punched his chest and wriggled to break free. "You're going nowhere until you tell me what I did wrong."

She extricated herself from his grip and jabbed her finger at his chest. "You . . . you died. Again." A tear escaped her eye.

"Well, that's entirely my fault then. I'll try not to die next time," he promised softly.

Orla sniffled and wiped the tear away. Realizing the ridiculousness of the situation, she snorted, "Infidelity and death are the two things I will not allow from you. Everything else goes."

He arched an eyebrow. "*Everything* else?" Before she could answer, he grabbed her and threw her on the bed. She landed on her back on the bed, but when he dove after her, she'd rolled off to the other side. She reached over and ripped his shirt open. He hooked a hand in the collar of her shirt and ripped open the front of her blouse. He pressed his mouth to hers, wincing at the sensation in his wounded lip. He sat up enough to look down at her face and her big brown eyes, full of challenge, and her lips, currently curled in a smug smile. She laughed and grabbed two fistfuls of his hair. She wanted devour him, one greedy bite at a time.

She groaned her pleasure as he ran his teeth down her throat. She wrapped her legs around his waist, moving herself on top so that he was under her. Then her mouth was on his. He pulled at her clothes like a man possessed by demons. Her smooth skin rubbed against his. Her hands and her lips took possession of him. He'd taken her beyond reason. Near delirium, he rolled over so she was once again on her back, and he devoured her.

Lips, teeth, tongues, and fingers demanded and took.

"You're mine. And I'm all yours," he whispered into her ears. "All of me."

"Now. Come to me now," she said as she arched her back. He drove into her, and she cried out, "Don't you ever die on me again."

"I promise."

And then they loved each other, moving together in rhythm, bringing on another into the glorious darkness of pleasure.

CHAPTER 5

The next day, Lorcan found Jay sitting on the back veranda, a cup of tea in his hand, watching the sun rise over the trees of the tropical forest in the distance. The horizon glowed in the glorious orange glow of sunlight.

"It's going to be a hot day," Jay said when he saw Lorcan approaching and gestured toward a chair. "I have tea, coffee, and things enough for a simple breakfast for you and your friends. You can help yourself before you hit the road."

Lorcan sat down. "I'd kill for a cup of coffee—any sort of coffee as long as it contains caffeine. But

Orla's very picky. She only drinks a certain type. Not only that, it has to be brewed in a certain way. She makes it very difficult when we're on the road, you know."

Jay laughed. "Women," he said and shook his head. "You and Orla are made for each other. I've been isolated from the human population for quite some time, but I can still tell. That says something about your relationship. Strong. Enduring . . ." Jay's voice hollowed out and he trailed off. Then silence.

"Where's your family now? I saw pictures in the living room."

Jay sipped his tea and looked at Lorcan over the rim of the cup. "You don't have to show an interest in my story, Lorcan. The truth is, if you're human, and you somehow got in to this town, you won't be able to get out. If you're not human, then you'll be able to come and go as you please. My advice is to leave as soon as you can."

"What happened here?"

Jay stared.

"Come on, I want to know."

"I taught English for a living in a community language center in New Jersey. I love travelling. You know—adventure, going places, meeting new and interesting people. This island was a treasure. Great for travel addicts like me. It was a real getaway. Apart from a connecting ferry, there's no other transportation in and out. I got on the ferry eleven years ago. Arrived and stayed for a few days. Then bam—we got hit by a heavy storm. That's about it. The humans were disconnected from the outside world. This island became heaven for creatures because of that isolation. Clans have been fighting over territories for a very long time."

"Do you know the number of humans remaining?"

Jay shook his head. "I don't know about the locals. I take care of the group of tourists. There are ninety of us . . . and the number is decreasing . . ."

They heard footsteps on the veranda, and Mori stormed out. "I can't find Roy. He's not in his room. He . . . he . . ."

Lorcan stopped Mori's stuttering, dragging her to the corner of the veranda. He lowered his voice, "He might have just gone for a run?"

"No . . . He told me he'd meet me in the front yard, and we'd walk into town. But he didn't go out."

"All right, calm down. Go get Orla, and then we'll look for Roy."

As Mori scurried away, Lorcan approached Jay. Sitting down opposite him, he stared into his eyes and said, "When we first arrived, there was a boy at the beach. He grabbed Orla's gun and tried to shoot Roy. When we saved your people at the Raven House, they thought Roy was one of the people or creatures that had imprisoned them. You know why, and I need you to tell me."

"What kid?"

Lorcan described the boy, and Jay nodded. "His name is Michael Harris. He's Rose's eldest son. If you head south for about four miles, there's a small forest, I think you might find Roy there, if he is who I think he is."

"And who do you think he is?"

"A creature. A werewolf, to be precise."

Lorcan shook his head. "Why is that such a big deal? Didn't you say the town is full of creatures?"

"But that's the most vicious clan. They feed on human blood. Were-creatures are bad news," Jay explained.

"There's one thing I can assure you of—Roy is our friend, and he's harmless."

Jay shrugged. "I hope so. Good luck with the search. You'll need your guns."

Roy ran as fast as he could. The werewolf in human form who ran in front of him was strong and fast. It carried a bag with little red fox Mori in it—

Roy could see her tail waving as the werewolf flew through the woods. It knew its way through the brush. Roy knew he'd be faster in fox form, but he wanted to be able to use his gun, so he remained human. He was stumbling all over the place. He was in a hurry and panicking, and he couldn't catch Mori's scent. He had to keep up with the man in front of him if he was going to save her.

Suddenly the man stopped running. He turned back with a grin on his face.

"Hello, brother!"

"Who the fuck is your brother? Let her go." Roy pointed at the bag. He could see the red tail poking out from inside and feel his blood boiling with fury, but he collected himself and tried to remain calm. He couldn't afford a wrong move.

"Let's go inside. My alpha is waiting for you. We can talk this out."

Roy glanced at the dark hole in front of him. It was the mouth of a cave, and he had no intention of going inside. The man wasn't as tall as Roy, but he was over six feet, and he was hulky. Roy knew the half-fox gene in him made him leaner and faster than a wolf, but not necessarily weaker. He adjusted his stance and checked to be sure his gun was still at the ready. If a fight broke out, he'd use his weapon first. Shifting and fighting in fox form was his last resource.

"Why aren't you coming in?" the man asked.

"Why don't you call your boss out here, and we can negotiate."

The man smirked. "You're scared. That's embarrassing. A disgrace to our breed."

"We don't share any DNA. If the head of your clan won't come out, I'm leaving."

"You jackass . . ."

"Language, Khulan. He's still a guest," chastised another voice. "I'll come out and welcome him to the family."

"I'm not your family. Not even close," Roy growled.

A formidable man wearing Native American garb now stood in front of him. The minimal outfit showed off impressive muscles that, when amplified by werewolf strength, could prove lethal to Roy. Ten more men emerged from the cave.

"Give me Mori," Roy demanded, firmness in his voice.

The well-built man arched an eyebrow.

"Tell me what you want from me," Roy asked.

"My name is Ganzorig, and I am the alpha of this clan."

Roy nodded. "What do you want from me so that I can have Mori back?"

Ganzorig smiled. "I can see you really care for your little firefox. One threat, and you trailed us all the way here. Did you mate her?"

"Don't you dare . . ." Roy clenched his teeth and his hand tightened on the gun.

"Calm down, Roy. Pointing a gun at me won't do you any good. I've heard about your reputation. The vicious mixed-blood renegade who chose to be a fox instead of a wolf."

"I'm asking for the last time . . . what do you want?"

"Who has the key of Psuche?"

"What key?"

"Don't play dumb, Roy. It doesn't suit you. You came here looking for the Indigo Stone. You've got to have the key."

"I don't know what you're talking about. I don't have any key. As much as it will humiliate me, I'll let you search me to make sure."

Ganzorig shook his head. "You're not stupid. You wouldn't have the key on you, but I know your people have the key. I'm sure of it. I saw you land from the sky. Quite a powerful toy you've got there. So you have the dragon in the water, and that big plane in the sky, and for some reason you think you're safe? You're wrong because we know your weakness. We're stronger. And we have the stone."

"No need to bluff. I don't have the key, and you don't have the stone. If you had it, you wouldn't have had to use Mori to lure me out here. Let's say we play by the rules—let's fight. If I win, I take Mori back. If I lose, I'll tell you all I know," Roy suggested.

Ganzorig nodded. "Sounds like a fair deal." He waved his hand at the other men. They nodded and shifted into wolves. They were enormous.

Roy looked at Ganzorig. Ganzorig let out a short laugh. "You didn't say it had to be a one on one fight."

Roy smiled. "My bad. You're right—I didn't say that." Then fast as lightning, he pulled his gun and blasted it at the dogs. In a few seconds, the wolves lay dead on the ground. Ganzorig howled and charged at Roy but was stopped by the muzzle of Roy's gun.

"Shoot me!" Ganzorig said.

Roy whacked him with the gun barrel instead, knocking him out cold. Then he ran immediately to the bag and pulled the little red fox out.

It wasn't Mori.

"Shit," Roy mumbled under his breath. He stood up and found it difficult to regain his balance. His vision was blurry, and his legs weak. He heard footsteps approaching in the distance. Thinking it to be Ganzorig's pack, he rushed to a tree to take cover behind it. It was then that he saw Mori frantically sniffing the air, searching for his scent. Lorcan and Orla were right behind her. Roy stepped out from his hiding place, and Mori saw him immediately. She ran to him, checking him up and down for injuries. Mori was saying something as tears streamed down her face, but Roy couldn't make sense of what she was saying. His body swayed, and his eyes glazed over.

Lorcan grabbed Roy's wrist unit. "Damn it. Ten percent. You only have ten percent energy left, Roy. How could it suddenly go down that fast?" On a hunch, Lorcan checked his own wrist unit. "Oh, no. The signals are all messed up."

Orla looked at Lorcan's unit. "It's broken?" she asked.

Lorcan shook his head. "No, it's either a magnetic force or energy movements underneath the surface." He moved away a few feet and observed the changes in his unit. "All right. It seems to be an issue with magnetic energy. Let's move Roy out of here. Can you walk, Roy?"

No response.

"We've got to get him out of here," Mori said and pulled at Roy. Orla and Mori flanked Roy's sides, helping him move in the right direction. Lorcan ran ahead, watching his unit as he went and giving direction to an area that seemed to have less magnetic influence. "Left. Left. Keep going." Lorcan scurried further ahead and tried a couple of options. "Veer right. Okay."

Roy was running slower and slower by the second. His wrist unit beeped a five percent warning. He gradually slowed down and stopped altogether. Before he flopped down to the ground, Mori slid her arm around his waist and wrapped his arm around her shoulders. "You have to get up and walk for me, Roy."

Howling echoed through the woods. Ganzorig's pack was coming. Orla darted back in that direction. She could see wolves' shadows.

"Orla, what are you doing?" Lorcan asked.

"I can wipe them out. You keep going." She dashed back toward the pack before Lorcan could respond. In a few seconds, fireballs were flying through the air, knocking down a few trees in their path. Lorcan darted ahead to check the magnetic field and then came back to Mori. "This way," he told her, "and keep it straight." He pointed then rushed to where Orla was fighting the wolves.

Roy dropped to the ground again. His wrist unit now indicated only three percent. She got behind Roy, wrapped her arms around his chest, and dragged him.

"Let go of me, Mori. Go! Run!" Roy whispered in his delirium.

"The hell I'll leave you here." She continued pulling him with all her strength, keeping it straight as Lorcan had said. She had to make it—he had to be okay. She fell a few times, but she got up and kept moving.

Mori could see a storm of fire in the distance and hear gunfire and the howls of wounded dogs. She kept moving. It was a bit of an uphill path, but it appeared to be the last leg out of the woods. She slipped a few times, grabbing tree roots, tree branches, rocks, and anything she could find to balance herself and keep moving. Her hand was scratched and bleeding. Roy was no longer conscious.

Reaching the edge of the forest, Mori flopped down on the ground, breathing hard. Roy lay beside her, lifeless. She looked at his wrist unit and saw a glaring red signal which stated zero percent. "Damn it! Damn you, Roy." She cried and punched his chest. From the woods behind her, Orla and Lorcan walked out, filthy with ashes and smears of blood. Lorcan had a new gash on his arm.

Lorcan checked his wrist unit—it seemed to be operating normally. "This is neutral ground. You made it." He opened a small lid on the back of Roy's wrist unit. Removing a small component, he did some coding and then snapped the part back in. The unit blinked red but quickly turned green and stated one percent.

Mori cried with relief. Orla gathered her into her arms and let her sob. When Roy got to fifteen percent, he regained consciousness and could walk by himself. By the time they got back to Jay's house, Roy had gotten eighty percent of his energy back. Jay met them in the living room.

"You guys look like crap. Which one of you needs the doctor first? There's only one medical doctor in town."

"No need to call the doctor. We can take care of ourselves," Roy said as he gingerly took Mori's injured hand and led her to her room.

CHAPTER 6

Roy took Mori to her bed. He fetched a bucket of water and sat at her bedside, washing the dirt and dried blood from her bleeding hand and checking the scratches that covered her arms. He focused silently on the simple task as if his life depended on it. He hadn't spoken since he'd gotten his strength back.

"I'll heal." Mori broke the silence.

Roy wiped off the last bit of blood. "Your healing process is always slow. This might hurt a bit."

"Why did you go to the woods to kill those wolves? Who were they?"

He shook his head. "I was stupid."

"That doesn't answer my questions."

Roy put the water away and sat back down by the bedside. He tucked away a stray strand of red hair on her forehead and looked into her eyes. "I saw a man tuck a red fox into a bag and run. I thought it was you, so I panicked and ran after him. Despite a gut feeling telling me it wasn't you, and the fact I didn't catch any scent of you at all, I chased him." Roy wiped away a tear that fell from Mori's eye. "There were countless moments during the chase when I thought I'd lose you forever if that man killed you. The fear clouded my better judgment."

Roy sank deeper into the bed, lowering his body, so close he could feel Mori's breath against his skin. His fingers trailed down her jawline as she looked up at him.

"What did you say to me when we were in the boat, and I was about to die from the poison?"

"But you didn't die." Mori looked away, avoiding his question.

"Unless you said something you now regret, or you lied to me, I'd like to hear you say it again."

"It makes no difference to our situation, Roy."

"What situation? I love you, Mori. You know that. I'd bet my life that you love me, too. So why can't we be together? Why can't we mate?" Roy was on the bed, almost lying on top of her. His body rubbed against hers, every muscle in him quivering as her body vibrated with desire. She said nothing, starting to wriggle out from under him. Roy's mouth hovered an inch from hers. She could see his eyes darken, submerged in the simmering heat of lust. The virility of his body seeped out from every pore. The wolfness in him was prominent now— dangerous, dark, and incredibly strong.

She wriggled again, and he grabbed her hands, pinning them to the bed. "Why can't you be mine?" he asked hoarsely and pressed his lips to hers. Her lips parted, and his heat rushed into her body like a tidal wave of energy. He kissed harder, breathing heavily. His body tensed. "Why can't you be mine?" he asked again. Mori closed her eyes. He was much too strong for her. If he wanted to take her, there was nothing she could do. Another tear ran down her face.

"No," Mori managed to utter.

But Roy didn't stop. He pressed down harder. He tried to kiss her again.

"Roy, I said no!" Mori cried out, struggling to escape Roy's grip. Regardless of how hard she tried, she couldn't get away. Roy's body didn't move an inch. She avoided the kiss, and he was now raking his teeth down her jawline to her neck. He was going to claim her. She tried to shove him upward so that she could see his face and look into his eyes. She knew she could stop him that way. But his thirst for lust was overwhelming. Mori couldn't get away. She cried out in frustration.

Mori's cry snapped Roy back to reality. He propped himself up on his elbows, breathing heavily, and looked into Mori's face, seeing her tears. His body was still shaking with desire, his eyes dazed with confusion. Before he could say anything, they heard a low growl, and Lorcan pulled Roy off Mori, giving him a punch to the face. He then dragged Roy to the veranda.

"You tried to rape her, you fucking scum bag."

Roy shoved Lorcan. "I didn't."

"When a woman says no, and you don't listen, what the fuck do you call that?"

"Were we that loud?"

"I have fox ears now, you jackass."

"I don't know what happened. I was just so drawn to her, and I tried to kiss her . . . I don't know . . . . I just wanted her so much that it took over. It's never happened before, I swear. I didn't mean it. I'd never do anything to hurt her."

Roy flopped down on the bench, raking his hands through his hair.

"You're telling me that you guys are as close as you are, but you've never kissed her before?" asked Lorcan.

Roy shook his head.

Lorcan knew laughing wasn't appropriate, so he cleared his throat and mumbled, "Well, that sucks. Anyone with half a brain could see you're head over heels in love with her, and she is with you. What's stopping you from going with your feelings? From loving each other? Whatever it is, it must be stupid . . ."

"It is stupid," Roy rumbled, staring at his hands. Then he looked up at Lorcan. "She cried. I must have hurt her." Roy jumped to his feet to go back inside.

"I wouldn't go in if I were you. You might risk injury to an important part of your body."

"Stop!" Orla's yell, coming from inside the house, accompanied the shattering of glass and sent Lorcan and Roy charging in. They arrived in the living room to see only a shadow of Orla outside the front yard, followed by Jay. The last light of the sunset wasn't enough for Lorcan and Roy to see what Orla was chasing. Whatever it was, she had lost it. When Lorcan, Jay, and Roy finally caught up, Orla stood still, bent at the waist, puffing and gazing into the darkness.

"What was that, Orla?" Lorcan asked.

"The kid we saw at the beach? He was in the house. I saw him in the living room."

"That's impossible," Jay said.

"He broke in?" Roy asked.

"No, he just walked in like he belonged there," Orla said, approaching Jay.

"You know Rose's son wanted to kill Roy. You asked us to stay with you, and you let the kid in. What's your game, Jay?" Lorcan raised his voice.

"No game," Jay defended weakly. A slice of freezing air whipped by, fierce and sudden, and the wind came in waves, blown by a gigantic flapping wings. It was too dark to see the creature coming at them. They heard Jay's scream. Orla waved her arms urgently, making a fireball and throwing it randomly to shed some light on the situation. The fire died out quickly, but it illuminated a gigantic pair of claws gripping Jay's shoulders and lifting him off the ground. The more Jay screamed and struggled, the more his flesh tore and his blood rained down.

Roy and Orla jumped up, each of them grabbing one of Jay's legs. The weight of their bodies hurt Jay more, but the creature couldn't lift the body weight of all three people. Lorcan drew his gun, aimed it above Jay, and fired. The sound of the gunshot dissipated in the air—followed by nothing, suggesting Lorcan had missed. He fired again. This time, they heard a squawk. He fired another shot, aiming at the same spot. There was a louder scream, and all three were released and fell to the ground.

They heard a tremendous flapping sound as the creature flew off into the night sky. On the ground, Jay was no longer conscious. His shoulders were soaked in blood, each of the cuts bone-deep. They carried him carefully back to the house, not wanting to cause any more damage. Once inside, they lay Jay down on the carpet in the living room.

"I'm not sure he'll make it," Lorcan said, concerned.

"He'd mentioned a medical doctor before. Let's get the doctor for him," Roy suggested.

Rose suddenly charged into the house from the front door. "I heard the commotion. . ." she started, and then saw Jay. "Oh, Jay!" she ran over, crouching next to him. She checked his pulse. "Still breathing," she said. She looked up and said, "I'll go and get the doctor."

"I assume there's no telephone network here?" asked Roy.

Rose shook her head and tucked Jay's head in between two cushions. She used the tablecloths to stanch the blood.

"I'll go with you," Orla said to Rose.

"No, you stay with him. I'll go," Lorcan objected.

"No, Lorcan," Orla growled.

Rose stood up and rushed to the door. Lorcan held Orla's elbow, stopping her from following. "Her son shot at us. You think I'd let you follow her out to the woods in the dark?"

"There's magic involved, Lorcan. I knew it. I don't recall magic being *your* expertise." Roy opened his mouth to say something but stopped as Orla jabbed her finger at him. "And you! Her son wants you dead, so you're not going, either."

"What if she doesn't come back?" Roy asked.

"That's not the worst scenario. What if she comes back with a herd of creatures?" Lorcan asked.

"Let her. There are four of us and we have . . ." Roy trailed off. "Wait—where's Mori?" Before anyone could say anything, he ran to Mori's room. Lorcan and Orla followed. Kicking the door in, they saw a trashed room with blood smears all over the white walls. Roy was half way out the broken window when Lorcan dragged him back inside.

"I left her here alone. They took her." Roy shoved Lorcan. "I'm a fucking useless piece of scum. I hurt her, then left her alone for those fucking hounds to get her."

"Are you talking about those wolves in the woods? Why would they want to take Mori?" Lorcan asked.

"They wanted the key of Psuche." Roy looked at Lorcan and Orla, devastated. "I know I should have told you. There wasn't any time in between . . ."

"You're telling us now. It's not too late. At least we know we have competition here," Orla said.

"Do they have the stone?" Lorcan asked.

"They said they do, but I don't think so." Roy gazed out the window. "They called me brother. I think they might be a part of the clan from my mother's side."

"Does that mean they won't kill Mori?" Orla asked.

Roy shook his head. "It's my fault."

"Don't be silly. You can't choose your blood. Plus, I don't know how much of the wolf blood is even left in you. You belong to another universe now. So when you go head on with the wolves, I want you to keep that in mind," Lorcan said.

"Creature," Orla said and ran back to the living room. Roy and Lorcan followed. In the living room, crouching next to Jay was a strange man. He looked up when the group entered the living room, and a flash of realization came across his face. He stood up. He was tall with round eyes, and he had a dark green reptilian skin. He shuddered, his skin glowing for a moment before returning to a more human state of pale skin, deep green eyes, and thick black hair.

Orla stared into those green eyes, trying to make sense of them. And then she recognized them. The recognition stunted her movement as much as the man's.

Lorcan grabbed Orla, shoving her behind him, and stepped forward. The man looked at Lorcan, realization dawning on him. His eyes lit up with fury, and his hands curled into fists. Orla held her breath and made fists as well, but she knew her fire was a child's toy compared to the blue fire forming in the man's hands. If the man shot that at them, there was no way she could protect Lorcan and Roy—they would all turn into pitiful piles of ashes.

Lorcan and Roy pulled their guns and aimed at the man.

"Don't shoot! Don't!" Orla commanded urgently.

"If he throws that at us, he'll have to take a beam from me," Lorcan snarled.

The man smirked and raised a hand, making a squeezing gesture in in the air. Lorcan shoved Orla further behind him and shot at the man. His beam flew out but was deflected into the air, dissolving into the nothingness right in front of the man. A crooked grin spread across the man's face as Lorcan slumped to the ground, dropped his gun, and grabbed at his chest, gasping for air. Roy charged at the man.

"Don't, Roy!" Orla yelled so firmly that he stopped short in his path. Orla held Lorcan. A stream of blood trickled from the corner of his mouth, and his face was turning blue. She turned to the man and glared at him. He continued to squeeze the air, simultaneously squeezing Lorcan's chest with an invisible hand. Lorcan continued to gasp for air, the skin on his arms turning blue.

Orla and Roy ran at the man. Still holding Lorcan with one arm, the man waved his other arm and Orla and Roy were knocked back on the floor, dazed with the impact.

Lorcan looked as if he was shifting into his fox form. The man pushed a harder squeeze at him. Lorcan grunted, and fire flashed in his eyes. The man yelped, withdrawing his hands as if electrocuted. He staggered back, looking at Lorcan, then raised his arms again to try something else.

On the ground, Jay opened his eyes and grabbed the man's leg. He said something in a strange language, and the man grunted a response. Jay said something else, and the man roared in anger, darted out the door. Then Jay passed out again.

Still gasping for air, Lorcan pushed to his feet and rushed toward the door as fast as he could. Roy grabbed him, pulling him back inside the house. It didn't take much for Roy to drag Lorcan back to his room, whacking him in the head once he got him there to knock him out cold. Roy turned to see Orla in the doorway.

"He's yours now." Roy said as he walked back toward the living room.

"You're not going after Mori now, are you?" Orla asked.

Roy shook his head and walked down the hall. Orla tucked Lorcan in. She pushed the bookshelf over to block the window, then locked the room door, securing a bedside table outside with a vase on top as a kind of alarm. If he woke up and tried to leave the room, she'd hear him. She left the room and went downstairs to the living room.

CHAPTER 7

Rose had come back with the doctor. Roy helped carry Jay to his room. The doctor checked him over and was happy the wounds hadn't been fatal. He gave instructions to Rose for Jay's care and was about to head out when they heard the vase crash.

"Damn it," Orla cursed and ran toward their room. Roy, Rose, and the doctor followed.

"Could you please stay here with Jay?" Rose asked the doctor. The doctor nodded and stayed back.

In the hall, they found Lorcan walking toward them, holding his hand against the wall for balance, wheezing and gasping for air. A stream of blood still flowed from his mouth.

Roy grabbed him, cursing. "You idiot. I thought you'd pass out and heal."

Lorcan shook his head. "I didn't know how long it would take, and I need to talk to Orla."

She wrapped her arms around him, steering him back to the room. "All right. We can talk." Her eyes gleamed with tears, but she refused to let them fall. "Could you get the doctor, Rose?" Orla asked. Rose nodded and scurried off to find him. In the room, Orla pushed Lorcan back down to the bed. He breathed with difficulty, his face was turning bluer by the second. "Your lungs are damaged. Lorcan. We don't need the doctor to tell us that. Hurry and tell me what you need from me. I need you to pass out and heal yourself before you die." Orla tried to keep her voice low and controlled.

"Who was that man? He knew you. I saw the look in his eyes." Lorcan wheezed as the pain in his chest intensified.

"I don't know who he was, but he could certainly wield magic. But you could tell that yourself."

"Don't ever try to play poker, Orla." Lorcan coughed out a bit of blood.

"Jesus Christ, what do you want from me? I said I don't know him." A tear escaped and rolled down her face.

"Promise me you won't go after him. He hurt me with his magic. And he blocked the laser beam with a dimensional shield. If he's a sorcerer, he's not an ordinary one. Not from this world."

Silence.

"You seriously can't promise him that? You really plan to go after that man?" Roy was astonished. "Well, I won't let you.' He turned to Lorcan. "I promise you, Lorcan. I won't let her go. You just do your thing and get better."

"No. I know that the moment I pass out, you'll go after Mori, and Orla will go find that man. I'll be lying here like a useless piece of shit." Lorcan grabbed at his chest, wheezing for air.

"The only way you can stop us is to get better yourself, Lorcan," Roy said.

Rose came back with the doctor, but when he approached, Lorcan pushed him away.

"Promise me, Orla!"

"I don't want to make promises I can't keep."

Lorcan sat up. Roy jumped on to the bed and held him down. "Doc, you have to put him out."

"That's dangerous—he mightn't be able to breathe by himself. I can't just—"

"Do it!"

"Don't you dare!" Lorcan protested but couldn't get loose from Roy's grip.

"Please, doc, I know he can get past this if you sedate him. I'm his wife, and I take full responsibility. You saw what happened to Jay? The people who hurt him will be coming back. We need to prepare, and I can't do that when Lorcan's in pain. Please!"

Lorcan protested again.

"Doc!" Roy yelled at the doctor.

"Please!" Orla begged.

Lorcan struggled, but Roy was too strong for him, and Lorcan was not at his best.

"We really need their help, doctor. They know what they're doing," Rose said. The doctor nodded reluctantly and approached the bed with a needle. In a moment, it was all over. Lorcan stopped moving, and his body relaxed.

"Lay him on his side. You should stay with him and make sure he's breathing okay," the doctor said and exited the room.

The riverbank was foggy and unusually cold for a summer day. Six-year-old Lorcan gazed at the empty sandy strip, watching the cool water rolling miniature waves onto lonely stones and rocks. His mother pulled at his shoulder when he tried to get closer to the river.

"She's not there, Lorcan."

"But she's always there." Lorcan's eyes filled with anxiety.

"Maybe her parents realized how dangerous the riverbank is and decided not to let her come here."

"What if something happened to her?"

"Don't think like that, Lorcan."

"But I know. I just know it, Mother!" Lorcan tried to run out to the river, but his mother held him back again, lifting him from the ground.

"Lorcan, if you don't calm down, I'll tell your father you've been coming here, and I'll never be able take you anywhere. I should never have brought you here."

Lorcan stopped struggling, so his mother put him back down. She crouched and wiped a tear from Lorcan's face. "I haven't seen the girl, son," she said, "but from what you've told me, I believe she is strong and resilient. I have a feeling she'll be fine."

"Really? You really think so Mother?" He trusted his mother. He was only six, but he knew he could rely on her and trust her unconditionally.

She nodded, pulled his tiny body into her arms, and rubbed his back. "There you go, good boy. You'll grow up to be a good, strong man, and you'll be able to protect your girl and build her a castle. I promise."

"I don't want to build castles anymore."

His mother released him and looked into his striking blue eyes. "Why not?"

"A castle is just a thing. If I build it, someone else can destroy it. I want to give her a happy life with me. If I make her happy to be with me, then the happiness is always hers. It will always be with her, and no one can take it away."

His mother looked at him, she merely smiled and kissed his cheek. "Now you make me want to meet that girl."

"I'll do the same for you and Dad. I'll make you happy. I'll make you proud."

A tear rolled down his mother's face.

"Why are you crying, Mother?"

She smiled again. "I'm just happy, Lorcan. I'm the luckiest mother in this world."

They heard a low growl from the bush nearby. His mother stiffened. She stood up, glanced around, and moved Lorcan behind her. The growl grew louder and closer. She grabbed Lorcan's hand and ran. They ran as fast as they could. Through the brush and over the other side of the hill was their home, where they'd be safe. They stumbled over rocks, tree branches, and tree roots that seemed to float on the ground like a giant's petrified fingers.

They had to make it to the other side of the woods. He resisted his mother picking him up because he knew he could run faster on his feet, and she could run faster if he wasn't her burden. At that moment, he regretted making his mother take him to the riverbank that his father had forbidden him from for this very reason. The peaceful and pretty Irish forest didn't help and wasn't trying to be particularly friendly. He thought he knew this area because he had spent so much time here but the trees didn't look so familiar now. It seemed as if they had rearranged themselves to make Lorcan and his mother run aimlessly deeper into the darkness.

Then they slammed straight into a large lump of fur and muscles. His mother fell backward, landing on Lorcan. In front of them was an enormous black wolf with glowing green eyes. The wolf bared its teeth and charged at them. His mother pushed him away when the wolf grabbed at her clothing. Lorcan pulled his mother's legs, but the wolf was too strong for him. It kept dragging his mother away. Then he couldn't remember much except that he knew he needed a weapon. He let go of his mother's legs to search for one. In a haze of confusion, he found a large rock, as large as his tiny body could handle. He hefted the rock up and charged in the direction the wolf had just gone, following the trail of his mother's blood. His fury intensified. Lorcan kept searching frantically. He didn't cry. He needed to protect his mother.

He found the wolf on top of her. From behind, he wasn't sure if she was still alive. But it made no difference now. Lorcan charged, pounding the rock on the wolf's head and body. He wanted to grind the animal into the dirt. He heard his mother crying out for him to stop. That meant she was alive. That was good. But the wolf had hurt his mother, had wanted to kill his mother. That he wouldn't allow. Lorcan kept pounding on the pile of fur and flesh. *"Flesh?"* He thought he saw some human limbs. Blood. There was so much blood that he couldn't tell where it was coming from. He attacked the thing on the ground until he heard his mother's voice and felt her hands pulling him away from the messy pile of blood and whatever else was left beneath the rock. He remembered nothing else.

In the room, Lorcan's body convulsed with the experience, and his fever shot up. Orla held him.

She didn't know what he was dreaming about, but she could feel the pain seeping through every pore of him, and it was terrifying. She could feel its intensity, but there was nothing she could do to take it away from him. She wiped the sweat from his face and wrapped her arms around him.

"You have to get through this. You have to do this for me." She held him until her body vibrated with his pain. For a while, he settled. She knew it more than a dream. It was a flashback, and it was excruciating for him. She knew he wouldn't tell her about it, but she promised herself that if they survived this, she would get it out of him—*if* she survived this.

His breathing was even now, and his body was healing.

Orla kissed him. She enjoyed looking at him in the dark. She propped herself up on her elbow and traced her fingers along his jawline, his eyebrows, his exquisite nose, and his kissable lips. She wanted to remember every line of his face, his body. She recalled his striking smile and the lust he stirred in her whenever he winked one those blue eyes at her. She kissed him again gently. "I love you, Lorcan." Then she climbed off the bed and went out onto the dark veranda.

Roy stepped out in front of her.

"I promised Lorcan I wouldn't let you leave."

"I wasn't leaving. I just came out here for some fresh air."

Roy nodded. "I can see you love him very much. The moving mountains and crossing oceans sort of love. There's nothing you wouldn't do for him. But you shouldn't lie to him and make false promises. You told him you wouldn't leave him. And now you are just coming out here for some fresh air? Do you think I'm stupid, Orla?"

"On the contrary, you're too smart for my liking. What do you want to do about Mori? I can see you love her. The moving mountains and crossing oceans sort of love. So you're just staying here, guarding this door while you don't know where she is at the moment?"

Orla looked straight into Roy's eyes. His deep brown eyes darkened, but he held his stance. "Mori will be fine. She's resourceful."

"What stops you from going out to look for her now?" Orla gazed deeper into Roy's eyes.

"Nothing. But I can't afford a wrong move. I need your help, both of you. So I have to wait until Lorcan gets better. If I act in haste and anything happens to Mori, I won't forgive myself. It's easy if they just want to lure me out. But they want the key, and that involves you both. As long as they haven't gotten what they want, they won't kill her." Roy shook his head to stay alert as his vision started to blur.

"You're coolheaded, Roy. I have to give it to you . . ."

Roy's body started to sway. "Huh?"

"I said you and Mori are perfect couple . . ."

Orla's voice sounded like a bell ringing in Roy's head. He flopped forward, and Orla caught him before he fell face first on the veranda. She helped him into the room and lowered him down onto a chair. "Sorry," Orla whispered and left.

CHAPTER 8

The winding road hugging the edge of the tropical forest posed more mysteries than threats to Orla. There was a sense of familiarity hovering in the air. She didn't need much light to see the path as she followed her instincts, ingrained in her since childhood. The wind whispered among the trees as if someone was chanting tunes from the days she had lived with magic. Insects silenced when she walked past, showing respect to her and what she was doing. Somewhere in the depths of the dark forest, she heard the hissing sound of a snake—the kind of snake that her branch of sorcery used in sacrificial ceremonies. Orla remembered vividly the struggle and the desperate hisses of the animal before the blood was drained from its body. She didn't care for the ritual, but at the time, she was a kid and was there to learn.

The forest came to a small clearing. She saw the strange man who had been in Jay's house earlier standing by a fire, finishing the last part of the snake ritual. His eyes were closed, but Orla knew his mind's eye had seen her. Not only now, but back in the house. He had known she would come and find him. The man took his time to finish, then opened his eyes and looked at Orla on the other side of the fire.

"You've grown up a pretty girl, Orla." The man's voice was earthier than his look. He smiled at her.

"Bricius, you've been gone a long time. Rumour had it you'd died," Orla said. Her body tensed up. She controlled her breathing to stay calm. She didn't come here to lose her life in a fight with one of the most dangerous sorcerers she knew.

Bricius laughed. "I'm impressed that you remember me. Rumor is good when it spreads exactly what you want it to. I needed to bide my time to create more power."

"It's been more than twenty years. I assume you got what you wanted? Otherwise, it wasn't worth your faked death, was it?"

Bricius laughed. "Indeed. You're right. This island is mine. Soon, there will be many more. Many many more. I respect your family, so I'm willing to share a part of what I've created with you . . . as a gift."

"You're a loner. You never share. And I don't remember having any kind of a bond with you."

"I've been fond of you since you were a kid. I hope you remember that. If you don't want anything from me, why did you come here?"

"You could have killed Lorcan in the house. Why didn't you? What did Jay say to you?

Bricius shrugged. "He said he needed your help."

"I know that."

Bricius snorted. "But he doesn't need you. I can help him. I didn't know the Yakuz hid these people in the Raven House. I didn't even know when they had gone missing—otherwise, I could have saved them. He didn't need your help. You just stuck your nose into our business."

"They asked us to stay."

"Well, they shouldn't have."

"You're one of the strongest sorcerers in your clan. Why did you take Jay's word at all? From what I know of him, he's an English teacher, not a creature, and he doesn't look like he has a fortune that could buy the entire Earth."

"I don't have to tell you anything."

"We might have the same enemies."

"I doubt that. I know you just want to save your lover, but it's not going to work. When this is over, I'll kill him, and there's nothing you or Jay can do about it."

"Why?"

"He must pay for what he did."

"What did he do?"

"Why don't you ask him?"

Orla nodded. "All right. I'll do that." She tilted her head slightly up, judging the direction of the wind. Then she turned to Bricius. "I knew you had come for Lorcan. I knew it the moment I saw you. Before you even realized it yourself."

Bricius arched an eyebrow. "Then you also know you don't have the power to go against me, right?"

Orla stepped closer to the fire, the shadow of the dancing flames reflected in her eyes making them spark with confidence. "Are you sure about that? You grow older while I grow stronger." Bricius shifted into the fire's light and gazed into Orla's eyes. Orla continued, "I come here barehanded. I didn't even cast a protection spell, and you know that. Does that say I'm afraid of you?"

Bricius narrowed his eyes. "Let's say we focus on the bigger picture, and then after that, we can talk about your lover."

"Oh, now you suddenly want to negotiate. I'm sorry, but I'm not interested. Lorcan is mine. You know my family. We protect our own kind. It's not negotiable."

"I protect my own kind, too, and that's nonnegotiable as well. Lorcan killed one of mine, and now he has to pay for that." Bricius raised his voice, his face turning crimson, and anger creeping into his eyes. His memories flashed across him like a tidal wave. He roared and glanced back at Orla across the fire, but it was too late. The fire surged up as if it was alive, surrounding him. Blades of scorching fire lashed out at him, cutting into his flesh with searing heat. He screamed.

Outside the fire ring, Orla stood watching. She was calm and collected, but a trickle of blood ran down her nose. She had to be strong, she might win this.

Bricius screamed. "You can never beat me, Orla! This isn't dark magic! You're betraying your ancestors!" He screamed again as his body caught fire.

"My family isn't all dark magic and hatred, Bricius. I'm sorry I have to do this to you, but I have to protect those I love."

"What have I done to you, apart from leading you to power?"

"Power? You call that power? All the girls in my class—they deserved every chance to live. But you killed them all. My cousin, Brian—you killed him, too. If you died a thousand times, it still wouldn't pay for the sins you've committed."

"Sins? What sins did I commit to solve your clan's problems?"

The fire surged higher. And then Bricius's eyes returned to their icy glare—and he smiled. The fire died down as a result.

Damn! Orla thought and knew she was in trouble. *Think harder.* Orla searched her mind frantically for what her aunty had told her about Bricius, about his weaknesses. She had to make him angry. She'd done that. He was furious, and he was now burning. The internal flame alone would kill him. Once it caught, he could never put it out. But it was dying down now. Why? *Think harder.*

Bricius started laughing. "You were the smartest, the best in your clan. I was fond of you, and I regret having to lose you like this." He laughed louder as the fire turned toward Orla.

She crouched and erected a protection boundary around her just before the fire hit. Its force was so strong that it knocked her out of her protection zone. She crawled on the ground, trying to avoid her own blade of fire. Regaining her feet, she raised her arms. The fire at her end died out, and the fire at Bricius's flamed up again.

He withdrew a step and swung his arms. A wave of icy particles appeared like a crystal arm. The arm extinguished the fire around Bricius, then twirled around, flattened like a sheet, and flew toward Orla. She only had barely enough time to turn away and cover her face before the ice particles rained down on her like a million pieces of broken glass. Orla slumped to the ground, bleeding.

Bricius approached Orla. "You're trying to be a good girl, aren't you? You think your pathetic little white spell can stop me? You'd do much better using dark magic."

Blood streamed from what seemed like every part of Orla's body, but she smiled weakly and said, "I pity those who love you." He approached as she dragged herself backward on the ground. She didn't understand why her fire had failed.

Bricius crouched. "I don't want to kill you now. I want you to live to see me destroy your lover. But with you bleeding like that in the middle of the woods, any creature coming around is going to devour you, and that ain't my problem."

"If I die, Lorcan will mourn. He loves me, you know. And my family will seek revenge. I have people who love me. If I die here, I'd die a happy woman."

"Your lover might seek revenge—if he lives. But your family? I doubt it. Do you really think I had nothing better to do with my time and power than to kill those girls? And just so that *you* are the first in line for the alpha role? Ask your parents for the truth! Oh, wait a minute—you can't, they're dead. We're not supposed to speak ill of the dead, but the truth is, they hired me to do that dirty job."

"Liar."

"Why would I lie?"

"Because you're lonely, Bricius. My family loves me. If my parents have done evil things to put me in power, they did it because they loved me. You have no family. You lie to me to make yourself feel better. What do *you* have, Bricius?"

"People love me, too. My family loves me . . ." Bricius's breath quickened.

A thought flashed in the darkest corner of Orla's mind. She had sparked the wrong fire of fury before. She hadn't touched Bricius's deepest emotional wound, and that was why it had died out. Orla caught a sign of Bricius's weakness now. She remembered.

"Now you're lying. You don't have a family, Bricius. Your magic won't allow a family. I know that much. Don't try to tell me the shapeshifter who died just before you disappeared had anything to do with you. You're the best in your clan, but that guy? He didn't have any skills. He was killed by a random human hunter. You wouldn't dare have such an embarrassment in your family, would you?"

Bricius roared, grabbed Orla by the throat, and shook her. "Shut up! Shut up, you little bitch."

Orla saw stars as he banged her head to the ground. She struggled to draw a breath. She knew she was dying, but she just had to get her last blow. "It wasn't a random hunter, was it?" she rasped. "There was only one human kid at that riverbank then who wasn't scared of were-creatures. Your son was killed by that kid. He died like a common dog."

Bricius threw Orla away, and she rolled across the ground. He screamed in excruciating pain as the fire erupted from inside his body. It burned and tore at his flesh and his mind. The fire of fury.

He stood up, burning like a torch, but he moved toward Orla. She lay on the ground, seeing him coming, but she couldn't move. She had no breath, no strength, and not much blood left.

Then she heard a familiar voice. It was Lorcan. He was racing to the scene, followed closely by Roy and Rose. He fired his gun, but just as before, the gun beam didn't work on Bricius. Lorcan pulled out his knife and stabbed. Bricius staggered backward. Lorcan's hands burned, but he kept stabbing until Bricius slumped to the ground.

Thinking him to be dead, Lorcan turned to look at Orla.

"Watch out!" Roy yelled and hurled a knife through the air at Bricius, who had gotten to his feet and was about to wrap his burning body around Lorcan.

Bricius roared as he took the knife to his chest. Calling up a spell, he once again conjured the icy hand, pouring the crystal drops over his body to extinguish some of the fire. He ran off into the darkness, saying, "Lorcan, I'll be back for you! Keep your stone and your key. No Flanagan is going to save you when I return!" Bricius's voice echoed back to them through the still night air.

Lorcan kneeled next to Orla. Her body was cold. He gathered her in to his arms to warm her and comfort her. "Hang on for me," he whispered as he carried her to the doctor's house. He was calm and tried not make any sudden movements. Lorcan concentrated as he had never before in his life.

"She's lost too much blood. We don't have any extra for transfusions," the doctor said.

"Take mine," Lorcan said. "I don't know my blood type, and I don't know hers. But please—just see if her body takes it. Please." The doctor shook his head.

"It doesn't work that way. If your blood doesn't match, it might kill her."

"So what do you suggest we do?"

"She has to heal herself."

"Not happening." Lorcan ushered the doctor and Rose out of the room. "Please jam the door, Roy," Lorcan instructed, pulling out his wrist unit to call Ciaran.

In a moment, a hologram appeared. Ciaran looked annoyed. "Can you handle anything by yourself, Lorcan?"

"Please, she needs blood." Lorcan pointed to the bed.

Ciaran turned toward the bed, moving closer so that he could see Orla with the light of the hologram beam. Ciaran frowned, reached his hand out as if to check her pulse, then remembered he was only hologram. He signaled Lorcan and Roy to step back and extended his hologram light beam into a holocast. The he moved the light circle over, encircled Orla, and checked her pulse. He took a small pin-like device from his unit and took a sample. He inserted the sample into his unit, and a short moment later, Ciaran looked up at Lorcan and Roy. "I need to get my doctor and do this properly. You two, wait outside."

Roy opened his mouth to ask something, but Lorcan had pulled him out the door and slammed it closed.

CHAPTER 9

The bright light shone out of the door frame, casting a rectangular shape on the opposite wall. It had been a while, and Lorcan kept staring at the door as if he could see through it. Roy paced back and forth, hands in his pockets, saying nothing. Roy knew the center of Lorcan's universe was in that room, so he respected that and didn't ask anything.

They had done this before when Roy was dying from poison. Ciaran and the doctor he brought from Eudaiz had fixed Roy using the most advanced technology in the cosmos. Lorcan had never been to the faraway universe that Ciaran governed, but he'd heard only good things, and from their dealings with Ciaran, Lorcan knew Eudaiz had the best medical technology in the cosmos, and that Ciaran's arrival in that universe could only have made it better. Before going to Eudaiz, Ciaran had been managing the most advanced and mysterious pharmaceutical company on Earth.

"Stop talking to yourself, Lorcan."

"Huh?" Lorcan snapped back to reality and saw Roy was staring at him. Lorcan nodded, raking his hands through this hair and pacing the corridor.

The light went out, the door of the room slid open, and Ciaran stepped out. He was in his solid form, not a hologram. Lorcan waited for him to speak.

"It's done. She's fine now. But it's the same deal for her as was for Roy—she will have to change her address to Eudaiz after this is done," Ciaran said.

"Of course. Can I go in?" Lorcan asked.

Ciaran nodded. Lorcan rushed in, slamming the door behind him before Ciaran could follow.

Ciaran had left a dim light on in the room, and Lorcan could see Orla lying in bed, pale and a bit dazed, but awake. He strode to the bed and sat by her side. Lorcan brushed the hair from Orla's face and smiled. She opened her mouth to say something, but Lorcan put his fingers over her lips.

"Don't do that to me again. Promise?"

She looked into his blue eyes and nodded. He gathered her into his arms and held her tightly. Every muscle in his body quivered with emotion, and she pushed him back.

"I'm sorry. I won't do it again," Orla said.

Outside the room, Ciaran turned around to see Roy.

"I'm sorry on Lorcan's behalf," Roy said. "He didn't mean to slam the door in your face."

Ciaran smiled and said nothing.

"Does that smile mean you forgive him? Or that you're not surprised because you've seen him like that before?"

"The latter. I've dealt with Lorcan and Orla before. I know how they are with each other."

Roy nodded. "Lorcan said you control a great deal of the multiverse. But then you handle this matter personally. It must be important to you."

Ciaran smiled again. "Yes, I do manage a lot of people and creatures. But only a few of them I'd consider friends. Lorcan and Orla are among them, and I don't take my friends for granted. If they need me here, I'll be here." He glanced around quickly. "Where's Mori?"

Roy inhaled sharply and informed him, "A clan of werewolves got her—well, that's speculation. The only proof I've got is the blood marks I saw on the walls, and the fact that the wolves threatened me the day before and used Mori to lure me out. So my guess is it was them who took her."

"May I take a look at the room they took her from?"

"It's not here. This is the doctor's house. We sent Rose—a local woman—and the doctor to the other house to take care of another wounded person."

Ciaran narrowed his eyes. "Your woman was captured, you don't know who took her or where she is now, and you're just standing here guarding this door?"

"I need Lorcan's and Orla's help. All the help I can get. I can't afford to make a wrong move. If anything happens to Mori, I'll never forgive myself."

Ciaran looked at Roy. He knew he would never be able to be that cool-headed if it was Madeline, his wife, who had been captured. He admired the way Roy handled himself. He'd sent them back here for the stone, but the Indigo Stone was not exactly their problem. Ciaran always felt a pang of pain and regret when couples got separated. "And you don't need my help?"

"No. I mean yes, of course, but I would just never expect you to help, never expect you to be here, given you're busy with your own business. But yes, we definitely need your help, especially now. The guns you gave us didn't work."

"I beg your pardon?"

"They worked before, but somehow the beams didn't work on the man we fought yesterday, and he almost killed Orla."

"What do you mean they didn't work?"

"He seemed to have an invisible wall surrounding him. The beams were sucked right into it."

"Dimensional shield," Ciaran mumbled.

"Sorry?"

Ciaran shook his head. "How did he hurt Orla?"

"He used magic. That's all I could tell. He almost killed Lorcan, too. But it seemed like someone called Flanagan had been protecting Lorcan, so he's okay."

"Who did you say was protecting Lorcan?"

"I don't even think Lorcan knows. Before running away, the man said he would come back for Lorcan and no Flanagan was going to save him." Ciaran paced as he thought, and he didn't like what he was thinking at all. Magic and Flanagan was a combination that would bring no good to any one. Adding a dimensional shield to the combination might make him impossible to defeat. Ciaran remembered vividly how he had killed Flanagan, and he remembered the carnage that the battle had caused in Eudaiz.

Maybe he hadn't kill Flanagan at all. If it was even the same Flanagan Orla had encountered . . . Ciaran shook his head, trying not to ponder things any further until he got more information.

The door of the room slid open, and Lorcan walked out with Orla. Lorcan had wrapped his arm around Orla's waist to support her. She could walk now, but she was still quite pale and shaky.

"You look as beautiful as always, Orla. It looks as though you put up a hell of a fight," Ciaran said.

"Thank you, Ciaran." Orla smiled and raised her right arm to display the wrist band Ciaran had snapped on it. "And now you've enslaved me to Eudaiz as well."

"With pleasure." Ciaran nodded.

"I'm sorry I dragged you here again. But this was urgent . . ." Lorcan began.

"Indeed, and it looks as though it's best if I stay a bit longer to help you with the problem at hand."

"Are you sure? We can handle this. We can . . ." Lorcan trailed off and let his arms flop down to his side. "I'm sorry, I really don't think we can handle this without further assistance from you. We're not catching a dragon here. We don't have any idea who we're dealing with. But we know they have armies of both humans and creatures. And now, it looks like there's magic involved and possibly forces from the multiverse as well. Mori used to have an army of firefoxes to help out, but now, there are only four of us. Three now, actually because—"

"I got it. Roy told me. They took Mori," Ciaran cut in. "I understand the magnitude of the problem. I'll stay to help."

"Really? That's great. Thank you," Lorcan responded. "Oh, and the guns, they . . ."

"Didn't work yesterday. I heard. I'll figure it out. For now, we'll have to use my all-time favorite—the most consistent and reliable weapon," Ciaran said, heading out of the house via the long hallway.

"Knives?" Roy asked.

"No, brain power. There are four of us now—we should be fine."

"I don't think my feeble little brain is working at the moment," Orla said.

"The next time you run into a sorcerer who could possibly wield magic strong enough to dilute laser beams from the most advanced technology in the cosmos, please call for help rather than trying to go it on your own," Lorcan chastised Orla.

"I'll get you better weapons, Lorcan," Ciaran promised. "But where do we go now?"

"To Jay's house. We're staying there. He's the leader for a group of humans. They were stranded on this island eleven years ago," Lorcan said.

"How so?"

"Apparently a storm hit, and then the whole island was disconnected from the world. Humans can't get in or out. Only creatures. I think it's some kind of a dimensional shift," Lorcan said.

Ciaran shook his head. "Perhaps. Can you find this island on a map?"

"No," Orla said. "They said it literally disappeared from the planetary map."

"An island doesn't disappear, especially an operational one. I could see it when you called me. That's how I got here." They were walking along the main street now. It was lively with people going about their business as if nothing had happened here a few days ago.

"We got into some crossfire here earlier. Many people died, and we just escaped by the skin of our teeth. Now they're all going on like it's business as usual. How weird!" Roy said.

"Can you tell which are creatures and which are humans?" Ciaran asked.

"I can only tell if they're werefoxes or werewolves," Roy said.

"I can tell," Orla said.

Ciaran smiled. "If only creatures can travel to and from this island, did you tell them exactly who you are? If they know out that we can open a portal to get out of here, they may want to leave, too. And I can't guarantee anyone else that I'll be able to transport them off the island."

"We haven't told them yet, but I'm sure they will eventually want to know," Lorcan contemplated.

"If they ask me, what should I tell them?" Ciaran asked anyone who could answer.

Orla stepped in front of Ciaran, looking him up and down. Ciaran was six foot three, slender with the toned muscles of a warrior, and had pale English skin. His long, black hair almost touched his shoulders, framing a face that God had created just to provoke men's jealousy and accentuating his smoky gray eyes. "Tell them you're a vampire!" Orla said.

Ciaran shook his head and chuckled.

Lorcan laughed. "They'd probably believe you."

They arrived at Jay's house.

"Creatures," Orla whispered. They pulled out their guns. Ciaran signaled Lorcan and Orla take one side, while he and Roy took the other side. The house was quiet. They entered easily, finding the house trashed and empty. A blood trail ran along the hallway and pooled on the carpet. They rushed to Jay's room—no one there. They searched everywhere and met back at the living room.

"Rose and the doctor aren't here," Lorcan said.

"Where's the room Mori was taken from?" Ciaran asked again.

"End of the corridor," Roy said and pointed. Ciaran went into the room and examined the blood spray on the walls. Then he asked, "You're saying they're werewolves, Roy?"

"That's my prediction."

"They wanted the key, and they claimed they have the stone, but Roy thinks they were bluffing," Lorcan added.

"Do you remember the eyes of Nick, the cowboy from Xiilok?" Ciaran asked.

"Yes, he looked like he had worms swimming inside his eyes," Orla said. "Are you thinking the wolves could have come from Xiilok?"

"Xiilok is a universe where multiversal outlaws stay. It's independent from all other universes, and thus the creatures living there could potentially bypass some standard physical laws of time and space," Lorcan explained to Roy. "Do you think the creatures on this island are from Xiilok, Ciaran?"

"Maybe. I have a theory, but I need more data to confirm it."

"The kid!" Orla yelled and ran to the window. She jumped through the window so quickly it looked like she was flying. They saw the kid standing at a distance from the house, smiling at Orla. Then he turned and ran away. Lorcan and Roy chased after him, following Orla.

"Don't chase him, goddamn it. It might be a trap!" Ciaran yelled at them, but they couldn't hear him, so he followed. This island must have many dimensional traps. Orla, Roy, and Lorcan ran straight to a narrow path with tall sand cliffs flanking either side, perfect way to be ambushed. He pulled his gun and gave chase to nothing. "Stop! I said stop!" Ciaran yelled again in a firm an authoritative voice. That stopped them just before the sand cliffs. "What are you doing?"

"That kid was in the house before and shot at Roy. I think he was looking for the stone," Orla said.

"What kid?" Ciaran glanced at the sand cliffs. He approached the cliffs and aimed his gun down the narrow path. "Nothing in there but a possible trap."

"Watch out! Shoot, Ciaran!" Lorcan shouted and pointed at the cliff. Ciaran turned around—and saw nothing—but pointed the gun in that general direction.

"You're aiming right at it! Shoot!" Orla yelled.

"I'm not shooting at a kid."

"Shoot, shoot now!" Roy roared.

Ciaran didn't see a kid—he didn't see anything at all. He wasn't about to shoot if there was a chance of hitting a kid. He felt some air movement, and his instinct made him step to the side. He felt a stab of metal in his shoulder and turned sideways. Looking at his left shoulder, he saw a long arrow protruding. Blood streamed from the deep wound.

Roy and Lorcan immediately shifted into two magnificent foxes and ran toward the cliffs. Orla approached Ciaran and helped him up.

"I'm fine. Go help them," he directed her.

"They don't my need help with these amateur shapeshifters," Orla smiled.

Ciaran narrowed his eyes. "Are there professional shapeshifters?" he asked incredulously.

Orla shrugged. "Of course."

"Did you see the whole thing?"

"Yes. You didn't?"

Ciaran grabbed his shoulder and winced.

"This is all pretty strange for you, huh?"

"Nothing really weirds me out. I just don't care for being at a disadvantage. I'll have to use all my resources."

"But if you can't see them, how can you fight them?"

Ciaran smiled. "I have my ways." He pulled the arrow out, setting free a spurt of blood. "This isn't good." Ciaran tried to stem the bleeding with his hand. "It might have hit an artery. Stupid," he mumbled.

"Let's go back to inside to see if we can find something to patch you up with," Orla said.

CHAPTER 10

Orla found a small medical box and was able to stop the bleeding from Ciaran's shoulder. Ciaran checked the house, searching for all communication devices and anything that resembled an electronic device. Once certain that there wasn't a spying bot in the vicinity, he pulled out his wrist unit and coded something in. A warm glow of light appeared in the air, and a holocast encircled the floor. A hologram of Madeline stood in the middle of the light. She smiled at Ciaran, and then narrowed her eyes at the wound on his shoulder, but she said nothing.

"Madeline, you remember Orla?"

"Yes, of course. Hello, Orla. How's Lorcan?"

"He's fine. Out hunting now!"

"Apparently, you're not in Alphi, Ciaran." Madeline kept the gracious smile on her face.

Ciaran shook his head. "I was. But I got this urgent call, and there are a couple of things I need to do right now. I just wanted to let you know that I'll be late."

"Can you make the council meeting tomorrow?"

"I'm not sure."

Madeline nodded. "I'll notified them if you can't make it. What do you need me to do now? You wouldn't call just to say you're going to be late."

Ciaran looked into his wife's brown eyes, and it killed him to see a hint of unspoken resentment. "On the holocast control panel, you can see the map with my location on Earth. Hit the record button on the panel to capture the location and save the information to a disc I store in our bed chamber. Then use our private channel to call my dad and transfer the file to him. Tell him that the Daimon Gate is fully responsible for this and that in order to solve this problem, his council has to use data from the EYE."

"Ciaran!" Ciaran could see the threat of tears in Madeline's eyes, but he pressed on.

"Please."

Madeline nodded. "I'll do it right away."

The looked on Madeline's face pained him more than the bleeding wound on his shoulder, but he had to live with it. He wanted so badly to caress the dimple on her left cheek and kiss her tenderly, but he couldn't do that with a hologram.

"Ciaran."

"Yes."

"Caed and Lyla spoke their first words this morning. Caed said 'mom' and Lyla said 'daddy'." Then a tear broke loose and rolled down her cheek. Ciaran instinctively reached out and touched the light beam, then withdrew his hand and shoved it in his pocket.

Madeline continued, "I swear both of them have your goddam sexy British accent." Madeline let out a wistful laugh. "You give your children kisses when you get back. They'd love that. Bye for now." Madeline smiled graciously and turned away as her hologram faded, and the holocast disappeared.

Ciaran stood in silence for a moment, gazing into the air where his wife had just been. He smiled sadly. "My twins. They spoke this morning. In English." He snorted out a short laugh. "They were conceived in the Daimon Gate, and were born in Eudaiz. We were afraid that they might speak

Eudaizian." He shook his head and muttered. "Such stupid thought. But anything could happen we you live across multiple universes."

"They must be beautiful."

Ciaran nodded. "And soon, they'll be too smart for their own good."

"You're asking too much from Madeline, Ciaran."

Ciaran nodded. "And I'm sorry for that. But it couldn't be helped."

"I'm no expert, but I know asking the Daimon Gate council to use the data in the EYE is a serious matter. I can't imagine what it's like from Madeline's perspective to know that whatever it is that you're trying to do could put your life in danger. And for what?"

"The magnitude of the problem is a lot broader than I thought. It's not just the key or the stone. All of you could see whatever was coming at us from the sand cliffs—I couldn't. It's because we were seeing different dimensions of the same thing. This island didn't disconnect from the rest of the world all by itself. It was a dimensional shift—and it was manipulated. There are only a few people who could do this. And if my theory is right, we are in bigger trouble than you could imagine."

"And what's your theory?"

"I'll let you know when I'm sure of it."

"Would our lives be in danger, too?"

Ciaran gazed into Orla's eyes. "I'm in this with all of you, and I left my family hanging because of that. I love my family, and I'm no hero. I'll do whatever it takes to get me back home where I can hear my kids call me daddy." Ciaran eyes sparked with fury. Orla could see his temper almost slip out of his control. Then he calmed down instantly. "My apologies. I shouldn't have raised my voice."

"No, I'm sorry. I shouldn't be so selfish." Orla shook her head.

At the door, Lorcan and Roy walked in, both covered in dust and sand. They could feel the tension in the room. "What happened?" Lorcan asked.

Ciaran sat down on the sofa. "All right, everyone, we need a plan. Please tell me what has happened since you arrived on this island," he said while laying out a portable liquid map on the coffee table.

The wedge of the forest where the werewolf clan had captured Mori was quiet. Lorcan was sure he and Orla hadn't killed them all while Mori took Roy away. But the most important thing they'd learned from that fight was that the area around the cave was blanketed with magnetic energy that had sucked the power out of Roy's wrist unit. And it would do the same to Orla because she was now equipped with the same kind of wrist unit. Thus, Ciaran had asked Orla and Roy to stay back at Jay's house.

"They were in there before." Lorcan pointed to the cave.

"It looks like a trap," Ciaran said and drew his gun, looking at it. "Will it work on them?"

"The only time it didn't work was when I used it on Bricius."

Ciaran nodded. "Speaking of Bricius, are you sure you have no recollection of when and where you or your family had come across a Flanagan?"

"One hundred percent sure. You look like you know who it is."

"Too soon to draw a conclusion." Ciaran followed a trail of paw prints in the mud. He heard slight movement. Pointing his gun to the top of a tree, he fired. A half-wolf half-man dropped down from a tree branch, howling in pain.

"Come on, choose your bloody form," Lorcan scolded.

The man shifted completely into wolf form and fled. Lorcan wanted to chase, but Ciaran held him back.

"Let him call his pack," Ciaran said. "Where's your gun?"

Lorcan pulled it out, brandishing it in front of him.

Ciaran nodded. "Okay, now don't shift into your fox form in front of me. Two reasons. Most importantly, I don't want to see you naked, and second, your gun will do a lot more damage than your teeth."

"But Ciaran, the rule is that when you fight were-creatures, you change into your were-creature form. Fair fight and all, you know."

"Your true form is human, Lorcan. Until I have evidence to prove otherwise, being able to shift into a blue fox doesn't make you one hundred percent werefox. Roy said you're different. You're not like him."

Lorcan nodded and held the gun tightly in his hands.

They heard movement in the bushes nearby, and a pack of gigantic black wolves crept toward them.

"I don't speak wolf," Ciaran said.

From the rear of the pack, Ganzorig stepped forward. "You know what we want. Do you have it?"

"And do you have what we want?" Ciaran responded.

Ganzorig signaled. Two men from the back brought Mori, standing her next to Ganzorig.

"Are you okay, Mori?" Lorcan asked. Mori nodded.

"Show me the key," Ganzorig demanded.

Ciaran took a small pouch from his pocket, sliding the key inside out to reveal its top. Then he put it back into his pocket. "The key is an important object. We want Mori—and all you have taken from us," Ciaran said.

"How much do you want? We don't have access to unlimited resources."

"Can you put a dollar value on the key of Psuche?" Lorcan asked.

"No, but money is all I have to deal with. I can't give you men or territories." Ganzorig scolded.

Ciaran and Lorcan exchanged glances—it didn't seem likely that Ganzorig had Rose and Jay.

"Well, this island isn't yours to start with, so you can't call it your territory. If I let you have the key, you must move away from this island," Ciaran said.

Ganzorig smirked. "Fair enough. Give me the key, and I will leave. You will never see me again."

Ciaran look again at Lorcan. They both knew that this was much too easy to be true. "Exactly how many men do you have here, and how can we be sure you'll stay true to your word?" Ciaran asked.

"I have two hundred and ten men on this island. You will just have to take my word that we'll leave this island. Once we have the key, there will be no reason for us to stay here."

"I think you should withdraw first, and I'll make arrangements to transfer the key to you elsewhere. The location can be your choice."

"Who *are* you?" Ganzorig asked, narrowing his eyes at Ciaran.

"You don't need to know who I am, but I have the power to destroy the people who hired you to do this."

Ganzorig paced. Lorcan was sure that even though Ganzorig had his men surrounding him at the moment, he felt vulnerable in front of Ciaran. He knew Ganzorig would give in. Lorcan relaxed his shoulders and the tension in his face.

"We don't have all day," Lorcan mumbled, loud enough for Ganzorig to hear.

"How can we be sure that you have the right key?" Ganzorig asked. Ciaran nodded and signaled to Lorcan. They stepped farther away from the wolves. Ciaran took his wrist unit and coded something in. He gave the key to Lorcan. In front of them, a portal opened in magnificent blue and white light. Lorcan stepped into the light and approached the door. He slid the key in, and the door slipped open. On the other side of the door was a smoky area, steamy and sparkling with electric red and purple lights. Lorcan stood back from the door, as if something behind it would eat him alive. Then he slammed the door closed and ran back out, leaping through the portal.

Ciaran closed the portal, while Lorcan breathed heavily. Ganzorig's jaw dropped.

"Are you okay?" Ciaran asked.

Lorcan nodded. "I'm fine. As long as you weren't asking me to go through that door, I was fine."

Ganzorig narrowed his eyes. "What kind of magic was that?"

Ciaran smiled. "The kind that can make whoever employed you agree to the terms I set out. Now, you've seen the key in action. It's not magic. That's what the key opens. You're welcome to try the door yourself."

Ciaran opened his palm to show the key to Ganzorig.

"What's behind that door?" Ganzorig asked.

"If your employer didn't tell you, it's beyond your pay scale," Ciaran said. "Do you want to try the door?"

Ganzorig shook his head. "No, it's not necessary."

Ciaran shrugged. "So will you give Mori back to us? Then when we're sure you and your men have left the island, we will deliver the key to a location of your choice."

Ganzorig nodded. "In three days. Kaihanshin Prefecture. At the old farmhouse called Ushiza."

Ciaran nodded. "Here are the terms. You withdraw your men immediately, and then we need time to check the island. After three days, we will deliver the key."

Ganzorig nodded, raising his hand to signal his men to release Mori. He turned, and his wolves followed him quickly, dashing off into the misty forest. Their howls echoed back to Ciaran and Lorcan for a while, and then the forest returned to its mysterious quietude.

"Well, that went more smoothly than I'd expected," Lorcan muttered.

Ciaran smiled at him. "I've just discovered a new talent of yours."

"I have plenty of talents, but which one are you talking about?"

"Acting. You could make a career out of it!"

CHAPTER 11

The late afternoon sun shined on the bright red roof of Jay's house, reflecting onto the row of mature pine trees flanking the sides of the house. However, it wasn't the harsh light of the sun that had Ciaran and Lorcan squinting. It was the sight of Roy sitting on the roof that had their attention.

"Well, Roy makes a perfect target for a sniper . . ." Ciaran commented and turned toward Mori, but Mori had left before he could finish his sentence. From the roof, Roy leaped down to the ground and sprinted toward Mori. The two embraced each other, rushed toward the house, and disappeared inside.

"I was admiring Roy for the way he handled himself before!" Ciaran said.

Lorcan laughed. "You'd admire him even more if you knew he's kissing Mori for the first time right now."

Ciaran arched an eyebrow. Lorcan shrugged. "I guess that's a werefox tradition. Some set of rules. I don't know really understand them, but they suck."

Ciaran smiled. "The rules or the foxes?"

Before Lorcan could answer, Orla approached, giving the two men a wink and nodding toward the house. "That might take a while."

"We have to head to the Raven House now. Roy and Mori know the plan. They'll follow us later. Let's go," Ciaran said.

"All right then," Orla responded.

"Ahh, I need to tell you this before we go, Orla," Lorcan said.

"What?"

"Ciaran and I . . ." he hesitated, then he cleared his throat. "It was Ciaran's idea to put on an act for Ganzorig, the werewolf, so we could get Mori back without a fight."

"I knew that already."

"Right. So the plan was that Ciaran would open the portal to the Daimon Gate, and I would insert the key to the front door of our house to open it in order to reveal some mysterious light inside. That way Ganzorig'd believe we have some kind of magical, mysterious power."

"Yeah, we talked about that. I knew that part, too."

"The thing is . . . to make it even more convincing, I wanted to add a smoke effect to the light. Ciaran had learned a trick from his cousin, George, and they'd done it safely before, so I tried it."

"And . . ." Orla narrowed her eyes.

Lorcan stepped backward a bit so he stood by Ciaran.

"We were short of time. We needed some colorful powder, so I sent a command to Gini asking him to sample the color from your makeup kit."

"Who's Gini?" Ciaran asked.

"Our home robot," Lorcan answered and continued, "Based on the amount of colored smoke, and the odour when I opened the door, I think Gini might have sampled your entire wardrobe as well."

"What do you mean by sample?"

"A chemical process involving the use of fire and some other bits and pieces . . ." Lorcan looked sheepish, but that didn't stop Orla from advancing on him, her hands on her hips. Lorcan glanced around and saw Ciaran backed far away from him.

"It was in the interest of the greater good, and I'm sure you'll get plenty of new clothes in Eudaiz, Orla." Ciaran felt obliged to help Lorcan out as much as he could.

"You see! Did you hear that? That's a promise from Ciaran. It's no big deal. He'll supply you with an entire new wardrobe when you come to Eudaiz. He's the king there, right?" Lorcan grinned, knowing his life might depend upon a favorable response from Orla. He moved in, kissed her face, and bit her bottom lip.

Ciaran rolled his eyes and looked away.

"An entire new wardrobe would normally be any woman's dream!" Lorcan whispered and deepened the kiss.

"Don't make assumptions, Lorcan. Women are not that shallow. Besides, I've been managing my own wardrobe since I was five. Women have specific tastes and preferences. An entirely new bunch of clothes from an unknown universe where I have no idea what their sense of fashion is? That's not necessarily desirable."

"Hmmm, only since five? So . . . you didn't wear any clothes before five?" Lorcan laughed.

Orla jabbed her finger into Lorcan's chest. "I'll have you know I wore *very* nice clothes before five. I lived with my parents in Paris, the fashion capital. Mother just didn't let me choose what I wanted to wear."

The smile faded from Lorcan's face. "I'm sorry. I didn't mean to make you talk about your parents."

Orla shrugged. "It's okay. They died when I was so young. I don't really remember much. But my aunt took good care of me."

"I know. But I'm sorry anyway," Lorcan said.

"Because we are on an important mission, and I don't want to be petty, I'll let the wardrobe issue go—for now. But there *will* be punishment, Lorcan."

Lorcan smiled.

As they turned around, Mori and Roy hurried out of the house. "You wouldn't leave without us, would you?" Roy asked.

"Never," Ciaran muttered as he headed to the road.

"You guys go ahead. I forgot something," Lorcan said and darted back to the house while the group left.

Back in the house, Lorcan ran to the bedroom and pulled out his computer. He didn't need to connect to the central network of the Daimon Gate to get what he needed. He opened a computer game he had been designing for Orla, a fun simulation, and pulled up all the historical data he'd imported into the program about her life. Orla Foley, born and raised in France until five. Her parents died in an accident, the rest of the family took her back to Ireland after the accident.

Lorcan stared at the data. He had never registered this information in his mind before. He thought he'd known every detail about her life. He put the computer away, sat back on the bed, and ran his hands through his hair. Then he stood up and rushed out to follow the group before anyone would ask questions.

The Raven house was the same as they had found it a few days ago, but it looked even more ancient now. The heavy, crooked wooden door was shut and covered in dust, as if it had never been opened, as if there had never been a fight, and as if there had never been sixteen people shackled inside, waiting to die. Ciaran stopped everyone at a fair distance from the house. He checked his wrist unit and turned around. "There's an unusual astronomical energy here. This isn't an ordinary house," Ciaran said as he saw the flashing signal of an incoming message on his screen. He read it and responded, then turned toward the group.

"The Daimon Gate council agrees to help and is gathering their resources. I suspect the dimensional shift that shields this island from human eyes is manipulated by forces from another universe. Who, where, and how is yet to be determined, and I can't do anything about it until I get back to Eudaiz. Our immediate task here is to save those individuals involved directly in this mission, get the Indigo Stone, and get off this island in one piece," Ciaran said.

"What about the residents here?" Orla asked.

"We'll see what we can do. But if this island somehow got stuck in the middle of a galactic war between unknown creatures and universes, lives will be lost, and there's not much we can do about it. If that's really the case, which I truly hope it's not, there will be other places facing the exact same destiny. When we get out of here, we'll try to find ways to save them, but we have to get out first. Understood?"

Everyone nodded. "Why can't the Daimon Gate send troops down here to help us?" Roy asked.

"The Daimon Gate doesn't have soldiers. They only have guards for internal use and don't involve themselves in battles or any affairs outside their universe," Lorcan responded.

"I can't take my troops from Eudaiz to Earth. This is not their war. The Earth is my personal interest, I can't justify sending resources here and sacrificing Eudaizians," Ciaran said.

"Then why did you ask Madeline to tell the Daimon Gate this is their responsibility?" Orla asked.

Ciaran smiled. "They need a good reason to get their act together, and this *is* partially their fault, isn't it? If they hadn't sent you to get the key, you wouldn't have upset the dragon, the stone and the key wouldn't have been separated, and you wouldn't have had to come to this island."

"Look!" Orla said. She felt the presence of the kid before she saw him. Everyone turned around and saw him standing in front of the house.

"What's going on?" Ciaran saw nothing. "Are the invisible shapeshifters back?"

"It's the kid who shot Roy," Orla said quickly.

"Kid, we don't mean you any harm," Lorcan began, "but you led us into a trap at the sand cliffs before, and you shot at Roy. What exactly do you want?" Lorcan asked.

The kid blinked his eyes, looked straight at them . . . and through them. "Shit, he's looking at Ciaran,"

Roy said. Roy ran at the kid to grab him, but Ciaran held him back.

"What does he look like?" Ciaran asked.

"Short, black hair, brown eyes, about nine or ten, average build," Orla said.

"What about his voice?"

Now that Ciaran had asked, they recalled that they had never heard the boy speak.

"I described him to Jay, and he said his name is Michael Harris, Rose's son. Rose is one of the sixteen people we rescued from this Raven house.

"I can take a bite and tell you whether he's human. He's definitely not were-creature," Mori said.

The kid stood still, gazing at them through the fence. He looked at Ciaran. Mori adjusted her stance, ready to make a move.

"Don't Mori, if he wanted to harm me, he could have done that at the sand cliffs."

"He led us into a trap and got you an arrow in the shoulder," Lorcan said.

"I don't think he knew the shapeshifters were at the cliffs," Orla said and turned toward the kid. "Hey, just tell us what you want. We don't have time to play around."

The kid didn't answer and kept staring.

"Let me try," Ciaran said and made his way through the group huddled in front of him. He couldn't see the kid, but spoke in the direction the rest were looking. "There must be a reason that others see you, and I can't. You approached twice since I arrived. What do you want?"

Silence.

"If you'd like me to do something for you, you have to at least give me a signal. Show yourself to me." As soon as Ciaran finished his sentence, the image of the kid flickered and became semitransparent. In front of Ciaran, he appeared, flickering like a poor quality hologram.

As soon as the kid opened his mouth to say something, there was a high frequency squawking. Ciaran grunted in pain, grabbing his ears, slumping to the ground with blood trickling from his nose. The kid saw that and stopped speaking. He was still half transparent, hovering between the two dimensions. Lorcan, Orla, Roy, and Mori couldn't hear anything, but they saw the movement of his mouth and saw also that Ciaran was in trouble.

Ciaran got to his feet and raised his hand, gesturing silence from the kid. "Don't speak." Then he turned around. "Did you hear anything?" Everyone shook their heads. Ciaran turned back to the kid. "All right, speaking doesn't appear to be the best form of communication between us at the moment. Can you move objects?"

The kid nodded.

"Can you write?"

The kid nodded again and crouched to pick up a small stone on the road. He drew one line but hadn't finished the first letter before they heard a low growl. From the end of the street, a large group of wolves approached, teeth bared. From behind the pack, a man made his way to the front. He wore a black robe, with a large sword tucked at the back. In his hand, he held Ganzorig's head by the hair. Blood from the head, its eyes still half open, dripped to the ground.

A corner of the man's scarred face quirked up as if smiling. He signaled the wolves with his empty hand, and the group stepped back. The pack of gigantic wolves charged at them. Ciaran, Lorcan, Roy, Mori, and Orla blasted their guns at them, but there were too many. The front line died, but the back line leaped over the bodies of the dead wolves to attack.

The group rushed to the door of the Raven house.

"Lorcan, stay with me. Roy, open the gate and check if there's anyone inside. Shoot if they come at you. Orla and Mori, keep in the middle," Ciaran directed. The group backed closer to the gate. Roy opened it and saw an empty courtyard. Ciaran and Lorcan continued to fire at the advancing wolves.

"Okay to come in," Roy said, stepping into the courtyard. Orla grabbed Ciaran and Lorcan from behind and pulled them roughly inside. She curled her hands into fists and pumped out two large fireballs at the coming wolves. While the wolves howled and barked, she darted into the courtyard as Lorcan slammed the door closed. They locked the door from the inside.

While Lorcan and Roy found logs inside and jammed the door, Ciaran stepped back, keeping his eyes on the top of the high fence. As he had predicted, the man in the black robe leaped to the top of the fence. His feet had not yet touched the fence when Ciaran shot at him. The beam hit the man mid body, he dropped Ganzorig's head to the ground inside the fence, and fell back outside.

Soon, they heard howling and the sound of paws scratching at the door.

They turned around and ran into the Raven house. The internal door seemed to be more stable and secured. The metal patch lock and chunky metal bars were in good condition. They locked the internal door and proceeded deeper into the main hall.

CHAPTER 12

The hall was dark and empty as before. This time, no creatures attacked them, but they held tight to their guns anyway. The bodies of the creatures they had killed before had been cleaned up. Lorcan frowned at the floor. It was *too* clean. It was as if the fight had never happened here, or someone had gone to great lengths to clean it. But why?

"Ciaran!" Lorcan called out as he proceeded to the next room.

"What?"

"Get behind me," Lorcan commanded.

"Excuse me?"

"I know you're used to leading, but we've been here before. I've seen the traps," Lorcan said.

"He's right, Ciaran," Roy said.

"I'll watch your back then. Ladies, in the center please." Ciaran went to the end of the line. They slowly made their way to a chamber and found the way down to the basement where the people had been kept shackled before. Ciaran glanced at the layout of the room and the decoration of the hallway.

"It's religious sacrificial ground here," Ciaran said.

"What? Why don't I recognize this?" Orla asked.

"This is a rare religion. I came across it when I researched for a small project a long time ago in London. Your magic is a practice not a belief. I can't explain and don't understand your practice. But I can explain certain pattern of beliefs and religions," Ciaran said.

Orla shrugged. "Do you always have a theory for everything, Ciaran?"

"Merely efficient." Ciaran smiled.

They arrived at the basement. Lorcan pointed to the dark wing at the far end. "I went in there before. There was a door, and as soon as I opened it, I blacked out. Orla said I looked like I was dead.

When I came to, there was no door. It was just a solid wall."

Ciaran stepped closer to the dark wing to peek in. Lorcan opened his mouth to protest, but Ciaran turned back before he could say anything. "Don't worry, Lorcan, I'm not an idiot." Then he approached the walls where the people had been shackled. He looked at the layout of the room, then pointed to a corner.

"There has to be a door over there," Ciaran said. Everyone looked at the solid wall. "I know this sounds strange, but this is the classic structure of a mind map. Mind maze, to be precise." Ciaran suddenly whirled around and shouted toward the middle of the room, "No!" Then he slumped to the floor, apparently dead.

Lorcan could see exactly what had happened to him the last time they were here. Whatever Ciaran had seen that made him fall to the floor, Lorcan had experienced before. It had come back to him twice now, targeting the darkest corner of his mind. Everyone has a secret they wouldn't want anyone else to know. A man like Ciaran would have many. Wherever this thing brought out in Ciaran, Lorcan knew it couldn't be good.

Lorcan could see himself on the floor, dead. He understood now, more than ever, how hopeless Orla must have felt. He froze, not knowing what to do. Orla sat on the floor next to Ciaran, rubbed his temples with her thumbs.

"Come on, Ciaran, you responded to me before. Do it for me again." His body was cold, and there was no response. "Come on, Ciaran. You have to get back home to hear your children call you daddy."

They could hear the wolves knocking down the courtyard door. Roy and Mori looked around. There was no way out except to go back to the hall and face the wolves.

Lorcan pulled his gun. "I'm going back," he said.

"There are too many of them," Orla protested. She shook Ciaran's shoulder. "Come on, Ciaran."

Ciaran stirred and slowly opened his eyes. Unlike Lorcan, who jumped to his feet right away, Ciaran seemed extremely weak. Although he couldn't move by himself, he was fully aware of what was happening. It looked as though he didn't have any physical strength, but his mind worked perfectly. "Do you mind helping me up?" he asked Orla.

"He's up! Ciaran's up!" Orla called out to others.

Lorcan, Roy, and Mori rushed over.

"I can't move," Ciaran said.

"Okay, let me." While Lorcan helped Ciaran sit up, he saw his wrist unit. "Jesus Christ, ten percent! Do you live on a wrist unit like Roy and Orla?"

"No. My wrist unit's energy is just for emergency. Whatever it was, it must have sucked out a significant amount of my natural energy. The reserve kicked in. It drew ninety percent out of the reserve." Ciaran paused to take a breath. "I have to crash."

"What do you mean?" Roy asked.

"You have to rest to recharge your natural energy?" Lorcan asked.

Ciaran nodded.

"You can't do it here. The wolves will break in any second," Mori said.

Orla stood, fists curled. "I'll handle them."

"No, Orla," Lorcan protested.

"Blast the wall," Ciaran said weakly.

"What?"

"Far end, left corner. There has to be an escape hatch. Blast it," Ciaran reiterated the information and then closed his eyes to preserve his energy. Lorcan, Roy, and Mori aimed at the wall and fired. In no time, the wall crumbled, revealing a short hallway. Lorcan and Roy rushed back in to help Ciaran. They all raced through the hallway just as the wolves knocked down the door.

At the end of the short hallway was a small wooden door. They pushed outside.

In front of them were endless rolling sand hills.

"Give me some space." Orla pushed everyone out of her way, curled her hands into fists, and threw fireballs at the brick dome that arched over the wooden door. The bricks collapsed, piling up in front of the door, blocking it from the outside.

The sand hills in front of them spread out in the scorching sun, having no resemblance whatsoever to the area in front of the Raven house they'd just been through. The island was tropical, and the sand hills in front of them were a desert.

"Another dimension. We just passed through a dimensional door," Ciaran muttered. He reeled toward a black rock poking up in the sand, then slumped to the ground, totally passing out. Lorcan and Roy carried Ciaran to the shady area of some crooked palm trees, then they themselves flopped down next to him. This dimension seemed to suck the energy out of every one.

A while later, Lorcan and Roy awoke, finding Ciaran already up, sitting on top of a small rock and watching over them, a gun in his hand. "Wake your women," he said. "We need to go."

"Out there?" Lorcan pointed at the desert.

Ciaran shook his head. "Too risky. It was bad enough to not know where we were on the island. There's no point charging into that unknown dimension. We're going to have to fight our way back inside the Raven house. It's been quiet in there for a while." Lorcan nodded and turned to wake Orla.

"Can you open a portal to the Daimon Gate or the transitional zone right here?" Roy asked.

"No. Someone with galactic connections called our bluff and killed Ganzorig. I'd be reluctant to open a portal now and risk being located by unfriendly forces."

Orla and Mori were up. Mori and Roy approached the pile of bricks Orla had broken to jam the door. It was very quiet inside the Raven house.

"What if we follow this building from the side to the front without going back inside?" Mori asked.

Lorcan pointed at the edge of the wall where it curved. "I checked, and it looks like a maze. I don't think it will lead us to the front of the building. The only sure way is to go back inside via this door."

Ciaran was about to get off the rock when Lorcan approached. "What did you see inside the house that made you pass out?"

"The kid yanked open a dimensional door, right in the middle of the room. I can't remember anything about it except the suction."

"I guess it's the same sort of dimensional door that I saw. You said you have to crash to recover your natural energy. It's the same with me—I have to pass out when I'm injured so that my body can start its healing process. Is that common in your universe?"

"What? The healing process or the recharging of energy?"

Lorcan shrugged. "Both, I guess. Roy said I'm not exactly a werefox. So I'm just wondering if there's any resemblance between our recovering processes."

Ciaran smiled. "I haven't been in Eudaiz long, but the moment I became a citizen of that universe, everything changed. I don't have total control of my energy, and it has to be recharged naturally every day like a battery. If I run out of energy, I'll die. So to answer your question—yes, there might be some connection between your recovery process and the energy charging process in Eudaiz. What I'd suggest is for you to have a test done in Eudaiz after we finish with our business here."

"Does that mean you'd admit me to Eudaiz? Orla will have to live there."

"You have some skills we can definitely use. Still, no promises."

Lorcan grinned. "That's good enough. I'll put my tech skills to good use."

"I can get any tech guy I need, Lorcan, no strings attached. Your most valuable skill is not computer crunching. It's what you did in the woods."

"Excuse me?"

"What do you think I saw when I passed out?"

"A secret. Me, too."

Ciaran nodded. "Yes, but it wasn't *my* secret that I saw."

Blood drained from Lorcan's face. He glanced toward the house and saw Orla, Mori, and Roy busy planning a predicted fight once they got inside. "Look, Ciaran, I don't know what you saw, but I was a kid. I wasn't exactly conscious of what I was doing. It was a wolf, and it was killing my mother."

"You knew it wasn't a wolf. You denied it in your subconscious and only saw what you wanted to see. It was your first kill. I know it was hard, especially as you were that young. No one else needs to know your secret."

Lorcan swallowed hard. "When was your first kill?"

Ciaran shook his head. "No one needs to know my secret, either."

Lorcan nodded. "I haven't told Orla any of this. I've never been so sure about what happened. My mother was never clear about it. I'm not sure what Orla would think about me if she knew that I had the ability to kill at such young age."

Ciaran laughed. "Bullshit. You think I'm an idiot?"

"What? No. I just . . ."

"You couldn't tell Orla because you were stalking her at the time. That was how you got attacked."

Lorcan sheepishly glanced back to ensure Orla was not listening. "You saw that, too?"

Ciaran shook his head. "No, that's my deduction from the conversation you had with your mother before the attack. Didn't need to use much brain power to figure that out. You two are made for each other. You're childhood sweethearts. Nothing to be embarrassed about."

"You heard us when we talked about the wardrobe back at Jay's house, Ciaran. She didn't come to Ireland until she was five. But at the time of the incident, she was only three. I wanted us to be childhood sweethearts. I always thought we were. But the girl I had been dreaming about at the riverbank might not have been Orla. It's not a big deal in reality, but we built our entire relationship on that fairy tale, the childhood love story. What if

I've been loving another girl, and then ended up with Orla by accident?"

"Your mind is very twisted, Lorcan. Orla would die for you."

"Yes, and I would for her, too. But all that was because of our fairy tale. I love Orla, and there is nothing that will ever change that. But what will she think if there's a chance that I fell in love with her because I once thought she was someone else?"

"You can't be so sure . . ."

"I'm not sure at all. But there's a big fucking fat chance that that's the case."

Ciaran nodded. "Your secret is safe with me. When we get this thing over and done with, marry her properly and get that doubt out of your mind."

"Are you two plotting our way in, because I can't see any other way than me sending fireballs inside first to clear the way," Orla called out.

Ciaran and Lorcan joined the rest of the group.

A short moment later, Lorcan, Roy, and Mori blasted the beams at the bricks. When the bricks loosened up enough, Ciaran wiped them away with one beam and kicked the door in. He withdrew quickly to make way for Orla. The pack of wolves rushed at the open door and were incinerated instantly by Orla's fireballs. When the last wolf dropped at the doorstep, Ciaran stormed inside, shooting at any movement he could detect. Soon, the Raven house reverted back to its eerie quietness.

Before Ciaran put his gun away, the flickering image of the kid came back, frantically waving his arm toward a corner behind Ciaran. Ciaran whirled around to see a dimensional door slide open and the man in the black robe charge out with sword raised high. Ciaran lifted his gun, but there was no need for him to even aim as the beam landed right at the man's neck, decapitating him.

The man's head fell from the hood of his robe, dropping onto the floor with his eyes still blinking, revealing irises with worms swimming inside them. The body of the man and his head began to disintegrate, turning into a black worm puddle.

"Xiilok creature," Ciaran muttered. He glanced up to thank the kid but he had vanished again.

Via the collapsed gates to the Raven house, wolves appeared. Hundreds of them. Countless numbers storming into the courtyard, heading toward the hallway. "No way we can kill them all," Roy said.

"Have to try." Lorcan raised his gun.

Ciaran glanced at the coming dogs and searched the room, contemplating. He raised his gun and called out, "Hold your women back, far right hand corner!" Then he raised his gun and strode to the center of the room.

"Ciaran!" Orla and Mori called out. Ciaran turned and glared at Lorcan and Roy. They grabbed Orla and Mori, dragging the wriggling women toward the back wall on the right. "Brace yourself behind that wall," Ciaran said. He stood in the middle of the room, staring at the coming wolves in challenge. Then he walked slightly toward the left, standing by the short hallway which led to the dimensional gate they had just fought their way through.

The wolves dashed through the main hall and ran straight toward Ciaran. He calculated the distance then pointed his gun at the opposite wall and shot. The wall shook but didn't budge. Ciaran shot again and got some protesting dust from the loose bricks. The wolves kept charging. He shot at a couple that had passed through the doorway and turned the gun on the wall again. It shuddered.

From the corner, Roy and Lorcan darted out, standing next to Ciaran. The trio blasted the wall. It shook and eventually gave in. As the wall crumbled, they saw a glimpse of dark space. "Run!" Ciaran shouted and dove toward the right, rolling toward the back wall. Lorcan and Roy did the same.

The suction funneled through from the dimensional door and the hole they just created. The coming wolves were sucked off the ground by the vacuum of air and tossed into space like rag dolls. Mori reached out, dragging Roy behind the protective wall. Orla grabbed Ciaran and Lorcan one by one by the hand and pulled them in.

They shot at any wolf that veered right toward the wall where they hid. The rest of the wolves storming into the room turned to the left to avoid the laser beams and were sucked into the deadly air funnel. From behind the wall, the group watched as the wolves flew out into nothingness.

"Enjoy the ride!" Ciaran laughed.

CHAPTER 13

A quietness had returned to the Raven house, the howling vanishing along with the wolves. The group stepped out from behind the wall, cautiously staying far from the spinning suction funnel. Ciaran muttered, "Now the Raven house has a gateway from one dimension to another."

"Seriously, how do you know that there is such thing behind that wall?" Lorcan asked.

"It's a maze, built by someone with galactic connections. Logically, the entry and escape hatches would be positioned at opposite ends. Classic mind game."

"Has this been developed into a hologame?" Lorcan's eyes sparkled with curiosity.

Ciaran smiled. "Yes. For training purposes only. "

"Come on, guys." Orla waved her arms in frustration. "We've got things to do. But we can't just leave a gigantic hole like this in the wall. What if someone falls into it?"

"They'd be sucked into oblivion and spend the rest of their natural lives staring into the darkness," Ciaran said.

"That was a rhetorical question, Ciaran!"

Ciaran smiled.

"How can we fix this?" she asked.

"I'm afraid there isn't a simple solution. A maze has entries, escape hatches, doors, traps, and keys. A mind maze like this would have connections to the movements of astronomical elements. Things will shift and change constantly. The hole might eventually cover itself up and vanish as if it had never been there."

"Or it might still be there, but someone might fall into it because they can't see it," Orla said.

"Yes and no," Ciaran said patiently. "They can only fall into it if they're in the same dimension. And if they're in the same dimension with the hole, they'll be able to see it."

"Why don't we just put a sign up saying 'Keep away from the gigantic hole unless you want free travel into unknown space,'" Roy grinned, and Mori laughed.

Lorcan was silent. He walked along the wall, trailed his hand on it. "They're here. Rose, the doctor, and Jay. This place is significant. That's why they shackled people here. The stone might be here, too."

"I agree," Ciaran said. They walked along the wall on the left-hand side, making their way back to where people had been held. Lorcan glanced around. The walls in the basement looked familiar. There had to be something more these walls. Why *these* walls?

While they were contemplating and searching, the kid appeared again in the middle of the room in half-transparent form, so that both Ciaran and the rest could see him. He opened his mouth to say something. Ciaran slumped to the floor, holding his ears. "Don't speak," Ciaran reminded him. The kid stopped. Ciaran picked up a loose brick and handed it to him. Taking the brick, the kid drew an arrow pointing toward a wall tucked away in another wing of the basement.

The group cautiously approached it. It looked like all of the other walls, nothing out of the ordinary. Ciaran turned, intending to ask the boy what he meant by pointing them to the wall, but he was gone again. Lorcan approached the wall, fingering the grooves of the bricks.

"Be careful, Lorcan." Orla said.

Lorcan turned around, looking at them. "The gatekeeper from Gate 131 was buried in the wall there because of the key."

"Are you suggesting that Rose, Jay, and the doctor are buried in this wall?" asked Roy.

"But if that's the case, they'd be dead," Mori said.

"Yes, if they are truly buried in the wall, in this dimension, they would be dead," Ciaran said, brushing his fingers along the grooves of the bricks as Lorcan had done.

"I supposed it wouldn't be wise to send a blast of fire at the wall if we think they might be in there," Orla said.

Ciaran stepped a few steps back, positioning himself in the middle of the room. "As I said, this is a mind maze. If they want to hide someone from us, they wouldn't put them in our dimension. But if this place is sacrificial ground, and if they were to sacrifice people to their higher power, there would be no point in keeping the sacrificial subjects in another dimension. They would have to be here, in this dimension."

"We can't see them, but it doesn't mean they're not here," Lorcan said. Then he looked at Ciaran. "Are you thinking what I'm thinking?"

Ciaran nodded. "It's quite disturbing to me when our minds share the same thought pattern, but yes, I agree with what you're thinking, Lorcan."

Orla had her hands on her hips. "Could you let those of with ordinary minds like me know what you're talking about so I can feel less useless?"

Lorcan laughed. "Come on, honey, this is just boys' talk. You hate computer and chess. Now could all of you walk to the far end of the room, please? Ciaran and I want to do some searching in here. If we trigger some kind of trap and it explodes into our faces, please be kind enough to save our asses."

Roy, Mori, and Orla moved to a quiet corner of the room.

"I'd prefer your ass just the way it is. No explosion, please," Orla told him.

Lorcan carefully searched the wall again, studying every groove. Ciaran stood in the middle of the room, gazing at the wall and thinking. Lorcan found a lever hidden behind a wooden column. He signaled to Ciaran.

"This column has no structural function whatsoever, so this lever is probably a trap," Ciaran said.

"I know, but we can't pretend it's not there." Lorcan stepped away from the lever. "I'll shoot at it. This is a fair distance, so if it turns out to be a trap aimed at whoever pulls the lever, we should be fine."

"Shooting is not your strong suit, Lorcan. I'll do it." Ciaran pulled out a knife. "Shooting would be too rough anyway. It might trigger a whole lot of different mechanisms," Ciaran muttered and threw the knife, hitting the lever precisely at the handle where it should be pulled. They heard a click.

"Watch out!" Lorcan shouted. Both Lorcan and Ciaran dove aside just before a rain of arrows flew from behind them toward the column and the lever. When the shooting abated, they checked the lever. The wall next to the lever had been peeled off, revealing a button inside the wall Ciaran was contemplating whether it was safe to press the button when Lorcan shoved him aside, turned around, and took a couple of arrows to his chest. Another ten arrows pierced the wooden column.

Ciaran pulled him out of the shooting range. "Your combat skills need much improvement, Lorcan. You should have turned sideways."

Lorcan's eyes started to close, and he wasn't saying anything.

Ciaran shook Lorcan's shoulders. "I'm going to pull the arrows out, and it's going to hurt, but you can't pass out until I say so. Got it?"

Hearing the commotion, Roy, Mori, and Orla darted toward them.

"Stay away! There might be more traps!" Ciaran warned, but they ignored him and kept approaching.

Orla said nothing, but she couldn't help a couple of tears ran down her face. "Open your eyes and look at me, Lorcan," Ciaran said. "I know you have to pass out so your body can start the healing process, but for it to begin, I have to pull the arrows out. I want to make sure pulling the arrows out will not be fatal. If I'm unsure, I'll make you wait until I can do a proper surgery and remove them."

"That would be too long and painful," Orla said.

"This kind of damage kills ordinary people, and it kills fast. But I need to be sure I won't kill him by pulling these arrows out now," Ciaran responded.

Lorcan opened his eyes. "I can handle it. Do it now," he said.

Ciaran nodded and glanced quickly at Orla, and she nodded, too.

Ciaran had seen Lorcan's survivor instincts when he killed the thing in the woods. He'd kill for those he loved, so there was no doubt he would live for those he loved. The way Lorcan looked at Orla gave Ciaran the confidence that he would survive this. Orla sat down next to Lorcan and held his hand. Ciaran inhaled, making sure his hands were firm and his action would be accurate. Then Ciaran pulled the two arrows out at once.

Lorcan grunted with the pain, and his eyes almost rolled back, but he regained his control swiftly. Blood spurted from the wounds, and Lorcan started to shiver with the chill. Ciaran took his shirt off and stanched the blood flow. They took Lorcan to the safe corner where he could pass out to start his healing process. Orla stayed with him.

Ciaran, Roy, and Mori came back to the wall.

"There'd better be no more freaking traps," Roy mumbled and pushed Mori behind him. Mori sidestepped, glaring at him. Ciaran signaled them to take a couple of steps back, then he pressed the button. The wall shuddered, loose cement dropping from the brick grooves. Then the wall detached itself from the connecting edges of the other walls and swiveled. Rose and Jay were chained to the other side of the wall. Jay was conscious, but Rose was not. Roy and Mori freed them.

"I thought there were three people?" Ciaran asked.

"This is Jay and Rose," Mori said.

"Where's the doctor?" Roy asked.

"I don't know. When I woke, we were chained here. Rose has never regained consciousness. Is she alive?" Jay asked.

Mori checked her pulse and nodded. Jay looked at Ciaran. "This is Ciaran, our friend. He's here to help," Roy said.

"Where are your other friends?" Jay asked.

"Lorcan is injured. Orla is with him," Ciaran responded. "So you are the English teacher that people have been talking about. Can you walk?" Ciaran asked. Jay nodded. Ciaran gave him a hand to help him stand up. Roy carried Rose to the other room. Lorcan was still out of it, but his wound had stopped bleeding. Orla gave Ciaran his shirt back. Jay flopped to the ground, sitting next to Orla while Roy put Rose down on the floor.

Ciaran looked at his blood-soaked shirt and muttered, "This would certainly scare young children."

"Come on, put it on. You'll stir up our women," Roy whined.

Orla glanced at Ciaran, noticing the incredible definition of his long lean body. He wasn't buff like a soldier, but his muscles were goddamn elegant. She was sure Madeline was pleased. They were a beautiful couple—now a beautiful family. She knew Ciaran longed to see them again. "Well, we might drool a bit, but we are very well-disciplined women, aren't we, Mori?" Orla smiled and played with Lorcan's hair, promising herself she was going to give him a kiss as soon as he came to.

Ciaran gave them a dismissive look, shook his head, and put his shirt back on. "It's not safe to stay here, but I guess your house isn't safe, either. Is there a place where we can go, Jay?" Ciaran asked.

"Where are we?" Jay asked.

"The Raven house. I thought you knew," Roy said.

"I know of it. Never been inside."

"Who owns it, do you know?"

Jay shook his head.

"We still have a wing of the house we haven't searched. We're on a mission. Will you be able to stay here and look after the injured with Orla?" Ciaran asked Jay.

Jay nodded. "What are you looking for?"

Ciaran shook his head. "It's best you don't know." Then he headed toward the other wing of the building with Roy and Mori. Once there, Ciaran asked, "What's your impression of Jay? Can we trust him to stay there?"

"I don't trust him—or anyone in this island. He has a connection with Bricius, and the man nearly killed Orla," Roy said.

"I'm more worried about Rose. Her son wanted to kill Roy," Mori said.

"It was a misunderstanding. He thought I was with the werewolf clan before. The kid has been helping us."

Ciaran nodded. "Still, he's been giving us half-baked information. He has an agenda. Let's quickly search to see if we can find any clue of the stone in here." Mori and Roy nodded and started looking around.

CHAPTER 14

Ciaran, Roy and Mori found nothing in the other wing of the Raven house, and they were now making their way back to the room where they'd left the four others. Lorcan had been up and was almost recovered, Rose had awakened, but there was no sign of Jay. Reading Ciaran's question, Orla responded in anticipation, "Jay said he needed to go home, and I couldn't stop him because Rose wasn't up at that time and Lorcan was still out of it."

Ciaran crouched next to Rose. "How are you feeling?"

"Not at my best, but I'll cope. Orla told me about you and what you can do to help. Jay had his own problems, but he's a good man. He was married to a woman shapeshifter. She died about five years ago, and since then, Jay has changed."

"How did she die?" Lorcan asked.

"Nobody knows for sure. My prediction was that it was the conflicts within her own family that resulted in altercations and brutal fights."

"What about Bricius?" Lorcan asked.

"He's a friend of the brothers in Jay's wife's family. That's all I know. They're very secretive."

"Do you know what the creatures on this island were fighting for? What are they up to?"

"They are always fighting over territories. Last time I heard, it was something about a key. I don't know which door it would open, but Jay's wife's family used to fight with the wolves in the woods for it. Then after she died, her family seemed to quiet down a bit. Then all the fights picked up again a couple weeks ago. I don't know why."

"Why does your son want to kill Roy?"

"What? Why do you say that? What does my son have anything to do with this?"

"Is your son Michael Harris?"

Rose nodded, then her eyes widened when the hologram-like image of the kid appeared. Tears rolled down her face as she stood up and approached him. "Michael!" He didn't respond. Rose reached out to touch him, but he turned slightly and disappeared into the dimension that rendered him invisible. He appeared again in the dimension where Ciaran could see him.

"He . . . My son . . . He disappeared!" Rose cried out.

"He didn't disappear, Rose. He just shifted from one dimension to another. I can see him," Ciaran said.

"What do you mean?"

"He can transfer himself in between different dimensions, or exist in multiple dimensions at once. Did you know about your son's special ability?"

Rose shook her head. "No, I knew nothing about this. Is he here, I mean there? With you? I should have taken better care of him. If his spirit can forgive me, please let me see him!"

"Spirit?" Ciaran arched an eyebrow.

"Yes. He died four years ago. You said his ghost can move between worlds. Can I see him again, please?" Rose cried out.

Ciaran looked at Roy, Mori, and Orla for explanation. He didn't have much experience in the paranormal.

"I don't think he's a spirit, Rose. If he is, trust me, I'd know," Orla said. "But at the moment, if he's only letting Ciaran see him, maybe he could ask him what he wants."

Ciaran nodded and turned toward the boy.

"Is Rose your mother?"

The kid shook his head. Ciaran turned to Rose. "He's not your son. He just confirmed to me that you're not his mother. I'm so sorry."

Tears ran down Rose's face. "How could someone appear as my son?"

Ciaran didn't have an answer.

"Shapeshifters can shift into human form, but it's rare, and it's evil. For me, it's only a myth," Roy said.

"The Yakuz can," Mori said.

Before they could speculate further, the kid waved frantically at Ciaran and pointed toward the back door.

"We can't go back there. We punched a hole in the wall, and it's now a dimensional funnel."

The kid then pick up a loose brick and wrote on the floor, "RUN."

And then the building shook violently as if it was going to explode. It felt like an earthquake. Ciaran checked his wrist unit and asked it to call the

Daimon Gate. He frowned at the screen then looked at the group.

"The Daimon Gate needs more time to gather the resources for us. But they confirm that they have received our request to shift the dimensional point of our location."

"What the heck does that mean? We didn't request anything!" Lorcan exclaimed.

The building shook harder. Dust, cement, loose bricks started to crumble.

"We have to get out of here!" Ciaran shouted and headed toward the doorway. A large column cracked and collapsed right in front of him, blocking the way to the entrance. They ran toward the back and headed toward the dimensional door. The suction had stopped, and the door was now closed. The building shook as if it was about to swivel. Lorcan, Ciaran, and Roy fired at the door until it collapsed. Then they all stormed out into the heat of the desert beyond. As soon as they exited the building, the doorway behind them swung away, and the building vanished.

"Oh my god, where are we?" Rose said.

"Don't worry, Rose, we can find the way back to the island," Orla said.

"How?"

"Werefoxes!" Mori cried.

Roy nodded. "Yes, and the other wolf clan was here as well."

They pulled their guns out and scanned the surrounding area. "There's nothing here but sand and heat," Rose said. Ciaran glanced at his wrist unit, then looked at Lorcan. Lorcan looked at his wrist unit and cursed. "We've lost all signals."

Sounds of howling came from the distance. "Only shoot when necessary. The beams are not unlimited, and that sounds like a lot of wolves," Ciaran said, trying to code his wrist unit at the same time.

Lorcan approached. "Is this a dead zone?" he asked Ciaran.

Ciaran shook his head. Then he looked at Lorcan. "It's not a dead zone, but someone has blocked us from space."

"Like the way they shifted and blocked the island?"

Ciaran nodded. "Not many people would have the power to do that. What exactly did Bricius say to you?"

"He said he'd come back to kill me, and when he does, there will be no Flanagan to protect me."

Ciaran arched an eyebrow in frustration. "And you really don't know a Flanagan?"

Lorcan shook his head. "Is he one of the people who could do this?"

Ciaran shook his head. "Maybe. But I killed him. He's the only one I know of who might be capable of combining magic and galactic matter and has an Earth connection. You've encountered him, Orla."

"What?" Orla asked.

"When I dropped by your place in the Daimon Gate a few weeks ago. The person who possessed you and used dark magic to attack me was Hoyt Flanagan," Ciaran responded.

"All right, but I have nothing to do with him. Why did he protect me, and when did I need his protection?" Lorcan exclaimed.

The howling had moved closer. It didn't sound like a pack attack, it sounded like an army. Lorcan and Ciaran looked again at their wrist units.

No signal.

They pulled their guns. From the horizon, packs of wolves appeared like ants, forming a dark line that separated the sand and the sky. They had no chance of killing them all regardless how many guns they had and how skilful they were.

"I'll fire at them," Orla said and curled her hands into fists.

"There are too many of them," Lorcan said. "We have no chance of opening a portal here, am I right, Ciaran?"

"Unfortunately, no," Ciaran muttered.

The line of wolves started moving toward them, slowly and surely. They heard a growl behind them. As they turned, they saw that Mori had shifted into a stunning red fox. She took a stance and howled into the air, a haunting sound that was powerful and heart-wrenching at the same time. Roy looked at her. There was no need for anyone to ask what Mori was trying to do. It was natural for her to take the position of alpha fox. She howled again into the air, calling for a response from the Firefox clan that she had never interacted with.

Roy gazed at Mori, the woman he loved with all his heart. He was filled with pride and love. Roy shifted into a formidable black half-fox half-wolf. Together, Mori and Roy looked magnificent. Ciaran fixed his eyes on the wrist unit Roy was wearing and smiled as it adjusted in size now fit tight to Roy's front leg.

Soon, responding howls to Mori's came from everywhere. From the side and from behind them, hundreds of red foxes appeared. They approached and formed a pack behind Mori and Roy. The army of foxes charged at the sand hills.

The wolves at the top of the hills howled and marched down. The foxes charged upward. The two armies stormed and merged. Howling, barking, and growling noises flooded the air. Lorcan wanted to shift, but Ciaran held him back. "You're more useful in your human form, Lorcan. Focus on shooting, not biting." They raced at the sand hills behind the Firefoxes and shot at any wolves that ran loose from the pack. They didn't want to hit any foxes. The fighting ground was so dense that Orla couldn't use her fireballs. They just had to wait patiently and let Roy and Mori take the front.

From a distance, the fighting ground looked like a gigantic sand ball.

Then the noise reduced. Bodies of foxes and wolves dropped in the sand. It was time for them to assist. Several wolves had run away. Ciaran, Orla, and Lorcan rushed in and shot at any moving wolves. The sand was soon littered with animal bodies and blood.

They saw a mass of moving bloody black fur that shifted into Roy. He reeled a few feet away to pick up a pile of red fur. The little red fox lay in Roy's arms. As a tear ran down Roy's face, Lorcan pulled Orla into his arms and turned her away.

Ciaran approached Roy. "May I take a look at her?" he asked.

Roy didn't say anything, he just released the fox. Ciaran checked her pulse. There was nothing. But he knew he could do something. There was no medical ground for this. He just had to use his instinct. He couldn't explain where this thought came from, but he pulled out his knife and stabbed at the fox's back leg. A cry came out, responding to the pain. Orla burst into tears. Roy pulled the little fox back into his arms.

"Come back to me. I love you, Mori." As his body shuddered with emotion, the little red fox shifted back into Mori. She moaned, and Roy held her in his arms and rocked her. He embraced the woman he loved as if his life depended on it. Indeed, his life might have depended on it, on her survival. For his entire life, that was all Roy knew—protecting Mori.

Mori opened her eyes and looked at Roy, her eyes filling with tears. She didn't need to ask him, but he knew what she wanted to know.

"All of your foxes are gone," Roy said. "I'm sorry, Mori."

"They followed the code of honor, they protected me, they fought my battle even though they're not even mine." A tear rolled down Mori's face. "I should have died with them."

"You are mine. If I failed to protect you, I would have no reason to live, Mori. But it's hard for me to protect you if you don't accept me. I know you won't accept my mixed blood, but . . ."

"Yes."

"I'm sorry?"

"I said yes, if that was a proposal. Not exactly as romantic as I've dreamt about, but it will do for now."

Roy paused for a moment to digest the information. He looked back at others, looked down at Mori, then he grinned and kissed her.

"Ow . . . you let Ciaran stab me," Mori groaned.

"I'll deal with him later . . ." Roy kissed her forehead and then turned to Ciaran, miming a thank-you. Ciaran nodded and stood, searching the horizon as he contemplated the next move.

CHAPTER 15

The desert sun had gone down, giving way to a harsh, chilly wind whirling around the random rocks on the sand hills. They had no shelter, no food, and no water. Mori and Roy had recovered from their injuries, but they wouldn't survive for long in this climate without food and water. They camped close to where the Raven house used to be, hoping it would reappear. Ciaran didn't want to rely on chance—he stuck to his wrist unit, continuing to code it and try to fix it. Then something sparkled in the horizon like lightning bolt. Ciaran called out, "Lorcan, check your unit."

Lorcan looked at his screen and got a glimpse of signal.

"I've got it," Ciaran said and strode to the open space, staring in relief at his wrist unit. He read the text on the screen, then glanced up to the top of the sand hills. "The stone is here," he said.

"I thought it was under water," Lorcan said.

"It is. But we're in a chaotic area of intercrossing dimensions right now. Things will change again, so let's stay close together," Ciaran said and stepped closer to the group. Then he looked up at the hills again. "The information I've got suggests the stone is hidden in a place that crosses two dimensions and is in the middle of nine thousand moving islands. Whatever that means," Ciaran muttered.

"Look." Orla pointed to a stone at the crest of the hill. It was glowing in a deep indigo shade.

"How can you fix that gigantic rock to the key?" Mori asked.

"The stone is either inside or underneath it," Ciaran said.

"Let's go," Lorcan said. They ran up the hill toward the glowing rock. They'd been running for quite a while, but the distance between them and the glowing rock didn't seem to change.

"It's shifting," Ciaran shouted. "Stay together." The sand under their feet flew like fast running water. In some areas, it sunk, creating enormous holes in the ground which sucked in anything on the surface. They looked up the hill and saw the same distance to the glowing rock. "We'll never get there," Rose said.

Ciaran knew the distance was illusional. He pulled out his portable liquid map. "Follow me," he said. He navigated based on the map, not on what they could see with their naked eyes. They appeared to run sideways. The sand kept sinking and flowing around them.

"The sand flows like water, Ciaran!" Orla shouted out. Ciaran stopped a moment and nodded.

"Yes. You're right. If the sand is the water, then the black rocks are the islands," Ciaran said.

"There are nine thousand of them to navigate around," Lorcan added.

They kept running. Ciaran's map seemed to lead them closer to the glowing rock, but not close enough before they were shifted away again by the flowing sand. Rose was not as fit as the young group of people with her, she fell behind and was sucked into a sand hole. Lorcan glanced back, seeing her sinking, he reached out to grab her and slipped in the sand. Orla grabbed at the edge of a small rock with one hand and gripped Lorcan's leg with the other. Sand flew everywhere, muffling their call for help. Sensing trouble, Ciaran stopped and looked back. He called out for Roy and Mori. They darted back, grabbing Orla's hand just before it slipped from the rock. They pulled Lorcan and Rose up.

"Thank you," Rose said. "You shouldn't have done that, Lorcan."

"If he hadn't saved you when he had the opportunity, he wouldn't be the man I love," Orla said as Lorcan grinned.

"The sand here isn't moving." Ciaran was astonished. "The sand around the rock was fixed, while the sand in the open space moves like a river. What if the rocks are not the islands but the gateways, and the flowing sand is the traffic," Ciaran spoke his thoughts out loud.

Lorcan chimed in. "The Daimon Gate has nine thousand gateways. The hunt for the key of Psuche began at gate 131. That can't be coincidence."

"It's moving!" Roy called out and pointed at the glowing rock. Ciaran looked at his map and could see that a surging energy beneath the surface was moving rapidly. Anticipating the direction of the glowing rock, he charged. They group jumped back into the flowing sand, heading toward the rock.

The sand seemed to move faster. They heard a rumbling noise from behind them, and saw a three-story high sand wave rolling toward them. Lorcan and Roy grabbed Orla and Mori. Ciaran pulled out his gun, increased the power, and shot at the sand wave and in a panning motion. The laser beam cut off the wave where Lorcan, Orla, Roy, and Mori were standing, breaking its structure. It collapsed and sand rained down on them. The tail of the wave hit Ciaran, lifting him from the ground and smashing into a nearby rock like a rag doll. He dropped to the base of the rock and was quickly covered by sand.

Lorcan, Roy, Mori, and Orla dove at the site, digging frantically with their bare hands. It seemed to take forever. They couldn't find Ciaran.

"Are we digging in the right place?" Orla asked. Mori and Roy shifted into their fox form and poked their noses into the moving sand. They whirl around, digging with their forelegs. They sniffed around, pushing toward the left, then the right, doing a circle. It had been five minutes. They searched more frantically. Seven minutes later, Roy wagged his tail and shifted back into human form.

"Here. Right here!" he shouted and dug at the same time. They all darted over and dug. Ciaran's hand came into view. They reached down into the sand, and grabbed his shoulders, and pulled him up.

"He's not breathing," Mori said.

"Come on, Ciaran," Lorcan said, checking his pulse and finding none.

"CPR," Orla said as she jumped on top of Ciaran and started pressing his chest. He gasped, opened his eyes, and took in a deep breath. He looked perfectly normal, as if nothing had just happened.

He squinted at the sight of Orla sitting on top of him and smiled. "Thanks for the offer, Orla, but I'm taken." Orla climbed down to the sand.

"You were just dead!" she exclaimed.

"No, I just shut my body down because I knew it would take you a while to find me. Thank you all for digging me up."

"How can you just put your body on hold like that?" Roy was astonished.

"That's what you get for being Eudaizian. How can you heal your injuries?"

"We've all got our talents," Lorcan commented.

"Where's Rose?" Mori asked. They looked around, and Rose was nowhere to be found. Mori and Roy shifted again and searched, but they couldn't find her.

"Does that mean she's dead?" Orla asked.

"Not necessarily. Until we find the body . . ." Ciaran said.

"There!" Lorcan shouted and pointed at a sand hill in the distance. There, they saw Rose racing up the hill, approaching the flickering image of the boy. They rushed in her direction, calling out for her, but Rose didn't seem to hear them.

"Are you seeing the kid?" Ciaran asked. Everyone nodded. They were approaching Rose, but she still didn't hear them calling, and she kept walking up the hill to reach the boy. Ciaran looked at the kid standing in the middle of the hill, gazing at Rose. There was something about him that wasn't right. "This might not be the same kid we saw in the house," Ciaran said quickly and stopped the group from running.

"What's that, Ciaran?" Roy asked.

Lorcan squinted his eyes, seeing a bright halo around the kid. "You're right, Ciaran. Something's wrong," he muttered. Feeling a prick at the back of his neck, the energy in his body started to surge.

"We're running away from the stone," Orla noticed. The group turned around. By running toward Rose, they had moved a great distance away from the glowing rock.

On the other hill, Rose smiled and reached her hand out for the boy. He smiled back, but Ciaran could clearly see it was not a smile on the kid's face, but a crooked grin that he had seen before and didn't want to see again. "That's not the kid! That's not him!" he yelled as Orla and Mori moved once again toward Rose. The sand under their feet flew faster, and they drifted even further away from the rock.

Close to Rose, a dimensional gate slid open, and Jay jumped out. He ran at Rose and called out for her. She didn't respond, hypnotized. Jay raced up the hill toward the boy. He glanced at Jay, then swung his arm in the air. The arm quickly turned into a blade, and before Jay could do anything, it pierced through Rose's body.

From this side of the hill, there was nothing the group could do. It was even too far for an accurate shot. Jay darted to Rose and held her in his arms. In front of them, the kid changed into the man in the black robe, then to Bricius, then to Ganzorig, and then into a bunch of people that they didn't recognize. The image flickered rapidly.

"What is that thing?" Roy mumbled.

The image flickered a few more times and raised the blade again. It was about to take Jay's head off. Ciaran grabbed Lorcan's gun and shot at the image. The distance was much too large for the laser beams to be effective. The thing was in an unrecognizable form at the moment, half-lizard half-dinosaur. It turned toward Ciaran. Orla moved to the front and threw two fireballs which quickly died out mid-air.

The creature seemed entertained by the group's effort. It turned to face them.

Taking the opportunity, Jay pulled a knife and stabbed the creature from behind. It roared, and Jay stabbed again. The creature staggered back.

"Our guns don't do much damage. How could he make such an impact with a small knife?" Roy asked.

"It's not an ordinary knife. He has the stone on the hilt of the knife," Ciaran said.

They then noted the sparkling indigo spot on the knife. They turned back and looked at the glowing rock to see that the rock had disappeared.

The creature regained its feet and was about to attack Jay again. Where the face of the creature should have been, images kept flashing, many faces. Among them, there was one that Ciaran didn't want to see—the face of Hoyt Flanagan. Hoyt was an ancient sorcerer and had more than once wanted to kill Ciaran. Their last fight had almost cost him his life, but Ciaran thought he had killed Hoyt. Who was Bricius, and why would he say Hoyt had been protecting Lorcan?

Ciaran clenched his jaw, trying to control his anger. The image of the man's face flashed rapidly and then vanished. The creature turned toward Jay now and raised its blade arm again. Jay fell onto the flowing sand and dragged himself backward. The blade stabbed and slashed into the sand. Jay stood up and ran toward the group while the creature slashed at his back. He fell but stood again and dove into the flowing sand.

"No!" Roy yelled and wanted to dive after him—not for the man but more for the knife he was taking with him into the deep sand—but Mori pulled him back. The creature had the same thought. It was about to rush after Jay but was swept backward by a gigantic wave of electric current. The creature stopped and looked at the group, and saw Lorcan standing on the top of the other hill, gazing at it. Lorcan's eyes were full of fire. The longer he gazed, the more electric waves came at the creature. It would soon disintegrate in the powerful heat of the electric currents. The creature withdrew a few steps.

Wave of electricity shot continuously toward it. Lorcan kept a firm stance, a drop of blood trickling from his nose. He reeled back. Taking the opportunity, the creature ran off down the hill. Lorcan stepped forward, shooting more waves from his blazing eyes. The current became apparent when it hit its target. The creature roared again. It stretched its arms, creating an invisible hand to grab Lorcan.

Lorcan grunted and was suddenly pulled forward, rolling down the slope. Ciaran dove after him, jumping into the flowing sand. Orla tried to rush toward the falling men, but Roy held her back. The sand became a grainy whirlpool, sucking everything on the surface down into its hole, the desert wind picking the surface sand up and swirling it in a globe in the air.

A moment later, the sand stopped moving, the wind calmed, and Orla, Roy, and Mori were alone with the desert sun at the top of the hill.

CHAPTER 16

The sand rained down into an empty space in the middle of the Earth, dragging Jay, Lorcan, Ciaran, and the creature with it. People, creatures, and unrecognizable objects tumbled one into another, rolling down a slope and eventually settling in the middle of the mud. All men jumped to their feet, taking a stance in preparation for whatever came at them. The creature rolled into a far corner. It rose up to a life-sized flickering image. Jay still had the knife in his hand and charged at the creature. The creature's image flickered and turned into the kid just before Jay's knife pierced its chest.

Jay's hand shook as he stopped the knife an inch before its pierced what use to be the creature's chest.

"No! No, it's an illusion!" Ciaran yelled at Jay as he hesitated to kill the image of the kid. The creature took advantage of Jay's second of hesitation, its hand turning into a blade, and before Jay could register the information, the blade pierced his body. Pulling the blade out, the creature used its free hand to grab the knife Jay was holding. It pushed him to the ground and ran away.

Ciaran still had Lorcan's gun in his hand, and he beamed it at the creature. It turned and looked at Ciaran, and he was sure it grinned at him. Its reptilian maw pulled upward in the shape of a smile. Then it opened its mouth and blew a jet of fire at Ciaran. He jumped aside to it. Suddenly, the creature staggered back. It had been hit by Lorcan's electric current. He did it again, shooting the current out by gazing at the creature with his eyes which sparked with blue fire. Lorcan shot again, and this time, the creature fell backward. It roared in pain and tried to get up to run.

Lorcan wanted to shoot again, but seeing the blood trickled from Lorcan's nose, Ciaran stopped him. "Let it go," he said.

Lorcan shot one more time and slumped to his knees. The creature staggered, then ran again.

"Goddammit. Don't use your ability so much when you don't know what it is or what it's costing you!" Ciaran exclaimed. "Now I know not only your combat skills need improvement, but you need training in logical decision making, too."

Lorcan smiled, wiped the blood from his nose, and said nothing. They heard Jay stir and ran to him.

"I thought you were dead. Come on, let me help you up," Lorcan said.

Jay shook his head. "I won't stay for long. I'll tell you what you need to know. But can you promise me one thing?" Jay closed his eyes to take a breath as blood flowed from of his body and pooled on the ground.

Lorcan shook his head to protest as he still wanted to take Jay back to the sand hill. Ciaran merely nodded and waited for the dying man to speak. "The place you come from, is it safe?" Jay asked Ciaran.

"Don't worry. I'll protect the kid if he comes to me. Is he your son?"

Jay nodded. "I'm sorry I lied before. Jacob is my only son. He was good friends with Rose's son, Michael. Four years ago, they were playing on the sand beach and were attacked by something in the water. I couldn't bear losing my son. Bricius is a friend of my wife's family. He offered to save one of the dying children, and I chose Jacob. I didn't know Bricius would use magic to make him live in Michael's body. I've never had the heart to tell Rose. If you see my son again, could you help him? Could you take him in? You seem to be a man of power . . ."

"I'll do my best," Ciaran promised.

Jay closed his eyes for a short moment to gather his remaining strength. "My wife was a shapeshifter from a powerful clan. We met in New Jersey, got married, and had Jacob. We took him to visit family on the island. Her family was estranged because of the hunt for the power of the key. Her cousins could shift into sea creatures. They're powerful and they've killed a lot of people. They wanted to expand their territories by flooding as many places as possible using the key of Psuche. My wife didn't know any of that and didn't want to get involved. As soon as we arrived, the island was disconnected from the world."

Jay closed his eyes again. Lorcan and Ciaran could see his life was drifting away. "My wife found out later on that the cousins had gotten together with some forces beyond this planet to somehow lock down this island and turn it in to a safe haven for creatures. Their base. She confronted them. She fought so hard to get the island back to the way it was. And they killed her for that. Before she died, she asked me to take care of Jacob. She told me I could trust Bricius."

"You know he's a sorcerer?" Lorcan asked.

"I knew he could wield magic and do a lot of other things that I don't understand."

"What's in this for Bricius?" Ciaran asked.

"Someone hired him to find the key. But he's on my side. Bricius paid a shapeshifter to take a young doctor form in Japan ..."

"Chiyo?" Lorcan asked referring to the doctor who stole the key from them in their last trip.

Jay nodded. "Chiyo formed and station in Japan. We almost got the key, but then the plan went south. She took the stone off the key and gave the stone to us. It was you people who interfered with our plans in Japan. Bricius had come to the house to tell me that—that's when you saw him. When he wanted to kill you, I told him you might have the key . . . Do you?"

"We're not giving the key to any creatures," Lorcan said.

Jay sighed. "It doesn't make a difference now. I can't keep my promise to my wife. I can't take Jacob out of here . . ."

"What about the werewolves and those you fought with when we arrived?" Lorcan asked.

"The Yakuz . . . they're everywhere. They want the key, too . . ." And then Jay drew in his last breath and died.

"How are we gonna get out of here?" Lorcan asked. Then he realized Jay was dead. "Goddammit." He glanced around. They were in what looked like a long, dark cave which curved in another direction. The creature had run that way, into the dark hole. It might not be a good idea to follow, but they might not have a choice, Lorcan thought. "Do you think we're in another dimension or just underneath the sand hill?"

Ciaran shook his head and tried to code his wrist unit. "We'll find out soon enough. Here we go." Ciaran's wrist unit flashed an operating signal.

Lorcan looked at his dead unit. "Why isn't mine working?"

Ciaran shrugged. "Not only is mine made in Eudaiz, but I also helped design it!"

"Smart ass," Lorcan muttered. Ciaran headed in the opposite direction as the creature. They didn't have to walk far before they arrived at a T junction. Ciaran checked his wrist unit again, but before they could make any more progress, a chill hit them from behind. They turned to see Bricius.

"Who killed Jay?" he barked out.

"Who are you?" Ciaran asked.

"Bricius, we didn't kill Jay. A creature in Jacob's form, the form you forced the kid into, killed him," Lorcan said.

"Who are you to judge me? What do you know about losing a son?" Bricius snarled, anger flaring in his eyes.

"The creature took the stone, too. And we have the key. We can work together to find the stone, and then we'll discuss the key."

Bricius laughed dryly. "You must be Ciaran LeBlanc. You might have a lot of power in the multiverse, but not in the middle of the Earth."

"I don't need power here to work our way out of this. If we fight, the consequence might be tragic, and neither of us will have a good outcome."

"I can't see how we can possibly collaborate. There's only one key, and we both want it."

"You don't want it. Someone hired you to fight for the key. I can pay you more."

"It's not just the money, it's a code of honor . . ."

Ciaran donned his most formal British tone. "Would you provide me with your services for free if the mission is honorable enough?"

Bricius shook his head and laughed. "You live up to your reputation, Ciaran. I was told not to talk to you."

Lorcan chuckled. "That's a compliment, Ciaran."

Bricius glanced at Lorcan, who was watching his every move like a hawk. "Money used to do the trick. But now, I want more. I want him dead." Bricius pointed at Lorcan.

"Lorcan is my friend. So if you kill him, I'll kill you. Then you'll get nothing."

"You don't even want to know *why* I want to kill him?"

"No," Ciaran deadpanned.

"Even if I can give you the stone right now, you wouldn't give him up?"

"That's worth considering, but I know you don't have the stone . . ." Before Bricius could respond, Ciaran pulled his gun and shot at him. It had totally slipped his mind that Bricius had a dimensional shield. The beam bounced off the shield and had no effect on Bricius. At the same time, Bricius waved his invisible arm and smashed at Ciaran's head. Ciaran fell to the ground, dazed by the hit. Bricius switched his focus back to Lorcan because he knew what Lorcan could do to him. But it was too late. Waves of energy flew at him, shooting from Lorcan's eyes. The waves cut through the shield and electrocuted Bricius, throwing him to the floor.

Lorcan staggered backward. The use of this newfound ability seemed to suck a lot of energy from him.

On the floor, Bricius used his invisible hand to grab for Ciaran, who was still dazed. He pulled Ciaran over to him and used him as human shield. Bricius's hand turned into a blade, pressing against Ciaran's throat.

"What do you want?" Lorcan asked.

"If I want you dead, it's going to be too easy for you. You killed my son, and you'll have to pay for that."

"I was a kid, and your son was in an animal form. He wanted to kill my mother."

"He'd never do that. Ask your mother. You were a kid, what do you know?"

"I saw it with my own eyes. He was going to rip my mother's throat out."

"Between sorcery and shapeshifting, do you think anything of what you saw from our family was real?" Bricius laughed. "We were powerful. Ask your little bitch, Orla. Even her family dared not cross us.

All this because of women. They are our weakness. They should be damned." He laughed again and let the blade against Ciaran's throat become slack. As fast as lightning, Ciaran pulled a knife, turned around, and stabbed Bricius. As he staggered back, Ciaran advanced and stabbed again. Bricius fell backward but managed to give Ciaran a kick on the way down.

Regaining his footing, he saw Lorcan was shooting at him again. He swung his invisible hand and pulled Ciaran up, shielding himself from the electric wave Lorcan was sending at him. As soon as the wave hit Ciaran, Lorcan pulled back, and the withdrawn current bounced back, hitting him just as hard.

Lorcan fell backward, lying on the ground, blood running from the corners of his eyes. Everything in front of him was a blur. He couldn't see anything, but he could hear the sound of Bricius approaching, his heavy breathing and the low growl of hatred in the air.

"If you want to kill me, then do it. Killing Ciaran isn't going to do you any good."

"Killing you is too easy. I'm going to kill those you love. Your family. Your little lover. And I want you to live to see it," Bricius's voice echoed.

Lorcan surged to his feet, reaching his arms out to navigate. In front of him was only a blanket of darkness.

"Ciaran!"

There was no response.

"Ciaran!" Lorcan repeated and heard Ciaran groan from the ground. He hurried in that direction, crouched and probed with his hands for Ciaran. "Are you okay?" He found Ciaran's leg and shook it. "Are you okay? I'm sorry. I didn't mean to hit you."

It sounded as if Ciaran had sat up. "It's okay, I've got it. Stop touching me, you're weirding me out! Jesus Christ, what happened to your eyes?"

"I don't know. I can't see anything. Are you sure you're okay?"

"Have you ever been electrocuted? If not, try a hundred thousand volts. That's what it felt like. I guessed you withdrew it. It could have been worse."

"Let's call it a draw—you took half the voltage, I took half. Now I'm blind."

"And I'm paralyzed." Ciaran chuckled. "Just stay here for a bit. Your vision will come back shortly."

"How do you know?"

"Just a theory."

"Another of Ciaran's theories!" Lorcan wanted to roll his eyes, but it hurt too much, so he let the urge pass. "So now in addition to being able to turn into a fox, without being a proper werefox because I don't have their genes and some of their supernatural abilities, I can electrocute people by staring at them. What the heck is happening to me?"

"I told you I have a theory. Do you want to hear it?"

"Spit it out."

"Remember Zach Flynn? He came to your place with Madeline and me once in the Daimon Gate."

"Yeah, how can I forget? He knocked Orla unconscious, and you tied me up so I wouldn't break his neck."

Ciaran smiled. He remembered the incident vividly. Orla was being controlled and was about to kill him, which forced Zach to interfere. Ciaran cleared his throat. "Zach is a sound bender. He didn't just knock Orla out physically. He can hit people with sound waves using his thoughts. He uses his mind as a vessel. So if he hits someone with strong resistance, the sound bounces back at him just as hard."

"So you think I can electrocute people using my eyes as a vessel. And because I withdrew the hit on Bricius when he dragged you in, it bounced back at me and hurt my eyes?"

"Maybe not just your eyes as a vessel, but your thought process as well. What did you think about when you struck him?"

"I wanted to smite him into charcoal, grind him into dust, and feed him to wild pigs."

"Well . . ." Ciaran cleared his throat. "I won't argue with you now, but that's a very long thought process for a strike that happens as fast as lightning."

"I can try one at a time, see which one works."

"Oh, no. No random shooting when I'm around, please. You'll miss even when you're shooting with purpose."

Lorcan shrugged. "I have a feeling Bricius will be back soon. Can you walk yet? We should get out of here."

"I can only wobble at the moment. Can you see yet?"

"About ten percent . . ."

They felt the cave shudder, and a rumbling noise hovered in the air as if the cave was moving.

"Shit!" Lorcan stood up, hauled Ciaran up to his feet, and they trekked down a quiet wing of the cave.

CHAPTER 17

The sun had almost gone down. The desert sand became hard, and the temperature dropped. Orla searched aimlessly while Roy and Mori tried to hold her back.

"We have to have a system, Orla. You've already looked in that spot," Roy said.

"The hole was there. And it was just here before," Orla exclaimed.

"But the sand has shifted. If we keep repeating the process, you'll never be able to find them," Mori said. Then she tilted her head up to sniff the air.

"You can smell them?" Orla asked.

"Not Ciaran, but yes, I can smell Lorcan from a mile in clear conditions. I bit him before, remember?" Then Mori gestured for silence. She sniffed again and raised her hand to point at a patch of sand.

"It's solid ground, Mori," Orla said.

"There will be a hole. She's guessing the movements underground," Roy said.

"Are they moving in this direction, Mori?" Orla asked.

Mori nodded. Orla looked at Roy, and they both pulled out their guns and aimed the beams at the sand. The sand loosened in large patches and soon funneled down, turning into a hole. Orla ran to the edge of the sand patch and looked down into a cave.

"Lorcan!" she called.

"Ciaran!" she called again.

There was no sound but the breezes blowing up from the hole. "Breezes!" Orla said, then looked at Roy who had arrived at the same thought.

Roy stood up, called out for Mori. "There are breezes. It might be a tunnel, not a cave. Can you find out where the other end is?"

Mori nodded, concentrated, and sniffed the faint scent in the air. She followed the scent, she strode, galloped, and pointed. "There, over there!"

Orla and Roy rushed in that direction. Around a curve at the top of another hill, there was the open mouth of a cave.

"Lorcan!" Orla shouted into the darkness. There was a low growl from a dark corner in response to Orla's call, and the enormous creature they had just fought on the hill stepped out, glowing on one side and bleeding on the other. It staggered a bit on the injured side. Orla pulled her gun and shot at it. The beam pushed it back, but the wounds weren't fatal. The creature spat out a jet of fire at Orla, and she rolled on the ground to avoid it.

Roy stood in front of Orla and fired. Similar to what happened with Orla's gun, the beams from Roy's gun didn't do much damage to the creature. It reeled, but then advanced again. "Technology doesn't do much for you," Orla said to herself, "but let's see how magic does." She curled her fists and threw two fireballs at it. Its tail and wing caught on fire. While it frantically tried to put out the fire, Mori leaped at it and pushed her knife into its eye. It roared and swung its free arm, throwing Mori several feet away to lie on the ground beside Roy and Orla.

Orla sent in more fireballs, but the creature had learned and spat out jet of liquid venom to extinguish the fire quickly. Orla, Roy, and Mori backed up to avoid the venomous spray. They hit the edge of a cliff as the creature limped toward them.

"Should we jump?" Orla asked.

"Too high," Roy said.

"We can jump in fox form."

"I said it's too high, Mori."

The creature advanced. This might be the end of them, Orla thought. The creature roared. It wasn't a sound of triumph, it was a sound of terrible pain. It roared again, reeling toward the cliff. Orla, Roy, and Mori rolled out of the way as the creature continued toward the edge of the cliff. Roy prepared to give it a final push over.

Behind the creature, Lorcan and Ciaran ran out from the darkness of the cave. Lorcan had electrocuted the creature twice, and he fell to his knees, drained of energy. Ciaran charged at the creature with a knife. "Don't let it fall off the cliff," he said, diving at the creature to grab its tail. Roy pulled at one leg, and Mori and Orla got the other leg. Ciaran jumped on top of the creature and arced his knife down into its brain. He stabbed until its life was drained.

When they were certain it was dead, they turned the body over. Ciaran yanked open a layer of wrinkled skin on its belly, pulling loose the knife with the stone tucked inside. The creature wriggled, its eyes sparking again with energy. Ciaran used the knife with the indigo stone to stab it in the heart.

This time, steam was expelled from its heart and brain. It was finally dead.

Ciaran flopped onto the ground, puffing.

Orla rushed to Lorcan, asking, "What happened to your eyes?"

"They bled a bit. But they're okay now."

Orla wiped away the blood on his face and looked into his striking blue eyes. She kissed his cheek. Lorcan brushed a tear that escaped from her eye. "I've only got fifty percent of my vision back now, but it's coming back slowly. I can see that you are still alive and beautiful." He smiled. Orla cried. He pulled her into his arms and said, "It's okay now, honey. As long as we're together, we're going to be okay. Don't cry."

Ciaran sat up and checked his wrist unit. "We've got a signal."

"We're getting out of here," Roy said and pecked Mori's cheek.

From the sky, a ring of light came down, encircling a large area of the sand. The light circled and spun, and the Raven house appeared at a position totally different from where it was before.

"We'll get back to the island now," Ciaran said and strode toward the back door of the Raven house.

The group pushed into the short corridor and through the house with no resistance, and they made their way onto the street. Ciaran kept looking at his wrist unit for new messages and signals. Then he turned toward the group with a grin. "They'll open the portal for us back on the beach. Once we're away, safe and sound, they'll rotate the dimensional shield on this island. Then everything here should be back to normal."

A flood of relief washed over everyone. Orla jumped up and hugged Lorcan. Roy pulled Mori into his arms and kissed her tenderly. Ciaran looked across the street, saying nothing, waiting until the scene of joy and affection was finished.

"What's that, Ciaran?" Orla asked.

"I beg your pardon?"

"Why were you looking at the bakery? Hungry?"

"No." Ciaran smiled.

Orla raised an eyebrow, then turned around. "Who's hungry?" The show of hands suggested that Orla was going to have to make a trip to the bakery. She winked at Ciaran. "And what would you like?"

He shook his head. "Nothing. Thanks."

"Come on."

"Okay, a bagel would be nice," Ciaran gave in. Orla grinned and sauntered across the street. Shortly, she was back with food for everyone. She gave Ciaran his bagel, and he thanked her and quickly shoved the bagel into his pocket. Lorcan laughed through a mouthful of pastry at the surprised look on Orla's face. Ciaran noticed it, too.

"I apologize if I offended you, Orla. The bagel isn't for me. Madeline mentioned how much she's missed bagels, so I thought it would be nice if I could bring her something."

A tear rolled down on Orla's face. Lorcan wiped it off and cooed, "Oh, come on, honey. I love you just as much as he loves his wife. I'd die for you! All he does is bring Madeline a bagel . . ."

"I love you, too," Orla said. Ciaran shook his head and smiled to himself.

"Let's go," Ciaran said. Before he turned to leave, he saw the boy standing at the corner of the street in full view. "Jacob!" Ciaran said to the group because he knew if Jacob was one hundred percent in his view, the others wouldn't be able to see him. Ciaran approached and crouched so that he was at eye level with the youngster. He looked into Jacob's tear-filled eyes. His skinny shoulders started to shake as he sobbed.

"You know your father died?"

Jacob nodded, and a tear rolled down his face.

"I'm so sorry for your loss. I know he tried really hard to get you off this island. Before he died, he asked me to take care of you. Did you know that?"

Jacob shook his head, and more tears rolled down.

"If you trust me, you can come with me to my place. I know people who will help you and take care of you."

Jacob picked up a rock and wrote on the street. "Where?"

"It's a place far away from here. A universe full of nice people." Ciaran smiled.

"Xiilok?" Jacob wrote. The smiled faded from Ciaran's face. He shook his head. "I live in Eudaiz. Xiilok is not a very nice place. There are many bad people living there."

"Bricius is a good person. He helped me. He told me Lorcan had killed my father."

Lorcan couldn't see Jacob, but he could see the words on the ground. He opened his mouth to say something, but Ciaran gestured for silence.

"Jacob, a Yakuz creature killed your father. Lorcan didn't do it. Bricius is not the good man you think he is."

Jacob shook his head. "He saved my life. He taught me how to hide in different dimensions."

"He didn't save you. He killed Michael and made you take Michael's body. That's not how someone should live, Jacob."

"He said he'd protect me."

"If you believe what Bricius says, why come to me? Lorcan is my friend, and I trust him."

Jacob started to cry out loud and shook his head.

"You don't know why you came to me?"

Jacob continued to shake his head and cry. Ciaran tried to look into Jacob's eyes. "Did Bricius hold you against your will?"

Jacob shook his head, then he wrote, "He was injured, and I left him. Am I a bad boy?"

"No, you're not a bad boy. You're confused. But you have good survival instincts. You took the opportunity to leave Bricius. It tells me that he'd threatened you in one way or another. Jacob, did he tell you if you ever leave him, he'll hurt your father?"

Jacob shook his head and cried again. "He said if I tell, the bad people will kill everyone on the island. I didn't tell anyone, but people kept dying." He wiped the tears off his face and continued to write. "When he told me my father was dead, I left him. I only worried about my father and not others. I am a bad boy."

Ciaran turned Jacob's shoulders so he looked into Ciaran's eyes. "How old are you?"

"Ten."

"Do you know what a ten-year-old boy should be doing?"

Jacob looked down at the pavement. Ciaran tilted his chin up. "You should be going to school, learning, and playing with other kids. You shouldn't have to worry about the fate of an island or whether someone will kill your father if you say the wrong thing. I can't change what happened to you in the past, but if you trust me and come with me, I promise you will have a home and people who love you."

"Nobody will love me for nothing."

Ciaran stared at those words coming from a child. He turned back and saw Orla and Mori had teared up. He cleared his throat. "Well, if you come with me, my wife, Madeline, will be looking after you. She loves kids. Maybe you should bring her something as a gift?"

Jacob contemplated then wrote, "Is she nice?"

Ciaran smiled. "She's very nice. I love her with all my heart. If you like me, you'll like her."

Jacob nodded, then pulled out a small stone box with exquisite carving on the lid. Ciaran didn't need extensive knowledge in antiques to know that this was a precious item. Jacob opened the box, showing that it was empty. Then he wrote, "Dad told me to put one hope in here a day, and my wish will come true when I have enough hope. But the box was always empty, so I took it to the beach to put some sand into it. Then Michael and I got attacked by something in the water. But I still put a hope in it every day. Do you think Madeline would like to have it?"

"This is too precious for a gift, Jacob. I am sure Madeline will love you even without it. But if it makes you feel better, yes, you can give it to her, and she will love it."

"It's still empty, though."

Ciaran smiled and pulled out his bagel. "This is my gift to Madeline from this trip. Why don't I fill your box with it?"

"It's just a bagel from the bakery! Don't you have anything more precious?"

Ciaran laughed. "Madeline used to live in New York, and she loves bagels. Where we live now, there is no such thing. So yes, a bagel is very precious to her now."

Jacob nodded. The bagel was too round for the box, so he broke it in smaller pieces and squeezed it in. Then Jacob put the box in Ciaran's hand and signaled him to hold on to it. Ciaran nodded, slid the box into the pocket of his shirt, and smiled at Jacob.

"Are you a guardian angel? Mother said she would get guardian angels to come and protect me and Father. But then she died, and the angels have never come."

"No. I'm just a man. But I'm lucky enough to have talented people to help me. People like Lorcan, Orla, Roy, and Mori. See, they are waiting for you. They are good people, and they will help you, too." Jacob nodded.

Ciaran's wrist unit signaled. He looked at it and then turned around to talk to the group. "Brandon is attacking one of the portals in the Daimon Gate to distract them from opening the portal for us. They'll still do it, but they can only hold it open for a very short time. We've got to get moving now." Then he turned toward Jacob. "Are you coming with me?" Jacob nodded and trailed behind Ciaran.

They had only gone a block when Roy and Mori stopped them. "Werewolves and a lot of were-creatures ahead," Roy said.

"That's the shortest way to the beach!" Orla exclaimed.

"We'll have to detour via the bush," Mori suggested. They veered right to a smaller alley which led to the bush and ran as fast as they could.

CHAPTER 18

The group exited the bush at the beach far from the spot where they had landed before. They raced toward the landing port. Ciaran kept checking his wrist unit while running, keeping an eye on Jacob at the same time. They felt the ground start to shake.

"What's that?" Mori asked.

Ciaran looked at this wrist unit. "Movements of energy underneath the Earth's surface. This is what we had seen before sending you guys back here for the stone."

"Can we open our individual portals, the way we always do?" Lorcan asked.

"No, not with the size of our group—and when every force in the multiverse that wants this Indigo Stone is watching out for the teleport so that they can attack us. We need to the Daimon Gate's teleport system. It's the best and the safest."

"Better than Eudaiz's?" Lorcan chuckled.

"I hate to admit it, but teleport is not our strongest suit. However, Eudaiz offers the safest destination for us, so we'll be using the Daimon Gate's teleport system to get to the transitional zone, and then we'll travel to Eudaiz from there."

"We're not going back to the Daimon Gate now?" Orla asked.

"No, that route is too predictable." Ciaran smiled.

They had almost made it to the middle of the long sand beach when they saw a wave surge up at the horizon.

"That dragon again!" Orla shouted.

Lorcan looked at the size of the monster's head rising up from under the water, and he knew they were in deep trouble.

"It's very ugly for a dragon," Ciaran said. "Jacob, can you hide in another dimension for now?" Jacob nodded, ran away and disappeared. "We have to kill that creature," Ciaran said.

"How? Last time Orla blocked its wave with the sand, and it gave us just enough time to run away. But now we don't have a portal to run to," Roy said.

"A dragon is a mythical creature. This one is not. It's a very big and ugly reptile. If it's an animal with a tangible form, there's a way to kill it," Ciaran said.

"But we need a realistic way to kill it *right now*. Any ideas?" Lorcan asked.

"Not yet."

The sea creature ascended higher above the water's surface and started moving inland. Each movement created a large wave which penetrated deeper inland. The group with withdrew, further away from the shoreline.

"Going back to town is just inviting the creature to drown the whole island," Ciaran said as the creature raised its tail fifty feet above the water and slammed it down, sending water flying inland to rain down on them. The creature whacked its tail again. A wave a story high rolled in and crashed on the shore. Orla charged to the front of the group.

But Lorcan pulled her back, saying, "No, Orla."

Orla broke away and darted toward the water. Her eyes had turned blank. She raised her arms and created a wall of sand that rolled upward toward the sky and smashed into the wave. But the water was stronger and broke through the sand wall, leaping onto the land. Although the water had been weakened, it still had enough force to hurl everyone like rag dolls, smashing them against hard objects, before withdrawing to the sea, dragging everything in its way with it. Everyone clung to the rock cliffs, trying to hold on through the withdrawing force of the water. As soon the water had cleared the beach, they flopped onto the wet sand.

"Any solutions, Ciaran? I don't think we can survive another wave," Lorcan asked.

Ciaran saw the creature raise its tail, about to create a second wave. Its beady eyes pierced through him as if enjoying the sight of the vulnerable humans before it. Ciaran raised his arms, indicating that he wanted to say something, and the creature stopped, its tail hovering in the air. Ciaran spoke quietly through his teeth to his friends, "It's listening to me. Is it safe to assume that it's a shapeshifter, and the other half it is human?" Ciaran punctuated the separate words shape and shifter to make his point.

"Yes," Roy responded quickly.

Ciaran looked at Orla. "Don't hate me, Orla."

"What are you—" Lorcan hadn't finished his sentence when Ciaran drew the knife with the Indigo Stone and pressed it against Lorcan's neck. Orla growled and threw herself at Ciaran.

"Keep her still!" Ciaran shouted at Roy and Mori. "We all want to live, but something has to give." He dragged Lorcan out onto the beach, pressing the knife harder to his neck. The creature had lowered its tail, focused on Ciaran. A stream of blood began to flow from where the knife had cut into Lorcan's flesh.

The creature recognized the knife and lowered itself for a closer look. "I don't know who you are, but I have nothing to do with this. I heard you wanted him because he killed your woman. And you want the Indigo Stone as well, so here it is. You can have both. Just let the others live. Can we make a deal?"

The creature growled.

"Don't come any closer. I'll leave what you want here. Take it or leave it. It's up to you." Ciaran spun Lorcan around and stabbed him. Lorcan grunted and dropped to the sand. Ciaran raised the knife, stained with Lorcan's blood, for the dragon to see. The knife with the Indigo Stone shone at the creature, stopping it from moving as if it had mesmerized it. Ciaran put the knife down beside Lorcan's body. Then he stepped backward slowly, turned around, and ran as fast as he could toward the rocks.

The creature appeared to frown at Lorcan's dead body, then it lowered itself to sea level and moved inland. The water raised up, hitting Lorcan's body and shifting the knife. Regardless of how gently the creature moved, the water hit Lorcan's body and washed the knife further away. The creature suddenly stopped moving, began to shrink in size, and then walked out of the water as a man in lizard skin.

When Ciaran saw that the creature had left the water and was moving toward Lorcan's body in human form, he charged at it and blasted his laser beams. It turned and roared at Ciaran. Roy, Mori, and Orla also ran at it, guns blazing, covering the creature in beams. It roared with pain and slumped to the ground. From behind it, Lorcan stood up.

"Yo!" he called. As soon as the creature turned to look at Lorcan, it jerked back, screamed, and burst into flame. Lorcan had electrocuted it. He did it again and again until there was nothing left. He slumped to his knees, exhausted.

Orla ran to him, and he pulled her into his arms and embraced her. The water gently lapped at their feet, cool and soothing, rewarding them for a battle won.

Over Orla's shoulders, Lorcan smiled at Ciaran, "You could have been a little gentler with the knife."

Ciaran picked up the knife with the Indigo Stone and tucked it under his belt. "You could have been gentler when you electrocuted me. You can heal yourself quickly, I can't. Besides, it was a cut, not a stab, don't be such a wuss."

"Bastard," Lorcan grinned, rolling his eyes.

"What?" Ciaran asked. Lorcan nodded toward the back. Ciaran turned to see Roy and Mori were drowning in a passionate kiss. "No need to teleport them. They're already in another universe," Ciaran muttered and turned to search for Jacob. He heard a sound from behind him— it was Bricius. He stood with Jacob in Ciaran's full view. When Ciaran glanced back, he could tell that the group didn't see either one. Bricius smirked, his hand around Jacob's throat now transformed into a blade.

"One wrong move, and I'll separate his head from his body."

CHAPTER 19

Ciaran froze. He couldn't even ask Bricius what he wanted because the others would see that he was talking to no one. As much as he wanted the others to read his eyes or his mind and do something about it, he wouldn't risk Jacob's life, which had already been savaged once.

Bricius approached and whispered into Ciaran's ear, "Don't speak to me. When the portal to the Daimon Gate opens, I will get in with you. Once we get to the Daimon Gate, you will lead me to the key of Psuche. After I get the key, you will give me the knife with the Indigo Stone." Then he stepped away from Ciaran and squeezed Jacob's neck a bit harder, causing him gasp for air, to make his point. Ciaran shifted his stance and gave a slight nod. His eyes fixated on Jacob's, and he let out a sigh of relief when Bricius eased his hold on the boy.

Bricius had to whisper because his voice could cross dimensions and others would hear him, Ciaran thought. He gazed at Jacob and got the strange feeling that he could communicate with Jacob with his mind. He made up a plan in his mind and sent the thought to Jacob. The boy blinked.

"That's a disagreement," Ciaran thought and sent his thought again to insist. Jacob's eyes teared up, and he look as if he might not cooperate. "Stubborn boy," Ciaran thought.

A few feet away, Lorcan was walking over to Orla, her back to Ciaran, Bricius, and Jacob. Lorcan glanced at Ciaran and frowned. "Did you find gold in the sand, Ciaran?"

Ciaran turned and smiled. "When we get to the Daimon Gate, there will be plenty of gold for you to dig."

"So stop looking for it here. Want to share a few rounds of air fencing while we wait for the gate?"

"Air fencing?" Roy asked.

Lorcan laughed. "People play air guitar, so why can't we do air fencing?"

"Ahhh . . ." Roy nodded with understanding.

"It still requires a lot of energy, and I don't really want to hear you grunt. It's not a nice sound." Ciaran grinned and turned around. He heard a low warning growl from Bricius. Bricius blinked a few times, revealing his wormy irises. Ciaran nodded as he understood that Bricius was now a Xiilok citizen and was invisible to the Daimon Gate's system. He could sneak into their teleport without being discovered. Bricius smirked when he saw that Ciaran realized he was at a huge disadvantage.

Ciaran turned to his side as if he was saying something to Lorcan and then, fast as lightning, he pulled his gun and blasted at Bricius's head. He knew the beam wouldn't work on him, but that was the only plan he could execute at the moment. As Ciaran predicted, he'd provoked Bricius and had broken his concentration. The blade arm pressed to Jacob's throat loosened a bit, and Ciaran flew at Bricius. He dropped his gun on the way, pulled the Indigo Stone knife, and stabbed at Bricius's head. Bricius had no choice but to raise his blade arm to block the attack. Jacob took the opportunity to duck down, and he disappeared from that dimension.

Ciaran's hand bounced back when the knife hit the blade arm. Half of Ciaran's body went numb with the impact. Attacking Bricius with his human strength was a stupid idea, but Ciaran knew he didn't any other option at the moment. Ciaran saw that Jacob had safely left this dimension, turning fifty percent transparent. It was time for Ciaran to flee, so he stabbed a few more times to keep Bricius busy blocking and then ran.

Lorcan had aimed like a hawk. The fifty percent transparent Jacob pointed at Bricius's position. Lorcan focused on that position.

Ciaran made it a few feet away from Bricius and yelled, "I'm clear." Bricius roared in fury. He could see he was in trouble, but he had allowed his anger to take over his rational mind. He extended his blade arm, pointing at Ciaran from behind. Jacob darted in front of Ciaran, pointing frantically. Ciaran stopped running and turned to see the sharp blade inches from his chest.

It was too late for him to do anything.

He felt the impact of the blade on his chest and, at the same time, the shape of Bricius jerked upward and turned red as he was electrocuted.

Then Ciaran saw nothing else.

Lorcan saw Ciaran go down and Bricius burning like a torch from the inside. He had been watching Ciaran closely. Ciaran had mentioned the Daimon Gate, which was not their destination, and he'd also mentioned gold in the Daimon Gate. Then he had hinted that he needed Lorcan to use his energy—meaning electrocuting someone. And that person was hiding in a different dimension, that person couldn't speak out loud because he could hide his tangible form, but his sound might cross dimensions.

Lorcan didn't think he could have done any better than he had given his limited time and information, but maybe he hadn't been quick enough to save Ciaran. Lorcan picked the knife up from the sand and charged at Bricius. He would burn to ashes anyway, but it wasn't enough. Lorcan stabbed at Bricius again and again.

Then Bricius's eyes fluttered open, and he chanted, "On this day, in this space, I curse your parents for the death of my son. I bind the curse with my soul and for that I shall go to Hell."

"Shut up!" Lorcan yelled and stabbed some more, but Bricius continued to chant the curse. It took both Orla and Roy to drag him off of Bricius's dead body.

Ciaran opened his eyes and saw Jacob and Mori sitting next to him. Jacob looked at Ciaran's chest and seemed to be happy with what he saw. He smiled. Ciaran smiled weakly as his chest hurt when he tried to move any muscle on the upper half of his body. He tried to sit up. Mori gave him a push from the back. "Slow and steady, here you go," she said.

Bricius's body had started to disintegrate into worm puddles. Orla and Roy dragged Lorcan toward where Ciaran lay.

"You see, he's already up. He didn't die. Don't be upset," Orla comforted.

Lorcan shrugged Roy and Orla off him and slumped to his knees, puffing in exhaustion. He knew Orla thought he was upset because he'd assumed Ciaran had died because he was too slow to shoot Bricius. He would let her think that. Lorcan watched Ciaran trying to sit up with difficulty and wincing with the pain.

Ciaran's shirt had been pulled open, and looking down, he could see a large purple bruise had formed at the position of his heart. Ciaran looked at Orla for an explanation.

"You were saved by a bagel," Orla said. Ciaran looked at his chest again and recalled the impact when the blade hit his body. Lorcan's strike had reduced the power of the blade and had pushed

Bricius backward, but he'd still managed to reach Ciaran's chest. When he hit the stone box, he must have thought he had done damage. Because Ciaran's shirt was covered in Lorcan's blood stains, Bricius wouldn't be able to tell whether he had wounded Ciaran. Still, the hit was, after all, hard enough that it had it ground the box into dust.

A beam flashed down in a large circle onto the sand.

"About damn time," Roy mumbled.

Lorcan stood up, squinted at the light, and then approached to give Roy a hand with helping Ciaran to the teleport. As soon as they entered the light circle, Jacob appeared in the same dimension with everyone. He could feel it when Ciaran and everyone else could see him at the same time. A smile flashed on his face when Orla crouched and opened her arms to him. "Hello stranger. Come give me a hug."

A short moment later, at a station in Alphi, a satellite station of Eudaiz, Ciaran manned the control panel and executed many complicated programs. Rows and waves of data and code flowed on the screen, each creating a visual change in a map-like picture displayed on another large monitor.

Ciaran pointed to blue dots in the middle of the map. "That's the island where it's supposed to be. Using the data and resources provided by the Daimon Gate, I have rechanneled some of the astronomical energy forces elsewhere and have shifted the shield that covered that island, blocking its dimensional view from other universes, including Earth."

"So everything is back to normal now?" Orla asked.

"Yes, for now."

CHAPTER 20

The spaceship they traveled on looked like a mini bus shaped like a capsule. There were no windows to see outside. Ciaran explained that these internal capsules travel in connected tunnels, and there was nothing to see. In addition, they traveled too fast for human eyes to see anything. Orla smiled to herself. Yes, Ciaran had called this vehicle a *capsule*. Ciaran assured everyone that English was the official language in Eudaiz, especially in the Sciphil zone— more terminology that they would have to learn. Sciphil was a short form of Scientist Philosopher, a powerful and important position in the committee that governed this universe of six hundred billion people. Orla shook her head, trying to register the information. It was a world different from the Daimon Gate, and it made what she and Lorcan had experienced there feel rather ordinary.

Lorcan turned aside and saw her smiling at him. He kissed her cheek. "What are you thinking about, dreamer?" he asked.

"This is a new life for us."

"Yes, indeed. Why aren't you happy?"

"I am. What are you talking about?" Orla shook her head and smiled. Something hovering in the air bothered her. The look in Lorcan's eyes was distance. She had caught him a couple of times avoiding eye contact with her. What was that about? Orla pushed away the black cloud in her mind, a dark thought that would only turn into a nightmare and made her weep for nothing—the fear of losing Lorcan.

"Orla, put that away," she told herself. Ever since childhood, she feared she might not be good enough for him. Her parents had died when she was only a kid and had left her nothing except a black magic debt and a dysfunctional family. Until now, she didn't quite understand it what was about her that Lorcan was head over heels in love with. He had left everything for her—family, wealth, connections, a world of opportunities. He had spent the life on the run with her and protected her as much as he could. Why? That fear, that question, clung to her body like a cancer cell, waiting to spread whenever her immune system was weak.

It was weak now.

The look Lorcan had given her after his encounter with Bricius was inexplicable. And then there were his nightmares, his hallucination when he was injured. When he was figuring out his werefox issues, Orla understood he was experiencing self-doubt and confusion, but he had gotten over that. So what was happening now was more than that, more profound. What was going on in his mind had to do not only with himself, but with her and their relationship as well.

They had never kept secrets from each other. Orla sighed.

Lorcan lifted her chin. "What's that, Orla?"

"Huh?"

"What are you thinking about?"

"Roy and Mori. They must be happily settled at their place by now. I was just wondering when we'll have a chance to visit them."

Ciaran turned around from the control panel. "As soon as tomorrow if you like. They live in the residential area in District Seven."

"What's the deal with the doctor you left Jacob with?" Lorcan asked.

"He's a good friend of ours. He helped Madeline and me when we first arrived to Eudaiz. He has a daughter Jacob's age. He'll take good care of Jacob."

A robotic voice announced their arrival at Ciaran's residence. Ciaran opened the capsule door and led them to the private platform.

"What a place!" Orla gasped. The private station shined with metal and stone, a mixture of contemporary design and medieval architecture. There were no green men walking around and no flying saucers in the sky. It was just like a palace somewhere in England.

The grand entrance led them to the main hall with gigantic columns, arched ceilings, and stone statues. A robotic butler approached, greeted them by name, and asked if they needed anything. "How does he know us?" Orla asked.

"The system must have updated and populated the moment we were accepted to Eudaiz," Lorcan said.

"Technology comes in really handy sometimes." Orla grinned. From a wing, Madeline stepped out. She smiled graciously and greeted Lorcan and Orla. Then she looked at Ciaran. She fixed her eyes on his left shoulder where the injury was. Lorcan saw Madeline's look and silently wished Ciaran luck. Because Ciaran didn't have the ability to heal himself quickly, the wound wouldn't look pretty when Madeline got to check it.

Ciaran approached and rubbed his thumb over the dimple on Madeline's left cheek. She touched his unshaven face, tucked away a strand of his long hair, and looked into those intense gray eyes that she hadn't seen for days.

"How are the kids?" Ciaran asked.

"They stopped talking to me. They must be waiting for you." She touched his left shoulder. "Is this bad?"

Ciaran shook his head. "Nothing is as bad as what I've missed." Then he kissed her.

Orla looked at Ciaran and Madeline, her eyes dreamy. Lorcan pulled Orla into his arms and kissed her. There, Orla let herself melt into his kiss.

Ciaran asked Orla. "Do you want to see the twins?"

"Of course! I'd love to!" Orla smiled.

"Madeline, would you mind taking Orla to the children's chamber?" Madeline smiled at him. She knew her husband, and that was a sign that he needed to have a private conversation with Lorcan.

"Come on in, Orla. The kids will be thrilled to see you." Madeline gestured to the corridor.

"Aren't you coming?" Orla asked Lorcan.

"Of course. But I just need to check out Ciaran's computer experiment first." Lorcan grinned.

Orla nodded and followed Madeline to the children's chamber. When they had exited the hall completely, Ciaran asked, "Are you sure about this?"

Lorcan nodded, raking his hands through his hair. "I have to leave now, or I won't leave at all."

Ciaran nodded. He knew what it was like to have loved ones threatened. But he thought Lorcan's decision was rushed. "I know what it feels like, Lorcan. But I think you should be better prepared. The threat wasn't solid and yet . . ."

"I know you don't believe in magic. I don't want to, either. But Bricius cursed my parents. I told you what happened to Orla and me in London. These curses are real."

"Bricius was a wannabe mind bender. He's not good enough to bend your mind. Don't let him succeed, especially after his death. But Hoyt

Flanagan, the one Bricius said was protecting you for unknown reasons, is a real threat to Eudaiz. I need you here to help me handle that."

Lorcan sat down, toying with his hair again. "My family still thinks that I'm in London. I checked the voice mail, and there was a missed call from my family without a message." He looked up at Ciaran. "My parents stopped talking to me when I left for Orla. I've never told Orla that. My sister calls a lot, and whenever she can't get me, she always leaves a message." He stood up. "My family knows nothing about magic. Do you think I can call them now and say 'watch out for a dead man's curse?' Would you do that if it were your family?"

Ciaran shook his head. "I'm sorry. My comment was careless. Of course, you have to go." Then he looked at Lorcan. "I promise I will keep an eye on Orla."

Lorcan nodded and turned on his heel.

"Take my private capsule, go to Alphi, and teleport to Ireland from there."

Lorcan turned around. "I can't take—"

"Take the fucking capsule!" Ciaran commanded. Lorcan nodded. He glanced back at the corridor where Orla had exited, then turned, put his head down, and walked out.

A moment later, Orla returned to the main hall of Ciaran's residence and faced a blast of hollow air. She drew in a breath. It wasn't the air that was hollow, but it was the emptiness of a space without Lorcan in it. She'd given him enough time to leave to do whatever it was that he had to do. She had left to play with the children because she knew if she had hung around him, he wouldn't have left. She wanted him to sort out whatever problem he was dealing with, otherwise it would haunt him for the rest of his life. But it still stung to face the reality of it.

Ciaran was looking out a window, his hands shoved in his pockets.

"I'd like to go to where you sent Lorcan."

Ciaran turned around. "I didn't send him. He went by himself, and I'm sure he'll be back soon. In the meantime, you'll stay here with us."

"I need to go with him. I know he has problem to deal with, but I won't let him deal with it by himself."

"I promised to keep an eye on you."

"Then watch me leave." Orla strode to the exit and realized that in this universe, she wouldn't have a clue how to even open a door manually, let alone everything else requiring technology. She stopped and turned. Ciaran wouldn't give in to her tears, so that was of no use.

"If there is magic involved in whatever Lorcan has to deal with, you know he's at a disadvantage, right? You know that regardless of your technology and your weapons, you can't help Lorcan when it comes to dark magic."

Ciaran shifted his stance slightly, and Orla saw it. "If the people Lorcan deals with have galactic connections, can use the sort of technology you use, and can also wield magic, then you know you are sending Lorcan to a dead zone."

Ciaran turned back to the window.

"Ciaran, if he's going back to Ireland without my help, he's heading straight to his grave."

Ciaran slowly turned around to look into Orla's eyes and saw vicious determination, the kind he found in Madeline's eyes whenever he was in trouble. It wasn't just love; it was the primal need to protect loved one. "Where exactly in Ireland do you want to go?"

"The riverbank where we met. I'll show you on the map." Orla smiled as Ciaran gestured her to the control room.

*****

PART TWO
RED MOON

CHAPTER 1

"**O**rla!" Lorcan's scream seemed muffled by the fog as he saw her turn around to look at him with tears streaming down her face. And then she vanished into the thick mist.

What have I done? Lorcan asked himself, not expecting an answer. He stared into the emptiness and felt the vibration of the energy Orla had left behind. A blizzard. It felt like thousands of blades of ice were slashing at his skin.

Was this the end? The end of Orla and him?

The Irish countryside blurred in front of him. This was the riverbank where they had become childhood sweethearts. But it had now become where their relationship ended. "Orla!" he called out again but expected no response as he remembered the vision of her blending into the smoky air of the mysterious river.

Why? Lorcan struggled harder to free himself, but his legs felt like they weighed a ton, and his body didn't obey him. He did his best to turn around.

Behind him, the woman pulled the upper half of her dress up to cover her breasts. She pulled her long, flaming red hair back to reveal her perfect face and the flawless skin of her delicate neck. Her striking blue eyes pierced at Lorcan at the same time as a smug smile crossed her face.

"What did you do to me?" Lorcan asked while summoning all of his leftover power to move.

"Nothing you didn't want." She smiled again.

Lorcan thought he had gotten things under control. Bricius, a nasty sorcerer he had fought and killed during his last mission, had cursed his parents before he died. Although Lorcan had no idea how to break a curse, he had traveled back to Ireland alone, without Orla. They had fought so hard to be together, free from the curse her family here had bound them with, and he couldn't take a chance she would get tangled up in that mess again.

He had landed at the riverbank after exiting the portal of the Daimon Gate. But before he even had a chance to congratulate himself for successfully sneaking back to Ireland without Orla, he saw her. He should have known. She always seemed to know where he was. She smiled at him. It was the usual Orla smile, but there was something more to it.

Lust.

It didn't surprise him. They had run away from this place to be able to love each other freely and be together. And now, here they were, back together—and at the riverbank. Love was the only thing he had in his mind, and he was sure it was in hers as well.

She's irresistible, he had thought and then grabbed at her. He kissed her as he always had, but this time, it was different. As soon as he touched her, the air around him seemed to turn into a vacuum of some kind, and he was 'sucked' into her. And that was the last thing he remembered, and that had been the last moment when he'd been able to control his movement. The eyes of the woman staring up at him were not Orla's. His arms were moving up and down her body, pulling up her dress. His mouth ravished hers. But it wasn't he who controlled the actions. His body seemed glued to hers, and his mind was numb. He heard himself screaming on the inside for it to stop.

He was watching himself from outside his body. *Bloody hell!* He was having sex with this strange woman, and he couldn't do a thing stop it.

Then he heard the most daunting sound, and it stabbed into his heart.

"Lorcan!"

Orla's shaky voice pierced his ears. She had followed him back to Ireland after all. He couldn't turned around himself—the woman had to push him. And nothing hurt him more than the look on Orla's face.

She walked away from him and vanished into the fog.

"Who are you?" Lorcan asked the woman.

"I am the one you were in love with. She was just a convenient replacement."

"What?"

"All the time you were looking at me at the riverbank, you think I didn't know? You were watching me from the bush. You were there for *me*. Remember? It was *me* that you wanted. You were going to build me a castle."

Lorcan stared at the woman for a long moment, then nodded. "It was you, my childhood fantasy. All those years, I was in love with you . . ." Lorcan whispered as he gazed at the woman.

The woman teared up. "You remember?"

"Yes, of course." He tried to walk toward her but failed. He raised his arms to reach out to her, to embrace her. But his body didn't cooperate. "I remember," he said. "Let me hold you again."

The woman smiled and waved her hand.

Lorcan felt as if a thousand tons of heavy air had been lifted from him. His body and his mind worked again, and the thought that instantly crossed his mind was rage. It gathered inside him. "Never ever call Orla names!" He grunted out the words and glared at the woman, a wave of electric current shooting from his eyes. It struck the woman, lifting her off the ground and throwing her rolling onto the wet grass. "No one can replace her."

Lorcan charged at the woman, hauling her up. "Who are you, and what do you want from me?" But his hands gripped a pile of clothes. The woman had vanished like smoke. A wedge of icy air hit him from behind. Lorcan fell, rolling on the ground. Behind him stood a woman who looked the same as the woman he'd just attacked—he recognised her eyes—but this time, she was twenty feet tall, and her face was ancient, marked with scars and veins. She raised sharp claws and made a sweeping gesture.

Lorcan's body was swiped off the grass, spun up in the air, and smashed down in the middle of the river like a rag doll.

From beneath the icy water, he saw the woman smirk. Her arm reached out, keeping Lorcan submerged. He knew shooting an electric wave from under the water wasn't wise. He kicked hard but couldn't free himself. He was running out of air when the woman started laughing. Lorcan reached for his gun and found it had slipped out and sunk to the bottom of the river.

Then the woman pulled him up to the surface. "You could have lived happily forever after with your bitch Orla out there. Why bring her back and take what's mine?"

Lorcan gasped for air. "I came back to visit my family. It has nothing to do with Orla. She doesn't care what's yours."

The woman let out a demonic laugh. "You fool. You think she follows you back here for love? Do you know who she is? Do you know what she would become in two weeks?" The woman dunked him in the water and pulled him back up again.

"I know who she is . . ." He gasped for more air.

"You know nothing. In two weeks, I will get what I want. If only she hadn't shown her face."

"I'll take her out of here. There's nothing here that we want."

"It's too late. They'll never let her leave this time." She brushed her bony fingers across his face. "What a pity! I thought I could have a taste of you. See what all the fuss was about. See what it's like to have the man she'd left everything for."

"She didn't leave here because of me. She left because she didn't want to be surrounded by people like you."

The woman laughed. "She will have to live with it now. Or should I say, *die* with it now!"

"If you want to kill me, do it. She wouldn't have come back if not for me."

"You'd die for her. How sweet! Let's do it."

Lorcan tried to yank her hands from around his neck, but they were clenched as tight as a vice.

"Were you really the girl at the riverbank?"

"You can't play the same trick on me twice, Lorcan. But yes, I was." Then she plunged his head under the water again. This time, it was for a very long time. He struggled for a while, and then he let go. He let his mind and his body flow free with the current. He hung on to nothing.

She pulled him up again. "She thinks she's protected here. Big mistake. She'll die painfully. And you'll have to help me to do that . . ."

Lorcan opened his eyes and shot the electric wave at the woman as soon as she lifted him out of the water. She screamed and released him. He swam to the riverbank while the woman burned like a torch.

As soon as he hit the riverbank, he ran as fast as he could. The woman whirled around and swung her arms. A wedge of icy air rushed over her, and the fire died out. Lorcan charged ahead. A few more feet and he would reach the bush and find a place to hide. But the woman clawed at him from behind with arms that had stretched out at him like two snakes. Blood spurted from his back as he fell to the ground. The woman flipped him around. *She's going to gut me,* Lorcan thought.

"I'll skin you and show whatever's left of you to the bitch Orla. See if she can handle this. See if she bursts into flame. No one is going to take what's mine."

The woman raised her talons. Lorcan used what energy he had left to shoot out the electric currents, but they died out like pitiful sparks before they reached her. Her claws came at him menacingly.

Suddenly the haunting sound of a lullaby wafted out from the other side of the bush. It was his mother's lullaby.

The woman screamed, "No!"

The song hovered in the air, and the soothing melody kept coming. The woman yelled again, "No! Stop!" She covered her ears with her hands and spun around. But it didn't seem to help. Her body burst into flames again, but this time, the fire was stronger and harsher. She raced into the woods, her haunting moans trailing behind her as she ran.

The bush returned to its eerie quietness. Lorcan thought he heard the woods sigh. Blood poured from the wound from his back and weakened him by the second. He needed to pass out in order to heal his wounds, but it wasn't wise to do it here. If wild animals, creatures from hell, or that mysterious woman came back while he was lying somewhere in a ditch shivering from fever, it would be the end of him.

He pulled himself up to his feet and darted in the direction of the place he had once called home. Trees and the darkness surrounded him, disorienting him. He kept running, and the pounding of his heart cause even more blood to gush from his wounds. He had run this very route with his mother once when he was six. He had killed for the very first time here to protect his mother. He couldn't see much, but the haunting lullaby guided him. He followed the song. The music floated on the wind, seemingly coming out of nowhere.

He didn't mean to throw a tantrum whenever his mother sang this lullaby. He actually enjoyed it, but he thought a boy shouldn't like a lullaby. Or at least so he thought when he was six. She had stopped singing it for a long time. So many things had happened between that time and now, and he had stopped talking to his mother. The words of the lullaby came to mind, and suddenly he began to mumble the lyrics under its breath. The song of a little lost boy finding his way home.

He hadn't been a little boy when he'd left. He hadn't been lost. He loved his parents, and he knew he had their unconditional love. But something in him told him that he didn't belong in the peaceful Irish countryside. And then he'd found Orla. It was like finding his other half. And he knew then where his life was meant to be.

It was Orla who stood between him and his parents. He had never told her he'd chosen her over his family because it was a wound that had never healed in his soul, and there was no point in her carrying the baggage.

But now it seemed he had lost from both ends.

Just before the last drop of energy drained out of him, he saw the gate of his family's mansion. The door swung open before he reached it, and once inside, he fell into the arms of his parents and his sister.

He had made it home.

CHAPTER 2

Cold reality slapped at Orla's face as she ran aimlessly into the woods. She had left Lorcan at the riverbank with a strange woman. The scene of him holding the woman had ripped at her heart. She knew infidelity wasn't in Lorcan's blood, but she had underestimated how much it would hurt her to see him with another woman.

They had been through so many life and death situations. She recalled the many times she'd held him in her arms, knowing that life was drifting away from him and having no clue how she'd ever survive if he died. But nothing compared to this! The knowledge that he was with another woman was worse than his death.

It wasn't jealousy that she was experiencing now, but just the shock of it. The pain knocked the wits out of her. She ran until her legs began to cramp and her breath hissed in and out of her lungs in painful spurts. When she finally collapsed onto her knees, when she looked up, the entrance of a graveyard loomed over her. She pulled herself up to her feet, using the low stone wall for support. She looked over the wall at the moss-covered gravestones, letting the misty fog and slight breeze soothe her broken heart.

The magic that her family possessed made it easy to keep private cemeteries looking scary enough so that they were left alone. She knew that the fog wasn't the ghosts of the dead, aimlessly wandering around their burial places. She finally caught her breath enough to stand up straight and limp her way down the gravel walkway toward the back of the cemetery where her aunt's grave was.

Aunt Siobhan had been more than just her mother's sister. Since her parents had died when she was five, she had known Aunt Siobhan as her mother. She had been a mentor in more than just magic, and she had been the one to give Orla hope that love was still attainable.

She set her feet on the familiar path, letting them carry her to the very back of the cemetery where the wild trees and grasses of the Irish moors began to creep up over the walls. She loved that her aunt's grave was here. Siobhan had been more of an elemental, using nature itself in her magic and spells. Now it almost seemed like nature was coming to be a part of her again, even after she was dead. As the fog rolled back, the grave marker came into view through the mist. The wild grasses and moss had started to grow up the stone, and Orla did her best to peel them off with her bare hands. She knelt down in front of it when she'd finished clearing the vegetation.

Then she thought of Lorcan again, and the fresh wound opened. She let her tears flow freely now, watering the grass at the foot of the stone.

"Don't go watering the weeds! There's no point in me coming here every month to do the weeding if you're just going to encourage them to grow."

Orla's head jerked up, her heart racing as she turned around slowly. "Maeve! Oh boy, am I glad to see you!"

Maeve was Siobhan's daughter, and she and Orla had grown up together. Maeve smiled at her and helped her up for a welcome hug. Orla stumbled a little, as her legs had cramped up from kneeling down on the uneven paving stones.

"You should be glad it's me instead of someone else. There's a bit of a storm brewing, and it'll be headed your way if they find you. You should stop by Mom's old house. It's empty and abandoned, so you should be able to stay there for a little while without anyone finding you." Orla gave Maeve a hug and an extra squeeze.

"Thank you. Your psychic read has gotten much better over the years, I can tell."

The smile faded from Maeve's face. "I saw clouds, Orla. You didn't come back by yourself. A storm is following you, and this one is bad."

The pain had crept up on Orla again, and she teared up.

"It's him, isn't it?" Maeve asked.

Orla nodded and wiped her tears away.

"It's poor timing, Orla. Couldn't you have waited another two weeks to return?"

"What's the difference?"

"It's a full moon in two weeks, and Bradan will become the leader of the clan."

"Bradan?"

"Your distant cousin, Orla!"

Orla squinted. "Oh . . . oh . . . Who would have thought!" Orla exclaimed remembering the skinny, freckle-faced, red-haired boy that all the girls, including her, had picked on all the time. She cleared her throat. "So I guess he'd grown up a strong candidate for the leadership. But what does that have to do with my timing? I broke my promise with the ancestors, and if they catch me, they'll burn me."

"The position has always been yours until replaced by the newly chosen. So that's Bradan, and that will be in two weeks' time. Unless you really want to . . ."

"Hell no."

"If you don't want to take up that post with the clan, why come back now?"

Orla had no answer. She had left and had been gone for years. She'd sworn to never set foot in the village again. There had been many times she'd wanted to come back to visit Aunt Siobhan's grave and Maeve, but her haunting past had put her off. She couldn't live the emotionless life of black magic again.

And then came Lorcan. He had found her in the city after she'd run off for a few years. He'd left everything behind for her. Before she knew it, he had become a part of her life that was more important than anything else.

Then came this trip. Bricius had cursed his parents, and he'd had to come back to Ireland. He'd thought he could get away and leave Orla in Eudaiz. But she had followed him anyway. Ciaran had helped her, warning that her trip was against Lorcan's wishes. Her thought circled back to the scene at the riverbank. *Who was that woman?* she wondered.

"Orla!" Maeve called out.

"Huh?"

"What's the matter?"

The image of Maeve became blurry and flickering in front of Orla. *Oh crap!* Someone was using black magic on her. Orla swayed and tried to hang on to her consciousness. She should have known. What had she expected, coming back to the land of black magic, to the place where she'd grown up, where she had been trained and where she owed a debt?

She hadn't been practicing for years. Her knees buckled. She heard Maeve calling out for her and felt her hands on her shoulders. Her best friend could help. Aunt Siobhan was a white witch, and Maeve practised white magic. She wasn't part of the clan, and she was Orla's only hope. They had been communicating in their psychic minds for years, and she was sure her trip to the Daimon Gate wouldn't have broken their psychic communication channel.

"Help me!" Orla managed. She couldn't get many words past her lips, but she remembered mind reading was one of Maeve rare gifts. "Read me!" She reached her hands out and tried her best to clear her mind to communicate with Maeve. She felt Maeve's cool hands grabbing hers and a slight energy passing through her body. The warmth of the energy helped.

"Concentrate," Orla told herself, willing the muddy clouds from her mind. The scene of Lorcan and the woman at the riverbank flashed back into Orla's mind. As much as it hurt her, she forced herself to analyze the situation. Someone was using the black magic on her. Someone was trying to break up her relationship with Lorcan. Someone wanted her to resent him.

A sharp pain pierced through her brain, and Orla suddenly slumped to the ground, breathing heavily.

"Hold on, Orla, keep thinking. I'm with you," said Maeve.

The resentment grew quickly into hatred. Orla could read her mind like an outsider and could see her conscious mind was leaving her. "I want to hate Lorcan." The words were demonic. It came deep from her throat and from her soul.

"What are you talking about? You confuse me, Orla. Your mind is confusing. I can't get hold of it," Maeve cried in a panic.

Orla's head was throbbing. She was losing it. She gasped for air as tears streamed down her face. She summoned a last thread of hope. "Someone is trying to get me to curse Lorcan from hatred. Please don't let me . . ." She groaned in pain, breathing heavily and trying to shake the thought from her head, but the mud was getting in again. The clarity was leaving her. She thought of Lorcan again, which was probably not a good idea. She almost lost control of her mind.

"Black magic!" she whispered. Lack of practice was doing her no good at the moment.

"Don't let go, Orla. I've got you."

She heard Maeve's voice in the distance. Everything seemed blurry.

"Tell Lorcan I love him."

"No, you tell him yourself."

Blood trickled from her nose. "Lorcan betrayed me. He kissed that woman." The words coming out of her mouth weren't hers. Tear streamed down her face, and her self-awareness slipped in and out. "He kissed that woman. I . . ."

"Don't say that, Orla. You'll put a curse on him, and you're going to regret it. You're strong. You can control it," Maeve's voice echoed in from a distance.

Orla cried. Her mind wandered back to the apartment she and Lorcan shared in London. She walked into the living room. She could sense him. She could hear his laughter. She saw him fumbling with the coffee machine, trying to fix it so the sharp lever wouldn't cut her next time she used it. He smiled at her. She loved his beautiful blue eyes. She smiled back .

The bed had blankets on it, and the pictures of them on the wall were hanging askew. Some of their pictures had fallen to the floor. Glass was everywhere. "Someone broke into our apartment! That woman—she stole him from me!" Orla yelled.

"You're hallucinating, Orla. Concentrate. Don't let it get to you. I can't help you if you let it take over your mind."

Her heart lurched painfully in her chest, thinking about how happy she'd been in London with Lorcan, but now all that filled her mind was Lorcan and that other woman. Rage began to build inside her, and she was beginning to feel a dull throb behind her eyes.

"It hurt!" Orla whispered.

"I know. Come on, Orla, look at me."

"It hurt so much," she said out loud, and once again, the words weren't hers. "I hate Lorcan. He'll pay for what he did to me."

"Stop, Orla. Stop!"

She heard Maeve yelling at her, but she couldn't stop. She drifted back to the apartment again. Looking at a picture of the two of them together was the last straw. She reached up and yanked the picture off the wall so forcefully that the nail behind it bent. As she threw it onto the ground, breaking the glass in the frame, the pain in her head grew worse. She tore through the room, ripping everything that reminded her of Lorcan off the walls.

At the graveyard, she could see herself hitting the stone marker and ripping weeds out. She saw Maeve trying to hold on to her. But then her mind slipped off again. The world became empty, and she burned with a desire to destroy.

"He has to pay for what he did to me . . ." She began to chant a curse while tears streamed down her face. The last drop of self-awareness was slipping out of her. Images of Lorcan flashed on and off at the back of her mind. "I curse . . ." She hadn't finished when a hard blow on the head put her out.

CHAPTER 3

A warm cloth wiped at his back with gentle strokes, as soothing as the hand holding it. Someone was checking his shoulders. Lorcan breathed in as much as he could, he wanted to capture and hold on to the familiar smell from the fresh bed linens and the comfortable pillow his head was resting on—it was the fresh floral scent from the pouch his mother always put into the linen cabinet. She said it was her secret formula, a scent that was unique and memorable to this family. He knew it now—it was the scent of home. He realized now how much he had missed it over the years.

"Good morning!" the voice sang like gentle and merry bell. Lorcan was facing the wall, but he didn't have to turn around to recognize his little sister's voice, Keeva Brody. He turned around to smile at her as he always did, but instead, his jaw dropped and he was speechless. Sitting at his bed side was a stunning woman with magnificent hair and twinkling eyes that he just knew smiled all the time and made people feel warm and happy.

Keeva rubbed at her face and frowned.

"I'm sorry, I thought you were my little sister! Would you like to go out on a date with me?" He grinned.

Keeva laughed and poked his side. Lorcan grabbed his sister and, in one swift move, pulled her onto the bed. He covered her with the blanket and held her tightly. He could feel her body vibrate with laughter. It had been five years since he'd last seen her in London after she had sneaked to the city to visit him. Regardless of her beauty and how much she had grown up since, she was still his little sister.

"You got a boyfriend yet?"

"Huh?"

"I would be surprised if you aren't seeing someone."

"Don't play, big brother. You should have seen yourself last night and the mess you put yourself in."

"Were Mother and Father really mad at me?"

"That was the first time they'd seen you in more than a decade. I'd definitely be mad if I were them. But surprisingly, they didn't say much. Just took care of you. It seemed like they had known you were coming home."

Keeva sat up in the bed. Lorcan sat up as well and glanced around his room. Everything was intact—just as it had been when he'd left. The decoration was from his teens, and he didn't think the comic book hero collection that he'd thought was so cool then was too cool now. "Where are they?"

"Father went into town. He'll be home shortly. Mother is . . . well . . . in the kitchen."

Lorcan raised an eyebrow. He didn't remember his mother cooking. There were more people who worked in the house than the family members themselves. Reading his mind, Keeva smiled. "She's supervising the chef. She's new, and Mother said she wanted to make something special for you."

Lorcan nodded as he hopped off the bed. His head was throbbing with a headache, and the purpose of this trip had come back to him.

"Before you go anywhere, Lorcan, can you explain to me how the wounds on your back healed in just a couple of hours? When I first looked at them, I didn't think you'd survive. If Father hadn't stopped me, I would have taken you to the hospital, or at least called a doctor."

"Father stopped you from calling the doctor?"

Keeva nodded. "He said you'd heal. I don't know what the hell he meant—he didn't explain."

Lorcan frowned. *His Father knew about his werefox ability?*

"Lorcan?" Keeva called out, waiting for an answer.

"I just found out about it recently. I'll tell you later. Right now, I've got to see Mother."

Keeva rolled her eyes and followed her brother to the kitchen. As they walked down the stairs and turned into a long corridor, the smile faded from Keeva's face. "What, Keeva?"

"Something's wrong." Her voice shook, and the blood drained out of her face.

Seeing Keeva's eyes darken, Lorcan darted toward the kitchen.

Keeva had never been an 'official' psychic. He'd always thought of it as an unfortunate gift that she had. She could sense death. The first incident was her pony. She sensed his death just before they had found him attacked and gutted by the wolves. The second was his parrot, who had died for no apparent reason. The third was the death of an old man who'd called himself a shaman. He lived in the woods and had nothing to do with the village and befriended no one.

The grand country kitchen greeted them with the inviting aroma of a freshly baked lemon and almond cake, Lorcan's favorite, a pot of jasmine tea brewing on the stove, and the undeniable fresh scent of blood.

There was no one there.

Lorcan rushed around the large table and found the chef lying face down in a pool of blood. There was no sign of his mother.

Tears started to stream down Keeva's face. Her shoulders shook with fear and confusion. "Her wounds . . . yours last night . . ." Her voice broke so badly that Lorcan could hardly make any sense of what she was saying.

"What about me?"

"The wounds on your back last night looked like those." Keeva pointed at the dead body.

"I need you to stay calm for me. Are there other people working in the house?" Lorcan asked, holding Keeva's shoulders.

She nodded.

"But I didn't see anyone on the way to the kitchen."

Keeva blinked in confusion. "But we have Mary in the kitchen, Shaun in the garden, and Susan in . . ."

"Keeva, there is no one else in the house, including Mother. I'm sure of it . . ." Lorcan picked up the handle of the phone mounted on the kitchen's wall. Static. He hung up and turned toward Keeva. "Phone line is dead. Do you have a cell phone?"

She nodded.

"All right, I need you to get the phone, call Father, and then come with me to look for Mother. I can't leave you here by yourself." Keeva nodded and scurried back to her room for the phone. Lorcan trailed right behind her, glancing around and scanning for anything unusual.

Before Keeva had finished dialing Father's number, they heard the bang of a door that had been swung open. They rushed toward the living room. At the door was Lorcan's father. He had a lot more gray hair, making him look wise and formidable, Lorcan noticed. His father had always been a powerful figure in Lorcan's mind. Sometimes too much for his liking.

"I was just about to call you," Keeva said.

"Something happened to your mother." It was a statement, not a question. He approached his father.

"Father," he greeted him, feeling like a robot. He'd never known how to behave in front of his father. He always felt foreign and awkward.

"I can see you're up and well. They took your mother." His father looked at him.

"And how did you know?"

"I'm not a psychic. Someone left a voice mail in my phone. They said they'd taken your mother because you took your girlfriend back home with you."

"I didn't take her. She followed me because she worried. Someone placed a curse on you and Mother. That's why I had to come back . . ."

"A curse! Jesus Christ, Lorcan, do you hear yourself?"

"Yes, I hear myself clearly. I'm not superstitious, but there are way too many things I can't explain, except by magic. How did you know that I can heal myself, Father?"

"That has nothing to do with magic, you silly lad."

Lorcan stared at his father. Ferris Brody was in his late sixties but possessed the brain of a man in his forties—a mind as sharp as laser. And there wasn't an ounce of sentiment in him.

"You're not worried about Mother?"

"Being out there on your own for that long, you should've gotten wiser, Lorcan. They won't harm your mother until they tell us what they want."

"Isn't it blatantly obvious? They want me to take Orla out of the country again. But there are others who wanted me here. That's why they cursed you and Mother. Are you sure if I take Orla out of here, they'll leave you alone?"

"Do not mention anything about magic in this house ever again, Lorcan. I won't tolerate it. Whoever took your mother won't kill as long as you do what they want."

"I don't know what they want, but they already *have* killed, and there is no guarantee they won't come back." Lorcan raised his voice as his father arched an eyebrow.

"They killed Mary, Father!" Keeva added and pointed toward the kitchen. Ferris's eyes darkened, and he scurried toward the kitchen.

In the kitchen, they found nothing—no dead body and no trace of blood. The teapot had been removed from the hot stove, and the cake had been taken out of the baking tray and put onto a crystal plate. Keeva's body shook. "I saw it . . . we both saw it. Tell him, Lorcan!"

He didn't know what to believe anymore. He used to believe in his own eyes, but what exactly did he see at the riverbank? Who did he kiss? Orla had walked away from him—had that been real or an illusion? And what about his mother? She was still nowhere to be found. Lorcan turned toward his father whose face was hardened as steel. "There was a dead body here, Father, but I don't have any proof."

"I can't say I believe it because there is nothing for me to believe or disbelieve. But they did take your mother, and that's a fact. And if you take your girlfriend out of the country, they might return her."

"Did they tell you that?"

"No."

"You're speculating on Mother's life?"

"What do you want me to think, Lorcan? We told you not to go out with that girl. You took off to find her, and you never came back. Then your mother rambled on all night last night about how she knew you were returning. Then you got here looking like a mess, and the next thing I knew, your mother was gone. I should never have given you to that woman . . ." Ferris ranted and trailed off at the last part as if he hadn't meant to let it slip out.

"*Given* me to her?" he stared at his father.

"I . . ."

Before Ferris could answer, Lorcan gestured for silence. "Please don't answer. I'm happy enough with what I know now." His mind was racing ahead with too many possibilities, none of which he cared for. This was the reality he hadn't wanted to know. "As I said before, someone threatened me with a curse on you and Mother. That's the only reason I came back. If you believe that me taking Orla out of here would solve your problems, then I'll do just that . . . As you wish, Father." His gaze paused on Ferris's face for a brief moment as if gathering some last images into his mind, and then he strode quickly toward the door.

"Lorcan!" Keeva called out and ran to him. She held him tightly just as she had on the day he left so many years ago. She had been a small kid back then, but her squeeze had been just as tight. Lorcan embraced her and kissed her forehead. "You always know how to find me. I'll leave a trail for you."

She nodded and wiped her tears away. Lorcan glanced at his father one last time and exited the house.

When Lorcan left the house, he ran back down to the river. It dawned on him now that he had no idea where Orla lived. She had never taken him to her home. They'd always met down by the river, and if what happened at the riverbank yesterday wasn't a hallucination, if it was actually Orla he had seen, then how the hell he was going to find her and take her out of here?

A rustling noise near a clump of bushes caught his attention. He turned around, shivers running down his spine. The noise was coming from behind a blackberry bush, and it made Lorcan freeze. Stepping out in front of him was a large, yellow wolf with red eyes. He didn't know if it was a normal wolf or something magical, but he wasn't going to take any chances.

He backed away a pace or two, as slowly as he could. The wolf advanced and then sat down.

"All right. So you're friendly. But I'm in a very bad mood right now and staring at me isn't helping at all."

The wolf stared at Lorcan for another moment and then spat out something on the ground. It back up a bit and sat again. Lorcan approached to see what the small object was. He crouched and picked it up. It was unmistakably his mother's wedding ring. He could feel his blood boiling and his body vibrating with rage. The yellow wold in front of him was obviously some kind of shapeshifter.

"What are you trying to tell me? If you want me to take Orla away, I'm going to do just that."

The wolf growled and bared its teeth.

"You don't want me to ? What do you want then?"

The wolf stood and turned around.

"You want to take me to my mother?"

It kept walking.

"I'll take that as a yes," Lorcan mumbled and followed the wolf. "I guess I'm going to meet the whole clan of shapeshifters now. I'm assuming you didn't do any harm to my mother. Also, if you decide to shift back into your human form so that you can speak, I have some things to ask you about the woman at the riverbank."

The wolf glanced at Lorcan and then put its head down to the ground again and continued walking.

"I think that woman is a witch—and a bad one." He heard a humming noise of agreement from the wolf. Lorcan chuckled. "I have to admit she was incredibly beautiful. But I would never have kissed her if she hadn't pretended to be Orla . . ."

The wolf growled.

"Yeah, I know. Thanks for the sympathy. I hope Orla understands. It felt as if that woman was raping me . . ."

A low bark came from the animal.

"I'm serious. As soon as I saw she wasn't Orla . . . It doesn't matter how beautiful she was, she was forcing herself . . ."

The wolf came at him like a sudden storm. Lorcan didn't have time to think except to remember he'd lost his gun. He knew fighting the wolf bare-handed wasn't a good idea, so he shifted into his blue fox form. The wolf was in the air and flying toward him, maw gaping. Even though he was only a fox, Lorcan wasn't much smaller than the tawny wolf, and his teeth were just as sharp.

He yelped when the wolf drew first blood, but he reared up on his hind paws and clawed at the wolf's face until it turned its head, then he bit down hard on whatever flesh he could reach. The fight continued for several long minutes, Lorcan trading a wound for every injury he received. Then the wolf made a mistake. He reached to snap at Lorcan's front leg, but when he stepped forward, the large rock he was putting his weight on shifted, causing him to lose his balance and expose his throat to Lorcan. Lorcan didn't hesitate. He moved his head, lightning fast, and caught the wolf by the throat. It went completely limp in his mouth, and he bit down a little harder before he shook the wolf and released his bite.

Lorcan watched as the wolf limped away, and then he returned to a pile of shredded material that used to be his clothes and lay down in them, nursing his own bite wounds and scratches. He was still amped up from adrenaline, and it felt like he could hear colors and taste sounds. He started to nose around in his shirt to assess the damage it had received. No, these clothes would never be worn again. He sighed.

He would just have to go home as a fox rather than walking in naked. Lorcan picked up the ring in his mouth and trotted home.

The house was as quiet as when he had left it. He walked right into the living room in his fox form. His father and his sister were glaring at each other as if they had just finished an argument. They turned and looked at him. Keeva stood there, mouth hanging wide open in shock, apparently unsure whether she should attack this animal or run . His father, on the other hand, sat down in a chair and just looked at him. If Lorcan wasn't mistaken, his father had recognized him right away. There was relief in his father's eyes when he saw Lorcan.

His father wanted him to come back.

Lorcan sat and dropped the ring on the floor.

CHAPTER 4

The haunting sound of an owl ripped through the air and woke Orla. She sat up abruptly and punched at something in front or her. She panted and glanced frantically around. The blurry vision become clear in a short moment. She was sitting in a bed, and the 'thing' she had hit was her distant cousin Alana.

"Oi, you crazy snit!"

Only Alana would call Orla a snit. It made no sense, but it was the nickname she had given Orla when she was just a grumpy kid in black magic class, and she refused to call Orla by any other name.

Orla looked around the room. She didn't recognize the place. "Where am I?"

"Uncle Daly's house."

Her head throbbed in incredible pain. Refraining from a sneer, she asked, "Bradan's father?"

Alana shrugged. "Yes, as long as I've know them, they've been father and son. What's the problem?"

Does Alana seriously not see the problem, or is she just playing dumb? Orla wagered on the latter. If Bradan was going into power in two weeks, having Orla back in the village was the last thing Uncle Daly wanted. Apart from Uncle Daly being a normally calm and collected man, Orla couldn't remember much about him, and she had no way of knowing who was friend and who was foe at the moment. "Where's Maeve?"

"She was the one who messed up your head?"

"What?" Orla straightened up, remembering the black magic that had attacked her in the cemetery. *How did Alana know that?* "What about my head?"

Alana thrust a small mirror toward Orla. "See for yourself. I bet it hurt!"

Orla frowned as she looked at her forehead and saw a nasty wound glaring back at her. "Did you find me?"

"No. Uncle Daly did. He brought you here and called me. He said he found you at Aunt Siobhan's grave. Only Maeve would lurk around there. That's what I said. But Uncle Daly didn't believe me. He said until he saw it with his own eyes, he wouldn't believe Maeve could do this."

"Do what?"

"Put that dent in your forehead!" Alana waved her arms in the air.

Orla nodded. She saw no reason to explain to Alana that Maeve had just wanted to help her. Between Maeve and Alana, she trusted Maeve more. She rubbed her head. "Do you have a bandage that I can patch this up with?"

Alana clucked her tongue. "You'll need more than that, and I have it ready. Nothing fancy." Alana put both a medical box and a makeup box on the bed. "Bathroom is over there. You'll find clean clothes in there, too. They're mine, but I think we're the same size."

"I don't need makeup. Just need to clean up and sleep for the rest of the night if that's okay."

Alana shook her head. "You have to at least go downstairs and say hi to everyone."

"Everyone?" Orla could feel the hair on the back of her neck stand up.

Alana grinned.

Orla scurried into the bathroom. Staring at her bruised forehead in the mirror, she knew Maeve was right—a storm was brewing her way. She had run off at the age of twelve, leaving her clan in limbo without a rightful leader. *But they had managed to organize and survive,* she told herself now as she had so many times before. She thought people in the clan were better off without a leader. They could live their normal human lives. But that was only her opinion. If they were sworn into the clan and made it flourish, what would they get? She hadn't seen evidence of it yet, but the myth was that it would bring immortality.

Orla shook her head. Why people would want to live forever in misery she would never understand. But she supposed that living an emotionless life might be a misery to her but a pleasure to others. She couldn't speak for them. She could see the point now after experiencing how much it had hurt to see Lorcan with the other woman. Just the thought of it now made her head start to throb again.

She cleaned up and walked downstairs with Alana. The hallway was too short for her liking. She walked as slowly as she could, but she knew she would get to the living room eventually. A good chunk of her family was here, and they were all staring at her. She could feel the heat of their gazes, and she felt like she had maybe grown an extra head or a tail. But no, she was just an older version of the Orla who had run away at the age of twelve. *What are they staring at?* She wondered.

The laughter and conversation in the room ceased as soon as Orla walked in. The air was as quiet as the calmness experienced before a storm. She could feel it brewing, ready to break on her like crashing waves on rocks. Orla pasted a smiled on her face. "Hi . . ." she said and internally cursed her awkwardness, immediately regretting it because there were some mind readers in her clan.

Uncle Daly approached and gestured toward a chair. "I hope you're feeling better. We won't keep you long. You see, the whole village wants to see you."

An elderly man pushed his way to the front of the crowd and glared at her. "You made a promise when you were younger, and again when you asked for help in London. You will take your place as the head of this family at the next full moon. There is no argument to be made. It is what you promised, and it will be fulfilled. You will be under watch until this happens because we will not risk you running away again."

"Tony!" Uncle Daly warned in a low voice.

"What? She was raised for this. We invested so much in her, and she is our best bet."

"It's not for you to say," Daly spoke calmly.

"You just want the post for your son. I knew it."

"Remember your place, Tony. Regardless, it's Bradan or Orla to lead the clan, and you are not in a position to say anything."

"And you are?" Tony glared at him again, but when Daly threw back an even harsher look, Tony turned on his heel and left the room.

No one else said a word, and Orla felt the silence pressing down on her like a weight. She could trust Maeve, but Maeve wasn't allowed to attend the clan meeting. She practised white magic, so within the black magic sorcery clan, Maeve was a 'black sheep'. *How ironic,* Orla thought. Orla realized that without Lorcan, nothing in her life seemed to work in a normal order.

She turned her face away from the family members who still stared at her and tried to give herself a false illusion of some sort of privacy. She wanted the tears to fall without anyone watching, but something told her that that wasn't going to happen. She wanted to run right out the door, but she was sure that would be a bad idea, so she let the thought pass. Orla had no expectation that these black magic workers who were supposed to live an emotionless life were going to be gentle with her. But she didn't care for them to gut her alive for a sacrifice, either.

She worked her brain hard to figure out a way out of the situation, but nothing came to mind. "I'm tired. Could I rest for tonight, and then we can resume the conversation tomorrow?"

"I see no harm in that," said a woman in her late fifties, sitting in the back of the room. If Orla's memory served, that was Aunt Anna, a very distant relative she had hardly talked to when she was a kid. She remembered Anna because she had broken into her conservatory and stolen a few rare plants for an experiment, trying to grow them with milk in her bedroom . Well, the plants had died, and Anna had never figured out where her plants had gone. Orla cleared her throat and tried not to think because if she was not mistaken, the old man sitting near the door was Pete, the shaman of the clan who also could read minds.

Daly looked at Orla. "Okay. We'll talk again tomorrow. Just so you know, I don't have anything against you taking the leadership. The position has always been yours, and it's written in stone. It has been an ordeal to train Bradan and get him up to speed to replace you. But if he can't use the skills in the position, I'm sure he can find use for them elsewhere."

"You don't have to speak for me, Father." Bradan walked into the room, and Orla's jaw dropped. The freckled, red-haired boy had turned into quite a formidable figure. "Orla," he nodded in greeting. "I'm glad to see you again."

Orla forced a smile and frantically searched her memory for Bradan's talent. Was he a mind reader? Was he good at compound? Spells? Nothing came to mind. Orla gave up and forced herself to stop thinking.

"If no one objects, I'll retire to the bedroom," Orla said.

Daly nodded.

"Someone should keep an eye on her," said Anna, her voice was as cold as steel.

"Are you imprisoning me?" Orla raised her voice.

"No, darling, we don't do such things. But it's two weeks to the full moon. It's no skin off my nose if either one of become the leader. But I would be annoyed if the post kept swinging from one hand to another," Anna said.

"Do you have a preference, Anna?" Daly cocked an eyebrow in challenge.

"Why would this old woman have a preference for this sort of thing? I just want to be left alone." Anna stood.

Braden wrapped his arm around Orla's waist protectively. "I think we should let Orla rest. I'll take her upstairs."

Anna chuckled. "You speak like a leader already."

Bradan stared at her. "I'm prepared for whatever comes my way, Aunty."

Anna gave Bradan a dismissive look. "I think you should let Alana stay with Orla tonight. I want to be sure you won't strangle her in her sleep."

"Don't accuse my son of something like that!" Daly raised his voice and advanced on Anna. Bradan stopped his father.

"All right. I think it's a good idea that Alana stay tonight . . . Alana?" Bradan asked.

Everyone turned to look at Alana, who was examining her manicure and looked as if she would rather be anywhere else.

"Alana!" Braden called again.

"Huh?" Alana jumped.

"Would you mind staying here tonight with Orla?"

"What? Why?"

"We just need you to stay with her . . . to make sure she's okay."

Alana rolled her eyes and looked as if she was mentally banging her head on an invisible wall. But she put a smile on her face and said, "Of course. I'm sure it's going to be a pleasant night." Then she turned on her heel and marched up the stairs. Bradan shook his head.

"Come on." He reached his hand out to Orla. She grabbed it and followed him up the stairs.

Braden entered the bedroom first, glancing around. "I've already been in here. Nothing suspicious here, Bradan," Orla said.

He shrugged. "You never know. The clan has developed a lot since you've been away, and there are a lot of people I don't care for."

Orla nodded. Bradan was so mature now, and she truly regretted picking on him when they were young. But they'd been kids.

"You should go to bed." His voice was deep and enticing. Orla shook the uncomfortable thought off and headed for the bed. Bradan opened the window and looked around. Seemingly satisfied with what he saw, he closed the door, locked it from the outside, and exited the room.

Alana had already lay down on the inside wall of the bed, and she'd put a long pillow in the middle, suggesting that Orla could take the outside half. She lay down and quickly dozed off.

Orla had lain in bed for a long time, listening to Alana's even breathing. When she was sure her bed mate was really asleep, she hopped off the bed and moved to the window. The roof arched over a porch below. Orla stepped out onto the roof and inched toward the edge. She looked down and let out a sigh of relief. It wasn't too high up from the ground. She looked up to the clear Irish sky in the middle of the night, breathing the clear air, and bent down to make a jump to the ground below.

Damn it! Orla cursed in her head as she hit the ground.

On the porch, next to the door, Bradan was sitting on a chair, smoking. She hadn't surprised him in the least by both trying to flee the clan in the middle of the night and landing from the sky in front of him. He squashed out his cigarette and smiled. Orla smiled back.

"You took longer than I thought you would," Bradan said.

Orla had her hands on her hips. "So you're a mind reader. Handy!"

He chuckled. "I wish I had such talent. My father trained me well in logical deduction. I don't have any magical talent. You'd be a much better leader than me because you're a natural."

"But I don't want to do it. Everyone knows that. You don't sound like you want to do it, either."

Bradan merely smiled.

"Oh . . . you *do* want the post!" Orla said. "That's good. Can we swap? Can you just tell them?" Orla put on the most gracious smile she could.

"I can't, Orla. If you want to see your man, I'll take you to him."

"Why help me?"

"You said it yourself—I want the post, and you don't. If you leave again, then the post will be mine. Simple!" Bradan smiled.

Orla narrowed her eyes. "I can go by myself. All you have to do is to pretend you didn't see me."

Bradan shook his head. "I can't let you go through that wedge of the woods by yourself. There's a nasty group of shapeshifters lurking around there lately."

Orla hesitated, and Bradan continued. "Now, I might kill you in the woods in order to take the position, but between me and these shapeshifters, I'm a safer bet. If you want to escape, now is a better time. Tomorrow, more family members will come, and it will become more difficult."

"Why are you helping me, really?"

"As I said, I want the post, so I have to help you escape." Bradan grinned this time. Orla wished she were a mind reader. It would certainly be a handy set of skills to have. Bradan appeared to be good, but he could be dangerous. Her magic might be better than his, though, because she had been trained earlier. Plus she had some white magic tricks she had gotten from Maeve. She was sure Bradan wouldn't have those.

He was right. The shapeshifters in the woods were dangerous. She guessed they were related to Bricius. Bricius had cursed Lorcan's parents, and his clan here had something to do with it. The more she thought about it, the more the option Bradan offered appeared to be more attractive. Orla put her doubts aside and nodded.

CHAPTER 5

Lorcan opened his eyes and sprung off the bed. He had gotten back to his room and crashed in order to heal his wounds from the fight with the yellow wolf. He couldn't have been out for long, he thought. There were so many questions he wanted to ask his father and his sister, and he was sure they had some for him, too. There was no way to have a conversation when he was in his fox form. Roy had told him once that most werefoxes didn't remember much of what happened when they were in the animal form, but some did. Mori had perfect memories and was well aware of what she was doing in any form because she was an alpha. Roy had such memory, too, but he was half fox and half wolf. Lorcan knew he was in none of those scenarios. As Roy had told him, he was different. In his fox form, his brain functioned normally and with clarity.

He put on the clothes he used to wear during his teenage years, grateful he had built himself up in the right places. His T-shirt fit more like a muscle shirt now, and his baggy jeans now fit him perfectly.

"Lorcan!" Keeva screamed out his name from the living room, a terrible sound that tore his heart and got him to his feet, running downstairs. Next to the fireplace, his father sat on the reading chair, holding his mother's wedding ring in one hand and a pistol on the other hand. His eyes were bloodshot, a sure sign of that he was trying to hang on to the last thread of consciousness. He didn't know where he'd seen this before, but he knew he had seen it.

Something was eating at his father's mind, and he was trying to fight it.

"She's dead. They've killed her." Ferris grunted out the words and pointed the gun to his temple. "It's my fault." Tears welled up in his eyes.

"Father, please don't do that. Give me the gun," Keeva cried.

Lorcan approached his father slowly. "Father, Mother is not dead. Someone tried to help us. That's why they gave us her wedding ring. Please calm down and give me the gun. We need to talk."

"It's my fault, it got her killed" Ferris brandished the gun. "I shouldn't have given you to her."

"What do you mean by that, Father?" Lorcan inched closer.

"Don't come near me. I knew I shouldn't have signed up for that. When I gave you to your mother, she was so happy, but I should have known that it wouldn't last long. You're such a disaster." He pointed the gun at Lorcan.

Keeva hissed and pulled at Lorcan, but he shoved her behind his back. "You adopted me?"

Ferris laughed. "I wish it's that simple. There is only one way to end this." He pointed the gun to his head.

"No!" Lorcan flew at his father and tackled him. He knocked Ferris to the floor and took the gun off of his father. From the floor, his father looked up at Lorcan with eyes that weren't his.

"Remember the curse?" The voice croaking out of Ferris was familiar. It was Bricius's voice. "No one can break my curse. Someone will die. I curse . . ."

"Stop." Lorcan yelled and muffled his father's mouth with his hand. His father wriggled hard. Keeva heard what her father just said, she jumped in helping Lorcan. Ferris roared, kicked and move with incredible strength, the strength Lorcan knew wasn't his father's. He didn't know how long he and Keeva could hang on to this.

Then he feel a wedge of cold breeze coming from the door. A woman appeared from nowhere stormed right into the living room uninvited.

"That's black magic. You can't fight that using physical strength," the woman said.

"Well, I don't do magic. Who the hell are you?"

"I'm Maeve, Orla's distant cousin. I'm here to let you know someone is using mind-control black magic on Orla. It tried to make her hate you and curse you. I can see it's now working its magic on that man."

"It tried to make Orla hate me?"

"I helped her before. The black magic didn't work on her that time, but it knocked me out. I'm not sure how long Orla can hang on. You're the key. The more Orla thinks about you, and the more she experiences conflicting emotions between love and hate, the more of a chance she's going to burst into flame."

"I have no idea what you mean. But if you helped Orla before, can you help my father now?"

Ferris grew stronger and almost pushed Lorcan and Keeva back.

"That's black magic. I don't know how to break it. You have to knock him out. That way you can temporarily keep him under control."

"You want me to hit my father?"

"The thing in his head is not your father."

"I don't give a shit, I won't hit my father." Lorcan shoved hard and pushed Ferris into a chair. "Get something to tie him," he asked Keeva. Lorcan all but sat on Ferris to hold him down. He still had a hand on his mouth to stop him from chanting a curse. Keeva came back with rope and tapes from the tool shed. They tied him up and stuffed his mouth with cloths.

Maeve stood there with hands on hips. "And how long do you think you can keep him like that?"

"I'll find Orla, and we'll work out a way to handle this."

"You don't sound like you totally dismiss the possibility of using magic."

"I don't have a choice," Lorcan growled. "Can you take me to Orla?"

"I can, but it's not going to help the situation. Before I figure out how to control the curse, you guys are best not seeing each other."

"If Orla couldn't figure it out, how can you ?"

Maeve smiled. "Are you saying I'm not as good as she is?"

"I don't know you. I just want to be realistic. They must want her to lead the clan for good reasons. There must be something she does that's better than others."

Maeve laughed. "I can see how she's falling head over heels for you. You guys are made for each other."

Lorcan narrowed his eyes. "I don't believe she's kept in touch with her family over the years."

Maeve shook her head. "We're have a psychic channel. You wouldn't understand."

"But can you help my father?"

"I use white magic. My mother and I are not friends with the rest of the family because of that. I'm not sure if I'm strong enough to go against them. That's why I'm here to tell you to stay away from Orla. I need a bit of time to figure things out, and the two-week deadline is coming faster than I care for."

"That two-week event again. What the hell is that?"

"It's the full moon when the clan chooses a leader. The other candidate is okay, but he's not as good as Orla. I don't think he's over-ambitious and would harm Orla or you to protect the leadership post, though"

"*He?*" Lorcan asked.

"Yes, as far as I know, Bradan is a male." Maeve raised an eyebrow. "I read in Orla's mind before she passed out about her encounter with you and another woman . . ."

Maeve's voice started to echo. Feeling the cold air creeping up his back, Lorcan withdrew and mentally braced himself to fight what was to come. His vision wavered slightly, and his head start to go numb. *You can't use the same trick twice on me!* He looked at Maeve, and a surge of lust rose inside him. *Control!* Lorcan distanced himself. The second he let the feeling grow because he thought the woman at the riverbank had been Orla was the very second he lost control of his body and mind.

He shook his head, trying to stay alert. He felt as if he was drowning in deep water. He turned toward Maeve. Her image flickered. And then in front of him was Orla. She smiled, and he couldn't breathe. His head was going to explode. He swayed. Orla approached to help him. But he knew it wasn't Orla. He stepped back.

"Stay away from me."

The image of the woman flickered and returned as Maeve.

"Lorcan!"

He heard Orla's voice from the door. Lorcan looked up and saw Orla with a man. This might not be her, he thought. "Stay away from me," he repeated.

Orla approached.

"Stay right there!" he yelled and that stopped Orla in her tracks. *That's how she looks when she's surprised. That's the real Orla.* "Orla," he whispered just before the hot rage took over. He hadn't experienced this before. He staggered back. The urge to kill and destroy consumed him. He hated as he had never hated before. *Why is Orla with this man? Who is he? Is he using the black magic on her and on his father?*

"You did this to my father!" Lorcan roared.

"I did what?" the man asked.

Lorcan staggered back, leaning against the wall, breathing heavily. He had to force his mind out of his body. He could see himself now—he looked like a madman, bloodshot eyes, yelling profanity, rushing at Orla, Maeve, and the man who had just walked into the house with Orla. He could see himself out of control, but he couldn't stop it. He saw a tear roll down Orla's face.

He had made her cry. Again.

Then he lost concentration for a second. That was all it took. He was sucked back into his body, and the next thing he knew, he had shot two waves of electric current at the strange man. To Lorcan's surprise, the man was as calm as still water. He waved his hand, and it seemed as if the current had hit a metal shield and diverted. It didn't come back at him but headed in his father's direction.

The heat burned the rope and set his father free. Charged with rage, his father grabbed a gun lying on the table and aimed it at Keeva.

That was all Lorcan could see.

At that very moment, his mind was as clear as crystal. He could shoot the electric wave and burn his father into ashes to stop him from pulling the trigger on Keeva. There was no other option except . . .

As quick as lightning, Lorcan grabbed at Keeva, pulling her backward. The momentum pushed him forward and into the path of the bullet. He could see the scene in slow motion. The penetration of the bullet into his chest wasn't bad at all. It was like a prick of pain at the entry point, and then the pressure of something disintegrating into his body, and then the heat of his own blood.

He slumped to his knees. Lorcan had a feeling he wouldn't be able to heal himself from this injury very quickly . . . if at all.

His mind was perfectly clear. It seemed as if the magic—or whatever it was that had caused the craziness in the room—had vanished. Everything was back to normal.

He fell backward and into Keeva's arms. His father appeared to snap back to reality as if the demon had just left him. And Orla, he could see her approaching him with tears on her face and determined eyes.

Lorcan leaned into Keeva's arms. Orla crouched in front of him and held his hands. "It's not too bad. You just need to crash and you'll heal," she said with a shaky voice.

"I don't want you anymore. I don't want to see you anymore. Leave me, Orla," he said.

"No way in hell I'll leave you. That trick doesn't work on me, Lorcan."

He didn't have enough energy to pull his hands from Orla's.

"Maeve!" Lorcan called out.

"Yes. You broke the black magic, Lorcan. If there was a black magic curse on your father, you broke it."

"Great news!" He smiled weakly. "Can I break the curse on Orla?"

Maeve said nothing.

Lorcan nodded. "All right. If I can't fix this, I don't want Orla near me. Can you keep her away, please?"

Maeve nodded.

"Maeve!" Orla hissed and withdrew when she saw Maeve glance at Bradan. Bradan approached from behind and snatched Orla off the ground. While Orla kicked, screamed, and struggled, trying to get out of Bradan's grip, Lorcan nodded a thank you to Bradan. In a short moment, Maeve and Bradan dragged Orla out of the house.

"Keeva!" Lorcan called his sister.

"Yes?"

"I don't want anyone to use magic on me. Promise me you'll keep those people away from me—even if I die because of it."

"I promise." Keeva's voice cracked with tears.

"I don't want a doctor, either"

"If you don't take magic, you have to go to the hospital," Keeva cried.

His father crouched in front of him. "Lorcan, tell me what you need." His eyes were calm and still, but his hands trembled.

Lorcan gazed into his father's eyes. "Am I your real son?"

"Yes. I can't take back the bullet, but I would like to take back what I said. You are my son, and I love you. Now if you want to know where you came from and your special conditions, you have to stay alive."

Lorcan smiled. His father was the same, a man with a mind as hard as steel. The world was blurring by the second. His father's image flickered in front of him.

"I'll have to take you to the hospital," Keeva said.

"No. I can't go to the hospital. I need Riley."

"Who?" his father asked.

"Your friend in London?" Keeva asked.

He wanted to answer his sister's question but darkness claimed him.

CHAPTER 6

Keeva checked Lorcan's bullet wound one last time and pulled the blanket up to cover him. Unlike the wounds on his back, this bullet wound was still bleeding and didn't appear to be healing. She didn't need medical knowledge to guess that regardless of whatever special ability her brother had, the wound wouldn't heal with the bullet still inside it. That was why Lorcan wanted Riley. From the little information she had, her brother's best friend Riley was a medical doctor.

Was he her blood brother after all? Where had he come from?

Things had happened so quickly she didn't have time to ask her father. He had gone into town to meet with someone who could help find Mother and send people to London for Riley. He had a lot of connections, and she hadn't yet seen anything her father couldn't handle. Well, maybe only the earlier incident.

Father didn't believe in anything magical. But Mother was a believer of magic, although she had never admitted it.

She needed to find Riley now, but she couldn't leave Lorcan here by himself, unconscious. She could go to the internet, but looking for what? There was something that looked like a watch that Lorcan always had with him. He had so many technological gadgets, she couldn't keep up with him. She stared at Lorcan's wrist unit, and it stared back at her. Then the screen flashed with an incoming message alert. She touched a green button. The screen flashed in red, punctuated by a loud beep. "Unauthorized access." The message startled her so much that she almost threw the device on the floor. She tucked it underneath Lorcan's pillow.

"Unauthorized my butt," she mumbled. Could she cut the bullet out herself? Keeva dismissed the thought. One minor surgery on an injured wild dog's leg when she was a little kid didn't warrant experience to cut her brother's chest open. She wiped the sweat on Lorcan's forehead and saw that his temperature had increased considerably. It was obvious that his body was trying its best to heal itself, but it couldn't do so with a foreign object inside his chest.

Keeva was in desperate need to hit something now, or maybe just to yell. Then she heard the doorbell. She cursed. People working in the house had mysteriously disappeared since yesterday, and their phone line in the house had been cut off. This may be a routine delivery guy who couldn't get into the kitchen from the back door.

Keeva opened the door. In front of her was not the delivery man but a man in his thirties and a boy of about nine or ten.

"Hello, my name is Riley."

"Riley? My brother's friend?"

"You must be Keeva."

The boy's eyes welled up with tears, and before Keeva could ask anything, he ran past her into the house. "I need to see Uncle Lorcan," his voice echoed back after he vanished up the stairs.

"Hey!" Keeva yelled. Riley grabbed her elbow, and when Keeva stopped and turned to look at him, he released her arm.

"I'm sorry. Lorcan was shot, wasn't he? I can help."

Keeva couldn't stop the tears filling her eyes. She wasn't sure if it was because of the anxiety or the fear, but the world around her had been moving too fast, and she had lost her bearings.

Without a response from her, Riley pressed on. "My son, Noah, he had a vision . . . he saw Lorcan get shot, and he's been nagging me for three days to come here. I know you probably won't believe me, but . . ."

"I believe you."

"Oh . . ."

"Yes, I said I believe you. I've seen some strange things here my whole life. A psychic vision doesn't surprise me. Please help Lorcan. The bullet is in his chest, but he didn't want any medical doctor except you."

Riley nodded and shifted the heavy bag he was carrying. "Is he upstairs?" Riley asked while heading toward the stairs.

Keeva rushed ahead to lead. "How did Noah know where to go?"

"As much as I hate admitting it, he's a psychic. I'm not." The bag he was carrying was so heavy he almost lost his balance on the stairs.

Riley chuckled. "Sorry, I didn't know what I'd need, so there's a portable hospital in my bag."

Keeva and Riley found Noah in front of Lorcan's room, tears staining his face. Keeva crouched down to his level. "Lorcan told me if I could get your father here, he'll be okay."

Noah nodded. He stepped aside to allow Riley entrance to the room. Keeva followed and felt a tug at her hand. It was Noah. His little hand was cold, damp, and a little shaky. She wrapped her hand around his and rubbed it to keep him warm. Noah looked up at her. His light green eyes were so much like his father's. Innocence. That was all Keeva could see. But what surprised her the most was that his hand in hers felt so natural.

Riley turned around, looking at Keeva after examining the wound.

"Oh God, please don't tell me you can't do it," Keeva said.

"The wound is so close to his heart. I'm afraid I have to do this at a hospital. It's too risky here."

"He doesn't want to go to a hospital."

"He always says that . . ."

On the bed, Lorcan stirred and opened his eyes. "Riley . . . I knew you'd come . . ." His voice was barely audible.

"Lorcan, I have to take you to the hospital. This is a major surgery—I can't do it here."

"Just take the bullet out. If I survive that, I'll heal quickly . . ."

"But I don't think you can survive it."

"I've had worse. Trust me. Just take the bullet out."

"I've seen his wounds heal themselves, Riley," Keeva added.

Riley shook his head.

"Please," Lorcan said and passed out again.

"Please do what he said, Dad!" Noah cried.

"Did you have another vision, Noah?" Riley asked.

Noah shook his head.

"Yesterday he came home with nasty wounds on his back. But in a couple of hours, they healed as if they'd never been there. But he can't do it with a bullet in his chest, Riley," Keeva said.

"Are you sure?"

Keeva nodded.

"Okay. Please give me some space and wait outside."

Keeva picked Noah up, left of the room, and closed the door behind her.

"Please keep an eye on her. I mean it, Alana." Bradan put an unconscious Orla on the bed.

Alana stood up from a comfortable reading chair in the corner of the room. "What happened to her?"

"Maeve knocked her out."

"Again? I knew it. Violent bitch."

"She was only trying to help."

Alana's hands were on her hips. "She's a white witch, Bradan!"

"She tried to help, and what she did was very complicated. Not just watching Orla as you do."

"You helped her run away. You talked to Maeve and let her do this to Orla. Now you're blaming me for not watching her!"

"I'm not blaming you for anything. If I could watch, I'd do so myself."

"I want to go home. I have a life, Bradan."

"Please!"

"What about all the aunts in the family?"

"You're the only young one, Alana. I can't put an aunt in here with Orla."

Alana rolled her eyes and walked around the room in agitation. "So what am I supposed to do when she wants to leave? Knock her on her ass?"

Bradan shrugged. "Apparently we can't just lock the door because she got off the roof last time. We might have to tie her up."

"You've got to be kidding me!"

"Do you have any suggestions?"

Alana rolled her eyes again. "What if she puts a spell on me and makes me free her? Or worse, what if she curses me?"

"Damn it, Alana, you're a sorceress. Don't you practice at all?"

Alana couldn't find a word to say back at Bradan. She stomped toward the desk and grabbed her books and her bag. "Well, if I'm not mistaken, you're asking for my help. I'm not good at black magic and will never be. I don't care for it. This clan's business is none of mine. Now get out of my hair!" She stormed toward the door.

Bradan barred her way. "Oh, come on. I'm sorry, Alana. Just stay one more day, and I'll see what I can do."

Alana glared at him.

"Please!"

"Never look down at me again!"

"Never. I promise."

"You owe me."

"Definitely."

"I need my laptop."

"What?"

"Do you seriously want me to sit here for two weeks, melting in boredom?"

"Okay. I'll get it for you."

Alana grinned. Bradan shook his head and left the room.

The sound of a computer game woke Orla. She opened her eyes to find that her hands were tied to the bar of a headboard. In the corner of the room, Alana was glued to her laptop. Orla sat up on the bed, but that didn't break Alana's concentration on her game.

It was rare that Orla had a chance to observe her distant cousin. She'd make a perfect movie star, Orla thought. Long sandy hair, big blue eyes, oval face, and perfect lips. She could play a princess in one of the Disney fairy tales. Orla cleared her throat, and that caught Alana's attention. She turned the volume of the game down.

"Damn, one more level, and I'll beat this. Bastard," she mumbled.

"Go ahead. I can wait." Orla jiggled at the chains on her wrists.

Alana shook her head. "That's all right. I can always come back and beat the hell out of him later." She grinned.

"What game?"

"You know games?"

Orla chuckled. "Not really. But Lorcan is a game fanatic. I hear a lot about them."

Alana's eyes sparked with curiosity. "Really? You should introduce us. When you become the leader, you won't be able to be with him anymore. I can take him. A good gamer is hard to come by."

"I'll consider it." Orla smiled.

"Please do. Are you hungry?"

Orla shook her head while Alana yawned.

"Bradan told me you went to Oxford. Why come back if you don't care about the clan's politics?" Orla asked.

Alana chuckled. "I miss that world. Really. My parents died. I'm sure Bradan told you that, too. I came back to make arrangements for the funeral. I thought it would be a short trip. Then one thing led to another. No one was taking care of the business they left behind. Before I know it, I was stuck here."

"Don't you want to go back?"

"Of course. Soon, actually. I promised to help out with the ceremony and then, after that, I'll be back to London. I've sold the family business here. Two more weeks, and I'm out of here." Alana grinned.

Orla smiled. "I can sense there's a man involved."

Alana blushed. "Can't tell you."

"I'm jealous, Alana. I don't want to take the post. Why can't they let Bradan? He wants it."

Alana shrugged. "It's not for me to say."

Orla adjusted her position. "I need to go to the bathroom."

"Don't try anything, Snit."

"You want me to pee right here?"

Orla smiled because she could feel Alana had put up her protective spell so she couldn't manipulate her mind. She opened the chain. "Try anything, and I'll hurt you, Orla."

Orla went to the bathroom and closed the door.

Inside, she turned on the tap and looked in the mirror to examine the bruise on her forehead. She waited for a bit and then cast her spell, a white spell she'd learned from Maeve. Shortly, she heard a thunk on the floor. She turned the water off and rushed out.

Alana had fallen on her face on the floor. Orla checked to see if she had hit her head on anything. Seeing no damage apart from a small bruise on Alana's forehead, Orla pulled the blanket off the bed and tucked Alana in. Then she crawled out onto the roof again. This time, she dipped her head down low and checked to ensure Bradan wasn't around. Then she hopped down to the ground and darted into the night.

CHAPTER 7

Keeva sat in a reading chair in a smaller room upstairs. She couldn't do much until she heard the news from Riley. It had been a while. She should feed Noah. She looked down and saw that Noah had fallen asleep while curling against her side. The kid had just met her, but the strange thing was that it didn't feel unusual at all that he displayed such affection in his interaction with her. Keeva always did well with animals, but she didn't think she would do well with kids. *What happened to your mom?* she thought as she looked at Noah's thick lashes, freckled cheeks, and fair skin. *She must be beautiful.* She played with Noah's hair but stopped when he stirred.

As soon as Riley walked into the reception room, Keeva sprung to her feet. Riley's hair spiked up as he raked his hands through it, and there was a blood smear on his face. "How is he?" Keeva asked.

Riley breathed out heavily. "Alive when I left. I took the bullet out, but I'm not sure about this at all. He lost a lot of blood."

Keeva darted toward Lorcan's room. Riley trailed behind. "I sedated him," he said, "so he'll be out for a while. But the most important thing is that the bleeding has stopped . . ." He trailed off when he got into the room and saw that the incision on Lorcan's chest that he had just stitched up had already begun to form scar tissue. The wound was healing by the second—right in front of Riley's eyes. "What the f—" Riley began but stopped himself when he saw Noah approach the bed, looking at Lorcan.

Keeva turned around. "Thank you." She tiptoed over and hugged Riley.

"You're welcome," he mumbled awkwardly when she released him.

She cleared her throat and pointed at his face. "You've got some blood . . ."

"Oh." Riley wiped randomly and missed the mark.

"Let me." Keeva pulled out her handkerchief and wiped mark away. She had to bite the inside of her mouth and look away after she finished. The contact was a bit too close for her comfort. She cleared her throat again. "Lorcan's wound will heal quite quickly as you can see. But it would be—"

"I'll stay until he's up and about," Riley interrupted.

"Oh . . . thanks. I'll show you to your room."

"Yes, please." Riley smiled.

He had a killer smile, Keeva thought, cursing silently. "This way, please." She pointed toward the door and scurried out.

Later, Keeva turned on the kitchen light and braced herself against the door frame on the off chance she'd see another dead body on the floor. But there was nothing there this time. She exhaled a sigh of relief and searched the cabinet for something with which she could cook a meal. It dawned on her at that point that the delivery man hadn't come, but it wasn't a big deal because the chef always kept enough stock available to make a feast.

Keeva frowned at the cabinet. Unlike her mother, cooking wasn't a skill she could earn a living with. She survived on what she cooked when she was in college because she didn't really have a choice. Hearing a noise at the door, Keeva turned around to see Noah standing there wearing his backpack.

"Where are you going?"

"I need some food."

Keeva uttered another internal curse . She had known it would come to this. How could she explain to the guests that she had found the chef dead in the kitchen, and therefore none of the house staff had come to work today? "Well, sure. Come in. Sit down." She pointed to the kitchen table.

"The food isn't for me." Noah placed his bag on a chair and pulled out the most beautiful kitten she had ever seen. He put the kitten on the table. "We were in a hurry, and I forgot to pack his food. He eats what we eat, but he doesn't like milk at all."

Keeva sat down next to him. The cat looked her up and down, seemingly judging whether she could be trusted. "I can take care of him." If her cooking was bad, at least the cat couldn't complain. "What's his name?"

"Aris. Short for Aristotle."

"You named the kitten after a Greek philosopher?"

"Yes. Aris is a very deep thinker. He just doesn't tell you what he's thinking."

"How do you know that?"

"Well, if he doesn't like something, he'll find a way to let you know."

"Humm . . ." Now she started to worry about the food she was going to feed this little kitten. She would go with the safest bet—a sandwich. The kind that required no cooking.

"Would you like a sandwich?" she asked.

"Do you have ham, cheese, and tomato?"

"Sure, I do."

"Toasted, please?"

"You're too demanding, Noah." Riley stood at the door, giving his son a disapproving look.

"It's easy enough," said Keeva. "But I can't guarantee anything fancier than that!" She stood up to make the sandwich. "And what would you like, Riley?"

"Anything is good. I'm easy."

She smiled. "Why don't I make you my favorite?"

"Thank you. I'm sure I'll love it." Riley smiled and scratched Aris behind his ears. Aris purred so loud it made everyone laugh.

"Come on, you seriously don't even care what I'm going to feed you?"

Riley shook his head. "I do care about what I put in my body. It's an occupational quirk. But it's merely the nutrition I think about and not so much tastes or preference."

Keeva scowled. "I feel sorry for you, Riley. Even Aris here has preferences."

Riley laughed. "Yes. That cat has preferences in *everything*. You should have seen his reaction when I called him Edward."

"Really?" Keeva looked at Aris, and she swore she saw the cat scowling at Riley. He saw it, too, and laughed. *He has such hearty laughs*, Keeva thought. Honest and from the belly, a giving-it-all kind of laugh. She shook her head, trying to clear out the inappropriate thoughts that threatened to invade her mind. "Well, given you won't tell me what you like, you're going to be stuck with my favorite—a tuna and cucumber sandwich."

Riley's laughter stopped instantly, and the smile vanished from his face.

"Not good?" she asked.

"Oh no . . . I mean yes, I'd like the sandwich." Riley said nothing else. He grabbed Aris, put him on his lap, and stroked his back. But Aris was no longer purring.

Suddenly the sense of death engulfed her. The room started to spin, and she couldn't breathe. She could sense death occasionally, but it had never been this strong. The plate she was holding slipped out of her hand and shattered on the floor. She stormed out the kitchen door to the back garden.

The cool air made her feel a bit better, but she was still quite dazed. In a corner of the garden stood a beautiful woman. She looked at Keeva with a smile on her face.

"Who are you?" she asked.

"I'm Michelle."

"I don't know you."

"You do. Not now . . . but in the future, you'll know me."

"What are you talking about?"

"You *are* me. Take care of Riley and Noah." The woman turned around and vanished into thin air. Then the world turned completely black. She couldn't feel anything except the sensation of floating in the nothingness.

Sounds gradually came back to her, and along with it, the familiar sense of air and life. She opened her eyes and found herself in Riley's arms. He was carrying her. She shifted in his arms. "Put me down. I'm fine."

"No, you're not. You fainted in the kitchen."

He was using what people often called his doctor's tone, and the best way to handle it was to be obedient. Keeva said nothing. Riley lay her down on the sofa and directed, "Stay down." He stopped her when she tried to sit up. "You cut your hand on the broken plate. I'll get something to patch it up." Keeva noted that her left arm was bleeding. As Riley left, he signaled Noah and pointed at her. Noah nodded and came to sit on the coffee table beside Keeva.

"He always like that?"

Noah rolled his eyes and nodded. "My friends at school used to call him Mr. Serious. But he just cares. Too much sometimes."

"You let your friends call your dad that?"

Noah shrugged. "They stopped after a while."

Aris approached, hopped on the coffee table, sat next to Noah, and started washing himself. Keeva narrowed her eyes. "I know how kids act. Your friends wouldn't just stop calling your dad names because you asked them to. What did you do to convince them?"

"Nothing. Maybe some weird things showed up in their lunchboxes. That happens to naughty boys, you know."

Keeva laughed.

"You saw my mom, didn't you?" Noah's tone was exactly the same as when he had told her about his friends' lunchboxes. The psychic kid must have lived with weird things his whole life. It had become a part of him. Keeva sat up and looked into his eyes. He looked straight back at her, waiting for an answer.

"How does your father handle your visions?"

"I'd never told him before. But they started to cause migraines , and it got so severe that Dad thought I had a brain tumor. So I told him about my visions, and he believed me. Since then, the migraines have stopped . . . Are tuna and cucumber sandwiches really your favorite?"

"Yes."

Noah nodded. "It's my mom's favorite, too. Dad doesn't like them, but he pretended to in order to please Mom."

She smiled. "That's very sweet. They must have been very happy together."

Noah nodded. "Before I was born, they were so happy. Mom told me everything. What they did. Where they went. She said Dad was broken when she left him, and if I'm a good boy, I'll take care of him."

"I'm sure you're a good boy. See, you stayed here and watched me just like he asked you to. You must miss your mom very much. When did she pass away?" She tucked a strand of curly hair back behind Noah's ear.

"When she gave birth to me. That's what Dad said."

"So . . . you talked to her . . . spirit?"

Noah nodded and a tear rolled down his face. "But she's stopped seeing me for months. I don't know why. I must have done something wrong." More tears rolled down his face.

"No, no, sweetie. I know she has her reasons." She reached out, pulled Noah into her lap, and cuddled him while he sobbed. It hadn't been for just a short period of time that he hadn't seen his mother, it had been a long while. He had lived with the vision of a dead woman for his entire life. She rocked the boy on her lap, rubbing his back to soothe him and thinking about her own mother.

Riley came back and stared at the scene before him. When Keeva stopped rubbing, Noah turned around and saw his father. He stood up, wiped his tears. Riley crouched. "What happened, Noah?"

"Nothing. I'd like to go to bed now." Noah walked out of the room. Aris trailed right behind him.

"I'll be right with you," Riley said.

"Don't need you," Noah's voice echoed down from the stairs.

Riley turned and looked at Keeva. "What did he just say?"

Keeva said nothing. He'd heard the boy well enough. Riley sat on the sofa and reached out his hand. "Let me see. I'll patch it up."

She snatched the medical kit from his hand. "I can do it myself, thanks. You go after Noah."

"No, it was just a tantrum. He'll get over it. He has to grow up sooner or later."

"He misses his mother. He's lonely. It's more than a tantrum, Riley."

Riley stood up. "You know nothing about us, Keeva."

"I know enough to know that you let your son starve emotionally because your heart was broken when your wife died."

His eyes darkened, and his face hardened. "I'm doing my best to give him whatever he wants. But I'm not his mother, and there's nothing I can do about it."

"Yes, there *are* things you can do to fix it."

Riley gave her a dismissive look and turned on his heel.

"Hey!" she called out loud enough to stop him in his tracks.

"What?" he growled back.

"You might think I know nothing about the pain of losing someone, that Lorcan and I come from privilege and have never had a hard day in our lives."

"I love Lorcan like my brother, but which part of what you said isn't true?" his voice was cold as steel.

"My mother has been missing for two days. Father went crazy and shot Lorcan. And now he's gone into town to look for Mother and hasn't answered my calls for hours. There was a dead body in the kitchen one minute, and then it had disappeared the next. I couldn't even call the cops because they would think I'm crazy. I can't look for my mother because I have no idea where to look."

"I'm so sorry."

"Your pain was so enormous that you saw nothing else. My mother's been missing for only two days, and it hurts so much. Imagine your son living with that his whole life."

"I . . ."

"No, don't say anything to me. I'm not in the mood to discuss who can handle more pain." She stomped out of the room. She didn't look back, but she knew he stood there for a while, staring after her.

CHAPTER 8

Orla ran as fast as she could in the woods. She remembered the general direction of Lorcan's house. If her calculations were right, she would be there in no time. The image of the bullet hitting him replayed countless times in her head and burned like fuel that made her run even faster. She knew he had to survive first in order for the wound to heal. When they were on the island and he was shot by arrows, Ciaran had to pull them out for his wound could start healing. *Who would do it for him this time?* Removing a bullet wasn't exactly the kind of skill that just anyone had.

She stopped when her train of thought hit a brick wall. Maeve was right. The moment she set foot in Ireland, she had upset someone's plan. She was the rightful leader of this clan, and a neat way to kill her would be to make her burst into flame. Conflicting emotions would definitely do the trick. Her clan's black magic worked on negative emotions, and conflicting emotions would kill the person who place the curse.

If she had put a curse on Lorcan and then realized it, her love for him would kill her. Regardless of how strong she was and how much she could control her mind, if she lost her concentration for even a fraction of a second, she would die. The love she had for him was ingrained in her and had become her living force. She couldn't pretend she didn't love Lorcan, and she couldn't deny it. Love came from the heart and soul. It was not a game.

Someone knew this rule well and was using it against her. But there was one thing that person or persons did *not* know, and that was that her years living outside this black magic community had taught her a lot, and she always had many tricks up her sleeves.

She smelled smoke. Someone was nearby. She caught a glimpse of a fire and crept among the trees to get closer. She recognized Uncle Daly and Bradan, and they appeared to be arguing, but she was too far away to hear anything. Uncle Daly paced back and forth, arms waving in the air. Bradan appeared to be listening and then responding, but he didn't seem to agree on whatever it was they were arguing about.

When Orla was about to move on with her task at hand, she saw a large shadow leap at Uncle Daly from behind. It was too dark for her to tell what it was, but she could tell from the shadow that the animal was enormous. Bradan physically attacked the animal.

Why didn't he use his magic? He ought to have some skills!

Orla darted in their direction with caution. She had nothing on her that resembled a respectable weapon, but she could throw fireballs, which by all means would be more effective than clawing back at the wild animal as Bradan was doing. When she was close enough, she threw her first ball at the backside of the creature.

It roared and turned, looking at her.

She could see it now. It was an enormous eagle with reptilian skin. "You're goddamn ugly!" Orla said and threw another fireball. The creature flapped its wings and lifted itself off the ground. Before it released Daly, its claw ripped his body apart. Brandan screamed in fury and charged at the creature. It swung a wing and threw him into a tree like a rag doll.

Orla threw more fire at it before it flew at Bradan, talons readied. The creature glared at Orla, and in that short moment, she saw a gleam of something familiar in its eyes. Her fire didn't seem to do much damage to it. She needed a weapon. She conjured a spell in her head, and the tree branches of a nearby tree peeled from the trunk.

The creature could hear the crack of the trees. It flapped its wings and spat a stream of blue fire toward Orla. *Hell!* Orla knew she couldn't get out of this one. She hadn't thought a 'bird' would have the ability to breathe waves of fire. There wasn't enough time for her to dart for cover. She could feel the heat heading toward her.

But just then the fire hit an invisible shield in front of her and bounced off, burning the nearby tree. She saw Bradan lower his arm. So *that* was his talent! He couldn't attack, but he could use some kind of shield to divert the energy elsewhere. The creature turned so fast that Bradan couldn't do anything about it. It flew at him and punctured his chest with its claws.

Bradan fell to the ground, grasping the feet of the creature and pulling it down with him. The tree branch Orla had broken free then became a sharp weapon. She swung her arm, and it stabbed deep into the creature's back. It uttered a horrific quacking noise, flapped its wings, and flew off into the darkness.

Bradan lay on the ground, gasping for air while blood gushed from his chest. Orla helped him up into a sitting position, hoping it would lessen his blood loss. "You fool! If you don't have any skills to protect yourself, why upset that ugly monster? Hang in there. If you die on me, I'll curse you at your grave and all the way to hell."

"I'll end up in hell, will I?" Bradan joked weakly. His head lolled back onto her shoulder, and his consciousness was ebbing.

Orla looked around. They were in the middle of the woods, and there was no way she could carry him back to the village on foot.

The sound of something behind her made her hair stand up.

"Who is that? Don't mess around with me, or I'll burn your ass!" she yelled.

Maeve rushed over to her. "Orla! Thank god it's you. It's so dark, I couldn't tell. I've been following the trail of a dark magic creature all evening and lost their trail . . ."

Orla made a small fireball and lit up a small tree branch on the ground nearby. The light stopped Maeve. "Bradan! What happened to him?"

"Got attacked. Possibly by the same creature you've been following."

"Put him down. Let me see."

"He's lost a lot of blood."

"Can you make more fire?"

Orla nodded and made the fire larger so Maeve could see. She opened the front of Bradan's shirt and looked at the wound. "It's not the blood loss that's killing him, it's the poison. That creature— whatever it was—sent poison into his blood."

Orla could see that the blood streaming from Bradan's chest had turned black. Maeve took a small bottle of potion she had in her little bag and tipped it into his mouth.

"Will it cure him?"

Maeve shook her head. "It helps ease the pain. But no, it won't save him."

"So what will?"

"There's a sacred black magic potion in the temple of the clan. That would definitely help, but they won't give it to anyone. But ask Uncle Daly—he'll find a way to save his son."

"I'm sorry to tell you this, but he's behind you. He was torn into pieces by that thing."

"Oh God . . ."

"Who made the potion, and what is it?"

"I think Aunt Anna made it. They're very secretive about it. It's for the next leader of the clan."

"So if they want me to lead the clan, will I have access to the potion?"

"Yes, but you have to swear in."

Orla narrowed her eyes. No one knew she *hadn't* sworn in with the clan. All the girls who had been groomed for the position of leader had sworn in on their first magic lesson. It was a sacred promise between the individuals and their god. But she hadn't sworn. That was one of the tricks that had kept her alive until now. All of her conflicting emotions and the fact that she would burst into flame because of them would only work on her if she had sworn in.

"What are you talking about?" Orla asked Maeve.

"Come on, you've never sworn in with your clan. I know that."

Orla lowered her voice. "*Nobody* knows."

"You don't suspect me, do you?"

"Nobody knows, Maeve. So what's your plan? What do you want?" Orla backed away.

Tears gleamed in Maeve's eyes. "Come on, don't do this to me, Orla!"

"I could kill you, Maeve, you know that!"

Tears rolled down Maeve's face. "You can do whatever you want to me. Just go get that potion and save Bradan, please!"

Orla looked into Maeve's eyes and mumbled, "You love him, don't you? Does he know that?"

"He's running out of time, Orla, please!"

Orla waved her arms in frustration. "Swearing in . . . that means I have to give up my life—and Lorcan—and stay here forever. How can you be that selfish, Maeve?"

"You can kill me if you want to. I don't care. I've had enough of this place. If you had sworn in, the black magic at the cemetery could have killed you. I knew back then that you hadn't done it. I *am* selfish. If you take the leadership, then Bradan doesn't have to, and then we will have a chance . . ."

"You would trade my life just for a chance with him?"

Maeve shook her head. "You are the rightful leader. You'll have to take that leadership sooner or later, Orla. I don't stand a chance with Bradan, even if he doesn't take the leadership. But I love him. So there, I said it. Do whatever you want."

"You fool! You could have told me," Orla mumbled. "Now you stay here. I'll go get the potion."

"Thank you."

"Don't mention it. But you owe me one."

Maeve nodded through tears.

The temple was as mysterious as she remembered it. Orla ducked low behind a stone wall and peeked inside from a distance. She remembered the layout of the temple but still couldn't made an educated guess about where about the potion might be. Her ex-profession as a thief might come in quite handy. She wanted the potion, but she had no intention of swearing anything to the clan.

There was no one around.

Very confident, Orla thought. They thought their magic and spells would protect the temple from thieves, which was probably true. But she was no ordinary thief. She entered the temple. Statues of her gods, ancestral remains, and numerous magical items were placed neatly on the altar. A large picture of a half moon, the symbol of her black magic sorcery clan, was located prominently. They didn't worship the moon, but their gods fed from its negative energy. Half-moon symbols were everywhere in the temple. Orla shook her head and chuckled to herself. Her clan was one third religion, one third magic, and one third emotion. While many magical branches relied on the harmony of the universe—the Ying and Yang and the composite of peaceful elements—what had possessed her ancestors to choose one that was destructive and unnatural? Why had they chosen to forbid love?

She looked around and couldn't see any potion jar or bottle.

Magic lock, she speculated. "Want me to swear in, I will," she said aloud, looking up at her god. She kneeled in front of the altar and stated her oath. It was a life and death statement, a giving-her-soul-to-the-devil kind of swear, and it ought to work, she thought. When Orla opened her eyes and looked up again, a small white bottle of potion was staring down at her from atop the altar.

"Thank you." She smiled and grabbed it. She turned, a quirk at a corner of her mouth appearing, but she quickly squelched it before her ancestors or any mind reader could catch it and strode out of the temple.

She rushed back to the woods. Bradan must have gotten worse as Maeve looked like a mess and was cradling him in her arms. Orla thrust the bottle into Maeve's hand.

"Are you sure it will fix him?" she asked.

Maeve said nothing and flipped the lid open. She nudged his lips open and carefully tipped the contents in. Bradan was white as a sheet. Orla thought he must have died ten times over. But in a short moment, in front of their eyes, he seemed to resume normal breathing.

Maeve laughed as she teared up. "It worked! Oh my god, it worked."

"I can see that, Maeve. Do you want him to know that you begged for his life?"

"What? No!"

"So put him down."

"Oh. Right." Maeve lay Bradan down on the grass. He opened his eyes groggily.

"Oh good, you're awake. Let's get out of here now. I'm freezing," Orla said, looking down at him.

"What happened?" He was still very weak due to the wounds on his chest, but the poison had been counteracted. Maeve shot a frantic look at Orla.

"Bradan, your father died, and you were injured. Remember that?"

Then he recalled. The pain on his face bought tears to Maeve's eyes again. Orla cleared her throat. "I have things I need to do. But first, we have to get you to safety, and it's not going to be the village," Orla declared.

"Why not?"

"Whatever attacked you knew you had left the village for the woods. Someone in the village tipped it off."

Bradan closed his eyes and seemed to agree with what she said. Orla continued, "You should stay with Maeve."

"What?" Bradan tried to sit up but flopped down again.

"You need to be taken care of. Nobody would guess you'd stay with her. Maeve, would you mind?"

"Yes, I mean no. Of course not. No one in the village knows my current place."

Orla and Maeve helped Bradan up. Orla saw no way out of helping Maeve taking Bradan to her place. He was still too weak to walk by himself. It took the two of them, flanking his sides, and they still had to walk one slow step at a time.

Orla looked up to the sky and saw a crack of dawn beginning to show itself. She sighed and thought of Lorcan.

CHAPTER 9

Keeva's scream sent Lorcan springing to his feet. He glanced down and saw that his chest had healed completely. Lorcan knew that Keeva slept innocently and deeply and would never remember ordinary dreams. But her nightmares were of the worst kind. Similar to her ability to sense death, her nightmares were all about death, and they were frighteningly accurate. Storming into Keeva's bedroom, he saw her sitting in bed and shaking, with tears streaming down her face.

Lorcan jumped onto the bed and pulled his sister into his arms to soothe her, but she backed away from him.

Her eyes were devastated, and she backed further away. What had she seen in her nightmare? Whose death? "Keeva, talk to me," he said gently, but she kept shaking her head.

Riley and Noah arrived at the door. Lorcan acknowledged them, then glanced back at Keeva. He vaguely remembered asking for Riley in his delirium last night. He remembered asking him to perform the surgery to remove the bullet.

"Thanks for coming," Lorcan said. Riley nodded, his eyes trained on the shaking Keeva.

Noah ran in and flew into Lorcan's arms. As he hugged Lorcan, Noah whispered into his ear, "She sees dead people. She dreams about them, too."

Lorcan eased Noah out of his arms and looked at his face, then he looked back at Keeva. "I know, Noah. I know about her visions and dreams."

Noah looked at Keeva, then in front of an astonished Lorcan and Riley, he climbed onto the bed and curled into Keeva's arms. Keeva embraced him as tears rolled down her face.

"Why don't you tell them what you saw? When I talked to Dad, it helped," Noah said.

Keeva shook her head. "I can't . . ."

"Do you mind if I tell them what you saw? I think Uncle Lorcan should know."

Lorcan stood up, bracing for the news. Riley flopped to the reading chair and put his head in his hands.

Keeva nodded to Noah. Noah turned around. "Uncle Lorcan, I think Keeva and I had the same dream. We saw each other in our dreams. We saw a big bird, blood, body parts and . . . Orla."

Lorcan braced his hands against the wall and inhaled deeply. Then he turned around and asked, "Did you see whose body parts they were?"

Noah shook his head. "It was dark. I saw Orla's face . . ."

"I need to see her," Lorcan muttered and charged out the door.

He thundered down the hallway. Keeva, Riley, and Noah chased after him. The lights in the house flickered, and a wave of fresh and lively air washed through the entire house. The eerie silence suddenly lifted, and they heard the hum of the forest and the wind. Birds flapped their wings, fighting for the small birdbath Keeva had made for them. Insects orchestrated soothing Irish country songs. And people chattered.

People? Lorcan came to a skidding halt and turned back. Keeva looked at him. They both heard the familiar sound of people in the house. Riley frowned at their expressions as they rushed down the stairs.

In the front garden, a man was holding a large plant trimmer, enjoying the birds in competition for a place in the bath. He turned and saw the group of people. "Keeva, your bath is very popular with the birds. I told you. Soon you will regret it because they make a lot of noise." He pointed at Lorcan. "And who might this be?"

"This is my brother, Lorcan, and his friends from England, Riley and Noah," Keeva said quickly and scurried after Lorcan as he made his way down the corridor toward the kitchen.

There were greeted there by the aroma of his favorite lemon and almond cake and the sight of his mother giving instructions to the chef. Lorcan's legs carried him into kitchen. His mind was numb with confusion.

His mother looked at him with her soft green eyes, which gleamed with tears of joy when she saw him. She opened her arms wide. Lorcan rushed in and embraced her, almost lifting her off her feet. She released him and cupped his face with her hands.

"Look at you, you're tired." Then she rubbed his back warmly. "How are your injuries?"

"I'm okay, Mother." Lorcan smiled. His mother had no memories of what had happened after he'd run into her arms with claw wounds on his back a few days ago. Keeva walked into the kitchen and stared at the chef—the same chef she'd seen dead on the floor. The chef frowned at the tears on Keeva's face.

"What happened, Keeva? Are you okay, sweetheart? Why are you crying?"

His mother approached Keeva and wiped the tears from her face. Keeva was dumbstruck and couldn't say a thing. Riley and Noah stepped into the kitchen.

"This is my friend Riley and his son Noah," Lorcan said. "This is my mother."

Riley nodded a greeting. "Nice to meet you, Mrs. Brody. Lorcan has talked about you a lot."

"Call me Jane." She smiled. "Have you just arrived? Stay with us for a while. There are plenty of beautiful sights to see. I'm sure Noah would enjoy it."

Riley was about to say something, but Lorcan cut in. "We'll go for a walk in the woods, Mother."

"That's a good idea," Jane said. "Come home early for brunch."

Lorcan nodded and strode out. Riley and Keeva rushed after him. Riley turned at Noah. "You stay at home, Noah. Don't say anything to anyone before I figure out what's going on. Can you promise me?"

Noah nodded.

At the edge of the woods, Lorcan turned around. "I broke the curse on my parents, and as a result, Orla died. Is that what this is all about? Is that what you saw, Keeva?"

"No. I don't know . . . You don't know that Orla is dead."

"What curse?" Riley asked.

"You don't need to know , Riley. But I need to see for myself." Lorcan turned around and hurried away. He tore through the forest like it was nothing, breaking through the tall grasses and young trees as he ran blindly.

He had no idea where Orla's house was, but he followed his instinct. There was a familiar trail of her scent in the air, and he followed it. He didn't know when his sense had become that developed, but he could feel every delicate scent and sound around him. He kept running.

And there it was. He stopped just inside the treeline, looking into the gardens behind Orla's house. He stood there, hidden in the foliage, as Orla walked out into the garden followed by a woman. She was alive. Lorcan was deliriously happy. She was walking and talking there, right in front of him.

But how could he know that this wasn't just another illusion? Lorcan stepped out and entered the garden.

Orla saw him, and tears immediately poured down her face.

"Lorcan! You're alive!" She ran toward him but was held back by the woman behind her.

"Stop right there or you'll kill her!" the woman yelled at him, and that stopped him in his tracks.

"Let me go, Alana!" Orla protested. Alana was the same size as Orla, but for some reason she appeared to be incredibly strong. Orla couldn't free herself from her grip and appeared to weaken by the second. Her eyes reddened, and he could see the vein on her forehead begin to throb. She grunted in pain. When Alana released her, she fell to the ground.

Lorcan charged toward Orla, but Alana warned him again. "She's sworn in with the clan and will be their leader. If she keeps thinking about you, she'll burst into flames."

Lorcan could see a shade of the fire in Orla's eyes. He withdrew, backing up so quickly that he almost fell on his backside. "Knock her out, Alana! Please!" he yelled.

"If you don't want her to think about you, don't come here."

"Lorcan, don't leave me!" Orla called out, lying on the grass. Her eyes glassed over.

"I'm sorry, Orla," Lorcan said and ran away as fast as he could, but he could still hear her whispering, "Lorcan, take me home. Don't leave me. Take me home with you . . ."

Lorcan ran and ran, not realizing that tears were streaming down his face. He'd lost her—not in death, but in life. Which one was worse, he couldn't say. He collided with Riley, and both fell to the ground.

Riley stood up. "What the heck, Lorcan?"

Keeva approached, panting. As Lorcan stood , Keeva pointed behind them, shaking. When he turned around, he saw the yellow wolf that he'd fought before. He faced it, putting his arms out in front of him and showing the beast he was unarmed. The wolf's eyes darted back and forth from his hands to his face, then to his friend and sister, searching for the biggest threat.

"I don't know why you're here, but I'm not going to shift, and I'm not going to fight you, either, unless you attack my companions." The wolf cocked its head like it was listening to what he had to say. It then hunched low to the ground, preparing to spring. Lorcan didn't move, and the wolf launched its heavy body into the air. When it landed, its front paws were on Lorcan's chest, and it closed its jaws on his throat.

Keeva screamed, and Riley dove forward to help, but Lorcan used his hands to wave them away. Obediently, they moved away , and then Lorcan lay still, arms flat on the ground, not fighting at all. The wolf's heavy breath made little eddies of dirt swirl near his ear, but still he didn't move. The wolf gently let go of his throat and backed up a little so it could see Lorcan's face. Lorcan just stared back at it, not trying to be intimidating or anything of the sort, just staring. The wolf climbed off of him and ran off, disappearing back into the green foliage of the forest.

For a few minutes, no one moved. No one made a sound. Then Riley came over and helped Lorcan to his feet. Lorcan had just opened his mouth to thank Riley for his help when Riley pulled back an arm with a fist attached and let it fly. His fist connected Lorcan's cheek with a satisfying crack, and Lorcan fell to the ground once more.

"You're pathetic, Lorcan. You wanted that dog to rip your throat out, didn't you?"

This time it was Keeva who helped Lorcan to his feet, but as soon as he was up, she yanked her hand back. Lorcan looked into her face and saw the same anger he had heard clearly in Riley's voice, maybe tempered with a little fear.

"Today is not a good day to die. I have lots of things to do. You got your punch in, are you happy now?"

Riley threw his arms in the air in frustration.

Lorcan continued. "I just saw Orla. She's alive."

"That's good, isn't it?" Keeva asked in a shaky voice.

"I'm sorry if I scared you. After I found out that Orla can never be with me if she wants to remain alive, and after I saw her running toward me even knowing the consequences, I wanted to let that wolf tear my throat out. I just couldn't think straight."

"What's the news?" Riley asked.

"Orla asked me not to leave her and to take her home. She would fight to the death for what she wants, and she's definitely not the kind to leave a dying wish."

Riley chuckled. "Couldn't agree more. So that's a hint then."

Lorcan nodded. "A way out for us, I think. I just have to figure out how to get there."

Lorcan turned and headed home with Keeva trailing behind. "Don't you feel the need to fill me in at all?" she said. "I met your girlfriend for the first time a couple of days ago, and Riley gets to know a load more stuff about your life out there." Keeva pointed at Riley.

"And he suffered for it, Keeva." Lorcan smiled and ruffled Keeva's hair. "Okay, for both of you—the condensed version is that Orla is a sorceress."

"What?" Keeva asked incredulously.

"Just accept it—*if* you want the rest of the story. Her family uses black magic and won't allow her to be with me. To save me, she made a promise to return to her family. Then she broke her promise, and we ran away together. We currently live and work at a place that you could say is . . . off planet."

"You're alien? I thought you were a werefox," Keeva said.

"I'll take the alien theory," Riley said and pulled out a piece of paper from his pocket. "I tested your blood last night in my portable lab. Only half of your DNA is human."

Lorcan cocked an eyebrow. "And what's the other half?"

"I need a more sophisticated machine to analyze that result," Riley answered.

"What about werefox?" Keeva asked. "I saw you turn into one."

"Werefoxes are mythical creatures, Keeva, and I don't understand their makeup. But even the werefox say I'm not one of them. On a mission in

Japan, I was bitten by a one, and the next thing I knew, I could turn into one and could heal my wounds quickly, as you've already seen."

"You make it too simple, Lorcan. And you left out the part that you nearly died a few times before heading off to that outer space place," Riley said.

Keeva turned, looking at Lorcan, her eyes welling up. "And you didn't tell me or our parents any of that! Didn't it ever occur in your brain that we're your family, and we care for you, regardless of where you are?" She stormed away.

Lorcan glared at Riley. "Did you need to stir that up?"

"It's a fact, that's life. She needs to know life out there is tough. Your life is hard and not cushy like hers. She thinks the last few days is proof that she's grown up and mature. She thinks having some psychic connections to Noah make her understand him more than I do, and that she can pass judgment on me and tell me how to raise my son . . ."

A clump of dirt hit on Riley's chest.

"Hey!" he yelled.

Keeva picked up more dirt and grass and kept throwing. "Now that you've fixed my brother, you can pack up your stuff, your kid, your cat, and your life and get the hell out of my head!" she yelled back.

"I have no intention of getting into your head given how muddy it is with all that psychic stuff. I have enough to worry about!"

"Hey! Stop it, you two. I have a curse to break. We have a life and death matter here. And you're going nowhere, Riley. I need your help." Lorcan pointed at his sister. "And you, young lady, I need you to help take care of Mother. Can you do that?"

Keeva glared at Riley and turned on her heel, stomping away. They all headed home.

CHAPTER 10

The heat was eating up her brain. Orla didn't know it would hurt so much. She had sworn in at the temple in order to get the potion for Bradan. But she thought she'd had it covered and had tricked her gods. She had sworn to death if she loved any man who hated her family on Earth. And Lorcan didn't hate the family. He had a temper, and he could kill. But he wasn't capable of hate. So it couldn't be her swearing in that was hurting her at the moment.

She wondered if Lorcan had gotten her hint. They understood each other, but given the situation, he might not be able to think straight. She needed him to take her out of here and back to the Daimon Gate and Eudaiz. She needed him. He had to be able to see through the haze of the pain and confusion.

How had she ended up back here? She had left Bradan in the woods with Maeve and had gone for Lorcan. What had happened next? She tried to remember, but her mind kept coming back blank. Then she recalled it. It was the wolf. A gigantic yellow wolf had knocked her out and had taken her back here. When she woke up, Alana was looming over her, ranting about how she had gotten out under Alana's watch again, making her look like a fool. Orla lied to Alana and said she'd gone out for fresh air and had gotten lost. She knew the excuse was lame, but Alana accepted it and didn't ask any more questions.

Orla tried to stand up, but her legs buckled and she fell to the floor. Alana cursed and helped her up.

"I want to go and get some help for you, Orla. Get Bradan and Uncle Daly. But I have no confidence that you won't run away again, even in your current condition. So I'm going to call Bradan's cell phone again, and hopefully he'll answer this time," Alana said, wagging her finger at Orla, warning her not to make a move.

She dialed and tapped her finger impatiently on the table next to the phone. "I'm going to get you a doctor, so sit still, Orla." Alana warned her again. "Damn it, Bradan doesn't pick up his cell. What's the point of having it?" Alana slammed the phone down.

Orla stood up again and staggered toward the door. "Sit down." Alana grabbed her from behind, but Orla elbowed her. Alana roared in pain, pulled Orla's hair, and slapped her so hard that they both fell on the floor.

Orla saw stars. The pain in her head was so unbearable that she could feel her life leaving her. She didn't know why her protective spells weren't working.

Maeve walked in and rushed over to help her up. "Are you okay?" Then she turned to Alana and asked, "What did you do to her?"

Alana stood with hands on her hips. "What did *I* do to *her*? I tried to help, and she hit me. What's wrong with her—apart from the obvious?"

"She's in agony. Can't you see that?" Maeve raised her voice.

"I'm the one in agony. I've had enough of this. I'll call the aunties and uncles, and they can come over and sort this out. And you? They won't be happy seeing you here, Maeve."

Orla's eyes were almost rolled up entirely in her head. She could feel someone using dark magic on her, but she was too weak and in too much pain to cast her protective spell.

"Why is she in so much pain?" Maeve asked.

"Ask her boyfriend. If I were her best friend, as you claim you are, I'd go and tell him to stay away," Alana said.

Orla leaned back in the chair and closed her eyes. She heard Maeve whispering in her mind, the way they had always communicated. *"Are you in physical pain, or is this the work of black magic?"*

"It's the magic. I need to raise my protective shield. The pain is stopping me," Orla responded in her mind.

"I thought you were going to find Lorcan?" Maeve asked.

"I did, but something attacked me on the way. I think it was a wolf. The next thing I knew, I was lying here in the front yard. Then Alana found me and took me inside," Orla responded.

"Why are you here?"

"I sensed shapeshifters in your direction just after you left, so I went to check on you."

Orla appeared to be resting with her eyes closed. Maeve pulled out a small bottle.

"Hey, what are you doing? She isn't going to take any of your white magic potion," Alana said.

"There's no magic in this, just pure medicine to help with the pain."

"I don't know that. And I don't know you. Everyone will be furious with me. Bradan and Uncle Daly will be so pissed." Alana approached and pulled Maeve away from Orla.

"You don't even want to know why I'm here?" Maeve asked.

"I don't care. Now get out of this house. I've called everyone. They'll eat you alive."

Maeve put Bradan's and Daly's chain necklaces on the table. They were unique symbolic clan items that only left their persons when they were dead. Alana stared at the items and froze. Taking advantage of Alana's distraction, Maeve poured the potion into Orla's mouth.

The medicine was like liquid gold. Orla could feel it wash through her system and her mind and ease the pain. She wished she could have a fraction of Maeve's skills in natural medicine.

"Are they dead?" Alana's voice shook.

"I'm sorry Alana, but yes. I found them, or what was left of them, in the woods."

Tears flopped down on Alana's face. "Oh God, oh my God." She walked back and forth, raking her hands through her hair. Orla glanced at Maeve, and they signaled each other and both stormed out of the door at once.

"Hey!" Alana yelled after them. In the front garden, Orla sensed a wedge of energy. "It's too late, they're here already. You go, Maeve. If you get to see Lorcan, tell him to get me out of here. As long as I am off this planet and with him, we'll be fine."

She pushed Maeve away before she could protest. As soon as Orla turned back, the entire family had flooded the front yard . Alana rushed out from the house. "She was trying to run again!" she cried. "Maeve helped her. It wasn't my fault. The two of them are wicked."

"Be quiet, Alana. Your only job was to guard her, and look at what happened," Aunt Anna scolded.

"Come on, she's young and inexperienced. And our up and coming leader is not exactly an innocent soul." Uncle Tony chuckled and wrapped his arm around Orla's shoulder. "Let's get you inside the house so we can talk."

Orla knew the arm around her shoulders wasn't there for protection. Uncle Tony hadn't seemed to like Uncle Daly much when she saw them a few nights ago, but she had a feeling that he wasn't exactly happy about their deaths, either."

Alana stood watching as he escorted Orla back into the house. Her lips trembled, and tears gleamed in her eyes. For the first time, Orla felt sorry for her. Her life here must be horrible. Orla wondered why she didn't leave when she had a chance.

Maeve ran as fast as she could back to her place. It wasn't exactly a mansion, but it was protected and blessed by love and cared for by her mother. It was comfortable enough. But now, apart from bringing back the memories of her mother, the house didn't give her much. There had been countless times Maeve wondered what kept her here.

Her mother had said she could leave at any time—go to a large city, make friends, have a life.

Didn't she have a life? Maybe she didn't. Bradan had entered her life and left her defenseless. She had met him at the village festival, one of those events that didn't discriminate against religion or theological belief. Then she'd found out he was her very distant cousin from the black magic clan. And with that knowledge came the end of her dream.

Bradan was a black magic sorcerer. She was a white witch. She thought her devotion to her God could do her good. But what she had gotten instead was a joke of faith.

Maeve stormed into the bedroom. Well, it was her bedroom, but she let Bradan sleep in it, and she slept on the couch in the living room. She touched his forehead and found that his fever was gone. Before she could withdraw her hand, he grabbed it.

"I was just checking your temperature, Bradan."

He let go her hand.

"I'll bring some food and water for you. The medicine and the instructions are on the table. Can you take care of that yourself?"

"Where are you going?"

"Someone in your clan wanted you dead. I let the news out to see who would do the happy dance."

"Where's Orla?"

"She's stuck. She was going to Lorcan's, but they caught her. No—she said a wolf got her and took her back. Now I have to go to Lorcan to ask him to get her out of there."

"The full moon is getting closer. If they think I'm dead, then they'll hang on very tightly to Orla. Getting her out isn't going to be easy."

"They should be happy. She's sworn in. They'll think they can hold her. That she dare not run away."

"She swore in? What the fuck?"

Maeve stared at Bradan. "I always thought it was required. Something you did at a very young age."

"It is, but I didn't do it, either. That's why my father was so upset in the woods. He wanted me to swear in before the full moon. We argued, and the next thing I knew, he was dead. And now it's Orla . . . why did she do that?"

"The claws from that monster bird had poisoned your blood. I told Orla that the potion in the temple was the only solution."

Bradan banged his head back down on the pillow. "And she had to swear in to get it! Fuck! Fuck! Fuck!" He punctuated the curses with the banging of his head.

"That's not very helpful, Bradan! Is there a way out of this?"

"Someone has to love her enough to take the challenge."

"What kind of challenge?"

"It's not possible, so don't ask."

"Just tell me."

"Maeve, no one is going to love anyone enough to do such a stupid thing."

"Is that what you really believe?"

"I am a black magic sorcerer, what do you want me to say?"

"If that's what you believe, why didn't you swear in when you were a kid?"

"As long as I'm here, as long as I'm with the family, that's what I am going to do. I will do the right thing, regardless of whether I believe it will work or not."

"If that's your plan, why argue with your father?"

Bradan turned to face the wall.

"Bradan!"

"Please leave me alone, Maeve."

"All right. But answer one last question. What would you have done if Orla hadn't come back this time?"

Silence.

"Bradan, we risked our lives to save you. We deserve an answer."

Bradan turned back and looked at her. "I would run, Maeve. I would do what Orla did years ago. That was always my plan. That's why my father was so upset."

She waved her arms in the air and was about to spit out a sarcastic remark, but then she realized she didn't have grounds. She let her hands flop to her sides. "Fair enough. If she hadn't come back, in a few days you would have just disappeared . . . would have run away from your black magic family. Oh God . . . I wasted my whole life . . ."

"Excuse me?"

"Don't worry. You don't have to run any more as Orla will take the shit for you. I have to get to Lorcan. We'll figure something out to save Orla. Take care of yourself. There's plenty of food in the house."

Maeve turned to leave. She heard Bradan try to get off the bed but fall back down again. She locked the door from the outside and left.

CHAPTER 11

As soon as Keeva walked through their front gate, she staggered back a few steps. Riley grabbed her elbow I support. She shrugged him off, but his grip was firm. "Are you okay?" Riley gazed into her eyes.

"What's wrong, Keeva?" Lorcan asked.

She shook her head. "Just feeling uneasy. I don't know what it is . . ."

"If you have a vision, I want you to tell me. Promise?" Lorcan asked. Keeva nodded.

Then she dropped to her knees, breathing heavily, and tears started streaming down her face.

Lorcan reached for her, but Riley pushed him aside. Riley held Keeva, rubbing her back up and down and rocking her, exactly the way he'd done to Noah. "Take it easy. Deep breaths. There you go. Calm down, Keeva. It'll pass."

She was gasping, and she nuzzled into Riley's chest as he kept caressing her back, but she couldn't calm down.

"What do you see, Keeva?" Lorcan asked.

"Nothing. I can't see anything." Tears streamed down her face, and at the same time, pain stabbed at Lorcan's chest. He knew it had to be bad news.

"Keeva?" he called her gently.

"Don't push her," Riley scolded.

"I can't see, Lorcan. I know it's bad, but I can't see." Keeva freed herself from Riley's hold and darted into the house. Jane walked out of the kitchen and saw Keeva, but before she could ask anything, Keeva charged past her and ran toward Noah's room.

In the guest room, Noah sat in the corner of the bed with tears glistening in his eyes. Aris sat next to him, meowing noisily. Keeva held Noah's hand. "Did you see anything? You saw more than me, right? Noah, please!"

Noah looked at Riley who had just entered the room. Riley nodded. Noah squeezed Keeva's hands. "I saw your father. I'm sorry."

"Oh God," Keeva cried out loud. "How? Where? That must be why he didn't answer his phone all night."

"Is he dead?" Lorcan asked.

"I don't know."

"Can you tell where he is?"

Noah shook his head. "It was dark. There were rocks . . . and water. He was in his car."

Noah looked up and toward the door. Everyone turned to see Jane standing in the doorway. She was quiet, and she didn't ask for an explanation. Jane contemplated and then said, "The cliffs. He's at the cliffs."

"It's a very large area if he drove back from town that way," Lorcan said.

Aris meowed louder and then began to hiss until he got some attention. Noah looked at the kitten, then he looked at everyone and said, "Aris knows where to find him."

The winter breeze cut into his skin, but Lorcan couldn't feel much. The cliff was high and steep, and any car slipping off the country road and dropping down there wouldn't have a chance of survival. His father, as far as he knew, didn't have any special ability with which to heal himself.

Pain pounded in his chest, and every vein in his head throbbed—it was the agony of loss. What had he said to his father last time they spoke? He couldn't remember. He had been on the verge of passing out after being hit by the bullet.

Lorcan's eyes were glued on the kitten, who strode straight ahead in front of them. The others were saying something, but Lorcan wasn't paying attention. He cursed silently. He needed to find his father. It would be his fault if he died. His father wouldn't agree, but hell, they never agreed on anything.

Aris stopped in front of a puddle. There was a fresh skid mark in the mud. He followed the track to the edge of the cliff and saw his father's car teetering on a rock ledge twenty feet down. The ledge wasn't too far down from where they stood, but from there downward, it seemed like an endless drop.

Lorcan turned, angled himself, and began to climb down. Riley pulled at him. "Don't! Let me call for help," Riley said.

"It'll be too late. With this wind, the car will slip off the rock at any second," Lorcan said and continued his descent.

"You can't hold the car back with your bare hands!"

"I'll pull him out."

"That's crazy, Lorcan!"

He ignored Riley and kept climbing down. It didn't take him long to reach the ledge. It was large enough to hold maybe half a car and maybe four people. He could see his father trapped in the dangling car.

"Father!"

His father opened his eyes and turned to look at him. He blinked a few times as if to make sure it was really Lorcan who was standing beside the car.

"Hang on, Father, I'm going to get you out. Can you undo your seatbelt?" he asked as he approached the car to open the door.

"Don't touch it! It'll fall!" Ferris waved Lorcan away, and his slight movement rocked the car.

"No, no, don't move, Father—just unbuckle your seatbelt for me."

Lorcan heard a sound behind him and saw Riley jump down onto the rock behind him. Lorcan could see his father release the seatbelt then lean toward the passenger side. The car rocked even more.

"Don't move, Father! Stay still!" Lorcan approached and gingerly grabbed the door handle. His father sat straight up, holding a small red box in his hand and reached out the broken window to hand it to Lorcan.

"Take this, son."

The car rocked more and slipped a bit. The handle slipped out of Lorcan's grasp.

"Don't move!"

"Take the box," Ferris scolded and thrust the box out. The car slid more with his movement.

"All right, all right." Lorcan grabbed the box and tossed it to Riley . Then he grabbed the handle and yanked the door open. The car was tipped precariously at the edge. Lorcan grabbed his father's arm.

"Let go of me, Lorcan. The hand brake broke and bent when the car went over the cliff and landed here. It pierced me—I'm stuck with the car. Don't hang on to me. You'll be dragged down, too."

Lorcan lifted the side of his father's jacket and saw that the handbrake had pinned him to his seat.

"I'll get you out of there." Lorcan grabbed his father's shoulders. The car started to tip.

"Let go!" his father yelled.

"No!" Lorcan pulled at his father.

"Don't do this, Lorcan."

The car rocked and rocked and slipped even further.

Riley braced himself against the rock and grabbed hold of Lorcan's belt from behind. Lorcan yanked his father out of the car just before it dropped into the nothingness below. Papers flew out from inside the car, floating in the air and raining down to the bottom of the gully.

Blood was everywhere.

Lorcan had his father half on and half off the rock ledge, and he could see a large gash on his father's stomach which extended all the way up to his chest. He pulled his father up into the safety of his arms. "We're going to get you up top. And you're lucky—we have a doctor handy. Riley!" Lorcan called out. Riley inched forward but said nothing.

"Say something, will you?" Lorcan asked.

"I'm afraid there's nothing I can do. This is too much damage, Lorcan . . ."

"You can help him. You're a good doctor. Please . . ."

Ferris opened his eyes. "The box . . ."

"Here!" Riley handed it over quickly.

His father looked at him with the eyes of a dying man. "You never belonged here, Lorcan . . . Your mother and I needed you . . . she loves you too much . . . I love you too much . . . we broke our promise . . ."

"Please don't talk. I'll take you to the hospital."

"We called the paramedics. They're coming," Riley said.

Ferris smiled weakly. "I've lived long enough. I wanted a child for your mother, but I had no idea of the consequences. I signed up for the project, but I thought it was just a scientific experiment. It was too late when I found out it was extraterrestrial. They took half of my DNA and with the other half they created . . . Your profile and your special abilities were documented on the papers in the car . . ."

"I don't care."

"You should, Lorcan. We were supposed to have you for only ten years. But your mother couldn't let you go, so we didn't give you back. When you took off with Orla, we thought it might be for the best. We would rather lose you, knowing you were safe on Earth and being human, than let them take you."

Tears rolled down Lorcan's face.

"The tears and the emotions are the human part of you. Treasure them, Lorcan. I don't know what the other part will do to those things, but I know you're special. You have several powerful abilities . . ."

"You didn't want to give me back, so now they decide to kill you?"

"Keeping my promise will save me. If I had pressed the button inside the red box, they would have done whatever I wanted within their power. But I don't need that. All I need is your mother, you, and Keeva . . ."

"Can they save you now if I press it?"

"No. I broke my promise, and that was the end of that deal . . . But that red box is my only connection to them. You are their subject, and they will save you, whatever it takes. I wasn't sure you'd survive the bullet at the house, so I went to retrieve the box . . ."

They heard the sound of the rescue helicopter hovering in the air.

"Father, you're going to be fine."

"Take care of your mother and Keeva, Lorcan."

"No, that's *your* job. You said I don't belong here."

"I'm afraid I can't do it anymore. Press the button in the box and find out your origin, but please try to maintain contact with your mother and sister. You're all they have now . . ." He closed his eyes to catch his breath.

"One more thing . . . I didn't drive off the road . . . There was a large puma . . . It jumped out right in front of the car . . ." he trailed off, and then he was gone.

"No, no! Don't die, don't leave me!" The pain was unbearable—he was losing a part of his soul. His was a family he had always taken for granted his whole life, and now he'd just learned that it had never really been his. Something was tearing at his heart, and he knew now that it was the human part of him.

The other part of him was heating up. Whatever it was, it was eating at him right now. Uncontrollable. He saw sparks of electrical waves in front of him. The energy surging inside him was unstoppable. More sparks and energy erupted everywhere like lightning in a storm. He heard Riley said something, ask him not to do something.

What was he talking about?

The air around him was chaotic. His mind was a mess. The helicopter hovered, but was being flung back and forth in the air as if it were a toy dangling from a rope in the wind. He heard the others yelling from the top of the cliff, and he could make out shouting coming from the helicopter and from Riley behind him.

Was he sending out that electric current again?

He looked around and saw large patches of rocks tumbling from the cliffs nearby.

More yelling. Were they yelling at him?

The helicopter approached. He watched as a wave of electric current hit it. There was screaming as it spun and dove downward. But then the chopper regained balance and flew back up again. Lorcan realized it must be him. But he couldn't control the electric current emanating from him. Riley called out again for him to stop.

He turned to tell Riley he hadn't done anything, and all saw was Riley staggering back and rolling off the edge, hanging on to the ledge by his fingertips. In a haze of confusion, he grabbed Riley's hands and hoisted him back onto the rock.

"Look away from me!" Riley shouted.

Lorcan didn't understand, but he obeyed. He turned away, facing his back to Riley. More patches of rocks at a distance where his eyes landed thundered down the cliffs. He felt a punch at his temple from behind, and then the world went black.

CHAPTER 12

Orla worked her mind frantically for a way out of the situation. She had sent Maeve to Lorcan with the message, but she couldn't totally rely on that. Lorcan might have gotten the hint from her before, but to act on it wouldn't be easy. He didn't have any experience in doing magic, and he didn't know the lay of the land in her part of the woods at all.

Uncle Tony seemed to be the one in charge now that Uncle Daly was gone. There were countless of others in the family that she didn't recognize or remember. They sat quietly in the house, waiting for Tony's instructions. Her magic class had had several kids, but the elite group had only a handful groomed for the leadership position. Now that she recalled , Bradan hadn't been in the elite group at all. But he was second in line after her.

How had this leadership line-up been determined? she wondered.

"We have only six days until the full moon. We can't afford any mistakes, or it will be another ten years of waiting," Tony said. "Now we don't have a choice now that Bradan is gone—we have only Orla." He turned toward her. "I'm sorry, Orla, we don't want to be rough on you, but I hope you understand the situation. You do have a track record of running away."

"What will happen if you don't have me?" she asked.

"We don't even want to consider that possibility now, dear," Aunt Anna said.

"I don't want this, so I'm going to be a very bad leader—or even worse, do something that harms the family!"

Tony chuckled. "Thanks for pointing that out, but don't worry. You don't have to manage anything."

Orla narrowed her eyes. "You just want a puppet leader? Maybe a sacrificial lamb?"

Tony laughed. "You can choose to be a puppet if you don't want to be involved or you're lacking in talent. As far as being a sacrificial lamb, don't worry, we don't kill our own."

"What exactly does the position require?" Tony glanced at Anna, and then back at Orla. She continued, "I'm entitled to know. You should know by now that I'm stubborn, and I have nothing to lose here."

Tony nodded. "All right. You're going to know sooner or later. This full moon is not like any others. This is the cycle when the full energy will be loaded onto the current leader. And of course, it will later be distributed to us."

"You want me to serve as a vessel?"

"You will be a pure channel to receive the power from our God. You will be powerful, and you should consider it an honor."

"What if I keep the power to myself?"

"You will always keep the power. Part of the power will be transferred to us via ceremonies because we are family, but the transfer will not weaken you as it doesn't take anything from you."

Orla smiled. "Only if I stay with the family forever, right?"

"Yes. That's the one condition. I'm glad we are coming to an understanding."

Orla smiled. "I'm afraid I can't help you with the mission. I'm no longer a part of this family. If I receive the power, I will not be transferring to you naturally."

A few uncles and aunts stood up, and the room hummed with discussion.

"What do you mean?"

"I was married to Lorcan in front of God. I belong to him and to his family. You can give me the power if you like, but you know where it will be transferred."

Tony's face turned red . "Why did you marry a man you don't love?"

"I love Lorcan."

Tony swung his arm, and a beam of fire hit the ceilings, burning a large hole. "If you love him, and you married him, you would be dead. Either you lied to us just now, or you didn't swear in!"

Someone sneaked into the room and whispered something into Anna's ear. "Hold on," Anna interrupted before Tony continued his rant.

"The potion is missing," Anna said.

"What potion?" Tony asked.

"The one at the temple. The *one*."

Tony's hiss was audible. "It wasn't in plain sight. Only the entitled can see it." He fired a deadly look at Orla. "You took it?"

"I took what?" Orla asked.

"You took the potion from the temple. The one for the ceremony," Tony growled.

"I don't even know what it is—why would I take it?"

Tony roared and blasted another stream of fire into the wall. "I can make another one," Anna said.

"There's not enough time," Tony roared again and paced the floor.

"I said I can make it—if I go now, and if you can handle the other housekeeping matters." Anna shot a look at Orla and scurried to the door. Chatter filled the room.

"Quiet!" Tony demanded. The noise died down instantly.

"How can I be sure that you were married in front of God," Tony asked Orla.

"You can't. But you can risk it and go through with the ceremony and see if the power is transferred to Lorcan's family."

"Someone has to ask Lorcan to denounce their marriage in front of our god at the temple," Tony said.

"I can do it," Alana said from the corner. "I don't want to be her warden, but I'll deliver the message for you."

"You do know that you have to cross to *that* side of the woods to do it, right?" Tony asked.

"I know." Alana bit her lip slightly. "Can I take a man with me for protection?"

Tony shrugged and pointed to someone sitting next to the window. "Sam, go with her." Then he turned back to Alana. "Tell Lorcan to be at the temple tomorrow at noon—or else." Then he move toward Orla. She maintained a stern stare and didn't back down. In a flash, she saw Tony's hand come at her, and then the whole world went black.

Lorcan groggily opened his eyes and saw the blurry ceiling and the headboard of the bed looming over him. Images of furniture and other decorative items floated in the air, flickered, and then settled. He blinked to clear his vision. His limbs didn't seem to belong to him, and each of his movements felt as if he was trying to move a mountain.

He remembered it now—the incident at the cliffs, the death of his father, and what his father had said before he died.

He was officially an orphan.

He must have drained all of his energy in electric waves at the cliffs in a haze of confusion and emotional pain. His human subconscious and the other part of him were tangled in a gigantic mess. He felt a tug at his hand and found Aris licking it.

"Thank you, Aris," he muttered. The door slid open and Noah walked in with a glass of water.

Lorcan smiled. "Since when can you read my mind, Noah?"

Lorcan sat up and gratefully took the water from him. The boy climbed onto the bed and hugged him. "I'm sorry about your father."

Lorcan held Noah in his arms and rubbed his back. "Me, too. Where is everyone?"

"Downstairs. Your mother and Keeva just got back from wherever they went to make arrangements for your father. Keeva was okay. She didn't cry much."

"Where's your father?"

"He's with Keeva. Glued to her. He said he had to keep an eye on her. Showing support and all that. But I know he likes her."

"And do you mind that, Noah?"

"Mind what?"

"If Keeva took the place of your mother, would you mind that?"

Noah shook his head. "No one will take the place of my mother. She's in heaven. But I think Keeva saw my mother, and they might have an agreement between them for her to take care of my father."

Lorcan chuckled. "Now you're weirding me out . . . What happened at the cliffs?"

"You shot something from your eyes—like a machine gun or something. It took down a lot of rocks on the cliffs and some trees, and you would've shot down the helicopter if my father hadn't knocked you out. I think he told the rescue people that you and he were trying to stop a special weapon that had automatically discharged. He said the weapon had belonged to your father, but it went over the cliffs."

Lorcan raised an eyebrow. "They bought that story?"

Noah shrugged. "They must have. It was chaotic. Stuff was flying everywhere, and it was foggy. Nobody saw much." Noah rubbed Aris's ears. "I had a vision."

Lorcan stiffened. "What did you see?"

"It was a happy one actually. I don't get it, though. I saw a beautiful blue fox, a golden wolf, and a black tiger."

Lorcan rolled his eyes. "The blue fox is me, just so you know."

Noah's jaw dropped. "Wow, really, Uncle Lorcan? It was magnificent!"

"Is there a reason you think I can't be a magnificent blue fox?"

"No, it's so cool. But about the wolf and the tiger? Who are they?"

"Why do you believe me that easily?"

"Because you never tell me lies."

Lorcan nodded. "I think you saw a puma, rather than a black tiger. Before he died, my father said a puma jumped out in front of his car. That was why he veered off the road. I've seen the yellow wolf twice. I'm sure it's some kind of magical creature."

"Werewolf?"

Lorcan nodded. "Are you scared?"

Noah shook his head.

"You said they were friendly in your vision."

"Yes, but I only saw one at a time. I'm not sure if they're friends or not. Was the yellow wolf friendly with you when you saw it?"

Lorcan shook his head. "Not exactly. The problem is I don't know what he wants. I think he might be friendly." Lorcan got off the bed, bracing his palms on the wall to keep balance and wishing he'd gotten a bit more rest to regain his energy. He shook his head to chase off his fatigue and went downstairs.

The living room was still the same, the air in the house was still the same. He found his mother in a black dress standing in the middle of the living room. Keeva was bringing her some tea, and Riley trailed just behind her. Everyone turned to look at Lorcan, and it was a different look from the way they'd looked at him before.

He just stood there in the hallway, finding his limbs useless. Jane stood up and approached Lorcan. She embraced him. That felt the same—his mother's embrace, the feel of her body, and the sound of her voice, a voice that had soothed his tantrums away when he was just a stubborn kid.

At this moment, he so needed Orla. She was the part of his life that he had never taken for granted. He had to fight for her. But his family—or what he had always thought was his family—he had taken it for granted. Now, he had nothing. He had no one.

When he didn't hug his mother back, she looked up at him. "I'm so sorry. I tried to save Father. I tried to pull him back. But the . . ."

Jane put her hand over his mouth to stop him from talking. "None of that was your fault. When you were six, you promised to build me a castle, and you promised to make me proud and happy. I'm still holding you to that."

"You don't hate me?" A tear fell from his eye. Jane wiped it and cupped his face.

"You are my son, my treasure, whether you like it or not. Come sit with me. I want to talk to you, and it will be your decision whether or not you still consider us to be your family."

When everyone had settled around the table in the living room, Jane looked at Lorcan over the rim of her cup of tea.

"We had been just married and were still on our honeymoon. Your father and I went for a picnic at the riverbank, the one he forbade you to go to. We were attacked by wild animals. At least that was the story for the official records. But I knew back then that it wasn't just wild animals."

"Shapeshifters?" Lorcan asked.

Jane nodded. "A whole pack of them. They were going to kill your father, and I couldn't take it. I was on my own in the middle of the woods. I didn't know what to do, so I begged and promised to do whatever it took if they'd spare his life." A tear rolled down her face. "The head of the clan wanted a daughter, and he was going to rape me. I told him I would kill myself if he did, and then he wouldn't have a child with me anyway. I don't know the reason why, but he needed a girl, and he need her within a certain period of time. So I made him a deal."

Lorcan looked at Jane. The tears had dried on her face, but he could see the pain was still raw and fresh.

"I told him if I got pregnant and our first child is a girl, he could have her. I said I would tell no one and lay no claim on the child."

Keeva gasped, and Lorcan saw Riley instantly grab her hand.

Lorcan nodded. He admired Jane—she was a strong woman, and she was fearless when it came to protecting those she loved. "That's how I came along?"

Jane nodded. "I wasn't pregnant at that point. We just had to make sure our first child wasn't a girl. Ferris never told me how he got you. He said it was best if I didn't know. And I always thought it was a closed adoption."

"Then you didn't know about the ten-year limit?"

Jane shook her head. "Not until a few months later. Had I known, I would never have accepted it. But the moment he brought you home, I fell in love with you. You became a part of my life the moment your father brought you through that door. The shapeshifter missed his chance, but he couldn't touch us."

"What stopped him from coming and grabbing Keeva or hurting you and Father if he found out?" Lorcan asked.

"It wasn't just a verbal deal. It was almost like an oath. For magical creatures, that's a big deal. We swore in front of his gods, and they gave me my protection. The lullaby that you always disliked, Lorcan, it would kill anyone in that clan if they broke their promise and tried to harm me or my family."

He remembered now—the lullaby had stopped the monstrous woman at the riverbank from killing him, the woman who had pretended to be Orla and then kissed him and controlled him to upset her. He didn't know much about shapeshifters, but he knew they were humans who could shift into animal forms. Maybe they could shift into other people's forms as well? He didn't know.

"How did you know they attacked me at the riverbank? How did you know to sing the song?"

"It was just gut instinct. I sensed you were coming home. I sensed danger. And the lullaby is the only protection I have for you. My senses when it comes to those shapeshifters are very strong. This time, it felt the same as it did so many years ago, when you came home after you kissed Orla."

"What?"

"Not long before Orla left, you came home reeking with the scent of that shapeshifter clan. You told me you had kissed her for the first time that day. And I knew she was related to them. I knew they were coming for Keeva, but I couldn't tell you why we wouldn't allow you to date Orla."

"But Orla had nothing to do with shapeshifters. Yes, her family does black magic, but it wasn't her choice to be born into that family. She wouldn't have anything to do with the shapeshifter clan you mentioned. Who's the clan's leader?"

"It's Bricius."

There was a buzzing in Lorcan's head. Bricius was one of the most dangerous sorcerers, the one who had cursed his parents and the reason he'd come back to Ireland this time. He was the one he had killed in another dimension. Bricius knew Orla and had taught in her black magic class.

Jane suddenly gasped. "They're coming now!" she said.

Lorcan looked toward the door and saw Alana and a man walking toward them with Maeve trailing behind.

CHAPTER 13

"**W**hich one? Can you tell, Mother?" Lorcan asked. He recognized Maeve, who had been with Orla before he got shot, and he recognized Alana, who had been holding Orla back when she'd tried to run to him. The two women had seemed to be on Orla's side. But he hadn't seen the man before.

Jane shook her head. "It was just the aura coming from them, but I don't know any of them," Jane said.

Alana walked into the house without invitation and spoke quickly before anyone could say anything. "My name is Alana. This is my cousin Sam. We're from Orla's family. We came to let you know that Orla has agreed to take leadership of our group, and in doing so, she will never see you again. But she did say that you were married in front of God. Therefore, you will have to denounce your marriage in front of our god."

"That's bogus. You guys are holding Orla against her will," Maeve said.

"Shut up, Maeve. You're not part of the family," Alana growled and turned back to Lorcan. "My family will be waiting at the temple at noon tomorrow. If you don't come . . ." She shifted her stance and glanced at Sam for instruction. Sam raised an eyebrow. Alana continued, "If you don't come, Orla will die."

"That's bullshit. It's a trap, Lorcan. They won't bring Orla there," Maeve hissed and pointed her finger at Alana. "And for your information, your family never kill their own."

"That's enough, Maeve," Sam growled.

"You come into my home without invitation, without permission, and you try to lure my son into a trap?" Jane said.

"It's not a trap. The temple is our place of family worship. Orla promised to be with us. All Lorcan has to do is to end their relationship—and do it for her sake. Why would he want to trap him?" Alana said.

"I'm warning you not to go there, Lorcan," Maeve raised her voice.

"It's not your call," Alana snarled.

"Which one of you is from Bricius's clan?" Jane's voice cut through the chaos like a hot knife through butter. She advanced. Lorcan had never seen such animosity in his mother before. "You can all leave except the one from Bricius's clan because that person is responsible for my husband's death."

"Hey!" Alana's voice shook. "We do black magic here!" She pointed her finger at Jane. Lorcan darted forward to stand next to his mother. Keeva and Riley advanced, but he gestured them to stay back.

Alana dropped her finger and withdrew. "We're just the messengers. Lorcan should go to the temple and talk to my family. You can come if you want." Jane moved toward her, and Alana backed away again.

"Let me ask once more, which one of you is from Bricius's clan." Jane's voice was as cold as steel.

Alana turned around. "Sam!"

"What?"

Alana grabbed him and pushed him forward, standing behind him. "Use some of your black magic! She's going to curse us," Alana said to him.

"All right, we've delivered the message. Take it or leave it—it's up to you. We're leaving." Sam turned leave, and Alana scurried after him.

Maeve glared at Jane. "Do you really think pulling a stunt like that is going to work on magical creatures?"

Jane smiled. "I have a very good singing voice. Let me sing you a song and see if you enjoy it. We can talk afterward." Lorcan knew his mother was going to sing the lullaby to see which one reacted to it.

They heard a crash. A large window shattered as a gigantic golden wolf flew through it and head straight at Jane. Lorcan pulled his mother out of the way, and the wolf landed on the table, smashing it to pieces.

Alana took one look at the wolf and fainted . Sam cursed and picked her up, rushing outside. The wolf bared its teeth and lunged at Jane. Lorcan shot an electric wave at the wolf. It dropped to the floor in convulsions. Lorcan dropped to his knees, exhausted.

Riley leaped at the wolf and grabbed it. It turned around and bit his right arm then sprung to its feet, running through the door. Lorcan stood up and charged after it, catching up to it at the edge of the woods.

"Hey!" he called out. Lorcan wasn't sure how much energy he had left, but he had a feeling he didn't have anything remaining to shoot at the wolf if it actually attacked him. But the wolf held the answers to many of his questions. He couldn't let it run away again. "Look, I told you before that I'm not going to fight you. I know you want something that I can offer. Let's work it out. I don't think you want to harm us unless we're threatening someone you care for, and that person belongs to Bricius's clan. Am I right?"

The wolf stopped and looked at Lorcan. It quickly glanced back to see if Riley or Keeva had caught up. There was no sign of them. The wolf's lips curled back from its teeth, and a low, rumbling growl came from its throat.

"Right, so we're friends now. Just tell me what you want, and we can work things out. I don't speak wolf, so you'll have to shift back to your human form."

On silent paws, the wolf took a step or two toward Lorcan, then hunkered down low to the ground and lifted its body up into the air in a giant leap, landing squarely on Lorcan's shoulders. The weight of the wolf made Lorcan stumble to the ground. Lorcan scissored his legs and flung the wolf away before it could take a bite of him. He planned to save the last electric shot he had for the worst case scenario. But for now, he could still handle it.

The wolf and Lorcan circled each other. It wouldn't shift its gaze because it thought he might shoot at it again, but Lorcan wouldn't waste his last beam that easily. The wolf ran out of patience quickly and charged at him again.

Lorcan braced for the impact. He'd learned an Aikido movement when he was younger. When a strong force came at a defender, a circling motion could utilize the force of the attacker. The harder the coming force, the worse the crash. As the wolf landed, Lorcan sidestepped in a half circle, grabbed its neck, swung, and released. The wolf flew through the air and smashed straight into a tree trunk. It howled in pain and crashed to the ground.

Riley and Keeva had arrived. Riley grabbed the wolf and jabbed a needle into it. It wriggled hard, biting and clawing at his arms. Riley held the wolf to the ground, and it whimpered under the pressure.

A wail from somewhere off in the forest made everyone cringe. It was a howl of pain and outrage, sadness and anger. While Lorcan was busy searching for the source of the sound, the yellow wolf bucked like a wild horse, throwing Riley off and rolling to its feet. Keeva jumped in to help. It took the two of them to force the wolf down again until the tranquilizer took effect.

Lorcan listened to the silence for a few more minutes. He didn't like it and did a mental check of his energy level. One shot was all he had left, he was sure of it. They heard the howl again, but this time it was closer. They heard a loud roar, and then a large shadow landed in front of them. It was a magnificent puma.

Lorcan cursed.

"Stay right here," he said to Riley and Keeva. Then he stood up and ran. The puma leapt after him. He knew he wouldn't be quick enough to outrun it, but he needed to get a bit of distance. The paws of the puma landed on his back. He rolled on the ground and felt blood gushing from his wounds. The puma was growling at him, advancing. He didn't have a good angle to shoot. He stood up and ran again. The animal pounced a second time, catching him in the side with one large paw. Lorcan jammed his foot at the puma's face, pushing it back a bit. He stood and raced off again, stumbling and falling to the ground. Taking advantage of the opportunity, the puma leapt up in the air so that it could land its front paws on Lorcan's chest. While flying, its chest and midsection were open to Lorcan.

He gave it one blast with all he had. The electric current shot out in a wave, curved up, and split into thousands of knives and spears flying at the puma. It roared painfully as the sharp blades hit it. Blood, fur, and flesh rained down to the ground. The puma dropped. It howled and clawed its way into the woods. Lorcan wanted to give chase but he lost sight of the animal as it loped into the cover of the trees.

Bradan ran aimlessly through the woods. Maeve had been gone for hours, and he couldn't let her fend for herself out there. They'd never been together, and he knew she would never consider him, but he wanted to tell her how much he cared for her. He couldn't bear the thought that she might never return to him, or that he'd die before he could tell her any of his feelings.

He knew he wasn't talented—in either black or white magic. He was just a guy who had stumbled into a bloodline of magical creatures and was lined up for a position of power. He didn't want it, but he had a responsibility, and people's lives depended on him. He was wrong to tell her he had planned to run away like Orla. The thought had crossed his mind, and he had planned on it—but he was a man. If anything, he had his integrity and honor. He was not going to run away like a little girl.

He had agreed to allow Maeve release the false news that he was dead in order to figure out who the traitor in the clan was and see who surfaced to claim the power. But he had never wanted her to risk her life to do so.

Where is she? he wondered.

He stopped by a tree to catch his breath, and then he saw them. Maeve and Alana, unconscious, bathed in blood. There were body parts scattered on the ground, torn into unrecognizable pieces. Both Maeve and Alana were breathing. He couldn't tell whose blood it was, but it was everywhere.

"Maeve!" He shook her shoulders. No response. He scrambled over to Alana and got the same result. He couldn't take both of them back to the village with him. He could barely walk himself. Bradan pulled them between two large trees and covered them as much as possible with whatever he could find—leaves, weeds, tree branches. Then he charged through the woods for the village.

The commotion in the house woke Orla. She wriggled but couldn't free herself from the rope. She was blindfolded. She cursed and struggled even harder. Someone kicked the door in and stormed into the room. She heard Bradan's voice. "Help her, or you won't have either of us." She felt the bed next to her sink down as if someone had lain down there. A burst of light assaulted her eyes when Bradan yanked off her blindfold.

She looked at the person next to her. "Oh God, what happened to Maeve?"

"I don't know. But they won't treat her." Bradan leaned against the wall, a jar in his hand. He was as white as a sheet. At the door, Uncle Tony stood, scowling.

"I don't care for being threatened, Bradan."

"I'm not threatening anyone. You need me or Orla. You care about this jar, so save Maeve."

Bradan removed the rope off Orla.

"Since when did you become completely reckless, Bradan?" Tony snarled.

"That's what we're all about. We do black magic, and we're reckless."

"You're wrong. We aren't reckless. We don't kill our own. And we don't destroy our ancestors' remains. Give me the jar. I will ask Anna to come and look at Maeve."

"I don't believe you. I told you we have a traitor in the clan. They killed my father. I don't know who's who anymore. You want a vessel for your energy at full moon, I'll do it. Just treat Maeve, and let Orla go."

"You're asking for too much, Bradan."

"I'm not asking. I'm telling." Bradan thrust the jar out as if he was going to drop it.

"Okay, calm down, son, I'll call Anna."

Tony backed out of the room. As soon as he'd left, Bradan flopped to the floor.

"Go, Orla. I know you've sworn in just to take that stupid potion for me. But if you don't come at full moon, you should be fine. Now run! As far away as you can."

"You think I'm going to leave Maeve like this ?"

"I'll take care of her."

"How can you take care of her? What if she dies?"

"She won't! Maeve wanted to tell Lorcan to get you out of here. She wanted you to be free. If that's what she wanted, I'll do it for her."

"If I leave you, they'll crush you in a heartbeat. And that will break her heart."

"What did you just say?"

"You heard me well enough."

"You . . ."

The door swung open, and Anna stomped in. She scowled at Orla and Maeve and pointed at Bradan. "You. Out. Unless you want to see the girl naked." Bradan scrambled out of the room and slammed the door behind him. Orla knew he stood on guard in front of the door.

CHAPTER 14

Lorcan awoke and found his chest bandaged and his arm in a sling. He shook his head. "You've got to be kidding me, Riley." He got up and pulled his arm out of the sling, put on his wrist unit, and went downstairs.

"You're butchering me!" Riley's voice shot to the hallway from the living room. Lorcan found Keeva cleaning up the gashes on his arms. The wolf had left quite a few bites on Riley even after it had been tranquilized.

"Stay still, Riley. I do this all the time," Keeva said.

"For rabbits and squirrels?" Riley hissed again. Noah sat in a corner rubbing Aris's ears. They both seemed to be enjoying the scene.

"Where's the wolf?" Lorcan asked.

Everyone turned to look at him.

"Apparently you don't need my sling," Riley muttered.

Lorcan chuckled. "But I need your help. Both of you."

Riley shrugged. "Anything except that which requires magical talents. We have two in the house, and that's a handful to deal with! Ouch . . . plus the cat . . . plus you . . . Ouch! That's enough, Keeva!"

Keeva let go of his arm while Noah giggled. She stood up from the sofa. "What do you need from me, Lorcan?"

"I'm going to the temple to get Orla out of there. I need you to back me up."

"The woman who came with Orla here before said it's a trap and Orla wouldn't be at the temple."

"That's why I need you. We haven't been married in front of any gods. By telling them that, Orla wants me to walk in there and not have to fight my way in. Once we're together, we can figure a way out. We can't do anything when we're separated from each other."

Riley shook his head. "What a wicked plan!"

Keeva smiled. "I like her already. What about the trap?" Keeva asked.

"I don't trust any of them, so I need you to back me up when I come in. But I don't want a fight."

"I don't see how it's possible without a fight," Riley said.

Keeva glared at him.

"No fighting for any of you," Lorcan said and trailed off when his wrist unit let out a beep. He glanced at it. "Fuck."

"What?" Riley asked.

"There was an accident, and Orla is no longer operating on her natural energy. We didn't have time to set up anything permanent before we came back here, and now her energy is running low. If it runs out, she'll die. I need to get going. Where's the wolf?"

"In the dungeon," Keeva said.

In the old cellar, Lorcan found the wolf chained to a column. His mother stood watching. When the wolf began to shiver, almost like it was cold, Jane took a rag and wrapped it around its body. Lorcan approached, standing next to Jane, and watched. To no one's surprise, the shape of the wolf began to change until it resembled that of a human. A flash of bright light later, and a young man lay upon the floor of the dungeon, still unconscious and clearly naked. Lorcan got up and grabbed some blankets and clothes out of a closet that stood against the stone wall.

Then the man opened his eyes.

"What's your name?" Lorcan asked.

The young man glared at him and looked away.

"All right, I' was trying to be polite, but let's cut to the chase. We've captured all of your friends, and I will use them to trade for Orla. To be honest, I'm no expert when it comes to magic, and I don't like being conned." The man shook his head and smirked. Lorcan grabbed his neck and shoved him against the wall. "Now, we've got a guy and two women. I will use one person to trade for Orla, I'll keep one until I'm sure Orla is safe and sound and out of here and there are no lingering effects of the magic shit, and I'm going to kill one to make my point. Which one of them you *don't* you want me to kill?"

The man glared at Lorcan. He shoved him against the wall one more time.

"Oh, sorry. I guess I should give you a way out, shouldn't I? Let me offer you something worth considering. I'll let you keep the one you care about, and I'll use the other one to trade for Orla. However, you have to tell me how to break the curse they put on her. I'm no expert, but I know with the curse on her, she'll never be free. If you've ever loved someone, you understand what it's like to be tangled up in a curse. You help me out, and I'll help you."

The man contemplated, then he said, "The curse is based on hatred. It can only be broken by love."

"How?"

"You have to challenge the clan to take your loved one out. They will offer you three choices—a dagger, poison, and a magic strike. If you don't know magic, don't choose that option. I don't know what the poison is, so your safest bet is the dagger."

"The safest?" Lorcan sneered.

"You're a werefox—you can heal quickly. Surely you know how to take a stab and make it nonfatal."

"Hummm. If I break the curse, will Orla be free forever?"

"In theory. *If* that's the only curse she has on her."

"But that means they can put another curse on her, right? And the whole hell cycle will start again?"

"We're were-creatures, not sorcerers . . ."

"There is no *we*. You and I are *very* different kinds, and trust me, you don't want to know what I am. Don't make assumptions. How can I stop them from placing another curse on Orla, or on anyone for that matter?"

"Are you stupid or crazy?"

"Try me!"

"As an outsider, you can challenge them to a fight to the death to take over their leadership. If you win, you can take the leadership and do whatever you want—including dismissing it. But you know what will happen if you lose."

"What's the challenge?"

"I don't know for certain. But they worship the moon, or its energy. If you destroy the source of their religion, then that should do the trick! Good luck."

"How do you know so much about them?"

The man sneered. "I was in the same boat as you. Didn't have any luck, though. But I've told you all I know. You can go save Orla. Can I have my woman, please?"

Lorcan nodded. "Which one?"

"Alana."

"Alana? The one who fainted at the sight of you?"

The man laughed. "She's a shapeshifter, you idiot. Bricius planted her as a kid in that clan . They trained her to do magic. She can shift in and out of that human form and do magic at the same time. In her true form, she's a hell of a puma. I have to give it to you for capturing her."

"Don't admire me. We didn't get her."

The man's eyes darkened. "What do you mean? You said you had them. I heard her howling before your friend took me out."

"I might have killed the puma. I'm not sure. But no, I didn't capture her."

"Fuck you, Lorcan. You bastard. You tricked me." The man's eyes reddened.

"Do you know how many people—including women and children—Bricius had killed? And God forbid how many people Alana killed. I can forgive her for trying to kill me at the riverbank, but I won't forgive them for what they did to my parents."

"It's not her fault. She was born into Bricius's clan and was chosen as a child. Please don't kill her . . ." Tears rolled down his face. "I've done my best to get her out."

"But did she want out?"

"She couldn't leave. It's her duty. She couldn't get out. Bricius's clan is vicious—you said so yourself. Please don't kill her . . ." Blood tricked from his nose, and he looked as if his head would explode. He pulled at the chain until it cut into his flesh and made him bleed.

"She will killing for power, wasn't she? That's her duty."

"She was born into it. It wasn't her choice. Let me go. I'll take her away. Please. Just let me go." The man kept tugging at the chain.

"If you couldn't do it before, why can you do it now? If you loved her that much, why didn't you ask your clan to help save her?"

The man roared in anger. More blood trickled from his mouth. "I am a rouge. I have no clan. No master. No home. Alana is all I have. Every time she goes into the woods, she's mine. Let me go!"

"I can't. If she's killing people, I'll have to kill her . . ."

The man roared and then let out a haunting howl. A projectile of blood erupted from his mouth, and then he passed out before he could shift back to his wolf form.

As a pang of guilt stabbed at his chest, Lorcan said, "All right, I'll spare her life if she promises she won't kill anymore . . ." Then he remembered his mother, standing quietly in the corner, listening to the whole conversation without saying a word.

Orla scrambled to the bed when Maeve opened her eyes. "Hey, how are you feeling?"

"Where am I?"

Maeve blinked. "You're at Bradan's place. He brought you here."

"Bradan!" Maeve shifted and tried to sit up. Orla pressed Maeve's shoulder to hold her down. "He's fine. It was his decision. He came back and blackmailed Uncle Tony into treating you. I think he's quite cool. I can see now why you love him, Maeve."

Maeve closed her eyes and blushed. Orla cleared her throat. "Thing is, because he's a cool guy, he actually asked me to leave. He said he could take the leadership for me. I can run, you know. But I can't leave you like this, so I stayed. But the point is that Bradan will tell the clan that he's willing the take the leadership, and I can deny it."

Maeve nodded. A tear trickled from her eye and dropped to the pillow.

"What happened in the woods?"

The memory hit Maeve, and she sat straight up. "Oh my God, where are Alana and Sam? Are they okay?"

Orla shook her head. "Bradan found you and Alana unconscious. He found parts of Sam, torn to pieces just like his father. Did you see anything in the woods?"

Maeve shook her head. "Everything was a blur. How's Alana?"

"Still out of it."

"I hope she's up and about by the full moon. They'll need a backup for Bradan. If you're not doing it, they'll need her even more."

"To do what?"

"Line up, just in case. She's the next in line after Bradan, but it's just a formality. After the ceremony, she'll go back to London. That's her home. She doesn't belong here."

"Alana is in line for the leadership of the clan?"

Maeve rolled her eyes. "I know. Talking about not wanting to do it, she's the worst of the three of you. I remember Uncle Tony had to drag her kicking and screaming all the way back here. He didn't have any success until her parents died."

Orla narrowed her eyes. "How did they die?"

"Hunting accident."

"Hummm . . ." Her wrist unit beeped, and she glanced at it. "Shit!"

"What's that?"

"I only have fifty percent of my energy left. Long story, but if this thing runs out, I think I'll die."

"Oh my God! How long do you have? What do you have to do?"

"I have no clue. I think I have to go all the way back to our place—very far away from here—with Lorcan to recharge this. I didn't think the energy would run out so quickly. I guess it wouldn't in normal circumstances, but in the last few days, we've been through a lot, haven't we?" She tapped the wrist unit.

CHAPTER 15

The temple was ancient and mysterious. It didn't have to be located in this spooky corner of the woods to emphasize the point, Lorcan thought. He adjusted his wrist unit, making sure everything was in working order. He had already said goodbye to everyone, his plan being to grab Orla and run at any chance he got.

It surprised him that so many people could fit inside the temple courtyard. It wasn't nearly grand as the Egyptian pyramids or Greek temples, but it was quite formidable with stone walls and lofty ceilings.

The double wooden door covered in symbols and letters that he had no clue what they meant. The door slid open as he approached. Lorcan stepped in and noted that the people in the courtyard didn't follow him. He figured that whatever it was he was going to do here was not entertaining enough for spectators.

There was no long aisle with columns or statues leading to a raised platform. It was a simple square room with an altar located right in the center. A large picture of a half moon was displayed prominently in the middle of the altar. The wolf had been right, they worshipped the moon.

His eyes landed on Orla. She was standing next to the altar, smiling at him. Illuminated by candlelight in the mysterious temple, she was beautiful. There were others standing around her. He glanced around, scoping out the number of people, location, and exits.

He heard a low beep and glanced at his wrist unit. But sound hadn't come from his unit, but from Orla's. She didn't look at it, instead keeping her eyes locked with his. He cursed silently. She knew her energy was running low.

An old man stepped forward. "Lorcan, my name is Tony, and I represent the family until the new leader is appointed. You are here to denounce your marriage with Orla Foley."

Lorcan smiled. "Her name is Orla Brody, and until we end our marriage, it will stay that way. I am here to take Orla with me, not to denounce the marriage."

"She owes a great deal to this family. And if I am not mistaken, your life is one of the things she owes us. You can't just walk in here and take her away from us. Who do you think you are?"

"With all due respect, Orla is my wife, and I can't let you force her into a position she doesn't want to take."

"She has sworn."

"Not voluntarily. And where I come from, a promise like that doesn't count."

"I know where you come from. That side of the woods isn't very far from here. But a promise is a promise regardless of where you come from."

Lorcan smiled. "Now that sounds like a threat. She promised to be my wife, and I'm going to hold her to that."

"You are not in a position to judge us . . ." Tony's voice came out so low it was almost a growl.

"I will take the leadership, Uncle Tony. Let Orla go," Bradan spoke up.

"Bradan, you are the second in line. Ideally, we should have Orla."

"Orla has the right to refuse, doesn't she?" Bradan advanced.

Tony narrowed his eyes. "Yes, under normal circumstances, she would have the right to refuse. But she made promises to save his life, and for that she has forfeited all of her rights. Do you want debate the rules with me, Bradan?"

"How can I repay her debts?" Lorcan asked.

"There is no way you can do that, young man. If you denounce your marriage, she stays as leader. If you don't, she will still stay as a magical slave. Either way, she stays and you go."

"There is no point keeping her. I have taken the potion for the ceremony," Bradan said.

"*You* stole the potion?" Tony stared at Bradan in surprise.

"We have a traitor in our clan who killed my father and tried to kill me. I was injured, and without that potion, I would have died."

"Who stole the potion for you?"

"That's irrelevant. I drank it, and the last I heard, Aunt Anna couldn't make a new one in time for the full moon."

"Don't you dare . . ." Tony swung his arm and sent a stream of blue fire at Bradan. Bradan put up his shield just as quickly, and the fire was deflected into a column at the corner of the temple, almost breaking it in two.

"You're not the subject today, Bradan. I know you have trained to be the leader, but at the moment, you are not. If you continue behaving in this way, I will not put you in that position."

"You have someone raising his hand for the position. Why insist on Orla?" Lorcan asked.

"You took a wife without honor, Lorcan. You might be married before your God, but you aren't before ours. She didn't have our blessing, and she will spend the rest of her life condemned."

"She doesn't need your blessing, and we don't worship your gods."

Sweat beaded on Orla's forehead. Lorcan knew she didn't have much left in her energy tank. He looked at the old man. If he denounced the marriage to pacify them, they would keep her, and she would die when she ran out of energy. He couldn't tell them about the Daimon Gate and Eudaiz. The multiverse was a secret, and he wasn't going to divulge it. He had to get her out of here, and he had to do it now.

Lorcan advanced. Tony and a line of men standing behind him closed in.

"A fight isn't necessary, Uncle Tony. I promised to take the leadership. Let Orla go," Bradan persisted.

"Do you think she can summon the spirits of our ancestors to save his life in London . . . by herself? I laid the path and connected her. I alone am the guarantor of her oath. She is in my debt. She can't walk away from that."

Bradan sneered, "So that's your true motive, Uncle Tony. I should have known. Because Orla owes you, you will have immediate access to the energy—and a larger share of it when she comes to power. I thought you cared for the clan."

Tony swung his arm, but this time it was too fast for Bradan to put up his shield. He was thrown into the wall like a rag doll and slid down to the floor in a boneless heap. Maeve squealed and crawled out from underneath the altar, scrambling toward Bradan.

"What on Earth is a white witch doing in our temple?" Tony exclaimed and prepared to hit Maeve. Orla yelled for him to stop. Bradan groggily pulled Maeve behind him to shield her.

"She doesn't belong to this clan. You are not allowed to harm her. So you want to start wars with other clans?" Bradan snarled.

"If you behave as you should, no one will get hurt," Tony growled.

With Tony and the clan distracted, Lorcan seized the opportunity to snatch Orla and make a run for the door.

Tony yelled for them to stop. Before he could swing his arm, Lorcan shot out an electric beam. It scraped the ground in front of Tony, digging a large hole and crumbling all the stone on the floor in the surrounding area.

"I can see you can wield magic, Lorcan. But Orla belongs to us until I release her. You walk through that door, and I will place another curse on her. Her debts will pile up, and she will live her life as a fugitive."

"I don't care, Lorcan," Orla said.

"You might save her now, but her soul will be forever in debt. She has a family, and all she needs is our blessing. She denied us for you, and all you can give her is a life of a thief? Is that how you take a wife in your clan?"

They were at the door, but Lorcan stopped. Orla pulled his arm. "I don't care, Lorcan. As long as we're together, I can live with it. Let's go."

"Don't dare set foot in Ireland again, Orla. Wherever you run to, consider this home lost to you. You came from dirt, and your parents died for nothing," Tony said in disdain.

Lorcan turned around. "I challenge you and your curses on Orla."

"Lorcan, don't do this," Orla begged.

Lorcan repeated, "I challenge you, Tony, and I challenge your curses and all the magic you've used on Orla. If I win, she will be free to walk out of this clan with no curses and no encumbrances. You will never be able to lay claim on her again."

"How do you know this rule?" Tony narrowed his eyes.

"Are you planning to break the rule, Uncle Tony? This outsider has challenged you. Will you accept or not?" Bradan asked.

"No, Lorcan," Orla cried.

He wiped the tears from her face. "I love you, Orla. If I can't give you the life you deserve, what kind of a husband am I?"

Tony went to the altar and opened a compartment. It didn't surprise Lorcan to see him pace a dagger, a bottle of poison, and a piece of dried bone on the table.

"You asked for it. Choose, and I will execute." Tony growled.

"No, Lorcan, no!" Orla cried again. Lorcan looked at Maeve. She nodded and held Orla back.

"I'll take the dagger. And just to confirm, there will be one strike, and if I survive it, Orla will walk free?"

Tony smirked. "Of course."

Lorcan saw the smirk, and he wasn't sure of what to make of it, but if he could take a bullet, he could survive a dagger. But suddenly, he felt a tangible click in his head, and at the back of his eye, a small screen popped up that said, *"Warning. Ten percent survival on execution of the mission."* Then the screen disappeared. Surely his survival chance was higher than that, he thought. Lorcan shook his head to will away his doubt and hesitation.

He stood and looked at Tony. Tony grabbed the dagger and charged at him. He felt a warm glow at his back and saw that Bradan had swiveled to stand right behind him. The force of Tony coming forward was like a raging storm. Lorcan relaxed his shoulders and prepared himself to subtly maneuver his chest so that the dagger wouldn't stab him in the heart.

Then it dawned on him. He could take a strike from a dagger if it was an *ordinary* dagger. But if there was magic involved, he would most certainly be killed. But it was too late now.

As Tony charged and swung the dagger, Bradan placed his palm on Lorcan's back. He felt a wave of warmth, and a shield pulsed forward from inside his body and hung like a curtain in front of him. It was too close for Tony to retract his movement, so he darted through the shield. His body was able to penetrate it naturally because it wasn't designed to block physical forces, but when the dagger hit the shield, particles splattered out of it like liquid and dissolved into the air. Lorcan knew nothing about magic, but he knew that the Bradan's shield had knocked the magic out of the dagger and that Tony planned to use magic on the strike.

The force of the blow pushed Lorcan back a few steps. The impact wasn't as severe as when the bullet had hit him, but he still felt the blow and slumped to the floor, smiling when he realized it had been an ordinary dagger. He saw his blood on the floor, and somewhere in the back of his mind, he heard Orla scream. But at that moment, he knew he had survived the challenge. He felt Orla's arms wrapping around his waist to help him stand up. Her body shook, but her grip was firm.

"I win," he said.

"Uncle Tony, you cheated. He chose the dagger, not the magic, but you combined them. You have disappointed us," Bradan said. "We don't want you as a member of the family anymore. Please leave."

Tony's face looked as if it was on fire, but he said nothing and strode out of the temple.

Lorcan knew he wouldn't be standing for long. He adjusted his wrist unit and opened the portal. In the distance, a flash of light appeared, and the portal opened. Lorcan and Orla could see it, but to the naked eye, it would look appear to be simply a strip of sunlight in the middle of the sky.

The crowd rumbled, "Look at the rainbow! He can create a rainbow in the night sky!"

"Let's go home," Lorcan said to Orla.

Orla helped him as they both walked into the portal, traveling back to Eudaiz.

CHAPTER 16

A beam of bright light assaulted Lorcan's eyes. He squinted and blinked, feeling incredibly groggy. Then he heard Orla's soothing voice and felt her cool hands on his face. The light was too bright. It blinded him, and he blinked again.

"There you are! Hello!" When the light dimmed, he was able to see her smiling face. She kissed his cheek and traced her lips down to his. He stopped the kiss, holding her face up so he could see her eyes.

"Are you okay?"

She grinned. "Perfect." Then she kissed him again.

"Are you okay, Orla? Tell me what's going on, honey." Then he saw a bracelet strapped to his right wrist, one similar to Orla's. "Crap." He winced and sat up. He was lying on a lab bench and wearing something that looked like a hospital gown. "What the hell is this?" He pulled at the gown that was a definite insult to his fashion sense.

"Orla, where are we?"

"Eudaiz."

"Oh, so we made it?"

"Not exactly. Ciaran got us half way."

He shrugged. "That's all right. He can brag for the rest of his life that I never complete a mission without his help."

Orla took a set of clothes over to him, and Lorcan slid into his jeans. Before he pulled his shirt on, he noticed that the dagger had left a large red scar on his chest. That surprised him because the injuries he'd suffered before hadn't left any trace after he'd healed himself, and they'd been, in his opinion, much more severe than this stab wound.

"Ciaran said your defense system, the one that helps you heal impossible injuries, was very low—or in his words, non-existent—when you took the dagger."

Lorcan nodded. "All right, I might have miscalculated a little bit . . ."

"Miscalculated?" Tears gleamed in Orla's eyes. "You knew your chance of survival was less than ten percent. You didn't calculate at all, but your artificial brain did. That robot warned you!" She jabbed her finger into his chest, tears rolling down her face.

He remembered the little screen that had flipped on in the back of his eyes, warning him of the danger. "How did you know that?"

"We almost didn't make it. My energy was running out. You couldn't walk anymore. I was sure that we would be dead halfway into the transitional zone. And then, Ciaran came to rescue us." More tears rolled down her face now.

He wiped the tears and kissed her cheek.

"And then you didn't wake up as you had before. The wound wouldn't heal. Ciaran said you were in trouble, so he brought you to this lab."

Orla walked over to the window and looked outside. Lorcan embraced her from behind and found her body shaking with emotion. She turned around and looked him in the eye. "Ciaran did an entire profile analysis of you. I don't know how he did it. You can ask him for the details."

"I only care about the details that draw tears out of your eyes."

She gazed at him for a long moment in silence. Then she sighed. "You are programmed to love me."

He released her from his embrace. "You think I'm a robot? You think my feelings for you have no emotional grounds?"

"I don't *think*, Lorcan. It's a fact." She waved her arms in the air. "Fifty percent of you was artificially created. Your brain was wired to tell you would fall in love with the first girl who made your heart skip a beat. That explains everything."

"What does it explain?"

"Why you always followed me. Why you loved me regardless of how I treated you. Why you loved me for no apparent reason. It explains the childhood sweetheart story. What you've got with me, you could have had with any girl, Lorcan. But why me? Because you were *wired* to love me."

The emotion coming out of her was like a horrific storm, and it stabbed at his heart. The pain was incredible.

"But what about my human half? My parents thought you were related to Bricius. They told me if I chose to leave home to look for you in London, they'd never want to see me again. But I chose you over those I thought were my family. Emotions can't be programmed! You can program a robot to do anything, but you can't program it to love. You can't program a robot to compare, prioritize, and choose between family relationships and romantic love!" He paced the room as he spoke, wanting to smash something. "Now that I've turned out to be a thing and not a person, my feelings mean nothing to you? Our lives together, our stories, what we have done together . . . you disregard everything because I'm not human?"

"No, it's not that . . ."

"It's not *that*? So what the fuck is it? What did I do with my fucking life—making fucking stupid decisions, giving up my family, and oh, hang on, that doesn't matter because they're not even my fucking family! I don't need a fucking family. Why? Because I'm arti-fuckingly created."

"The profanity is unnecessary, Lorcan."

He waved his arms in the air. "Sorry! There's nothing I can do about it because it was fucking wired in my brain that way!"

The tears in her eyes had dried. She simply looked at him and waited until he finished his rant. Then she sighed. "I'm sorry, Lorcan. It was just one of my weak moments."

"You don't have weak moments, Orla. You kicked me around like a soccer ball for years." He went to the window and looked outside. He noted that the garden outside the lab was artificial—the lawn, the flowers, the trees, and maybe even the air as well. The garden looked perfect, but he was far from being perfect. He was defective. He turned and looked at Orla, and he would have rather seen tears than what he saw on her face.

He had hurt her.

He wished she would yell at him, call him names. But she didn't. "Lorcan, I was just wondering if you would ever choose me if your attraction to me were natural? Before all of this, there were countless times I asked myself if your love for me was real. But I love you. I've given you all I've got. It hurt too much for me to contemplate the slightest chance that you didn't love me back. So I just pretended I didn't question anything."

He didn't have an answer—for her or for himself. The pain stabbed at his heart, at his brain. He wondered if that was artificial, too. Surely pain couldn't be programmed. He didn't ever want to cause Orla pain. He wanted her to know his love was natural, and he wanted to know that for himself as well.

Maybe there was only one way to find out.

His knees buckled, and he slumped to the floor. He felt Orla's grip, and then he felt nothing else. But he could still hear her. He heard Ciaran's voice, too. He was glad nobody asked him anything because he couldn't seem to speak.

"The wound healed. Why is it bleeding now?" Orla asked.

"His body is too weak to handle the injury naturally. He's relying on other parts to help him survive until he can naturally gain some strength back. His body is rejecting the supernatural part. If he totally disengages with it, he'll die."

"What are you talking about?"

"Orla, the supernatural part of him is like an implant. His body accepted it well before. I don't know why he's rejecting it now. What did you say to him?"

"I just asked him if he would naturally love me, even if he wasn't programmed to."

"Jesus Christ, Orla! The human brain drives emotions. It can't be programmed. Love is not in DNA—it's in the heart and soul. You guys are soul mates, and if you can't see that, there's nothing I can do to help you—or him."

"It's my fault . . ." Orla cried.

"Beat yourself up later. Grab that machine. I need to resuscitate him. He's shutting his robotic part down."

"No."

"What? If he doesn't reconnect with that part of him, he'll die."

"Will resuscitation connect the two parts?"

"No. But I'm running out of options here!"

"Let me talk to him."

"Orla!"

"Let me talk to him. Please."

And then he heard her voice whispering in his ear, "Lorcan, I love you. If you want to love me back, you have to stay alive. I need you to borrow some of the supernatural power. I know I've made you hate it. But please try . . . for me . . ."

He wanted to try, but he was just so goddam tired. Maybe he just needed to sleep. He blocked her voice out and drifted to a dark and quiet place for some peaceful rest. But suddenly it was like lying on a train track when the train was near. He felt his shoulders shaking, and he heard Orla's voice again. She was saying something, crying maybe. Maybe if he tried a little harder, she'd let him sleep.

He didn't know how much time had passed.

A beam of bright light assaulted his eyes again. He squinted, blinked. Then he heard Orla's soothing voice and felt her cool hands on his face. "Here you are! Hello again!" When the light dimmed , he was greeted by her smiling face.

"How long was I out?"

"Too long. And before you ask, let me say this . . . I love you too much to lose you again. I know you come with extras, like the supernatural part of you and all the cool tricks it can do. So if you ever try to disconnect from your superpower again, I will go back to my clan and figure out a curse to hunt you down regardless of where you may be in this multiverse."

"Now I'm scared. Can I sit up?"

"Sure."

Before he hopped up, she planted a kiss on his lips and pressed him back down again. Her hands were busy on his body, and his breath caught so damn quickly. He could feel his body vibrating uncontrollably.

"Are we on a lab bench?" he asked while his hands pulled at her clothes as if he was possessed.

"Yes, and I think this session is being recorded."

"Anything for research." He flipped her over so that she lay on her back, and then he ravished her.

Orla was curled into his side, sleeping. The lab door opened, and they scrambled to their feet. Ciaran walked in. "I see you're up and well." He sat down opposite the two of them. "You've got quite the supernatural makeup, Lorcan."

"What kind of creature am I exactly?"

Ciaran laughed. "Yes, for lack of vocabulary, I think we can settle on *creature*. Your human DNA comes from your father. You knew that part. But your emotional and psychological profile comes from your mother. And that fascinates me because you're the perfect combination of nature and nurture."

Lorcan scowled. "I'm not your lab rat."

"Certainly not. But you're sombody's, and I happen to know the person who created you and what she tried to accomplish."

"When will you give me that information?"

"I can't tell you about your maker, but I can let you know everything about yourself . . . when you're ready."

Lorcan nodded and raked his hands through his hair. "We have to go back to Ireland to finish our business there. Then I'll be ready. How long has it been since we left?"

Ciaran stood. "A couple of days at the most. Do you need my help this time?"

Lorcan nodded. "Not you personally, but we'll definitely need people."

Ciaran smiled. "I'll see what I can do."

CHAPTER 17

Tonight was the night. Orla gazed at the altar in the temple from a distance. The doors of the temple were open, and a large group of people gathered outside. In front of the altar, Bradan stood in his ceremonial robe. All the senior members of the family flanked his sides. They were waiting for the magical moment.

Outside the temple was a raised platform, set up so that the new leader could receive the energy from the moon.

There was no sign of Maeve. Orla knew her friend wouldn't be anywhere near this place during this moment. She would be crying her eyes out somewhere in the woods. She felt a tug at her arms and felt Lorcan's warm hands holding her.

"We will stop all of the suffering. Do you trust me?" he asked.

"I do."

They hear the chanting sound of praying from the temple and saw that the moon had come into position. Bradan left the temple and went outside. He walked to the raised platform and looked up to the moon. He was quite a formidable character and would make a good leader if not for the dark magic.

Among the senior people in the family, Alana stood solemnly.

"There she is," Orla pointed.

Lorcan nodded. "What do you think she'll do?"

"I'm not sure yet. None of them know she's a traitor and a shapeshifter. I can't see how she could take the leadership naturally while Bradan is alive. After he absorbs the energy from the moon, there will be nothing anyone can do to remove it."

"Can she use black magic to kill him?"

"No. There are so many senior people around, she'd get caught. Plus he could shield himself from the energy and magic."

The crowd had finished their praying and started to cheer as the magical moment crept closer.

"She signaled. Did you see that?" Orla asked.

"Yes," Lorcan responded as Alana twirled her hair and angled the ring she was wearing to the sky. He saw it let out a faint spark. Lorcan adjusted his wrist unit to signal his people.

Bradan winced and touched the back of his neck.

"They shot him," Orla said and jumped out of their hiding place.

Lorcan pulled her back. "We have to wait, Orla. Don't ruin the plan."

On the raised platform, Bradan swayed and slumped to his knees. The crowd gasped and grumbled in confusion. Aunt Anna rushed to Bradan. A stream of dark blood trickled down his nose.

"He's poisoned," Orla said. "I have to help him."

"How?" Lorcan asked.

"I don't know."

From the chaotic crowd, Maeve jumped onto the raised platform and grabbed for Bradan who was turning bluer by the second. Blood started to come out of his mouth. He tried to say something to her, but all that came out was blood. She pulled out her potion and tilted it into his mouth.

The crowd protested.

"White witch, what's she doing here?"

"White witch, get out of here!"

Maeve ignored the crowd. Bradan coughed out some red blood and leaned into her arms. She helped him up. The crowd yelled for Maeve to get off the platform.

"He needs treatment, or he'll die," Maeve explained.

"Let them go," Anna said.

The crowd quieted down and split in half, leaving a path for Maeve and Bradan. She shifted, taking most of Bradan's weight, and walked down the path. Someone in the crowd objected, yelling and insulting Maeve, but no one touched them. Maeve and Bradan struggled through the crowd, heading toward the woods.

"I have to help them," Orla said.

"I'll wait here. Be very careful, Orla. In case we get separated, I'll open the portal at the riverbank. Promise me you'll make it there." Lorcan grabbed Orla's hand.

"Yes. Promise me you will be there, too."

He nodded. She kissed him and headed in the direction of Maeve and Bradan.

The crowd grew noisier as Bradan and Maeve disappeared into the woods. Aunt Anna stood on the platform, glancing around. Alana smiled to herself. She had worked her whole life and sacrificed everything she for this moment. Her clan should be proud of her. She glanced up to the platform and met Anna's eyes.

"Alana," Anna called out.

Alana smiled openly. "Yes."

"You are the third in line. Step forward."

Alana wished she could tell Anna how much she hated the look on her face, her magic, her medicine, and everything else about her. The minute she became the leader of this family, Anna's garden would be the first to go. It would give Alana so much pleasure to see Anna suffer. Anna looked at her with disdain and said, "Kneel. Swear to our gods right here. No need to go inside the temple."

Of course she would do it right here. She kneeled and swore to the gods of this family. She would do whatever it took to take this clan over, and then to wipe it out and grind it into dust to make them all pay for her suffering. Her whole life had been leading up to this moment—swear in, become the leader, take the power from the gods. And then she would let them in on the bad news that the power would not be distributed to their clan but to her shapeshifter family.

Bricius had to be proud of her, wherever he was .

Alana wanted to laugh out loud. She hated this clan so much. She would eat them alive right now.

"Alana!" Anna scolded.

"Yes."

"Are you done?"

Yes, of course." She stood and looked up to the moon. It was almost time.

Bradan fell to the ground, exhausted. "Leave me here, Maeve. Go back to the ceremony. Whoever wanted me dead is causing trouble there. Alana is third in line, but I'm not sure she is up to the task."

"Wake up, Bradan. They treated us like that, and you still worry about them? I wonder sometimes how on earth you belong to that black magic clan. Keep going. I don't want to be dinner for the shapeshifters."

"Too late, it seems," Bradan said. With the strength he had left, he lifted Maeve up, and she grabbed a tree branch and hopped up onto it. They heard the movements of several animals accompanied by deep growls. Maeve reached down to help Bradan climb up, but he didn't take her hand. Instead, he drew out a pair of hunting knives.

Three leopards leaped out from the bush. Maeve had to admit that Bradan was quick as lightning. Although weakened by the poison and knowing no magic, his combat skills were more than respectable. With a few moves, he took down two animals. The third one tore up his shoulder before he killed it.

Maeve jumped back to the ground. Before they could move, there was the sound of animals moving in a herd. "Holy crap." Bradan shook his head. He turned around, wanting to lift Maeve up into the tree again, but she backed away. "There's no way you can take down this many. I'll stay with you."

Before Bradan could protest, they saw the reflection of wild animal eyes scattered among the trees. They advanced on the two of them. Bradan pushed Maeve against a tree trunk behind him. He turned to a press a deep kiss onto her lips. Then he gripped his knives.

The animals came.

From behind them, Orla charged forward, hands curled into fists and fireballs flying at the animals. The howled in pain and burnt like torches. In a short moment, there was no more movement. Orla turned around to see Maeve and Bradan gaping at her. She shrugged, "I've done this before. Once or twice."

She looked again at a dark corner of the woods. "Crap. They're heading toward Lorcan's home."

Orla stood at and looked in the direction of the ceremony, the opposite direction to his home. She looked at her wrist unit but had no idea how to operate it.

"Hell!" She rushed off toward Lorcan's home. Maeve and Bradan followed her. "What are you doing? You can hardly walk! You'll slow me down, Bradan."

"You'll need my shield," he said and let Maeve help him run after Orla.

Lorcan glanced around . What was taking Orla so long? He might have to finish this himself. Alana had sworn in and was proceeding to receiving her leadership. The next step would be receiving the power from the moon. It was critical they intercept her after she had sworn in—but before she received the full moon's energy.

Alana stood on the platform and was proceeding toward the last step. Lorcan had no choice but to execute the plan. He came out from his hiding place.

"Stop!" he said.

On the platform, Alana turned at look at him. Her expression was priceless.

"What?" It was a growl loaded with tons of explosive fury.

"I can see that you are the new leader of this clan, and I am here to challenge this clan and your leadership."

"You're *what?*" Alana roared.

"I challenge your leadership," Lorcan repeated.

"You wouldn't dare!" Alana whirled , her eyes bloodshot and beads of sweat running down her forehead. She adjusted her stance, and her eyes went blank. Lorcan knew black magic was coming his way. He concentrated and shot an electric wave at the platform right in front of Alana. It dug a large hole and cracked the surface. The crowd withdrew.

Alana jumped down to the ground.

"Now we're on a level playing field." Lorcan smiled. "You look like you'd like to use magic on me. That's not an appropriate response to an outsider's challenge of the leadership. If you are too new to the position to know, this is your second chance to respond properly."

Alana smirked. "Do you know what will happen if you lose?"

"I don't plan to lose, but yes, I know the consequences."

Alana smiled. "All right. To win this challenge, you have to burn our energy source . . ."

"I do indeed." Lorcan looked at the crowd, which had backed several feet away. Even the senior clan members stood at a distance.

Alana and Lorcan circle each other, looking one at the other like predator and prey. Lorcan smiled. He glanced at the crowd and then concentrated. He turned his face up to the moon, gazed at it, and shot a large wave of electric current into the air. He used so much energy that it sent him staggering backward.

A funnel of smoke appeared, twirled, and flew straight at the moon. He heard a clashing sound, and the image of the moon cracked and shook. There were sparks, and each spark of purple light sent the crowd staggering back further. Lightning stretched across the sky, straight to the moon. Explosion after explosion burst blood red in the dark sky.

The moon caught on fire. The round shape of the moon became redder by the second. The heat of the fire burned the trees around them. They could smell the smoke and feel the heat. People in the crowd cried out, tears in their eyes. They slumped to their knees and started praying.

Lorcan cast a dismissive glance at Alana, who looked as if he would set him on fire if she could.

The moon still glowed red. Lorcan had burnt the moon, the source of the clan's energy.

"You trick me? You must be cheating. This isn't possible," Alana roared.

The entire clan was on their knees.

"They don't think I'm cheating." Lorcan gestured at the crowd.

"Liar. You have to be." Alana advanced and raised her arms, ready to perform magic. Lorcan shot another electric wave at her. She jumped and rolled on the ground to avoid it.

All senior members of the clan approached Lorcan. Anna stepped forward. "You have won the leadership challenge. What would you like to do?"

"I want Alana out of the clan. I want Maeve to be leader. If she doesn't accept, then I want Bradan. All rules of the clan that restrict positive emotions and relationship are to be abolished. New rules will be formed, and it will be up to the new leader—either Bradan or Maeve."

"No!" Alana roared and charged at Lorcan. Anna swung her arm, and a stream of fire shot at Alana. Alana twirled to avoid the burst of fire. Her body stretched out, and she grew to twenty feet, her arms becoming gigantic claws. Lorcan looked up and wasn't surprised at all to see a hideous version of the woman at the riverbank. Her long, sharp claws stretched out like iron snakes. They pierced Anna and lifted her off the ground. Blood rained down on the people as Alana laughed. People trampled each other, running to get away.

"This is the price for stopping me from getting what I want. Do you like this, Lorcan?"

"Give up, Alana. You've lost," Lorcan said.

"Over my dead body. I am the leader of this clan. It is mine!" Alana screamed and shot fire at Lorcan. The force lifted him up and threw him into a tree. From the corner of his eyes, he saw Riley running toward him. Lorcan smiled and glanced up at Alana.

"This is your last chance, Alana. Give up your leadership."

Orla ran as fast as she could. The air vibrated with the energy of the coming shapeshifter. Maeve and Bradan trailed right behind. Orla worked her head frantically, searching for the information Ciaran had gathered about Lorcan and his parents. Why were they attacking Lorcan's home? If Alana was the key to their plan, and she was to get them the power, what would attacking Lorcan's home give them?

She kept running.

When she got a glimpse of a small group of shapeshifters, she charged straight at them and let her fireballs fly. She took them down quickly—too quickly for her liking. She was missing something.

She kept running toward Lorcan's home. She could see the entrance from the distance. She skidded to a halt, and Maeve slammed straight into her.

"Holy crap," Orla said.

The leopard shapeshifters had surrounded the house. There was no way she could take all of them down. The people in the house, aware of the attack, had turned the lights off, but that would put them at a disadvantage. Darkness was what these animals were used to.

Lorcan had said Alana was from Bricius's clan, and the wolf he'd captured was her lover. How much she loved the wolf, Orla had no clue, but maybe she was sending other leopards here to rescue it. There were problems with her theory. First, the number of leopards present here was definitely overkill for rescuing a single wolf from a group of defenseless women and children. And second, Alana didn't know Lorcan had the wolf and was keeping it here.

Then something dawned on her. Lorcan's father had been on his way to give Lorcan information about his origin when a leopard caused the accident that had cost him his life. That meant the leopard—or Bricius's clan—knew about Lorcan. They knew he was not their biological son, and therefore knew that Keeva was their first child. Jane had promised their first child to Bricius if the child was a girl.

It was obvious to Orla that the leopards weren't trying to rescue the wolf. They were going for Keeva.

CHAPTER 18

Lying on the ground and looking up at the demonic version of Alana, Lorcan said, "Give up your leadership, Alana. I know you've worked your whole life for this, but it's over, and I want to spare your life."

Alana laughed. "How kind of you! Sparing my life!" She laughed again, but the laugh grew bitter.

Lorcan saw a broken soul beneath the evil facade. At the riverbank, he knew she had meant some of what she'd said. She'd read his mind and had stumbled upon the memories of him stalking

Orla during his childhood. She'd tapped into it, and it had chewed up her subconscious and had become her own memories. When she'd said she wanted a taste of him, what she had meant was she'd wanted a taste of true love—and not with him but with someone special in her life.

There had been countless times Lorcan had thought the same thing about Orla and their relationship—he either had her, or he had nothing. The human half of him was fed by his mother's emotions and his father's logic, and the supernatural part of him made him act for a larger duty, whatever it might be. But his human part had been the stronger component for his entire life, and thus, love and a relationship was high on his list of priorities.

But Alana either didn't believe in love enough, and the supernatural duty had taken her over. She simply had no choice, and he pitied her. Had she ever loved at all? If she hadn't, his plan was ruined, and she would kill him and do it quickly.

"You're outnumbered, Alana. Let this go and live," Lorcan said.

"Do you think I'm stupid enough to fight this whole clan by myself?" She snapped her fingers, and herds of pumas and leopards emerged from the depths of the darkness, stealthily walking around and closing everyone in. "This is my true family," she said. "I'll let this clan live, but they will live the way they I tell them to. As for you, Lorcan, you destroyed the source of energy I've worked years to get. I can never forgive you for that."

Lorcan glared at the animals. Maybe his plan was ruined after all. Riley was getting closer, and he regretted that he might get Riley killed, too. His next plan was to make it to the riverbank so that he could open the portal and get away from Earth.

"Sorry, Lorcan," Alana said and signaled.

Two pumas jumped at him. He leaped back, fixed his stance, and shot a large electronic wave at them. They howled, dropped to the ground, and disintegrated.

Alana smiled and raised her arms. She was ready to call the group of them to attack Lorcan.

But just then they heard a loud, haunting howl. The shadow of a warrior and army of wolves appeared. Lorcan smiled. They had made it in time. It was his friend, Roy, a half-wolf, half-fox were-creature. Obviously, Ciaran had given him an army of creatures to lead. And they weren't ordinary werewolves, they were space were-creatures. They would be unbeatable because Ciaran had created them.

The shapeshifter leopards and pumas cringed and shrunk into disorganized small groups. The space creatures were double their size.

Alana glanced at her surrendering clan. "You cowards! Fight! Don't just stand there!"

From behind the line of space creatures, Roy stepped forward and approached Lorcan. "Sorry I'm late," he said. "We had a change of plans." Lorcan looked behind Roy and couldn't find Mori. He thought it odd because those two would never be separated. "The shapeshifters split," explained Roy. "Half of them attacked your home, and Mori is handling that half," Roy whispered into Lorcan's ear.

The hair at the back of his neck stood up, and a surge of fear stabbed at this heart. Attacking his home? With this mother, sister, Noah, and a kitten inside? How could he have made such mistake? Why hadn't he thought of that?

"How many?" Lorcan asked.

"Don't know. We split half of what we've got."

"Did you see Orla?"

Roy shook his head. Riley arrived, holding a bag in one hand and a rifle in the other. "It was harder than I thought, but we've got it."

Lorcan felt sweat running down his spine. He had to finish the business here quickly, find Orla, and get back home.

"As I said, Alana, you're outnumbered. I've given you a chance to withdraw, and you didn't take it. So I guess you'd rather die."

A corner of Alana's mouth quirked up. "Intriguing. I am the best of the shapeshifters. Even if I don't take this leadership, killing me isn't possible."

"You have no clan, no group, and no master now. I'm guessing you'd like to be a rogue. So go with your friend. You can be together in hell."

Lorcan tossed out the contents of the bag Riley had given him. On the ground lay the golden wolf skin, the fur soaked with blood.

"Your friend wouldn't give up your location or your identity. He died protecting you, Alana." He could the blood surging beneath her skin. "The reason I gave you a second chance was because beneath that mask, I know you are a woman who could love. Or should I say, a woman who used to love. The wolf told me all about the time you spent in the woods with him."

Alana roared and grew larger. Then she shrunk considerably and fell to the ground.

"He said you left him for power, and he would rather die than live without you. When he found you, he didn't want to be a rouge anymore. He thought he had found his other half. A life partner."

Alana opened her mouth to say something but it came out as a guttural animal growl. Lorcan's plan might work. If she'd had a fraction of true love for the wolf and had sworn in to this black magic clan, the conflicting emotions would kill her. She would burst into flame at any second. That was, if she had ever loved the wolf.

"Before I ripped his skin apart from his body, he was telling me about the time the two of you had run together in the woods. He treasured that and said he would do whatever it took to free you from your duty to your clan. But you loved power too much. And that broke his heart."

Alana roared one more time. Riley aimed his rifle. Roy pulled his gun.

She leaped toward Lorcan and then dropped to the ground. Alana fell, curled up next to piles of dirt and the bits and pieces of Anna's body she had torn apart. Then she stretched her arms out, and for a moment, her hands turned into the gigantic paws of a black puma. The black magic clan roared in anger. They yelled and cursed and wanted to trample her to death.

Lorcan stopped the crowd. "She'll die soon by herself because of her own curse and her betrayal to her true love."

She couldn't shift. The paws turned back into human hands, and she turned back into a beautiful and dying Alana. She lay on the ground, tears pouring from eyes that had begun to burn with fire. She didn't beg, and she didn't talk. She just waited for her death.

Lorcan crouched next to her. "Why did you send your clan to my home?"

"I didn't. They found out about your make, so now they want Keeva. I am not that important to them. I'm just a pawn."

His heart skipped several beats. His little sister was what they wanted. Lorcan turned to Riley who had no idea what was going on back at home. Lorcan could feel the heat seeping out from every pore in her body. She was going to burst into flames. They still had the wolf locked up—the fur had just been a decoy. Surely Alana's clan knew the wolf was important to her. Keeva and his mother would be smart enough to use it to bargain for their safety—or to at least bide time.

"I won the challenge. Is there anything I can do to help you?" Lorcan asked.

Tears rolled down her face. "Did he really think I left him for power?"

Lorcan couldn't lie to the dying woman. "No. He loves you."

Alana nodded. "Thank you." And she closed her eyes.

They heard a low growl and saw a shadow fly out from the woods. The yellow wolf leapt out in one swift move, flipped Alana onto its back, and charged into the woods. People roared and wanted to give chase, but Lorcan stopped them.

"Let them go. Your clan isn't exactly saintly. So for all the sins you've committed and the people you've killed or harmed with your black magic, let this even out the game. Let's forget and move on," Lorcan said to the crowd.

He turned toward Riley and Roy. "Shapeshifters attacked my home. The wolf is here, so I don't know what's happening at home or why they released it." Then he ran in the direction of his home. Riley and Roy followed. The run home through the woods seemed to take forever.

In the house, Keeva grabbed the rifle and walked toward the door. Jane banged at the door of her room and shouted for Keeva. "Keeva, let me out. I won't tolerate this."

"She's really mad, Keeva," Noah said. Aris sat on his shoulder, giving Keeva a disapproving look.

"Now, for you two, I'll lock you in your room, too." Keeva picked Noah up. Noah wriggled and protested.

"I can do magic, Keeva. Orla taught me. I can help."

"I can't let a kid fight."

"Let me down. You just wait here. Father will be back. He always keeps his promises. If I let you go out there and you get hurt, he'll be mad."

"Stop wriggling. I'll wait if I can. I thought we had a wolf to use to bargain with the shapeshifters. They lurked around for hours and didn't attack because we had the wolf. It's one of them. But Mother let it go, and now we've got nothing, Noah. Do you understand that? They will storm in here shortly, and I need to put you somewhere safe."

"But how many can you kill with that rifle?"

"I don't know, but I won't go down that easily."

"No one is going down. Let me go. I had a happy vision, and if you stay alive, it will happen."

Keeva put Noah down. "What was your happy vision?"

"You and Father, me and Aris were having a picnic at the riverbank."

Keeva looked into Noah eyes. "That's a happy thought. But no one is having picnic at the river bank in the middle of winter. You're making this up, aren't you?" Keeva tiled Noah's chin up and looked into his eyes. Noah pouted and tears threatened.

"You promised my mother!"

"I didn't promise anyone anything!"

"You promised you'd take care of me and Father. Please—just stay in here and wait."

They heard a crash. The side window broke, and a gigantic shadow leapt in, landing smoothly and quietly on the floor. Keeva raised the rifle, aiming at the creature. In front of them was a magnificent leopard with glowing green eyes. Keeva aimed the rifle. "I never harm animals, but I'll make an exception this time. You're not just an animal, and I have a kid to protect."

The leopard whirled around stealthily, then its fur glowed for a second before it turned into a man—tall, lean, and young with striking green eyes.

"There you are. You weren't hard to find at all. What a magnificent creature! Now I understand why he wanted you so much." He looked Keeva up and down.

"Who?"

"Our late leader. But don't worry, regardless of whether he's with us or not, we'll treat you well."

"Thank you very much, but I'm the one with the gun, and I am *not* in the mood to treat any one well at the moment. What do you want?"

"You, of course."

"Well, you are not going to get me. Aside from me shooting you, what can I do to get you out of here?"

In the blink of an eye, the man shifted back into leopard form and leapt at Keeva.

She pulled the trigger.

CHAPTER 19

The sound of the bullet terrified the wild animals in the woods as much as the shapeshifters around the house. The shapeshifters closed in, howling, barking, and roaring to intimidate.

From behind the shapeshifter lines, Orla, Maeve, and Bradan rushed in. Orla threw fireballs at them, nonstop, one after another. As the ones in the back howled in pain and burned like torches, the front line turned around. They ran in circles to surround Orla, Maeve, and Bradan.

From this end of the woods, the moon was full—bright yellow and clear, and shedding enough light for Orla to see that they were outnumbered by the were-creatures. She kept hurling her fireballs, but she wasn't sure how long they could hold on. They stood, their backs toward one another, while the animals ran circles around them. The animals closed the circle, tighter by the minute. They were so close she could hear them breathe.

"Behind me," Orla said. Bradan and Maeve can fight with magic, but when the animals commenced a physical attack, there was nothing much they could do except engage in hand-to-hand combat. Orla threw more fireballs to the front of her. At the back, Maeve and Bradan fought some shapeshifters off when they got close.

Orla turned to throw a couple of fireballs and heard a growl at her back. A puma's paw slapped at her shoulder, throwing her a few feet away. She scrambled to her feet and tossed more balls of fire in the directions of her attackers. Maeve and Bradan stood back to back. They wouldn't be able to hang on for long.

The door of the house opened, and Keeva yelled, "In here!" Orla, Maeve, and Bradan raced inside. Before Keeva could close the door, a smaller puma leapt toward it. It was too fast for Keeva to use her rifle . Orla was running in and didn't see it.

They saw a small fireball the size of a tennis ball hit the puma right between the eyes. He howled and ran away. Keeva slammed the door closed and saw Noah behind her, hands still curled into fists. "The fire was small, but it did the job," Noah said when Keeva glared at him.

Keeva pointed to the broken window. "The others are secured with thick wooden doors. That's the only window broken." They guarded the one window, hitting any shapeshifters that attempted to enter with a fireball or a bullet. The animals seemed to understand the risks, and eventually none tried to invade through that window.

Orla saw the leopard, now a man, tied to a chair. "He thought I wouldn't shoot him, so I got him in the leg," Keeva said.

"You're a hell of a shot, Keeva. Ask Lorcan to shoot at an elephant at two feet, and he'll still miss," Orla said.

Keeva laughed. "I'm glad there's something I can do better than him. Now that he's turning supernatural and all that, he'll be unbearable."

"No one can compete with you in being his sister, Keeva. You and your mother are the two most important women in Lorcan's world. Trust me."

"What about you?"

Orla merely smiled and said nothing. Lorcan and she were soul-mates. There was no need for reassurance.

"Your shoulder is soaked in blood, Orla," Maeve said. Orla looked at her injury, realizing she couldn't heal as fast as Lorcan did. "I'm okay. Where's Jane?" Orla asked Keeva.

"She released the wolf, and Keeva got mad and locked her in her room," Noah said.

"Thank you, Noah! I guess I'm not able to speak for myself," Keeva said and pinched Noah's nose lightly.

Orla peeked through the window and looked outside. The shapeshifters were lurking around, waiting for an opportunity to attack. "Bradan and Maeve, could you watch the window?"

"Sure," Bradan said.

"I need to talk to Jane. Can you keep an eye on Noah?" Orla asked Keeva. Keeva nodded. "Mother is in the room at the end of the corridor on the left."

Orla went to Jane's room. She knocked and removed the chair Keeva had used to jam the door from the outside. Orla entered and found Jane sitting at the side of her bed. It wasn't just a room, it was a grand master suite. The room was elegantly decorated and there wasn't a single wrinkle on the bed linens. Not a single thing out of place.

From years working as a high-end antique thief, Orla knew exactly how women in upper class families behaved, reacted, and dealt with life. She knew them so well that she could walked through their doors and stolen without having to break in most of the time. After so many years, she had seen so much. She knew how they handled pain, loss, happiness, family, and lifestyle and—in rare instances—maintained their sanity. The room in front of her was an example of how much pain this woman had suffered and how much control she had. Jane was a role model for controlling emotions.

Jane stood when she saw Orla. Her movements were gracious, but Orla knew there was a storm of turmoil inside her. Not exactly the ideal situation to be introduced to a mother-in-law. She cleared her throat and spoke, "I'm Orla . . ."

Jane smiled. "I know. I've seen your pictures."

Orla nodded. "I shouldn't be so naive as to think that you didn't keep tabs on Lorcan's life."

"Not as much as I would have liked to."

"The shapeshifters are surrounding us. I think we should get everyone out of here. If they decide to attack us all at once, we'll be trapped inside the house. If we are outside, at least, we can run."

Jane looked Orla squarely in the eyes. She was much smaller than Orla, but her inner strength made Orla squirm a bit. "Why did you come here?" Jane asked with a voice as cool as water.

"I saw the shapeshifters moving in this direction. I didn't have time to get to Lorcan, so I came straight here. This is Lorcan's home, and I'll help him protect it as much as I can."

"But he left this home for you."

Orla looked straight into Jane's eyes. "We are soul mates, Jane. Without each other, our lives have no meaning. I left my family because they forbade me to love him. When you forbade him from loving me, it was like asking him to refuse his life. What did you expect him to do?"

"I'm sure Lorcan has told you by now that the reason we have him is because of Bricius. When Lorcan was six, he killed one of Bricius's shapeshifters in the woods to protect me. The day he came home and told me he kissed you for the first time, he was covered in Bricius's aura . . ."

"He taught my magic class. I practiced some of his magic, and of course, it carried his aura. I have no blood ties with him."

"At that time, Keeva was a toddler. Bricius was our biggest fear. We worried that he'd come for her at any time. How do you expect I'd react when Lorcan came home with our worst nightmare?"

"You asked him not to see me again without even giving him a reason."

Jane nodded. "That was exactly what I did."

"Lorcan killed Bricius in our last mission."

"I knew that. I felt a deep wound in my soul suddenly stop bleeding. I don't know how, but I just knew that the nightmare had stopped, and Lorcan was coming home. I didn't know that Bricius would get his last strike, and that it would cost Ferris his life."

"Yet you released the wolf so he could save Alana, a descendant of Bricius's clan?"

Jane smiled. "I will never forgive Bricius, but this is no fault of his descendants. Now he's dead. And so is Ferris. I now consider that chapter of our lives closed. Keeva and Lorcan have to move on . . . And you have to move on."

They heard a bang on the back door. "Come with me." Orla took Jane's hand and ran toward the living room. "They've start attacking already. Are the rooms upstairs secured?" Orla asked.

"Yes," Keeva said.

"Noah, can you go upstairs with Jane? Go into a room and secure all the doors. Don't open for anyone except us. Take the cat and use the fireballs if you have to. Can you do that for me?"

Noah nodded. Aris jumped onto his shoulders.

"Give me your knife," Jane said.

"Mother!" Keeva exclaimed.

"Take mine." Orla gave Jane hers.

Jane nodded and took the knife. "I'll take care of Noah." Then she rushed upstairs.

"You have a hell of a mother, Keeva." Orla mumbled. There was more banging on the back door. Orla grabbed the captured shapeshifter and used him as a shield. She opened the front door and walked outside. All the pumas and leopards in the front hunched down, growling, preparing for an attack.

"Withdraw, or I'll set him on fire." Orla said and threw a fireball at a tree in the front yard. The tree burst into flames. "Now, withdraw!" Orla yelled at the animals. They kept growling, unsure of what to do. There were rows and rows of them. A sea of shapeshifters walked stealthily around them.

They heard a haunting howl, the coolest howl Orla had ever heard. "Mori!" Orla exclaimed under her breath and grinned. Beneath the moonlight, Mori appeared—a magnificent warrior with an army of space foxes. "This is the end of you!" Orla threw the shapeshifter she was holding hostage to his frontline and ran back to inside the house.

Mori and her foxes attacked the shapeshifters from behind.

From another direction, more howling came. Roy and his space wolves charged toward them. The banging from the back of the house had stopped, replaced by the groaning of wounded dogs. Lorcan and Riley stormed in from the back door.

"Your mother and Noah are upstairs!" Orla told them. They heard a thumping sound from above. Lorcan and Riley raced up the stairs. Orla turned and threw fireballs at some pumas that had gotten past Mori's foxes. Another leopard jumped for the broken window, but Keeva gunned it down instantly. Maeve and Bradan rushed toward the back door to guard it.

Lorcan arrived at the landing upstairs and was in awe. His mother had her knife held at the throat of a puma, and Noah had thrown a leopard off balance with a fireball. The animal rolled off the roof and landed outside. By the sound of it, the shapeshifter was finished off by Maeve and Bradan in the backyard.

The puma wriggled and got free from Jane's knife, and it jumped at Noah. Riley darted at the animal, aiming his rifle upward, and shot. The dead puma landed on top of Riley, sending him rolling and sliding down the stairs.

Then everything went quiet.

"We've got the outside covered at the front," Mori yelled.

"I've got the back," Roy added.

"The upstairs is fine," Lorcan said and darted down the stairs.

At the bottom of the stairs, Riley lay beneath the dead puma. Lorcan dragged the puma off his friend. Riley was lying upside down, and Lorcan was worried he'd broken his neck in the fall. When he approached, Keeva pushed in front of him and gently put her hand behind Riley's neck and back. "No blood. Doesn't seem to be broken. He might have a concussion, though," she muttered more to herself than to the others in the room. Riley opened his eyes groggily.

"There you are. Give me a smile so I know you understand me," Keeva said.

Riley winced.

"That doesn't qualify as a smile, but it should do for now. I'm going to try to move you, okay? Tell me where it hurts."

"Left shoulder," Riley said.

"Welcome back, doctor." Keeva smiled.

Later, Lorcan and Orla saw Mori and Roy back to the portal. Bradan and Maeve helped to clean up the mess in the house. From the sofa in the living room, Lorcan heard Keeva's voice, "Don't be a puss. Stay still. I'll fix it."

"Have you done this before?" asked Riley.

"I fixed a pig's tail. He was alive and healthy."

"What about his tail?"

In another corner, Noah was sitting on a bench with Aris on his lap, enjoying the scene of Keeva playing doctor with his father.

Lorcan fixed the bandage on Orla's shoulder and kissed it. "How does it feel?" he asked.

"Better." She smiled at him. "Sorry I missed the show at the ceremony."

Lorcan chuckled. "It wasn't much of a show. Ciaran did a spectacular job with the special effects, though. The moon really looked as if it was on fire. And I don't know how the hell Riley pulled off the fake wolf fur stunt. It looked so real that Alana couldn't tell."

"I'm sure it wasn't easy. I'm sorry I left you alone to do all that."

He kissed her cheek. "That's okay. You were busy saving my family." He kissed her, but she stopped the kiss.

"Should we go and talk to your mother?"

He cringed, and Orla laughed.

Epilogue

The riverbank was cold as usual. Lorcan wasn't sure that walking along this riverbank before going back to Eudaiz was a good idea. It was associated with too many painful memories. But Orla had insisted. Perhaps she valued the good memories over the daunting experiences. She wanted to remember the good times they had spent here during their childhoods and the moment they had become childhood sweethearts.

They approached the large rock where Lorcan had always hopped up first and reached his hand out to bring her up with him. He always felt good doing that. It made him feel like a prince. Recalling the experience, he chuckled.

"What?" Orla asked.

He looked at the way her long hair blew in the wind and the way she squinted her eyes when the hair tangled in her face. He did what she always expected—he untangled the hair on her face and kissed her squinting eyes, then her exquisite nose, working his way to her lips.

They heard children giggle in the distance and saw a group of families gather for a picnic. It wasn't exactly a summer picnic under the glorious sunlight. But considering this riverbank always seemed to be the territory of creatures and black magic, the signs of families gathering was quite a treasure.

Orla smiled.

"What are you smiling at?" Lorcan asked.

She looked up at him, twirled her finger in a strand of his hair, and gazed into his eyes. He loved the way she looked into his eyes, so intense, as if she was examining them, memorizing them, and savoring the moment. He knew he wanted to do the same to her, but hell, he wouldn't be able to do it as well as she did.

"I'm just happy, that's all," Orla said.

"Would you be happier seeing that?"

"What?"

Lorcan realized that with her human senses, she probably couldn't see and hear what he could. Across the river, deep in the woods, Bradan and Maeve were walking, hand in hand. He described what he saw to Orla.

"About last night, you weren't disappointed, were you?"

Orla shook her head. "No. Your mother was tired. She'd had a hell of a day."

Lorcan looked down at the sand. "Still, I'd love to see you two talk before we leave."

"No, you wouldn't. You squirmed when I suggested it."

"I did not!" Lorcan laughed as Orla punched him lightly in the chest. Then the smiled faded on Orla's face. Lorcan turned to see his mother approaching.

Jane smiled. "So you two are leaving now?"

Lorcan nodded. "We'll be back to visit you in no time."

Jane looked at Orla. "I thought it was too soon for me to come to terms with everything. Too hard to forgive and forget in such a short time. But I thought about it all night, and you were right. Life is short and precious. I have to treasure every moment of it."

Lorcan put his hand on Orla's back and rubbed it lightly. She had his support in whatever was coming.

Jane pulled out a necklace. "This belongs to my mother. I had kept it for Keeva, but now I'm giving it to you." She put it around Orla's neck. "Keeva will always have me. But you don't have anyone. You two can take care of each other. But when you are out there, I want you to know that you always have my love and my blessing."

Orla embraced Lorcan's mother. She closed her eyes and a tear rolled down her face. He was glad they had come back to Ireland and thankful that they had worked things out and the riverbank was now at peace. He was grateful she had given him the little rock as a promise of their childhood love. He thanked the person who had created him as a supernatural creature, just so he could prove that it wasn't his creation that made him who he was.

It was his mother's nurturing that had guided his emotions and made him the human he was today.

The end
Check Out Other Books on the Next Page

D.N. LEO'S LATEST NOVEL LIST
http://www.narrativeland.com/dnleo-novels

Check out all the latest series and novels

Thank you for reading.

If you enjoyed reading **Uncursed** I would appreciate it if you would help others enjoy this book, too.

<u>Recommend it.</u> Please help other readers find this book by recommending it to friends, readers' groups and discussion boards.

<u>Review it.</u> Please tell other readers why you liked this book by reviewing it at Amazon or Goodreads. A few sentences will make a significant difference to me. If you do write a review, please send me an email at info@dnleo.com so I can thank you with a personal email.

Connect with me online:

Web: narrativeland.com; Twitter: @dnleostory

To join my mailing list, please click here

Facebook page of the Outlanders of the Multiverse series
https://www.facebook.com/Outlandersofthemultiverse

GET FREE BOOKS FROM D.N. LEO
http://narrativeland.com

COPYRIGHT

UNCURSED
Spectrum Duology – Volume 2

By D.N. Leo